TAKE MY SUNSHINE

TAKE MY SUNSHINE

M.E. Glinz

MOONGATE
books

First published in the United States by Moongate Books, an imprint of Moongate Press.

ISBN 9798988938002

For my family,

1

"No, no, no, no..."

Devon's papers flew everywhere as he rounded down the stairs of the history and arts building. The old stone and ivy carved into the foundation of Mt. Hope University, one of the largest schools in Michigan, flashed by him as he hurtled through the corridors. He gathered the papers together in a flurry—matching the weather outside—and cursed as the leftover remnants of melting snow prints dampened them.

Why did his History of the Ancient Worlds class have to be located at the end of the furthest wing in the basement?

Devon was not a good student at Mt. Hope University. In fact, he was one the worst, which was why he overslept and nearly missed another class. In his first two and a half years of school, he had barely skirted by in his gen eds. But as the pressure of his junior year and upcoming LSAT mounted, he began to turn to drinking and sleeping in over prioritizing his classes.

Like a reverse Dean's List, he had gotten an email a few weeks ago, outlining his terrible GPA (2.09), poor likelihood of making it into law school to follow his father's suit, and the warning if he missed any more classes, acquired more than 35% class tardies, and failed to get a C+ or higher in all his classes, it was goodbye to his soccer scholarship—the only way he could afford to study.

And goodbye college.

If he slipped up, Devon would have to leave the sport he'd played since he was four, the insatiable college parties Mt. Hope hosted, and most importantly, his girlfriend, Lindsey, and the life they lived together in their little apartment off campus.

And although he still had wiggle room on his tardies, he had less than a minute to make it to class before his professor and history major advisor, Dr. Asan, considered it an absence. That would be his final allowed absence, leaving him unable to miss any more.

As he turned the final corner, the door was in sight. With a stretch, he grasped the doorknob with his heart still pounding. A turn.

Nothing.

Devon rattled the knob, but it wouldn't budge. The door had never been locked before.

He swore again and pounded against the wood. The window in the door allowed him to watch his professor, Dr. Asan, roll his eyes, hold up a finger to the rest of the class, and—with a click of the door unlocking—step out into the hallway.

"Mr. Camburn," Dr. Asan sighed, clearly disappointed in Devon's chronic tardiness. Asan's face held a perpetual frown of frustration. Nearly every class period, it seemed, Devon would either fail to appear or would come, tap-dancing in for the last fifteen minutes.

Most of his classes he could at least sleep off his hangover in the back, but Dr. Asan's eight a.m. lecture was a constant battle to get up in time for.

"This is my class—is it not?" He raised his scarred eyebrow—another of his classic signs of disapproval.

If anything could have motivated Devon to arrive early, it was to avoid this interrogation. He hated being spoken to like a child.

"Yes, sir, I know but my—"

"History is a collection of recorded events that have shaped the world. Each time you walk in late, I have to log it into your attendance." Asan folded his hands and laid them along the roundness of his belly that had expanded with age. He wore his age well; with a tweed jacket and horn-rimmed glasses he was probably required to wear the moment he turned fifty to complete his professor persona.

"And if I'm not mistaken, Mr. Camburn, you're running low on tardy tolerance, and since it is now eight-ten, I have to report this as an absence."

His last one.

"C'mon, Dr. Asan," Devon pleaded, "Please don't do this. I have to pass and play soccer. It's not my fault—my phone died so it didn't wake me up." A lie, a simple one, but a lie nonetheless. He hoped his mint toothpaste could cover up the lingering aroma of alcohol on his breath.

"And I have a class to teach waiting for me inside," Dr. Asan responded without missing a beat. He ran a hand along his brown cheek wrecked with wrinkles and sighed. "Mr. Camburn, college is a time to sort out your priorities. If soccer is one, you put in the work, go to training sessions, and don't let your teammates down. If you can do it for soccer practices, you need to give your education and processors the same respect by attending and completing your assignments, which requires you to be punctual. I suggest you invest in an alarm clock."

"Okay, okay, I'll be on time next time, okay? I was literally only a minute past tardy..." Devon said as he attempted to step around and get into the room but was met with his professor mirroring his movement like a stilted tango, blocking his path.

"I'm sorry, Mr. Camburn, but you can't come to class today." Asan glanced down at Devon—but gave a small smile of pity. "Everything you need is online. Check the syllabus, do the work, and I expect to see you here promptly on Monday."

Without giving Devon the opportunity to respond, Asan turned back into the classroom and clicked the door locked once again.

Devon's eyes fell to the floor. He bit his lip and tried to hold back a scream of frustration. Every night when he opened another bottle of beer, he told himself he would do better the next day. But now here he was, twenty-one years old and one mistake away from losing everything he had worked hard for his entire education.

He walked back to his apartment, just off campus, unsettled by his interaction with Dr. Asan. Despite rather annoying habits like drumming his podium with his fingertips, Dr. Asan taught the majority of the history classes Devon needed to prepare for law school, and now he's blown his chances of getting a good recommendation letter.

Lindsey would be in ceramics right now, Devon remembered as he passed by the art studio, while he should have been listening to a lecture about—Devon checked the syllabus on the Blackboard app on his phone—Ancient Greece & their Mythology. He groaned—Greek mythology and history was much more interesting than the Bronze Age they covered Wednesday.

If his parents, who were devout Christians, knew Devon enjoyed studying mythology more than the Sunday school he began skipping at age ten, his poor mother would keel over.

He figured it would be better to sleep than wait around to go to his next class at three, so despite being briefly lectured by Asan about the importance of going to classes, as soon as he got home, Devon shrugged on his sweatpants and plopped into the bed he had only recently vacated. It still smelled like Lindsey after sex and the four IPAs he downed before he fell asleep.

Nearly four hours later, Devon woke up to his alarm he had set to make sure to make it to his afternoon classes and checked his phone. A few social media notifications popped up, but the one that caught his eye was a text from Lindsey.

Are you going to Kyle's tonight?

Kyle Weller was a senior and considered Mt. Hope royalty. His family was "has a private jet" rich and owned nearly half the business in town and the surrounding areas. Kyle had inherited a house near campus with its own cleaning service specifically to accommodate for the wild parties he threw every weekend. Rumor was he continued to flunk Chemistry 101 so he could continue to attend the university and put off real life.

Devon had been to his fair share of Kyle's parties—anyone who was anyone had—so he didn't know why this should be any different. But if he was being honest, Devon was tired from the previous night that he and Lindsey had spent at Prickly Peer, a local academia bar. He had gone to try and scope out law students to ask questions so he could prepare for the LSAT. With no success, he turned in early, but not without getting drunk enough for the repercussions of today.

Sure. Lunch?

After receiving a smiley and thumbs-up emoji from Lindsey, Devon pulled himself out of bed, and tried not to dwell too much on what Dr. Asan said about impacting his future—he'd think about it after the party. This time would be different.

2

Kyle must have raided an entire liquor store for the party as Devon had never seen so many people scrunched together in the house. It was slated to be the last big party before Christmas break starting next week.

As Devon looked around, he spotted Lindsey, who had headed to the party right after her night class, sporting her personal Jackson Pollock drinking glass that was already being refilled by a butler. She was wearing her custom-painted dress that was nearly as colorful as her glass. For a project last semester, she had popped balloons full of paint on a white dress, à la that scene in *The Princess Diaries*.

Devon grinned as she caught his eye. He had helped her pick the colors for that project, and loved the blue that matched her sapphire eyes.

"Devon!" she shouted. "Get a drink and get yourself over here! I have to tell you the craziest thing!"

Devon got himself a Scotch on the rocks and walked over to her.

"So I was in the library yesterday," Lindsey began, "and—I really can't believe I forgot to tell you at lunch, Devon—anyway, I was in the children's book section since it's the quietest. I was studying for an exam for once," she giggled, "and I started hearing this really weird noise behind the shelves. I'm curious, you know, so I went and looked and bam!" Lindsey exclaimed. "Kyle and his girlfriend were having sex with a Dr. Seuss bean bag propped up against the corner!"

Devon scoffed and took a long sip from his glass. "That's your 'story?'" he guffawed. "I've heard better. What's so shocking about seeing Kyle and his girl doing it in the library? I've seen them in his bed, on the floor, even against this *clear* door," he said and knocked on the slider behind him. "There's nothing—"

"President McGrumpy was *two shelves down*," Lindsey whispered excitedly, like the highly anticipated punchline to a bad joke.

Devon sputtered as he sipped his drink, and in trying to suppress a cough, he dropped his cup and it shattered, sending shards of glass across the floor. Annie, the maid working tonight, immediately began to sweep it up.

Devon wasn't shocked that Kyle and his girlfriend were rounding third base heading home in the library while Present McGrumpy was *right there;* what he couldn't understand was how President McGrumpy didn't notice them or hear them, as they sounded like barking seals.

President McGrumpy, whose real surname was McCarrell, was an ancient man. He had been the president of Mt. Hope longer than any other, moving through the past few decades like short sprints, and was now as much a part of the fabric of the institution as the old brick clock tower.

He'd earned his nickname when Devon was a freshman. Someone set his begonias on fire—accidentally, of course—from a cigarette butt. He was able to save some, but ever since that explosion, people began to call him McGrumpy. Dr. Asan was somehow annoyed for two weeks after that, too. He sulked around the campus and shot glares at students. The culprit never admitted to the crime, but 'McGrumpy' stuck.

Despite his old age, President McGrumpy had perfect eyesight and acute hearing. While Mt. Hope had a party reputation, it was also an incredibly distinguished school, and McGrumpy was always cracking down on anyone mixing fun in the academic buildings. He didn't need to remind students of that when he passed through the corridors. He could hear even the quietest of whispers and the crisp pop of a beer can. In mere seconds, President McGrumpy could spot the delinquent and stare them down. His body may have aged, but his mind and reflexes were as sharp as ever.

"He must be dying," Devon reasoned. "Nothing gets past him."

"Or he doesn't care anymore," Lindsey countered. "I mean, he's been president here for what, 40 years? That guy's got to be sick of reinforcing the rules over and over again."

"No way," Devon insisted. "McGrumpy is never going to lighten up. His iron heart has failed or something."

Before any discussions of McGrumpy could continue, Lindsey spotted a friend over Devon's shoulder.

"Ah, Marianne, hold up, girl!"

Devon grinned as Lindsey sashayed away. He never would have thought his Intro to Arts class freshmen year would have brought her to him, but he was so thankful. While they still had a year and a half of school together, the pressure to decide what happened between them after they crossed the graduation stage was an unspoken rule that they didn't talk about. Living in the moment was much more Lindsey's style, which is what had attracted Devon to her in the first place.

Devon meandered around to some acquaintances. He continued to talk and drink, losing count of how many he'd had at this point. He slurred during conversations and his vision blurred but he could still make out simple shapes: squares for chests and circles for heads.

After one drink too many, Devon felt a pull on his belt loop, and he spotted those bright blue eyes that made him fall for Lindsey. They hooked up occasionally at parties, and while he wasn't expecting it tonight, it wasn't unwanted. Kyle had three guest rooms upstairs just for this, while the housekeeper had the unfortunate task of stripping the beds in the morning.

In a matter of minutes, Devon and Lindsey were upstairs, their bodies against the door, and completely out of their clothes. Lindsey wasn't normally this brazen, but Devon liked this change.

He kissed her body slowly, starting from below her navel until he was at her neck. He scrambled with his hands, but soon she let out a groan of pleasure as he thrusted.

Devon continued to kiss up until he reached her lips. Lindsey normally loved teasing.

And immediately, his stomach dropped. Lindsey's mouth tasted like cigarettes. While Lindsey smoked on occasion, like at parties, it was another taste and a feeling that sent Devon reeling backwards, as he pulled out of the woman before him.

It was warm metal from a tongue piercing, but Lindsey only had pierced ears.

He didn't even try to look at the woman before him. The more he focused, the blurrier his surroundings became.

"Oh no," Devon mumbled as he staggered around trying to find his clothes which were scattered around the floor. He swore as he hurriedly put on his clothes. "What have I done…" he groaned. "I'm sorry… I can't—"

He stumbled out of the bedroom and barreled down the stairs, unwilling to even look at the girl he left in the bedroom. He tried to look for Lindsey, but the room before him just contained a blurry sea of dancing students. What was originally supposed to be one last night of fun before the end of the semester had turned into a nauseating mess. His head pounded in time with the techno music he recognized from some viral video, and he did the only thing that made sense.

He left.

Devon stumbled away, out the door and into the great darkness, unaware of where he was headed, but just knew he couldn't spend another second in that house. He gritted his teeth as he met a blustery snowstorm—he hadn't thought to bring a coat. It served him right to think he was impervious to the December weather in Michigan.

Determined to make it back home, he shivered as he zigzagged along the sidewalks, but before he could work out where he was heading, he stumbled on something hard and hit his toe. He howled out in pain.

One eye dared to open; it was the fire hydrant in front of the library. He had somehow stumbled back onto campus.

Overcome by the pain and unsteady from how much he'd had to drink, Devon's knees buckled. In just ten minutes, he had gone from being in a happy relationship with the most beautiful girl in the world to being filled with dread and guilt over what he'd done. He felt queasy, and unable to stop himself, he wretched onto the ground beneath him.

As he tried to pull himself up to his feet, something else caused Devon to halt, and this time, he swore and wished for the fire hydrant over again.

"Mr. Camburn?" came a familiar voice.

3

This nightmare of an evening could not get any worse. Not only had Devon cheated on his girlfriend, but now he'd been found nearly passed out and drunk by his professor to whom he had just promised he would be more responsible just twelve hours ago.

Perfect.

"D-Dr. Asan," Devon sputtered, before he was sick again.

"Oh, Mr. Camburn," Asan sighed, his tone different from anything Devon had heard before. He almost sounded concerned.

"It's not what it l-looks..." Devon dry-heaved this time and let out a cry. "O-ow..." When was the last time he had thrown up? It hurt so much more than he remembered.

"No, no I know what this is, "Asan harrumphed as he pulled Devon up to stand. "I remember the days..."

Slowly, through the snowy grass, Asan walked Devon into a yellow house behind the library, lit up with a Christmas tree, providing a warm glow into the cold snowy night. The siding was a bright shade that Devon was pretty sure was able to be seen from space. Even the door was baby yellow with a mustard yellow trim.

Before Devon knew it, he was sitting in a velvet dining chair in Asan's mint green kitchen with a bucket between his knees and a warm washcloth on his forehead.

"Don't be afraid to use that," Asan, gesturing to the bucket. "I have children—it doesn't bother me."

Devon barely registered what Asan said. He was too busy looking around. The house was single-story, and to his right was a living room, also yellow, with photographs on a fireplace mantle too far for him to see what they were. The fire crackled gently in the background as a nearby Victrola played Christmas music. It seemed much more comfortable than the bright light staring down on him from the kitchen.

As if he could sense Devon's thoughts, Asan cleared his throat.

"The living room is far too cozy. I can't have you fall asleep here. You can stay until you sober up." And there was the stern Asan back again, as if he had caught himself in an act of kindness.

Devon nodded—he was thankful, nonetheless.

Asan began to busy himself in the kitchen. He scooped ground coffee beans from a little yellow bag into a filter and turned on his Mr. Coffee maker.

"Good thing I was already planning a cup to help me stay up…" he muttered to himself, but loud enough that Devon could hear. "Have you had any food?" He asked Devon.

"Um, l-like at five…?" Devon mumbled. He braced the bucket suddenly as his stomach tightened. Thankfully, it was just a burp.

"Have any allergies?" Asan shot back, already prepared with his question.

"N-not that I—"

"Eat this, then." Asan handed Devon a box of corn flakes. "Our daughter hates them, and they've been in our pantry for nearly three months now, and I cannot stand the sight of that green rooster staring at me every morning." After a pause, he added, "and I'll make you some eggs and toast. Is scrambled with cheese okay? It's my usual late-night snack."

Devon blinked back at his professor, who was pouring the freshly brewed coffee into two yellow mugs that looked just like the style of ceramic mugs Lindsey made in class the previous month.

"Coffee was always my remedy of choice when I needed to sober up quickly—careful, it's hot," Asan said as he passed Devon the mug. He sipped it, hoping it would do the trick.

"Y-you got drunk?" Devon almost laughed into his coffee. "Sorry, sir, but I can't really imagine that." Devon hadn't ever pictured his old professor to be the wild type.

"Oh yes," Asan said as he cracked four eggs into the skillet. "Drunk nearly every weekend my first two years of college. I had more notches on my bedpost than school assignments. And several other things I probably shouldn't share as your professor." Asan smirked for the first time since Devon had known him. "But anyway, I put all that behind me long ago. It wasn't all that worth it anyway."

"Why not?" Devon asked. "Isn't that just part of the c-college experience?" He coughed spittle into the bucket.

Dr. Asan's nose scrunched, and he turned back to the scrambled eggs.

"Yes, it is, but there was a moment I quickly learned that my life had far more to experience than getting drunk or high, and blacking out large sections of my life." He paused as he added the cheese. "Do you have a girl in your life, Mr. Camburn?"

Devon's stomach began to tighten again at the thought of Lindsey. At the way her face would fall when she found out he had cheated on her tonight. How she would probably cry. How she would make the decision for him when it came to what happened after graduation—now probably long before graduation. She would break the unspoken rule.

He took a deep breath to steady himself, determined not to use the bucket again.

"I did—or I do... I-I hope I still do," he stuttered out. "I just... Tonight I-I made an absolutely huge mistake. And I'm worried that if I tell her, I will l-lose her forever." Devon ran his hands through his dark hair, that still had flakes of snow sticking to the ends. "You probably don't get it, you're too old."

There was silence for a moment as what Devon said hung in the air, and he desperately wished he could take it back.

But Dr. Asan just plated the eggs. He pulled the toaster out of a cupboard, plugged it in, and paused.

"Mr. Camburn, do you remember how I said there was something that pulled me out of the same rut of life you're in right now? I know it's hard to believe I was young once, too, trust me, I sometimes even forget..."

Devon nodded but was too afraid to speak—his stomach was on the verge of lurching again.

"I need you to listen to me, Mr. Camburn, *really* listen. We are not too different, you and I." Asan took a deep breath as he popped bread into the toaster.

"My life changed when I was a junior at a track meet, and I saw Allie Johncox."

4

April 7th, 1990

Hold. One two three four five six seven eight nine ten, I counted as I gripped my knee to my chest. I never understood how people could stretch—I was always too excited to just start running. But I kept a smile on my face as I switched to my left leg at Coach's whistle. I shook out my lean body with a long exhale, and then I began to stretch my arms with the team. Over my head…across my chest…over my head…across my chest. We must have looked like the weirdest army until the whistle blew, and we all relaxed as we shook out our limbs. Ten more minutes until the 200m.

"Ben!"

I turned quickly and spotted my best friend, Spencer, jogging toward the field. I had time before my race, so hurried over to meet him at the fence.

"Hey Ben," he breathed out. He spit scarily close to my shoes, and I took a few steps back to avoid any more flying sunflower shell-and-spit cannons. "Do you know how long the track meet will last today?"

I shook my head and beads of sweat dropped from my black wavy hair and my nose. Despite the fact I hadn't even run yet, I was sweating like a frog in boiling water. It was hard to believe I was a first-generation Indian American with the way I handled the heat—*I didn't.* My dad would often scoff at my preference for cooler weather. My mom always said it was my Irish genes coming through.

"I don't know, maybe two more hours? But once this is over, I'm doing two things," I said as I held up my fingers with each point, "eating so much food I can't move and sleeping—that's all. Why?"

"Oh, well," Spencer sighed, losing his enthusiasm. "I was just thinking that you and I could hang. I have baseball practice from ten to one tonight, and I don't have anything to do until then—"

"Hold that thought," I said as the whistle blew for us to line up, and I jogged back to the start.

I was going in the first heat, which was reserved for the fastest sector of all the schools. When the blank was set, I immediately got into position to be ready until…

Bam.

I was off.

People always have stories as to how they first got into something. For example, Spencer began to play t-ball after he went to a Tigers game and caught a foul ball. His father was a special correspondent for the team. After the game, he brought Spencer into the locker room and got his ball signed by Al Kaline. Now a committed baseball player himself, Spencer made sure to shine that first ball before every game for good luck.

I never thought I had a story as to why I ran, it was just something I did. But my mother told me a story that I hadn't heard before during my freshman year at Mt. Hope.

Apparently, I got my itch to run from what happened on a beach.

When I was seven, my parents took our family—just me at the time—on a vacation to North Carolina. While on the beach, my mother—a very adventurous person compared to my fern-watering, Encyclopedia-reading father—began to dig through the white sand. She unearthed the usual things—shells, pebbles, plastic—and as a seven-year-old, it all fascinated me. Of course, that was until she "playfully" threw a crab in my face.

Okay, she didn't *throw* it in my face. She held onto it and mimicked a crab-like voice as she inched it closer to me, but I was done either way. I spun on my heel and pelted down the width of the private beach, like the road runner screeching away from Taz. I zoomed to the road where our car was parked. My swim trunks were falling, and I had lost my flip flops when I sprinted off, but it didn't matter to me. I just needed to get away as quickly as I could.

I was furious at my mom for a week afterward, but it didn't last. I was seven, and she made PB&Js to get me back on her good side. However, I had reached a revelation. The halfway out-of-breath, head reeling, stomach-crumbling feeling from running was invigorating, and I was never going to stop.

Never stopping was kind of a bad thing for me. When I set my mind to something, I don't stop. At all. Whether it be running, laughing, or sweating, I always had trouble stopping. Literally when I ran, I found it nearly impossible to stop without running into something.

"Asan!" I heard Coach yell, and luckily, I stopped inches before crunching into the fence.

"Thanks, Coach!" I hollered as I turned around. I jogged back toward the track and wiped my forehead to remove the sweat. "Sorry, sometimes I get so fast I can't stop!"

I smirked and looked over to the fence where a gaggle of girls usually blushed at my comments. However, all I saw was a blonde girl with a camera in her hand looking down, seemingly uninterested. Her nose was scrunched as she assessed the camera in front of her. She exhaled, sending wisps of hair fluttering out of her braid into her eyes. She turned to her raven-haired friend who gave her a look of utter disbelief. Neither giggled at what I had said.

Odd.

I frowned. Most girls thought that "Ben Asan—Track Star" was a handsome and perfect wonderboy. It was unusual to see a girl ignore me. I didn't recognize her. Perhaps she needed an introduction…

Once my heat was done, I swaggered over to my water bottle which was conveniently near the girl. As I took a sip, with water dribbling down my chin as I watched, distractedly, the girl's friend waved goodbye. With the plop of my water bottle hitting the ground, I wiped the sweat off my hair and face with my already soaked jersey.

"So, you're a photographer?" I asked when I came face-to-face with her. I leant over the fence to try and get a peek at her camera.

The girl in front of me wasn't beautiful in a typical way, but something about her seemed different from other girls, and I liked it. She had her hair—a soft, dirty blonde—

pulled back in a braid on the side. She wore a strappy black dress over a white T-shirt and white Converse.

"Yep," she said plainly, popping the "p" for emphasis.

"So," I said with my lips puckered in an attempt to look cool and flirtatious. But she seemed to have no interest in my moves.

I took that as a challenge.

"You take pictures?" I tried again. *Obviously, she took pictures, you idiot,* I thought to myself. What kind of pick-up lines did you use on photographers? How's that shutter speed? I was used to flirting with tennis players and asking if they had room for more than a tennis ball down their skirt.

"Not just pictures," she answered firmly, finally looking up. However, she looked straight past me, over my shoulder at the field. I saw someone attempting the long jump, I saw, as I followed her gaze. She replaced her camera with another one that she produced from a bag on her hip.

She tested the scope once more before pressing the red button on the top. A series of clicks sounded with another resounding one at the end.

"I create stories," she said. "Every snapshot is another moment. When placed all together, you get the story of today, a track meet." She sighed and looked back down. "Not my favorite client to create a story of, but it'll do for today." She pulled out several squares I recognized as polaroids. Each one featured me—talking to Spencer before the race, at the starting line, at the end, when I glanced over her way. "I reinvent lives," she explained before dropping them back in her bag.

"Am I a good candidate for your 'client?'" At this point, I was leaning so far against the fence that it was poking me in the ribs. It was definitely cutting into my skin, but I hadn't really noticed. Perhaps the closer I got, the more she would realize how perfect I was.

The girl shook her head.

"Not typically. I usually shoot portraits or landscapes, not action shots, but I take photographs for stories in many local newspapers, now including the *Mt. Hope Herald*, and they wanted the winners." That was the newspaper I had always read the comics in every Sunday as a kid. "Also, I do some work for campus, taking pictures for the pamphlets they send to prospective students."

"How'd you know I would be a winner? Or do you just like taking pictures of me?" I asked with a wink.

The girl rolled her eyes but let out a chuckle.

"Oh, no... You were standing in the first lane. I just assumed," she shrugged, and as she turned on her heel toward another area of the track, eyes bright and focused on the race before her. My eyes held her hips—they swiveled with each step she took.

Okay, she was definitely strange if she hadn't already fallen in love with *The* Ben Asan. Whatever. I thought at this point in my junior year at Mt. Hope, my reputation would precede me. I was the epitome of the tall, dark, and handsome man of romance novels that everyone swoons over, or so the girl I had been with last weekend had described me as.

I rolled my eyes and hustled back to the starting point. I nearly missed the 400m. I went in the first heat again, and I took a deep breath. With the sound of the blank, I took off with my head straight forward.

Was she flirting with me? She had to be, right? But she deflected every smirk I teased her way, like she was just being friendly. The thoughts ran through my head with every step I took. I shook my head to dislodge them and kept moving forward.

I felt strong about my performance and didn't see anyone in front of me, so I continued at my pace. It wasn't until Coach blew the whistle and screamed that I stopped.

"Asan!" he harped, and I turned over my left shoulder to glance at his large figure from afar. Coach Nickels could tremble the earth with his deep stern voice alone. "What the hell are you doing in the outside lane?"

What? In the outside lane? I was way ahead of the… Oh.

I glanced around and saw that I had been running alone. I had drifted as my mind did, and I was nearly in lane 5. The rest of the group were in the first two lanes, finishing the 400m in the proper lanes. I had lost an easy win. Heat prickled my neck and my cheeks, this time not from the scorching sun as I flushed with embarrassment. How didn't I realize?

I was alone on the field as my team members chatted with each other. Too humiliated to talk to them, I headed back over to the fence to talk to Spencer. He wasn't my only friend, but he was the only one who cared enough to come.

Once I got over there though, I stopped. Spencer's friend and one of our roommates, Brennan, was with him, who notoriously disliked me. Brennan thought I was selfish, annoying, and slept around too much. He was right, but I didn't want to be reminded of that. So, most of the time, I avoided being with Spencer when he was around.

"Asan!" Coach Nickels yelled, and I sped up my steady jog back to the team. "What the hell happened back there?" he asked and lowered his voice slightly as the rest of the team turned to look. "This isn't Opposite Day. You're supposed to go *into* the inner lanes, not stay on the outside," he enunciated as if explaining it to a child.

"Sorry, Coach," I mumbled and wiped my mouth with my soaked cut-off. "I don't know what I was thinking. I *wasn't* thinking. Won't happen again, promise."

Obviously, Coach suspected something was up, but he didn't say anything.

"Alright, Asan, I'm letting this go because you're one of my best runners. But if there's something going on, I better not find out." He eyed me to make sure I knew exactly what he meant, and I nodded quickly. Drug abuse in collegiate athletes had been all in the news lately, but I would never risk it. Alcohol was one thing as a college student, and often part of the culture in Mt. Hope, but I never touched illegal substances.

"Of course, sir," I promised before joining the rest of the team at the water cooler. A few guys were still sniggering, and I pretended like it didn't hurt me, but before the next run, I made sure I was focused on the inner lanes before the next blank was shot; I took off at a sprint once more, determined to prove to myself and everyone else that I could regain my top spot and cross the finish line first—this time in the proper lane.

Dinner came, and Spencer was sitting at our usual spot on the high stools in the middle of the dining commons commotion. While on weekends I found myself surrounded by strangers at parties, when it came down to it, I really just enjoyed being with Spencer. There were some other spots that were quieter, but I liked our little circular high table seats. We heard everything—including multiple hilarious breakups over ridiculous things—from our little nook of the world. We saw the world as we knew it, and we were kings.

As I moved through the line to get to quesadillas, the most beautiful food in the world in my opinion, I spotted a flick of dirty blonde hair that reminded me of the girl from earlier. I glanced around in that direction only to be disappointed; it was this grunge guy in my philosophy class who had long hair he often wore in a low ponytail. I didn't realize how far I had moved up in the line until the server clanked her tongs against the counter in impatience, breaking me from my distraction.

Spencer side-eyed my three large quesadillas when we sat down. I gave a small eye roll before grabbing the first one and taking a bite. Grease dripped down my chin, and I smiled as I licked my lips.

"So," I began shortly after I licked my fingers clean of grease. "You've got practice tonight? How late again?" Ever since that girl had seemed incredibly turned-off by me, I had rethought my night. Instead of sleeping, I wanted to be awake and on-campus just in case I saw her.

"Ten at night until one in the morning, training for night games," Spencer answered as he cut a piece of his pink sirloin. "I hate these late practices; I can barely stay awake for them."

I shook my head and gave a small chuckle.

"Spence," I said and pushed aside my plate. "You're the only one on the baseball team who goes to sleep before twelve on a regular basis." It was true. The baseball team was notorious for staying up late and pranking Mt. Hope's dorms.

"You should come. We're just practicing for the tournament next week. I could use a distracting audience member to help me power through."

Mt. Hope had an amazing baseball team, much better than our terrible track team, me excluded. They went to multiple tournaments in the spring and always won several championships.

"Oh, yeah," I said, trying to remember. I finished my third quesadilla and dug into my chocolate mousse. "The one down in Florida, right?"

Spencer shook his head.

"Georgia," he corrected.

Yeah, I didn't know that.

I didn't pay the closest attention to Spencer's life as much as I expected him to pay to mine. I mean, he was a good friend, but *I* was the one being scouted by Olympic coaches.

"I'll just have to keep you up to date on all the drama that goes on during dinner."

After an additional quesadilla that I told myself I deserved, I got up to leave.

"I'll meet you at the field at ten," I promised. "I'm going to take a quick nap, do some homework, and I should be good."

Spencer just nodded and continued to pierce his food with his fork.

As I walked to the dirty dishes belt, I looked around the dining commons just in case she had come by. But my search for the beautiful blonde girl was deemed fruitless.

5

April 7th, 1990

"Hey batta batta!" I hollered out to the dark field lit only by a few ancient stadium lights. "Hey batta batta! *Sa-wing,* batta!" I gave a laugh as I chewed on the Big-League Chew gum Spencer so kindly let me have—it was expired by two days, and Spencer wouldn't even use expired laundry detergent.

Strike.

Spencer *had* asked for a distracting audience member.

"Ben, you're supposed to say that when the *opposite* team is batting!" Spencer exclaimed, wagging the wooden bat at me like an extended finger. His face reddened as he struck out, and he sulked back to the dugout.

I shrugged and spat the wad of Pepto-Bismol colored gum out onto the stands.

"I don't care. Ferris can't be wrong!"

"That was Cameron!" Spencer yelled back and threw his bat to the ground. He fixed his white baseball pants before settling back in the dugout.

"Whatever!" I called back and filled my mouth with more stringy gum.

Practice continued, and I found myself becoming increasingly bored as the Mt. Hope Ocelots played against each other. They were so good, someone would either strike out or hit the ball up, up, up into the air and get caught by an outfielder.

No one ever scored.

It was extremely dull.

Eventually I decided that the sky littered with stars was much more enjoyable. So, I laid on my back, feet propped on the highest bleacher, and began to count as many stars as I could. I got to about forty when I realized that I had no chance of ever counting all the stars and gave up. I wasn't much of a number person anyway. Or an English person. Or science. Or history. I was really only good at running, and that's all I wanted to spend my time focusing on.

The stars were unusually bright tonight, and I thought it would make a beautiful background for a picture or a painting.

I never really noticed the stars because during the night I was usually inside hanging out with Spencer or at some party getting wasted.

Behind the baseball field was a rather sturdy hill which Mt. Hope was named after. Or the other way around. It was most famously used for sledding in the bleak winter months, October through March. Despite growing up near MHU, I never went sledding. Some other people I knew from track or school really liked it, but they would, since they were childish. I considered giving it a try this past winter, but there hadn't been much snow, so I promised myself I would sled next year—my last winter at Mt. Hope, hopefully ever.

But as I looked towards that normally vacant hill, I noticed a body sitting about halfway down it. It was too far away to see exactly who it was. I squinted as much as I could, but it just made the picture even more blurred than staring at the stars.

I had decided to give up but then I saw a flash of a camera bulb. It was quick but left a hazy glow that lingered in the black and white sky. I smirked immediately—it had to be the girl from earlier today.

I didn't know her name or much about her, but something deep inside compelled me to find it out. Not only did she completely disregard my greatness earlier, but she was also unconventionally attractive. It was the kind of attractive that was interesting—almost as if her eyes had secrets buried within them that I needed to discover. It was as if her entire face was a scavenger hunt, and you needed to look closely to truly understand its beauty.

That is how I found myself walking toward the hill. Most girls didn't push me away so coolly as she did, and I was determined to win her over.

Apparently, in the time it took for me to walk over, the girl must've gotten bored and headed out. When I reached the top of the hill, finally, with its emerald bushes combing my feet, I realized she had gone. She seemed so real, but had I imagined her?

Either way, I had decided right then and there, on that hill, the girl I had seen not even twelve hours ago was thought up by my subconscious. It was the only way to make sense of a girl not impressed by me. I was not prepared to deal with the alternative—dare I say it?—that my looks and charm *were* deniable.

I sat on top of the hill, slowly forgetting the girl I had made up when I felt a playful slap.

"Hey," I heard Spencer say in a rather raspy voice. I wouldn't be surprised if he was sick; these late-night practices weren't doing good to his required eight hours of sleep. "Whatcha doing over here?" he asked and slid down next to me. It wasn't with the tone of a concerned friend.

"I was just trying to see if I stood at the highest point on campus if I could see everything. You know, like parties that I'm not at," I added with a hint of sarcasm.

"It was your choice," Spencer replied with a laugh. "Besides, I gave you gum," he said and pointed to the packet in my hand. "That's gotta count for something."

I chuckled under my breath and rolled my eyes.

"Sure." I stood up and shoved the gum back into his hand. "I think I'm turning in for the night."

"Don't forget, you're coming with me on a run in the morning!"

I waved him off and walked back down the pathway from the hill. A thud hit my back, and I turned around to grab the packet of Big-League Chew.

The next morning, I rolled out of bed with the song of mattress springs and the cracks of my spine as a musical accompaniment. With a groan, I finally realized the importance of fully stretching before running and not half-heartedly doing it as I usually did. I shuffled into the bathroom of the house Spencer and I shared with Brennan. I knew there was no time for a shower, so I dressed and dragged my sorry butt outside where Spencer was waiting for me.

"You know what time it is?" he asked as we began to tie up our laces. "Eight! And now we have to run six miles."

"You know, Spence, you're the only one who's making us do these runs. We could both go back to sleep."

"But how else would we lose the beer weight?" Spencer teased.

Mt. Hope was an expansive campus, but we tended to stay on the west side—near our house, the library, and the local church. The whole area made up about three miles, so we typically did the loop twice.

As we ran past the library, the smell of the Callery pear trees assaulted my nostrils. While pretty, they famously smelled awful, so I avoided breathing through my nostrils as we passed the blossoming white petals.

Different from the humidity of the day before, early morning springtime in Michigan was crisp and cool, with the sun shining down on us through puffy white clouds, hinting at the warmth ahead.

But every time we passed by the church, I shuddered, knowing who was in there, and the fact that I wasn't.

I had never been a Christian. My mother was, though, but her faith was more personal. She grew up Irish Catholic, then converted to Protestantism in her early twenties. She tried to speak with me several times about it, but I usually just smiled and nodded. My father was Hindu, and he always encouraged me from a young age to learn more about his faith by reading me passages of the *Bhagavad Gita* and encouraging me to pray to Ganesha and Shiva at the *murti* every morning, but I didn't feel connected to the gods like he did. At different points in my life, I spent Sunday mornings with my mom at Mt. Hope Methodist, and others I spent burning incense at the *mandir* with my dad. But as a teenager, overcome by the pressures to choose a side, I chose my own path, which was to disengage with religion altogether.

So, as we ran past those doors, I wasn't surprised to see my mom walking in with my younger siblings. I just put my head down and kept running.

After the first loop, I felt good, but Spencer was struggling about twenty paces behind me. I circled back to catch up with him a few times, and by the time we were back home at 6 miles, Spencer was panting and sweating, while I was just feeling warmed up.

"Thanks for helping me get out of bed," I told Spencer as sweat plopped off the tips of my hair. I used my shirt to wipe my forehead dry. "It really is worth it."

"O-oh yeah, for suuuure...." Spencer coughed and leaned over. "Gosh, I need more sleep." He shuffled toward the front door. "You coming?"

"Actually, I might do another loop," I said as I stretched my arms and yawned. "Before it gets too hot out."

"Suit yourself," Spencer groaned as he disappeared inside.

I cleared my throat and kept going forward. It was easy to keep running once I started—not because my muscles were warmed up—but because unlike every other moment of the day, my mind was clear. The voices driving me, pulling me between the expectations of my family and my friends, quietened. I could simply just be.

After a mile, I turned down the street with the church again, and I stopped in my tracks. Standing at the base of the steps was the girl from yesterday. I hadn't imagined her at all, she was really there. She had her hair clipped back, wore a lilac floral dress with puffy sleeves, and had a small purse over her shoulder. Her heart-shaped face was pulled into a smile as she spoke to an elderly woman.

I stopped running all on my own.

This girl wasn't like the girls I knew, and I had absolutely no idea how to approach her. She wasn't impressed by my good looks or my charm.

Before I could decide what to do, her eyes met mine. She gave a small wave of goodbye to the woman she had been talking to, and before I could begin to run off, she was in front of me.

"You're the track boy," she said matter-of-factly.

"And you're the camera girl," I replied. "I know we didn't speak very much yesterday, but I felt bad I never got your name. Calling you 'camera girl' in my head isn't as personal."

"You've been thinking about me?" she smirked. "Is that why you've been standing outside the church instead of going inside it?"

I chuckled.

"I, uh, woke up too late this morning. I missed it." *Yeah, for the past five years,* I thought.

"But not too late for a run?"

"Less concern of appearance when I'm running."

The girl nodded.

"Touché."

"But if I'm honest," I continued, "I have been thinking about you. And I have two questions for you."

She raised one eyebrow.

"One, what is your name? Mine's Ben Asan, by the way. Wonderboy Ben, if you will."

Now both eyebrows were up.

I coughed, trying to pull myself together.

"Um, or just Ben. And, uh, the second question is would you like to get a drink with me sometime?"

The girl before me bit her lip, deep in thought.

"That's uh, a very sweet proposition, Ben. But I don't think I'm the kind of girl you want to be with."

"Why not?"

"Because I'm not going to drop my pants for you."

My mouth fell open in shock.

"I've gone here for the past three years, and everyone wants the same thing from me. And even if that's not what you want," she looked at me, almost hoping I would jump in and agree, "dating just isn't going to work for me. Now, or really ever."

I hadn't known what to expect from my mystery girl, but talking about dropping her pants in front of a church was definitely not it.

"Now, I really should go back inside—I'm helping to set up for the potluck. You can join us if you want."

A potluck meant my mom was inside, socializing with her friends before the meal like she always did. We were close, but I wouldn't dare walk into church covered in sweat. I may not have gone to church any more, but I knew the decorum.

"Thanks, but I should probably finish my run."

She nodded, her lips in a tight smile.

"Well, have a good day," she said as she turned away.

"Wait," I shouted, "you never told me your name."

She turned back to me and walked slowly backwards to the church. "Allison Johncox. You can call me Allie."

6

"Why did you ask her out?" Devon asked as he scraped the last bits of egg from his plate. "You didn't even know her name!"

Dr. Asan was a surprisingly fantastic storyteller, and Devon was already feeling more awake.

It became difficult for Devon to imagine his serious, old teacher as a young and strong ladies' man. Even the thought of Asan buying condoms was enough to make Devon cringe.

"Well," Asan began, "I thought she was really pretty. She was nice, but not wooed like I was used to." He laughed. "Not a good start, right? But at the time, beautiful girls caught my attention, and I caught theirs. I thought if she went out with the wonderful Ben Asan, I could convince her I was amazing." He let out another small chuckle, like old men do when they hear a classic joke for the first time in years. "Because when she ignored me, it affected my self-esteem. When I was your age, I basically needed compliments to live. Compliments and girls fawning over me, you see?"

Devon raised his eyebrows and mouthed a disbelieving, "Okay…"

"I know it seems like girls would never chase after your professor, but I was quite a catch in my day."

"So, this Allie girl who didn't want to talk to you, she somehow made you so...soft?" Devon asked. He thought about Lindsey, about how his relationship with her had developed over that Intro to Art class, and how she had opened him up to a kind of joy he never knew was possible, even in those early flirty moments.

"Okay... One more sketch and my series of skeletons in office jobs should be complete!" Lindsey had exclaimed during the last half hour of class one day. She and Devon had sat next to one another every day, teasing and chatting since they first met, and now she was entrusting Devon with a sneak peek at her newest project.

She flipped the sketches onto Devon's side of the table: one had two skeletons seemingly joking around a water cooler, and the other was a close up of a skeleton boringly staring at a computer screen.

"Wow," Devon had said as he picked up the pictures. He truly was impressed – in awe of her talent and not just acting interested because he liked her. And he knew that he did from the first time she sketched out Boba Fett skateboarding for fun the second week of classes. "How is it possible that you can show emotions when they have faces?"

"Just me and my raw talent," Lindsey had teased and snatched her sketches back.

For a moment, Devon could forget everything and just remember that interaction. But then the bright lights of Dr. Asan's kitchen fled back, and the dread set back in at what he had done tonight.

"She was a big part of it, of my 'softening' so you say," Dr. Asan chuckled. "But of course, I didn't know it at the time. And I was still lost in my mind as this macho-man, thinking I was better than she could ever do. Hence why I was acting like such an idiot around her."

7

April 16th, 1990

About a week later, I was staring at myself in the mirror. Track practice had just finished before one of our final meets, and the last month of school was creeping up on me. I was never a big fan of college, but the summer off was definitely worth all the homework I hardly ever did.

I tousled my damp black hair, just starting to curl up against my brown skin and grinned into the mirror.

"You are a beast," I said in preparation for our meet the next day. The majority of the Olympic coach scouts who had been tracking me would be there. No pressure. "You are a beast, and you're going to do absolutely perfect, because you are." I could've sworn my teeth sparkled, and I gave a small wink to myself as I went back to change at the lockers.

To my utmost luck, as I swung my bag over my shoulder and walked toward the clear front doors of the fieldhouse, I spotted someone I hadn't seen since Sunday.

"Oh, hi, Allie," I said with my award-winning smile. "Taking pictures again, I see." I pointed to the vertical camera she had around her neck. It was resting on her chest.

I may have lingered my gaze by a millisecond.

Allie glanced down at her neck and nodded, unaware of my gaze.

"Yeah, well, it's sort of my hobby. Sort of like you're always running, competing, and trying to hit on me." Allie didn't meet my eyes, to my disappointment. I had made it my personal goal to get this girl to like me, no matter what.

"I like the competition," I teased and chose to overlook her last statement. I kept my shining smile as I continued. "It makes me feel good. And it reinforces my looks and my fantastic running ability."

Allie finally looked up, her eyes seeing right through me. The sun made her face especially bright, and especially pretty. She chuckled and crossed her arms beneath her camera.

"Of course you would say that," she muttered under her breath. "I don't even understand why you're talking to me."

"Because I like you. Will you get a drink with me?" I asked hopefully. I grinned from ear to ear and eventually crossed my arms to mimic Allie. "Go out with me."

"I already told you—I'm not the kind of girl you'd want to be with. Do you really think asking me this over and over again will make me want to go out with you or even talk to you?"

I grinned and rocked back and forth on my feet.

"But you are talking to me. You might say you don't like me, but you aren't walking away," I pointed out.

Allie pinched the bridge of her nose and sighed.

"I'm sorry, Ben, I can't." When she glanced up, her eyes trailed past me, and she waved down a girl in soccer shorts. "Audrey! Come on, let's go see how the light in the science hall is now!"

Allie Johncox hurried off without a goodbye and went off with her friend toward the classrooms. She turned around after she sprinted across the road, and I would've bet money that I saw her eyes glimmering on her pouty face.

My plan had failed once more. What was I doing wrong?

Allie's and her friend, Audrey's, silhouettes became smaller and smaller until they were two dots in the distance.

Her friend, Audrey, popped into my mind. I'd seen her before. She was in my Microeconomics class on Tuesdays and Thursdays. Maybe she could be of some help to me.

I kicked a small stone with my foot, thinking about Allie and about the meet. But my mind drifted to one more than the other. Allie Johncox. Her name was like a celebrity's before they made it flashy. A name that was perfectly fine all on its own.

Tuesday. I'd try something different on Tuesday.

After Microeconomics that day, I followed Audrey out of class and to the library.

"So, you're Audrey, right?"

Audrey had short dark brown hair that stuck up on all sides, completely the opposite of how it was on that Saturday. I assumed—and thanked my science professors—that it was the humidity. This week was getting hot. She wore rectangular glasses that made her boxy face even more square. She wasn't ugly, but she wasn't naturally pretty like Allie. I had barely talked to her before since she never looked up much—she mostly kept her nose down at her shoes.

"May I help you?" she asked.

She chose expensive-looking clothing, but she still wore black everything, had five earrings going up her left ear, and dark red nail polish on every finger except for black on her thumbs.

"Yeah, actually. You're friends with Allie Johncox, right?"

"Oh yeah, you're that track guy she turned down." I don't think she meant it as an insult, just being honest. "Weird, you're cuter than I remember."

Normally a compliment like that would propel me into full flirtation mode and imagine us finding the nearest coat closet, but that wasn't important to me anymore.

"Uh, thanks," I mumbled, "but I just wanted to ask you why I keep striking out with Allie."

"Oops, sorry," she said and tucked a strand of hair behind her ear, "that's not really my place to say. Just leave her alone. Allie's more of a steady girl, not one you can just drop when you're done with her."

"So, I'm guessing you mean she's a have-to-ask-my-father-for-my-hand kind of girl?" I guessed.

Audrey rolled her eyes. "I guess you could put it like that. We both know you, Ben, know *of* you. We know who you like and what you like, and you're wasting your time with Allie. She's a fragile flower, and you will crush her."

But I didn't care. Maybe Audrey hadn't realized it, but she just gave me a great deal of information. I knew exactly what I was going to do.

On Thursday, I spotted Allie heading to the fieldhouse after lunch, so I hurried up behind her.

Eventually, Allie turned around with her eyes mid-roll.

"What do you want, Ben?"

But her weight shifted a bit. Her eyes met mine for a moment and then looked away.

"I want you to get a drink with me, go out with me, Allie Johncox, anything," I said as I kept my winning smile plastered on my face. "Come on, Allie, give me a chance. You have no idea what you're missing."

Allie blushed. Audrey had described her as a fragile flower, and I began to see her tough exterior crack.

"I think I know what I'm missing, and I'm happy. I won't bring any joy to your life, and you won't to mine." She spun on her heel and hurried toward the dining commons. But again, it happened—she couldn't help looking over her shoulder at me.

Although I'd been rejected once more, I still hoped Allie might give me one more chance for me to prove I wasn't like what she'd heard.

But no matter, I was determined that the next day, Friday, would be the day she said yes. And I promised myself, it would be the last time I asked. A record of an infinite number of girls saying 'yes' to one 'no' was still good numbers.

I had an idea, and I was hoping I'd be able to put it into motion. So, without further ado, I went to the fieldhouse for practice. Sure enough, as if desiring to see me too, Allie was there observing the trees and the blue sky, taking pictures, and creating her little stories.

When practice finished, I quickly showered and dressed. If I was lucky, Allie would still be here. Thankfully, she was standing at the vending machine, playing with a few silver coins. She moved them from one hand to the other, while biting her lip nervously. Her eyes darted from the corner of the glass to her hand, and back again.

I walked over toward the water vending machine, trying to be nonchalant, which was by the snack machine—right next to Allie. I glanced over at Allie to see her check the time on her watch, and then quickly feed the machine her coins. She groaned, and I looked back to the water machine. I always had money in my pocket, but I carried my Nalgene bottle in my bag, so I really didn't need anything.

"Oh no," I heard Allie mutter. "Does anyone have a quarter?" she asked around, looking at other athletes in the fieldhouse lobby. There was a boy kicking a soccer ball who shook his head, and a few girls in bright Spandex apologized before hurrying away.

After a pause, Allie's yellow sandals turned toward me, and she looked between us at the ground.

"Ben?" she asked. "Do you have a quarter to spare?"

This could finally be my moment. Allie needed my help, but I wasn't sure how to play it, feeling more unsure of myself after being rejected twice.

"Oh, Allie!" I said as if I had just spotted her. "How are you doing?"

"I'm fine," she sighed. "Do you have a quarter I could borrow, please?" She spoke so quickly that if I hadn't heard her question earlier, I would've thought she was speaking baby gibberish.

"A quarter?" I repeated in a much slower voice, trying to seem casual. "Hmm, let me check..." I reached into my pocket and pulled out two dollars, one crisp, and one wrinkly. "Take your pick."

Allie went for the crisp dollar, as I assumed, but I pulled them away too quickly for her.

"I'm not going to give them up so easily. First, you have to promise me something."

"I'm not going to get a drink with you!" she exclaimed. Allie pushed her forehead up against the vending machine glass and groaned. "Please, Ben, I'm in a hurry. You're wasting precious time. I just want to get my Funyuns and go. Please." Her lips parted, and her eyes looked up to me and softened like a puppy dog. Normally patient and calm, Allie was breaking.

"I'm not going to ask you to get a drink with me," I corrected. "I was going to ask you something else. If you borrow a dollar, you have to go on a *date* with me. And I promise to be a perfect gentleman." I could have been mistaken, but Allie's eyes looked as if they lit up slightly. Her shoulders relaxed, and she stood up straighter.

"Why," she breathed out, "do you want to go on a date with me so badly?"

I hadn't expected that response, but I understood it. Although no girl ever questioned why I wanted to go on a date, I thought my intentions were always obvious. But maybe not to someone like Allie.

"I like you," I said simply.

"You don't even *know* me," she protested. "Please, just... I'm kind of in a hurry. What's your honest answer?"

"That is my honest answer," I said honestly. The words started to tumble out of my mouth before I could stop them. "I like the way you talk about photography. I like the way you create stories just from a few stills. I like that unlike many other girls I've met, you're not falling over yourself at me. You're sassy—you actually have a personality. I think you're one of the most fascinatingly beautiful women on this campus. And all I know is that from the moment I met you almost two weeks ago, I haven't been able to get you out of my mind. I want to have the opportunity to get to know you and don't want to imagine my life not knowing you, and I don't even know why!" I said exasperatedly. My own words shocked me. "All I know is there's a little part inside of me, that from the moment I met you, has gravitated towards you, and I want to know what else there is to know about you, Allie Johncox."

Allie had finally met my eyes again. Her lips broke apart, but no words came out.

"I know I haven't gone about this the best way," I said and scratched the back of my neck, "and maybe you're right, and I should just give up. But I just had to try one more time, because I think you're worth getting to know."

I held out the dollar to her.

"Take it. Don't worry about paying me back. Not even with a date. I shouldn't have lorded it over you like that in the first place," I sighed. "Maybe I can be an idiot in how I approached this, but you really are something else, though, Allie."

I turned around and headed out toward the door. Behind me, the clatter of change from the vending machine told me Allie got her Funyuns. I pushed open the door to head outside, but the door didn't close behind me.

I turned, and Allie caught the door behind me. She looked up at me again.

"That was… one of the kindest things anyone has ever said to me," she said softly. "I've never… I don't… I don't date often. Ever," she admitted. "I don't really know how to respond when someone shows interest in me, so I guess I just get defensive and put up a wall. It just doesn't really happen. But…did you really mean all of that? Or was it just a sneaky ploy to get me to sleep with you?"

Ah, there it was, the sass again. Or, I guessed if she was anything like me, self-preservation.

We stepped out into the afternoon sun, walking side by side.

"I meant it," I reassured her. "Every word. Even the ones I didn't know I was going to say."

The silence within us was filled with expectation. I didn't know if Allie wanted me to speak next, or if she was building up her courage. But then, she spoke.

"No drink, no date," she said. "But what if we just… talk? You seem to really like me, and I—" she hesitated before continuing, "I've heard some rumors about you that may have clouded my judgment. I think you deserve a chance to show the real you. Is that a deal?"

Allie held out her hand, and I stared at it for a moment. She had turned things around. It was now *my* yes that was needed. Very sneaky.

I took my chance.

"Meet me outside the library tomorrow at seven?" I offered. "We can walk around my favorite spots in Mt. Hope?"

"I can't do it tomorrow, or Sunday at all. Monday?"

"Monday it is."

"Okay. Bye then, Ben."

Allie began to walk toward the parking lot, her Funyuns still clutched in her hand. But despite being in a hurry earlier, she turned to look back and wave at me before she headed off.

With a wide smile on my face, I waved back at her.

And with the excitement about seeing her on Monday still pounding in my chest, I watched the wonderful Allie Johncox drive off in her yellow Jeep, with the Funyun bag sitting on the dashboard.

It wasn't a proper date with Allie, but it was a start. I felt my chest twinge as I thought of the words I spoke to her. The truth about how I'd been feeling wanting to burst forth.

My brain was buzzing, thinking over the conversation repeating in my head. I couldn't focus on anything else, so I hurried to the track and ran and ran until I could no longer feel my legs, but Allie's smile and wave stayed stamped in my mind.

8

April 23rd, 1990

Waiting for Allie outside the library for our not-a-date was painstaking. I felt a nervous pang in my chest and kept checking my watch. I wanted to play it casual, so I'd worn my favorite black t-shirt that looked sharp against my brown skin. The night was young and warm. The sun had not set yet but was illuminating the sky near the horizon.

I glanced at my watch again. 7:15.

I sighed and leaned against the rusty railing. She was either running late or must have had a change of heart. That would be crushing after I'd admitted to myself—and to her—how I felt about her.

Then, on the top of my head, a cool, hard object pressed onto my curls. At first, I thought it was just a drop of rain, and I groaned. Rain wasn't much better than intense sunshine. However, nowhere else was wet, and when I patted my hair, I pulled off a bright silver quarter.

"I wanted to pay you back," said Allie, who suddenly appeared behind me.

She walked around the railing and stepped up the stairs back beside me.

"Well, sort of. Think of it as a down payment. You'll get the rest if you behave." Allie winked. She was back. Whatever stressor was plaguing Allie when she was desperate for Funyuns was gone, her playful teasing was back, and she seemed lighter.

"No, no," I said and pocketed the quarter. "It's great. Uh, thank you." I normally didn't trip over my words around girls. but Allie made me nervous. And then again, the girls I usually talked to were so horny I could've said, "I make my clothes out of potato skins" and they still would've followed me to my bedroom. Perhaps I didn't realize how nervous I got in front of girls until there was one worth bumbling over.

"I thought we could walk along one of my favorite running routes, if that sounds good?"

She shrugged and pulled the strap from her yellow tank top which had slipped off her shoulder.

"Alright."

I bit my lip, and for good measure, stuffed my hands deep in my pockets.

"Well, come on then." I headed down the faded white cement walkway that crisscrossed through the campus. But it was only wide enough for one person. "You go," I told Allie and made my path alongside her on the damp grass.

Allie looked hesitant but stepped along the dry walkway.

"Tell me about yourself, Ben," she said and watched me from the side as I trampled through the grass. She chuckled when I tripped over my feet and flung out my arms to steady myself. I quickly jumped my feet together, arms up like a gymnast.

"And he sticks the landing," she laughed.

I laughed along with her and already began to feel myself relax around her company, my nerves fading.

"Well," I said as I went back to her original question, "what do you want to know about me?" I asked as I skipped over the bump between the sidewalk and grass. I couldn't help but notice Allie had already relaxed next to me.

"Anything. The basics, really. Favorite color, birthday, if you've ever met a celebrity. You know, the gist. But I want you to give the background too for why, not just the answer!"

I shrugged and played along with her game.

"Okay. Well, you know, my name is Ben, which I really like by the way. I was named after my grandfather on my mother's side, and he was in the Air Force during World War II." I saw Allie nod approvingly, and I continued. "Oh, you said birthday, right? It's April 1st. April's Fools jokes are not fun when your grandparents tease that they got you tickets to the Olympics as a birthday present."

Allie guffawed in shock.

"Oh, that's terrible! How old were you?"

"Seven. The '76 Olympics in Montreal."

She burst into laughter again. "Seven? You poor kid!"

I laughed along with her. It was a funny story now, no matter how much it had hurt at the time.

"Sorry," Allie said, collecting herself, "you're supposed to be talking, right? Please, continue."

I harrumphed.

"Anyway, my favorite color is black," I said, gesturing to my shirt. My eyebrows threaded together as I studied Allie, who was waving her hand for me to continue. Then I remembered: background. "Um, I wear it a lot, like now," I pointed to my shirt, "because it makes me sweat more. More sweat means less fat," I rhymed. Allie stifled a chuckle. "I also wear a sweatshirt when I work out over a black shirt to make me sweat even more. I've heard some Olympians do it, and that's my ultimate goal—to be an Olympian."

Allie nodded as she hopped across a square of cement, jumping from crack to crack.

"Olympics, huh? That's… really cool. I had no idea. Honestly, I thought you were just the same as all the other jocks, that's… a big goal."

"I'm headed that way, hopefully," I explained. "The meet on Saturday had a lot of scouts for the Olympics. I'm still too slow to qualify, but if I keep it up, I hope I can get my times down."

"Too *slow!?*" Allie exclaimed. "I saw you the other day. It's like you're spring-loaded when you run. How are you still too slow?"

I scratched my neck again—a nervous tic of mine. "Eh, it's all based on milliseconds at this point. And trust me, when it comes to the Olympics, you can be fast but still too slow."

Allie must have sensed I didn't want to go further into it.

"So, *have* you met any celebrities?" she inquired, changing the subject.

"I actually have," I teased, and Allie's eyebrows raised in interest. "Last year, my buddy Spencer and I went on a little road trip to Los Angeles. We saw, uh, that one girl from the movie with Tom Hanks. The mermaid?"

"Daryl Hannah?"

"Yes, that one. There were a bunch of people like, crowding around her and asking for an autograph. She was so hot that I—" I stuttered. I was not coming across as Amazing Ben Asan as I thought. I blushed and ran my fingers through my hair.

"So, yeah, I've met a famous person. Have you?"

Allie sighed and shook her head as we began to walk along the dark road. Loads of potholes littered the streets of Mt. Hope with makeshift slabs of asphalt to decrease the holes and increase the bumps. I stepped on one such bump that looked almost like melted black chocolate chips and picked at it with the tip of my sneakers.

"I wish. That's something I want to do someday before I die, sort of like on my bucket list." She gave a satisfied sigh and smiled. "But I shouldn't worry. I have my whole life, hmm?"

"Yeah, you shouldn't," I agreed. "Because you've already met somebody famous."

"What?" Allie asked, and her eyebrows knit together. Her eyes flashed up to mine and narrowed.

God, she was beautiful.

"You've met someone famous: me."

Allie rolled her eyes and continued walking.

"You are completely full of yourself," she laughed. "This is why I won't go on a date with you." She took a few longer strides ahead of me, and I jogged up to meet her speed.

"It was only a joke," I insisted as I continued to jog to keep up. "I'm not full of myself. I'm the right amount of myself. It's just a joke."

Allie turned to face me slowly with a face of utter disbelief.

"It's not a joke about how conceited you are. No one likes to be around someone who just talks about how great they are, and how the girl is missing out without them. Your fishing for compliments is uncomfortable. No one likes being put into a corner like that, Ben." While sounding strong at first, Allie's voice dropped into a whisper.

I clicked my tongue and stuffed my hands into my pockets. My eyes glanced back up at her almost expecting to see my father yelling at my teenage self. The shame spread inside me like the rising tide; at once, and then lingered. I had spent years perfecting this confident, Wonderful Ben Asan version of myself, that I had no idea how I really came across to someone who could see right through me.

"I'm sorry," I responded. "You said you wanted to get to know the real me outside the rumors, and I have not done a good job of showing you who I really am. But please let me start over." I held out my hand. "Hi. I'm Ben Asan. I'm not as confident as I make myself out to be, which is why I put on this front because I just want people to like me." I gave a silly grin, hoping to ease the tension.

Allie tucked her arms across her chest.

"Hi, I'm Allie Johncox," she said with a chuckle. "And I appreciate your apology, Ben. And your willingness to be honest. But I need you to understand that I've been hurt by guys just like you in the past." She sighed. "I guess you would say I'm cautious. It would be easier for me not to get involved with you at all."

"I understand," I began, and Allie raised an eyebrow of disbelief. "Okay, I can *try* to understand. If you'll give me time..." I wanted to say more, but I didn't want to press her. "I do really like you, Allie. What I said on Friday? That was a glimpse of the real me. I've just gotten really good at hiding, because..."

No, I shook my head. I couldn't go into that right now.

After a pause, Allie spoke.

"I'm sorry for calling you conceited."

"It's fine, really," I insisted. "I hear worse stuff from my father, and he's not even defending himself."

There, now we both said something personal we regretted.

After a few minutes, she spoke again.

"People don't normally like me."

"Well, I like you," I reiterated. "Even when you make little sassy remarks. It makes you interesting. Or endearing—I just learned that word this week on my friend Spencer's desk calendar." I looked Allie up and down with a coy smile playing at my lips. "It describes you pretty well, I think."

Normally, when I complimented girls, they'd blush and wink, signaling my success. But Allie, however, looked at me with wide eyes and her mouth slightly opened as though in disbelief.

"Interesting is just a nice word for weird," she recited like it was the state capital. "Besides, you barely know me, remember?"

I shrugged and kept walking, my hands still tucked in my pockets, now nervously twisting the fabric inside. Allie's hand lay against her side and swayed as she walked.

"I'd like to get to know you," I said, turning towards her. "Even if you are weird. Funnily enough, I think I'd like you less if you weren't."

Allie's eyes were looking at mine when I finally dared to look at her.

"I think people like you. More than that, I think you are very likable. I want to get to know you so I can prove you wrong like you wanted me to prove you wrong."

Allie belly-laughed so loudly and unexpectedly, I nearly jumped.

"Really? Is that the line you give every girl on the tennis team?"

Oh, so she *really* knew my reputation.

"I've used it on one other girl," I told her with complete honesty. "My younger sister."

Her laughing ceased.

"Now I know everything about her." I could tell Allie had to suppress an eyeroll. "I'm serious. The lines I've used on girls have been awful. Have I used any lines on you?" I asked to prove my point.

"I guess not," Allie mumbled. "What would you like to know about me?"

And we kept walking and talking. At one point, I tried to grab her hand, but Allie quickly shot it away. I took the hint and stuffed my hand back in my pocket.

She apologized for prejudging me, and I told her she had a right to, with a reputation like mine, and that she should stop apologizing so much.

"It's a thing of the past," I explained and that quieted Allie. The words I used to encourage my sister were universal it seemed. "And if you keep apologizing to people, you'll keep thinking they don't like you—"

"Why are you *so* interested in me again?" she asked with a laugh.

"Like I said before," I explained, "you are endearing. You are creative. I can just tell the cogs in your brain are firing at all hours of the day, and I want to know what makes them tick. You intrigue me, always walking around with a camera in your hand. Which is, by the way, very strange to see you without one tonight."

Allie shook her head and gave a soft chuckle, relaxing with my words.

"I always have a camera with me," she corrected, and out of her pocket she pulled an orange disposable camera out. "Even if this isn't one of my favorites."

An oak tree loomed above us, and Allie brought the camera to her eye and tilted her head back. It seemed like an eternity had passed before I finally heard a faint click, and the familiar scroll of ticks.

"What's your favorite camera?" I asked as she quickly pocketed the disposable camera.

"Um," she said, biting her lip in thought. "I guess a Polaroid or a Nikon FA which takes amazing exposure shots." Her face lit up, and her eyes sparkling beneath the dim light seemed to dance. "But when it comes to—wait!"

"I wasn't going to—"

"I said wait!"

With the gracefulness of an ostrich, Allie hurried down the road at a sprint. However, in a few strides of a good jog, I could pass her. She wasn't exactly the fastest runner. In fact, I wasn't sure what she was doing *was* running. She'd almost tripped over her own feet twice already. To make her technique worse, she simultaneously reached for her small camera and fell to her knees once she reached the grass.

With grace and speed and only *five* strides, I reached Allie's side. I extended my hand to help her up, just like a gentleman would, but she quickly popped up like a spring, brushed the staining green grass and smashed dirt and rocks from her kneecaps, and hurried over to the fence that blocked off the perimeter of the track. She tried to climb onto the fence by squishing her toes in between the small diamond shaped wires. She scrunched her big toes to hold on, but I knew once she let her hands go, she wouldn't be able to balance.

Allie groaned and tried to stand up.

"Darn it! Ben, can you please help me?" she asked and looked back at me with a pouty face—she knew how to play her cards. "The sunset looks so beautiful, but I can't get a good angle. Can you try and hold me up?" She batted her eyelashes and turned the pout into a winning smile.

"Can I hold your waist?" I asked to make Allie comfortable. My hands wavered by her hips, and I made sure not to even brush her. If I planned on getting anywhere with this girl, I couldn't press my luck.

"Yeah, yeah," Allie mumbled, waving me off. She didn't really seem to hear my question as her mind was too focused on the sunset before her.

With Allie's permission, I set my hand on the smooth curve of her waist and steadied her with a soft squeeze.

As if suddenly getting the courage to stand, Allie straightened her legs and pushed her hips against the top of the fence as she tried to balance. She exposed her lip, which had small bite marks on them, and her eyes dropped, losing the hope of a beautiful, albeit low-quality, photograph.

I gave her waist a gentle squeeze to reassure Allie I was still there, and it seemed to help her. From beneath her, I pushed my head to the side and saw her face brighten, her dimples deepen, and her white smile widen. She brought the camera up to her eyes, looked through the lens for just a moment, and pressed the plastic button.

It gave a hollow click. She scrolled and scrolled, and it didn't stop.

"What? Oh no. No!" She groaned. "No film…" she said after a moment of denial. I kept a grip on her waist as she hopped off the fence like a failed dance lift.

"I must've used the last film on the tree…" Allie looked back at the setting sun, whose hues of orange, purple, and pink had now begun to fade. "Oh well," she sighed and pocketed the now-useless Kodak disposable camera. "I have a lot of sunset pictures anyway," she mumbled. But by Allie's slump and her quieted voice, I knew she was disappointed.

"Where are your other cameras?"

"Don't worry about it," Allie whispered, her voice losing its honey tone. "I told you. I may have a thousand pictures of sunsets. It wasn't that pretty anyway." That was a complete lie. Allie would later describe The Sunset That Got Away as an exploding array of shades in hot colors, bursting against the pinking strips of clouds on the horizon.

We began walking again, and my hands wormed their way back into my pockets. Our shuffles were quiet, and we talked no more.

Allie ended up leading us back toward the dining commons entrance, still looking rather down.

"Well, I guess this is the end of our 'not-a-date,'" she said, adding air quotes with her fingers.

I shook my head.

"Not now. Not exactly. I want to take you to one more place. And I want you to show me something." I held out my hand. "Close your eyes."

"No! What? How do I not know you're not a Ted Bundy type?"

Now she was just being ridiculous.

"Am I pretending to be injured to gain your sympathy? No. I simply wanted to go to the art gallery, which is a brightly lit public place, to hear some of your thoughts on the photographs there." I held up my hands in defense and shrugged innocently. "I just wanted it to be a surprise."

Allie's face fell and she glanced at her feet. "I'm sorry," she said as we headed in the direction of the art gallery. "I just always have my guard up."

"Any particular reason why?" I asked, curious.

"Do I look like an open book you can peruse, looking at each of my chapters with your own sick leisure?" Allie explained, but she immediately burst into laughter. "Sorry, sorry," she said, this time with a smile on her face. "I've just always had that comeback in my mind after thinking of it two hours after some girl asked me if I had kissed some guy. I've just been *dying* for the perfect moment to use it."

"Smart," I said with my eyebrows almost disappearing into my black hair. "So, *did* you kiss that guy?"

Allie's laugh echoed as we stepped into the stone foyer of the art gallery. "I knew you'd ask…" She spoke as if we'd known each other for years. "As a matter of fact, I did. Or, well, he kissed me if you're picky like that… It was years ago, though. I don't even remember his name," Allie chuckled as if it was funny, but it came out far too sad. "He was actually my first and only kiss. It was after high school and he was talking to me by my locker, right in the corner of the building, and when no one was looking he pecked me right on the lips. Not very romantic, I must say."

"No, it doesn't sound like it," I agreed. "My first kiss wasn't much better. I was walking with this girl. I don't remember much about her, but her name was Jan." I internally groaned. I hated this story, but Allie had shared something personal, so it felt only fair to share the disappointment of my first kiss with her. "She told me she wanted to kiss me, and before I knew what was going on she pushed herself against me, completely missed my lips, and kissed my eye." In my peripheral vision, I saw Allie stifle a laugh.

"She was really embarrassed and tried again. The second time she got my chin. Finally, I just held her head in place and kissed her. She ran off and never talked to me again," I sighed. "Good old Kindergarten," I joked.

"Aw," Allie chuckled. "That's a sweet story. Better than mine at least."

Suddenly, our conversation ceased as Allie had opened the door to the photography section and walked in as if greeting the gates of heaven.

"Allie, I was thinking—"

"Shh," she hushed me and held up a finger for silence. Her eyes widened as she observed the hundreds of photographs —black and white, color, sepia— and soaked in the art.

"But I just—"

"Shh." Her voice was breathy, like she was speaking to butterflies and bluebirds. Never had I ever seen a girl so in love with photography. She seemed absolutely bewitched by the gray walls sporting even grayer squares of glossy film.

It was mad, however, that I wanted to keep talking just to hear the soft "Shh," fall out of her mouth.

After a few moments of distant observation, Allie turned to me with a grin spread wide from ear to ear.

"Okay, okay, I'm done. What were you saying?"

"Don't worry about it," I mumbled. "I was just thinking we could go around and talk about what we thought each photograph was about, but if you don't want to..."

The next smile I had never seen before. It was mischievous, exciting, and completely pure.

"That's divine."

And so, we did.

Allie decided that the fat man trying to squeeze into a little pink inflatable ring was about how people were always trying to mold into the world's perfect society. I said it was about how the man needed to lose weight to achieve his goal.

"Same thing," Allie shrugged. And we both thought the eye containing the galaxy meant this person was God, knowing and seeing all.

"What about this one?" Allie asked curiously and pointed to a photograph of a girl's feet. At least I assumed it was a girl. Men didn't normally have chipped blue nail polish on their toenails. They were covered in dirt, wrinkly, and all scratched up.

"You see," I began, tilting my chin up to observe the photograph. I added a stuffy English accent to top it. "I believe the photographer is trying to say that it is raining outside, and she is dying, that's why the feet look shriveled up."

Allie raised her eyebrows as she studied the photograph more closely.

"Good guess," she said, "but I think the photograph means that even the most clean, proper, rich people, whose lives are quite in order are easily destroyed and affected by the changing, evil world."

"Wow," I scoffed. "A bit dark, don't you think?"

Allie gave a shrug and turned toward a photograph of a dissected frog.

"Maybe. What do I know? You could be right."
As she walked off to another corner of the room, she brushed the frame, and my eyes spotted a small slip of paper in the lower right corner. My face immediately flushed as I read it, and I looked toward Allie. Something in my chest tightened. Neatly typed, it read:

The Destroying World by Allie Johncox

9

Devon stood up and stretched, and his back cracked down his stiff spine. His head was throbbing, and as if he knew, Asan had gotten him a cup of water as well. Devon's neck strained to look behind him, and he spotted an Audubon clock with the numbers as different types of birds. The long hand pointed to the Eastern Meadowlark, and the short hand to the Hermit Thrush, displaying the time: eleven thirty.

Time had flown by; Devon had been at Asan's for an hour. It took him a moment to figure between Asan's pauses of thinking and his random, off-subject comments like, "I got this little artifact from my trip to India," he held up a little wooden elephant on the kitchen windowsill "do you like it?" —Devon said yes, genuinely—that the time had merely disappeared. He was starting to feel a lot better, but he wasn't sure he wanted to tell Asan that. He was enjoying learning about Dr. Asan as a young man and was reassured that Asan had made some of the mistakes Devon felt like he'd been making lately.

"Allie's just so... I don't know..."

"Unique?" Asan suggested, though Devon would have disagreed. "Yes, I thought so, too. There was some sort of feeling I got from being around her. At the time, it was unexplainable. She was beautiful—well, still is beautiful. She's never stopped. But she was just cautious about me back then. She built up a wall against people like me."

"How did you get into history?" Devon asked suddenly. "Not to change the subject or anything, but how? You said you hated it back then." He sat back down in the velvet dining chair, skeptical with an eyebrow raised. "Some old man didn't tell *you* a story when you were his student, did he? Is that what this is about, some sort of inception?"

Asan shook his head and laughed.

"No, no. That is a part of the story that doesn't come up until the end, I'm afraid. You don't hear the end in the beginning because the story is much better when the ending is at the end." At a second thought, he muttered, "or not there at all."

Devon tried not to think too much on what he meant by that—he hated things ending as well. His stomach turned again at the idea of possibly losing Lindsey when she found out the truth.

"What is your life like, Mr. Camburn? I bet it is more interesting than mine, at the moment," he laughed. "I'm currently spending my time spilling my life story to one of my students now, apparently, and the occasional game of poker with my fellow colleagues." He paused. "You have a girlfriend, you said?" Asan asked. "Miss Huff, am I correct?"

Devon nodded.

"Yeah, Lindsey's my girlfriend… But I don't know if she will be for much longer," he admitted.

"Trouble in paradise?" Asan seemed genuinely concerned. "That sounds like a question of history, uncertainty, and murkiness."

"It was fine, everything was fine. Until tonight." He gagged for a moment. Maybe he wasn't feeling better yet after all. "I'm sorry. I-I don't think I'm ready to talk about it yet. I-I'm so ashamed of myself."

Asan held up his hand in surrender.

"Of course, Mr. Camburn, sorry to intrude…" He winked over at Devon. "But as your professor and advisor, I just want to let you know if there is some stress with Miss Huff, I am here for you." He cleared his throat and glanced out of the window; it was still snowing.

"I love winter," Asan remarked, changing the subject. He raised his coffee to his lips—now on his second cup. "It is *much* better than summer. Summer has been my least favorite season for years. It is too hot, I sweat more, and I am altogether uncomfortable. On the bright side, this town is always quieter without all the students…"

"So, you like your peace and quiet, huh?" Devon confirmed. "You would rather sit in a noiseless room than go to a party?"

Asan laughed and shook his head.

"Of course not! Well, maybe now, but when I was your age, about twenty-one, I would rather have music constantly playing or be around lots of people at once. It was a nice distraction." His eyes looked over Devon's shoulder, perhaps imagining his life before that point. "But I cannot say that now. Peace and quiet suits me best, I think. That's why I talk so much," Asan added as an afterthought as he scratched at his neck, "because when

I'm in my moments of noise, I think, and so in times of quiet, I speak."

Asan looked back to Devon, his gaze far from the window now.

"I hope your girlfriend issues get worked out. Young love separated by something repairable is truly tragic. You still have time to make things better. There's always time."

With a watery look in his eyes, Asan poured himself a third cup.

As far as Devon was concerned, cheating on Lindsey was beyond repair. He knew he couldn't keep it from her and pretend it was all okay. Thinking of her made his stomach flip again.

"I-I really love the way my girlfriend smiles," Devon started. "She has this cute little dimple—just on one side—that stands out when she smiles and laughs. She's an artist—like Allie is—but she does mostly painting and sculpting."

Just earlier that week Lindsey had revealed her newest project to Devon, with that perfect dimple marking her joy.

"Is that…?" Devon had queried.

"Two pigs salsa dancing, yes," Lindsey had confirmed with a squeal. She had covered Devon's eyes with her hands and led him into the pottery studio. There, in her corner of the world, stood two clay pigs, sculpted together, with intertwined hooves and bodies. One was sculpted wearing a salsa skirt; the other, a Latin body shirt, complete with a deep V-neck. The male pig looked a bit like Antonio Banderas.

"I still have to fire it, but what do you think?" Lindsey bit her lip in anticipation, but she didn't have to be nervous.

"It's brilliant. You're brilliant," Devon had said and kissed her.

Devon shook his head at the memory, and his mind transported him back to the present.

"Do you have any of Allie's photographs around?" Devon asked. "I know how proud I am of Lindsey's work."

Asan thought for a moment.

"I mean, I have so many it's hard to pick, but…there's one in particular that may interest you…"

He shuffled past Devon – "Excuse me"—over toward the living room. He pulled out a flat, leather book at the base of the bookshelf. At first, Devon thought it was a portfolio. But placed in his lap, he saw it was a yearbook.

Plastered beneath the words *Mt. Hope University 1990-1991* was a black and white picture of what looked like the track team out by the fieldhouse. The camera was angled parallel to the ground, and two legs in a running formation could be made out. Right behind the mystery legs was a blurry figure with its elbows in, chest in mid-rise, and its cheeks inflated with air. However, the runner's dark features, strong jawline, and wide eyes outlined a young Asan. Devon's first glimpse into the past.

"Try page thirty-eight," Asan advised.

Devon flipped through the yearbook. He made it to the page and found Asan standing in the back row furthest on the left. At the bottom read: (L to R) Asan, Ben (Sn) Samson, Jeremy (F) Pogski, Warner (J).

Asan had unruly, curly, black hair. Devon smirked as he glanced up at his professor. There was no evidence of that in the present. And unlike the cover photo, which was serious, he was smiling with the other track runners.

Devon's eyes traveled to the side of the photograph. In bold, black print read: **Photographs taken by Allie Johncox**.

"Flip once more," Dr. Asan instructed, and Devon listened. But it wasn't a yearbook page that stood out, but a loose photograph, one of Dr. Asan—Ben—smiling directly at the photographer, nearly laughing out of joy.

"That's my favorite photo," he said, "taken August 1990, right before move-in day senior year," Dr. Asan explained. "Allie's always been tremendous at capturing emotions in her work. And she really found a way to showcase how I felt about her."

10

May 4th, 1990

I kept seeing Allie's name everywhere now that I knew who she was. Her name was in the Mt. Hope newspaper; on a forgotten homework assignment in the hallway; in the art gallery on more than just one photograph. It was sort of like that feeling you get when you buy a new car, and then you constantly start seeing that car because you're more aware of its existence.

Occasionally I'd see her in the dining commons. I would give a nod to her, and she would give a smile and a wave back.

"I heard you're 'smitten' about some girl," a voice said behind my ear as I sat down on the couch one morning with a bowl of cereal.

I whipped my head around and saw it was Brennan. We didn't speak much in the house, so I had no idea where he would get his information. I had a reputation to uphold, and me taking things slowly with a girl I had actual feelings for would tarnish it.

I frowned slightly before laughing it off.

"Smitten? I'm not smitten about anyone. And what is this, *Pride and Prejudice*?"

It was Brennan's turn to chuckle.

"At least you've heard of good literature."

I shrugged and turned my back in hopes the conversation would end. But alas, it did not.

"I know you went on a date with Allison Johncox."

I whipped around and stared at him over the back of the couch.

"Where did you get that idea?"

"So, it's true?"

"No, actually," I said. "It was 'not-a-date.' And it's none of your business."

"It's plenty of my business," he said. "If you did go out on a date with Allison Johncox, then I have to warn you."

"Warn me about what? Allie is harmless."

Brennan ran his hands through his straw-blond hair, sighed, and crossed his arms.

"She's harmless, but I'm not. Allison is my cousin. And if you're trying to add her to your lay list or something, then don't bother. I've seen her get hurt too many times, and I don't want a stupid boy, especially you, to make her life even worse."

It was a sincere request. But Brennan had me pinned wrong.

"Yes, because I plan on hurting girls the moment I meet them," I said tersely. He glared and raised an eyebrow, but I stood my ground. "You have no idea what my business with Allie is, or is going to be, and you don't need to." There were a lot of people looking out for Allie, more than any other girl I'd ever pursued.

I thought Brennan was going to be upset at me, but he remained calm.

"So, you're serious about her?" he checked, all pretenses dropped. His shoulders, which were tight before, relaxed slightly when I nodded, and he let his arms fall to his sides. "Then.... Can I help you?"

"What?" I was thrown. Brennan and I barely talked, but he wanted to help me?

"Help. I want to help you," he said. "If you're really serious about this, let me help you. I know the things she likes, and how to get on her good side. She may actually begin to like you and she deserves to have someone who makes her happy."

It was my turn to cross my arms. He must really care about his cousin if he was prepared to help me out.

"You mean, like me *more.*"

He raised an eyebrow.

"I mean, *like* you."

Allie and I had gone on two other not-a-date walks at this point, never straggling beyond the borders of MHU. At the end of that second not-a-date, she let me hold her hand. Allie was slowly warming up. Our last date, she greeted me with a hug, and we proceeded to walk the same route, holding hands.

I turned my attention to Brennan and let him give his advice, thankful for his help.

For our fourth date, we would still walk, but I planned things out a bit more, thanks to Brennan. We would be walking my running route in the backroads of Mt. Hope.

I chose to wear my gray bomber jacket, which I usually wore picking up girls because I thought it made me look cool, like a sexy Indian Tom Cruise from *Top Gun*. But I wanted to wear it for a different reason.

At first, when Allie hurried up to me, all I could notice were her eyes. They stood out as a bright green, with specks of gray around the center. It took me a moment to notice her hair, which normally was left down, was tied back neatly with a scrunchie.

"Hi," Allie exclaimed as she threw her arms around me. It still shocked me, her newfound enthusiasm, but I was ready for it to be an expectation. She turned and headed out on our normal route.

"Hello yourself, Allie Johncox," I laughed, but guided her in the opposite direction. "C'mon. Let's walk a new route."

Allie smiled and followed me. I was still impressed with her change in demeanor toward me. I thanked the stars for my luck at the art gallery, which I continued to cite as a game changer.

Tonight, Allie had a dark camera bouncing against her chest as she dropped my hand. Soon, my long strides separated us, and she jogged to catch up.

"Still not-a-date," she said, passing me with a wide grin.

She kept insisting this, with each not-a-date, that it wasn't *really* a date. I played along, even though we both knew better at this point, but I was okay with whatever made her comfortable.

We playfully raced all the way to a side road. Normally an easy run for me, the distance seemed to stretch, and by the time Allie passed me again, I was out of breath from laughing at the silly faces she'd shot at me in an attempt to distract me. I had not been fazed by her tongue sticking out sideways with one eye squinted, but when she grabbed her ears and puffed her cheeks to mimic a monkey, I lost it.

"Yes! Victory!" Allie exclaimed once she halted at the entrance. She celebrated her win with her own slow-motion touchdown dance. As I watched Allie shamelessly party, I roared so hard until I was wheezing.

"Sorry," she blushed and stopped. "Only my sister should see that side of me." She took a deep breath and casually walked back to me—where I had gotten pins and needles in my legs from laughing so hard and was now laying on the ground. "Shush, it's not funny!" she said with a chuckle and took my hand to help me up from the asphalt road.

I slowly got back on my feet, and the laughter subsided.

"A sister?" I asked as we began walking again. "How are we on our fourth not-a-date, and I didn't know you had a sister?"

Allie rolled her eyes jokingly and swept back a small strand of hair that had fallen out.

"I don't know, Ben. You just talk about yourself all the time," she stretched out each word littered with sarcasm. "Her name is Essie and we're nine years apart. She's thirty."

"Thirty?" I asked in surprise. "That seems so old."

She happily graced me again with her cute laugh and swung her arms back and forth as we turned a corner onto one of the main backroads.

"It does seem sort of old. One day I'll be thirty," she whined.

"You'll still be as pretty," I added in as slyly as I could. I watched Allie blush, and I stood half an inch taller.

"And I'll probably be a thousand times hotter, so you'd really be reaching out of your league," I teased.

My reward was a playful slap for that one.

"Anyway, her name is Essie," she continued, "and she's married to this really nice guy named Jack. You should meet him one day." It took Allie a couple seconds to realize what she said, and her face turned scarlet. "I-I didn't mean that we'd keep—I-um—this still isn't a date!"

I chuckled and took her hand as casually as flipping off a light switch.

"I know what you meant," I whispered into her ear. "You look good in red, by the way."

I wrapped both of my arms around her and pulled her closer to me.

"It's like you're a red Popsicle. Or the most adorable fire hydrant." Fire hydrant? How could Allie still make me stumble over my words?

I could see Allie struggling whether to make a retort or just accept the compliment. Finally, her lips turned upward, and she giggled.

"I can't believe you. You're ridiculous, Ben Asan!" She spun herself out of my grasp and ran ahead again.

Like a little copter seed, she spun around, letting the wind, imaginary or real, whip her around.

"I think you're crazy." I stepped forward with sharp movements and took her hand. "Completely mad." My eyes wandered down to her pink cheeks and then her red shirt. The sleeves went down to her elbow where little strings of yellow were stitched on the end. "But seriously, you do look so beautiful in red."

Allie's face wouldn't stop blushing.

"It's actually plum," she corrected, glancing down at her shirt.

I groaned.

"What's the difference? Isn't it a shade of red? You're throwing off my groove," I protested.

Allie Johncox rolled her eyes.

"There are different shades of red, and they mean different things, according to my color theory class," she began. "A little pink can mean teasing or playfulness," she explained.

Although we were standing two steps apart, it felt as if we were only a hair's breadth away. We'd walked together for hours over the last few weeks, talking about anything and everything. Colors were a new topic.

"A deep red, like crimson, can be spicy, hot, or lustful," she clarified. "Plum is a shade of purple."

I took one step forward and placed my hand perfectly on her cheek. I maintained some space, but I kept the most intimate of things—hands—touching skin.

"Well, what's purple?"

It took a moment, and Allie's face contorted as she was deep in thought. I had no idea how her brain worked. Did she have imaginary filing cabinets like me, or was everything she knew plastered on a giant white easel, and it took a keen eye to seek the desired information?

"I don't remember," she murmured after a pause.

And that moment was forever plastered in my mind. Her eyes seemed almost glassy, like she wasn't seeing anything of the outside world, but just lost in her own world. She wasn't just unlike other girls I had been with, but unlike anyone I had ever met. Allie saw beauty in everything.

As I bent closer to Allie, my eyes shifted from her gaze down to her lips.

"May I?" I breathed.

Allie answered in seconds, but it felt like an eternity to me. In response, Allie gave a quick nod.

Our lips only touched for a few seconds, but I couldn't imagine a better few seconds. When I pulled away from the short, innocent peck, Allie pushed her face into my chest and took a long breath.

At first, I thought I had done the cliché of taking her breath away, but then I noticed that she was sniffing me. I suppressed a laugh and kissed the top of her blonde head instead.

"You smell like pine," she blurted out.

Pine? I smelled like pine?

To be fair, I leant down and sniffed her neck, too. Probably not one of the most romantic things I'd ever done, but Allie had started it.

"You smell like lemons," I decided, then let out a snort. "I guess we'd make a good air freshener."

I didn't know if it was my great humor or my pathetic charm, but Allie gave a small chuckle against my chest before pulling away. "Alright, air freshener, lead the way."

So, we kept walking with our hands interlocked. Eventually, Allie began to swing our hands as we rounded a corner and passed a few houses. Her smile had grown even wider; I was unsure if it was from the kiss or the idea that we were air fresheners, but at the sight of her joy, the corners of my mouth upturned, too. Seeing Allie happy made me happy.

"Hey, I was thinking—" I started, "with my business degree, and your degree in photography, maybe we could start a photography studio together."

Allie's laughter echoed mine from earlier.

"Definitely not. You would make little babies cry!"

I rolled my eyes and pulled her closer.

"Gee, thanks," I snorted. "My mom actually *owns* a photography business, so I have helped her before. And *no,* I don't make babies cry." Allie's face brightened when I mentioned my mom's profession. I knew she was in school to become an art teacher, but we all had our practical job and our dream job. I believed I'd just stumbled onto Allie's dream career.

When we finally began to walk again, we didn't speak, but were comforted by the sounds of distant birds singing their lovers' farewell serenades.

"What's this place?" Allie asked as we made our way past a small store off the side of the road.

"A little farmer's stand." In front of the deep red door lay a few crates of squash, tomatoes, and corn. "I've never really been there before. I usually just run by, but my mom has gotten vegetables from here before."

Allie pulled us from the road to the little shack.

"Let's look at it, then."

"No. No, I don't think we should. I don't really need anything, or—"

"It'll be fun!" Allie exclaimed and pushed me in. With her smile and glowing face, I couldn't help but follow.

The little barn that made up the market was no bigger than a gas station bathroom, but the multiple shelves holding the baskets of produce made the little space seem even smaller and cozier. Right in the center was a little green shelf with matching green plastic containers filled with raspberries, blueberries, blackberries, strawberries, and a few with an assortment of them all.

Allie stepped forward to the berries and pulled out her camera. I heard her mumble something about a texture shot, but then she was absorbed in her world of photography.

Lined up all around the market were little crates full of baked goods and vegetables. Eggplants, potatoes, bell peppers, and barrels of beans and peas filled the first few. In the corner, a small wicker basket held suckers, multicolored tops, miniature M&Ms, and loads of homemade caramels. A few sparse Pez dispensers lay on the top next to a doll and parachute men.

When I was younger, I used to time myself when I ran. But I didn't really enjoy using a stopwatch, so I would spin a top instead.

It was blue and as curvy as the women I'd soon find in my company. I would take the handle and practice spinning it before I timed myself to run around my house, and if I could do three laps or so before the top fell, I would be satisfied.

I reached forward into the small basket, picked out a yellow top, and rolled it through my fingers for a moment. It wasn't as smooth as mine had been, so it must have been hand carved.

Just like old times, I gave it a spin. It shook for a moment before steadying out.

"Ben?" Allie's voice rang. I whipped my head around and smiled when I saw her arms brimming with fruit. "Do you want anything? Like an apple, or a peach?"

I looked down at the buckets of fresh fruit. I reached down, clutched a seemingly perfect peach, and rolled it through my hands. "Yeah. I'll just have this."

Her face fell slightly, perhaps, because she felt bad for getting so much when I grabbed so little but shrugged it off and was smiling once again.

As we left the little shop, I looked over my shoulder at the top, now fallen over. Time had run out.

"So, where exactly are we headed?" Allie asked as we trekked up a small hill while avoiding passing cars. She was popping raspberries in her mouth, then blackberries, leaving the strawberries for last.

I shrugged and stole a blackberry from her carton.

"I usually go down to the left, but if you want to stop now and turn around, we can."

Allie shook her head, and as I led her to the first part of Brennan's plan, she suddenly gasped.

"Are those horses?" she exclaimed and crossed over to them. Two horses and a small foal were grazing in the center of their pen. "They are! I used to love horses!" Allie started to ramble about different breeds of horses, and explained that they were Clydesdale, one of the largest breeds.

Thank you, Brennan, I thought, for his insight which had delighted Allie.

"How do you know all of this?" I asked as I stepped forward. The fence was barbed, so I held a hand in front of her for protection.

"I just do. I loved horses when I was little, so my mom bought me tons of horse books, so I could own one when I got older. We couldn't, um, afford it at the time..." She gave a half-hearted chuckle. "Funny. I never got a horse." Her voice trailed off, but she smiled again. "I've never seen this part of Mt. Hope before. And I can still see the clock tower! Strange, isn't it?"

I nodded. When my hand met her waist, Allie relaxed to this new touch.

"Oh! Can we get closer?" she squealed. "I love photographing horses."

"Actually," I began, and pulled her down my normal running trail, "I can show you something better than horses."

Allie's eyes widened, and she nodded.

We talked the whole way about classes, our favorite childhood cartoons, and if the Tigers had a chance in the World Series this year.

Halfway through, Allie mentioned offhandedly that her knees were hurting, and within a second, she was up in my arms, shrieking and exclaiming that she should be let go. After a minute or so, her body relaxed, and she stayed quiet with her head on my chest. I told her stories about our huge family get-togethers when I was a kid only for Allie to interrupt periodically with questions or little comments like, "Must've been fun, huh?" With each question, my smile grew.

"We're almost there," I whispered in her ear.

Allie was rather mellow, keeping just to herself as we rounded the final corner. She was lighter than I thought she would be, and became easier to carry over time, as if her entire body was made up of lace unraveling as we walked.

"Close your eyes," I instructed as we approached the farm. "Okay… Now open them."

I had never met someone as clumsy as Allie in my life. She jumped out of my arms faster than I could advise her not to, and she fell flat on the ground. Her bag of fruit spilled over in the road, but she wasn't too worried about them.

"I WANT TO TOUCH THEM!" she shrieked happily and pushed herself against the wooden fence. Allie Johncox was simultaneously childlike and the most beautiful woman in the world. "Which are they?" she asked after a moment. "Caribou or reindeer?"

I chuckled and pushed myself up against the fence with Allie.

"Caribou, I think. I'm not sure that reindeer actually exist."

Allie shook her head quickly and scrutinized the animals a few feet in front of her.

"No. They're real. Hmm… I think these are reindeer. They're smaller." She reached her hand out, wiggling her fingers. "Come here, reindeer."

A rather large reindeer stared at her but stayed still. It waited a moment, then began to walk away.

"No! Reindeer, come back! Please? Please!"

Allie bit her lip, raised one eyebrow, and reached for her camera.

"Let's do something fun," she whispered, her eyes ablaze with whatever mischievous thoughts were running through her mind. "Help me over the fence, Ben."

Immediately my eyes widened.

"No, *no*, Allie, you are not! You aren't trespassing and getting hurt!" I said firmly.

Allie rolled her eyes.

"I just want to get a good photo, okay? The fence is too high." She gripped onto the fence and looked back at me. "If you won't help me, I'll figure out a way to do it myself." She hoisted one leg up and pushed her body over the fence without caring that my hand was on her ankle.

I sighed, knowing it was fruitless to try and stop her.

"Just be careful, okay? I don't want to see a headline that says, 'PHOTOGRAPHER DEAD FROM ATTEMPTED CARIBOU PICTURE.'"

Allie stuck out her tongue.

"Reindeer," she corrected before hopping off the fence and onto the grass. She landed mere feet away from the nearest reindeer and inches away from its latest excretion.

I rolled my eyes but pulled myself to the top of the fence, balanced with better grace than Allie attempting to take The Sunset That Got Away, and hoisted over to meet her.

"You're gonna die."

"I am not going to die," she giggled dismissively. "Come on. Be at least a little adventurous."

"I'm adventurous!" I countered. "I just don't think going into a fenced area with cow-sized caribou-reindeer is a good adventure."

"They're reindeer, I'm telling you." She took another tentative step forward, then another, as she held her camera up and kept it steady.

The reindeer hardly even moved—for a moment. It just grazed on the grass and was content. The other reindeer, twenty at least, rested in multiple places around their giant pen. I spotted a pair of males fighting in the distance.

Everything was quiet. The only sounds that reverberated in my ears were the crushing of dry grass beneath Allie's feet; the scraps of antlers, rough and barbaric unlike the sectile sound of slicing blades; the final, single tick of a camera grasped between untainted fingers.

Then the harmony of noises broke when a grunt sounded, and the clicking of hooves against the grass caught my attention.

I swore as I pulled Allie aside from the reindeer's path.

See, it would have been a rather awesome movie-like boy-saves-girl moment if the reindeer or caribou had been headed for Allie.

"Ben!" Allie laughed and pushed me away. Immediately, the reindeer started heading for me.

As I sped deeper into the pen to escape the beast, I thought, *Thank God I'm a runner.*

The pen's perimeter didn't seem large on the outside, but it felt like miles when a reindeer was charging after you.

At one point, I thought I was done when I slipped on some wet grass, and it almost caught up to me.

The first time I looked back, I saw Allie snapping photos of a different reindeer. Glad she got her shot, while I was losing steam every second.

By the time I was rounding third, Allie was back by the road, yelling at me to just 'Speed up and jump over' as if I was a magical giant.

As the perimeter was close, I increased my speed, and with all of my strength, I jumped as high as I could over the fence.

Then I met the ground with a thud, thankful for adrenaline and Allie, and out bubbled a great bellow of laughter.

Allie sat beside me, slow clapping.

"Perfect job," she said as she laid down beside me, both of us in the ditch. She handed me a Polaroid. "I particularly like this one where your face screams 'I am terrified, I am going to pee my pants.'" Allie's laughter, although playfully cruel, was contagious.

"Wonderful," I said sarcastically through deep breaths. I laughed through her slide show of the rather horrible memory that began to soften into a funny one. I looked away about halfway through the photos and sniffed. "Ugh, now I smell like reindeer."

Allie chuckled.

"That's attractive." She leant over and gave a whiff. "Wow. You *do* smell horrible. Almost like a dying pig who rolled around in his own vomit and urine."

"You're so sweet! And I thought smelling like pine was bad." I smirked. "Oh, Allie! I think you need a hug!" She shrieked as I wrapped my arms around her. I rubbed my arms up and down her body, and soon we both smelled like we had just sloshed around in a sewer.

"That's repulsive, Ben," she laughed. "And if you cared to know, our hot water isn't working in my dorm!" Now I was in for it.

"You can take a shower at my place if you want," I offered, trying to smooth things over, as we began to walk back. Somehow, we had only passed the entrance to the field, although it felt like hours since I jumped the fence. Our hands, though inches away, had not wandered back together yet.

"Oh, definitely not," she insisted. "There is no way I'm going to be naked in the same building as you, let alone in a dorm room."

Ooh, that burned.

"I don't live in a smelly dorm," I countered. "I live in the house behind the library. The white one." Although, they were all white so there was no way to distinguish between them.

Allie sighed.

"Guess it'll have to be a cold shower. But I shouldn't complain," she said quickly. Her cheeks pinked as she did, which I couldn't help but grin at. "Some people in the world don't even get a shower or a toilet. I have both," she said.

"You'd better have a toilet," I teased.

Allie rolled her eyes and pulled me down the road by my *Top Gun* jacket.

"Come on, let's just go home so I can shower."

"Hey, Allie," I paused as I realized where we were. "If you're serious about not having hot water, I know a perfect alternative to a shower."

It took about five minutes in the opposite direction to get to the Hopso's pool.

A long time ago, during a hot August day, I had gone for a short run. The humidity was blasting, and I had already sweat through two shirts, which I had abandoned in the ditch on my route, to pick up on my way back.

Close to my death, I smelled chlorine—a pool was nearby. I practically sprinted toward the scent and found myself standing in front of an old, worn mailbox which was once painted a light blue with bronze letters, but now the letters were faded or missing, and the family name had turned into 'Hopso.' The cheap paint job meant it must have been done by the owners, who were probably frugal or the elderly. Either way, I was sweating out any fluid my body could find, and I couldn't handle it much longer.

Ever since that day, if I was running and ever got to the point where I could hardly breathe, I would take a detour to the Hopso's, climb over their fence—always get picked by a thorn bush—and eventually relax in their nice, eighty-degree pool.

"What are we doing?" Allie asked skeptically. I held my hand out to her, and she took it hesitantly, jumping over the fence.

"We are getting you clean."

I led her through the bush— "Watch out, there's thorns," I warned—but when she halted, I knew it was too late.

"It's fine, just on my shorts," Allie chirped and pulled off the thorns like she was picking out individual snowflakes. Every movement she made was as if it were a part of some classical ballet, and every lift, touch, and motion was graceful.

Well, except for her running.

When Allie was finally picker-free, we made it through the gate. I reached down to my waistband and twisted the brass button free.

As I shimmied out of my shorts and flicked them away, Allie turned on her heel. At first, I thought she was going to leave, but instead she covered her eyes. She was purposely not looking at my partially naked body. I unzipped my jacket and tossed it near my shorts haphazardly laying on the concrete.

"You know you're allowed to look, right?" I asked. Allie stayed firmly in place, so I let my bellows echo out as I flipped into the fresh, chlorinated water.

When I resurfaced, my hair fell just in front of my eyes. Drops of water plopped either above my upper lip or back into its home from the tops of my hair. I shook my head back and forth, and I froze when I saw Allie laughing at me. She pointed to my face, and I felt the strands of black hair sticking to my cheeks.

"You look like my puppy, Linus!" she laughed. "Whenever he gets out of the bathtub, he shakes his body just like that, and I get soaked in the dirty bathwater."

Everything she told me went straight over my head except for a single part.

"Why did you name your puppy Linus?"

Allie blushed.

"Because I'm a really big fan of Charlie Brown and the whole Peanuts gang. Linus was always my favorite." I knew by her scrunched-up face that she was worried. I would laugh at her. To calm her nerves, I shrugged.

"My favorite has always been Sally," I said simply and ducked under the water.

"Dare me to do a cannonball?" Allie asked when I resurfaced as she climbed onto the rickety homemade diving board. Splinters of wood stuck out at every angle, just waiting to penetrate some unsuspecting victim's soles as a horrible paint job left each visitors' feet a shade of blue. The rusty bedsprings creaked beneath the board as Allie shifted her weight from side to side, and it spoke more.

My eyes wandered up and down her covered body.

"You're, uh, not lessening your layers?" I tried to ask in a polite way, but there was no medium between sounding like a player by saying 'strip' or an aristocratic man of the 1800s practicing asking a girl to let him court her.

Allie raised her eyebrows.

"'Lessening my layers?' I may not be a prude who wears sweaters and long skirts in the summer, but I don't drop my pants either," she said. "Especially not on the fourth date."

With those final words, Allie rolled her body back and surged forward in the spherical cannonball, straight into the pool. The spot ricocheted its waves to the edges of the pool and back, and I almost didn't notice Allie's head bobbing between them.

"I thought these were not-a-dates," I countered mockingly as I swam to her.

"Um, it isn't!" She tried to backtrack and ducked under the water. I followed her to the shallow end, where she sat on the edge, pulling at wet strings of her hair. She untangled the scrunchie from the midst of her damp hair and set it aside.

I rolled my eyes and took her hand as she hopped back into the pool.

"I already kissed you. That means it's a date."

Allie shook her head.

"Not necessarily. We could just be two people hanging out who just happened to kiss." She leaned back and balanced on her knees as she wet her hair to untangle the knots. Her hands raked through it as the blonde strands began to curl under. "Nothing more than just two people together."

I chuckled. She was trying so hard, but from her own smirk, I knew she didn't even believe her explanation anymore. Allie slipped up and finally admitted it was a date.

Allie floated out to the middle of the deep end now with her hair stretched in every direction. She ducked beneath the water and swam as far down to the bottom as she could. Through the discombobulated view, I watched Allie brush the rather dirty base with her hand, then pull her body up into a handstand. She pushed off the grimy blue floor and twisted her body into a frontward flip. Allie's body, suspended in the fluid, as if gravity had no effect, rocked into the fetal position before she dug her heels down, pointed her toes, and kicked her feet to meet me back at the surface.

"I think I'm ready to start heading back," Allie began. "I was too busy finishing my photography collage to eat, so I have Cup Noodles waiting for me." Allie pulled herself out of the pool, and her shirt looked slightly darker than before from being soaked, and I finally understood how plum was a shade of purple. She picked at it, which had stuck to her body like a suction cup.

"You could just take it off," I suggested with a smirk as I hoisted myself out. My feet stayed within the water-stained concrete as I fumbled for my own shirt.

"Very funny, Romeo," Allie said as she picked up her camera. "I'm fine like this, really. My clothes will dry with the walk." However, the moment Allie looked down and noticed I could plainly see the texture of her lacy bra through it, I tossed her my *Top Gun* jacket. She swiftly covered herself while her face tried hard not to blush.

"Thank you," Allie spoke with such delicateness, it hardly seemed like words, but music instead.

A car engine rumbled to life and crackled over the rocky driveway. My eyes widened.

"The Hopsos are home! Run!"

The thorns caught us on our way out, and both of our legs got scratched up and scarred. I had been caught once or twice by the old couple, but I never cared. Neither did Allie, whose golden hair was already drying. Just seeing her face brightened the situation.

Beauty was Allie Johncox, and she spent her life trying to bring beauty into the world through her art.

As we walked down the quiet road, Allie snapped quick photos of the grass or some other part of nature. She scuttled across the side like a bird searching for worms to give to her young. Eventually, she held down the power button and just let it swing on her chest.

"Ben," she began.

"Yes?" I asked.

"Why did you kiss me in the middle of our date, instead of the end?" she asked quietly. Maybe I had overestimated her happiness at the kiss after all.

"I don't know, really."

"Just give me a reason," she urged. "Even if it's off the top of your head."

Our hands found their way to each other, and my mind buzzed with thoughts. After a moment, I spoke.

"I guess… I like kissing in the middle of the date. The idea of an end-of-the-date kiss seems so restricted, so planned. It can't be too long of a kiss because the date is over. Also, you probably would have expected it, right?"

Allie shrugged and nodded.

"That's why I kissed you in the middle of the date. It's spontaneous—you can kiss for as long as you want without everyone telling you to stop, and there could be more kisses later on because the kiss didn't seal the end of the date. It heightens the moment."

Allie nodded and squeezed my hand.

"I like that. Middle of the date kisses. Kisses just because." And when she leaned towards me, that next kiss lasted much longer than the first.

When we parted, Allie's face blushed again, a common occurrence I've come to find increasingly cute, and she swung our hands back and forth as we walked back toward the university.

"You smell like chlorine."

A third kiss.

"You still smell beautiful."

By the time we reached campus, we had kissed a total of six times, and each one made me want another. But I wanted to be a gentleman and treat Allie right like she deserved, so my hand stayed appropriately at her waist, and when we turned the corner, the final stage of our date was in place: the ice cream truck.

Ned, a friend of Spencer's whose dad had an ice cream truck, leaned out of the window, holding out a Bugs Bunny ice cream bar Brennan had told me was her favorite, and a drumstick for myself. To fit the mood, instead of playing the annoying and high-pitched, "Pop Goes the Weasel" or "Do Your Ears Hang Low," Brennan brought me a mixtape he grabbed from Allie's car about God or some Holy Spirit.

"Ben Asan, did you set this up?" she asked, eagerly grabbing the Bugs Bunny bar. "How much?" she asked Ned.

"No charge," Ned replied. I had prepaid for all the ice cream Allie could ever want.

Allie's eyes widened, and I winced as she slapped my chest.

"You're crazy, Ben! You really are!" she laughed. Allie reached into her pocket anyway. "Here," she said. "A soggy dollar. I owe you one, didn't I?"

"Seventy-five cents, technically" I said and pocketed the drippy dollar. "I'll get you back a quarter when I actually have money. This cost me far too much. I will pay you back when I'm 82."

Allie smirked and kissed my cheek.

"I guess I'll have to stick around until then."

Allie's voice interrupted us, but not the Allie before me—the one in the ice cream truck speakers. It was thick, like she had been crying, or teetered on the edge of a meltdown.

"Day twenty-five. December 6th, 1986. I tried to have another support meeting today. I set up all the tables—"

"Skip it," Allie exclaimed, her eyes widening. "Skip it, skip it now!" Her voice rose in volume. She whipped her head at me. "Ben, where did you get this?!"

"...I blew up the photo of the fair..."

"SKIP IT!"

Ned fiddled with the stereo, turning the volume up and down as he worked on skipping the track. I didn't know how hard it could be or how long it would take, but apparently it was too long for Allie.

"Skip it! I SAID SKIP IT!" she screamed. In one fluid motion, her hand unclasped from around the stick of her bar, and she threw herself up into the window of the truck before Bugs even hit the ground.

The tape buzzed, fast-forwarding. When it lifted up, I saw Allie's face in my mind, full of tears.

"GOD, WHY DO THEY DO THIS?" screamed out from the speakers.

With a single click, the sound around the lot died out, but the echo remained in all our minds. Allie pulled herself from out of the truck, looking sickened with herself. In her hand was the orange tape marked, "Oh, Jesus, I Need You." With all the force she could muster, she slammed it against the counter of the truck. It barely cracked. She didn't seem to have the energy to do anything else.

Ned and I stared at her, both with the same gaped expression.

Allie glared between us, her hair a mess and her eyes brimming with tears. She breathed deeply, closed her eyes, and a tear slid down her cheek. She wiped it away immediately. Her face painted remorse and embarrassment, and I stepped forward to comfort her, but Allie stepped back, wiping the fresh tears falling from her face. Her gaze finally found mine, and she handed over my jacket.

"Thank you for the date. Goodnight."

My stomach dropped as Allie briskly walked away. Her hands wiped her tears away, and as much as I wanted to go after her, to ask her to talk to me, to explain, that I would understand—*take the time* to understand her—I already knew Allie well enough to know she needed her space.

I just didn't know for how long.

11

"What was that?" Devon exclaimed.

"I'll get to it, "Asan stated calmly.

Devon's mouth gaped open in shock.

"So, you obviously stopped seeing this girl, right?"

Dr. Asan shook his head. "Of course not. My feelings didn't change. And as much as Allie wanted to, hers didn't either."

Devon sat back—he didn't even realize he had jumped forward in the velvet chair. Allie and Dr. Asan got back together after that fiasco—so maybe all hope was not lost with Lindsey...

"Wait," Devon interjected. Suddenly the coffee had made it to his bladder. "Where's your bathroom?"

"Oh, of course," Asan stuttered, a little jilted at the reminder of reality. "It's just behind me, to your left."

Devon set aside the bucket and stumbled to his feet.

"Do you, ah, need a hand?" Asan outstretched his, but Devon shook his head.

"I got it, thanks..."

After he shuffled past Asan, his elbow brushed something on a table in the hallway, just outside the bathroom. He quickly caught it. He had almost knocked over a vintage camera. As he steadied the expensive antique, his eyes drifted to the bottom. Written in shining silver marker read, "Allie Johncox," with a small, distinctive smiley face just after the 'x.' The camera had been preserved in time, and the only little piece that didn't seem perfect was her scribbled name.

"This is Allie's," Devon noted as he set the sash behind it.

Asan turned around and raised his eyebrows.

"Yes," he said slowly. "Now, please don't touch it—she wouldn't like it touched."

"S-sorry. I just bumped into it." Devon figured Asan must have taken it out of their room and forgotten to put it back.

Devon used the bathroom, and when he finally looked at himself in the mirror, he cringed. No wonder Asan stared at him with so much pity. His eyes were glazed and unfocused. His hair was standing up like it always did when he nervously ran his hands through it. His shirt wasn't buttoned properly and, as he noticed at the toilet, neither were his jeans. And, of course, he had dried vomit sticking to the collar of his shirt.

As Devon washed his hands, he tried to dissect Asan's story. Asan hadn't been much different than Devon himself—maybe even more of a player. Devon had been loyal to Lindsey for their over two-year-long relationship. But he had also spent so much time drinking, losing himself on the weekend. Lindsey deserved better. She deserved to know. He had to tell her what happened and face the consequences.

As he reached for the towel to dry his hands, he felt his phone vibrate in his pocket. He was incredibly lucky that it hadn't fallen out when he was stumbling around drunk. Thank goodness for deep pockets.

Hey babe, where are you? It's getting boring and I miss you. I've searched everywhere. Did you leave?

Then another one.

Can we put on our PJs and watch New Girl? Meet you at home <3

He had to go. He had to, right? But he couldn't face Lindsey. Not yet. He needed to cling onto hope, however faint it was, that nothing would change between them when he told her.

Devon looked back out of the bathroom door and saw the bright light of Dr. Asan's kitchen, a beacon for him. Dr. Asan had turned his own life around. He had been through college before—been through the difficulties of love. If anyone could help him now, it would be his professor. He had to know what it took to change his life.

12

May 17th, 1990

Spring finals came around, and as it did, lovebirds fluttered around the campus of Mt. Hope ready for their summer romances to bloom.

Every spring, after the last exams, the staff threw a party for everyone. I had just finished my last exam for Microeconomics. Like most college athletes, I majored in business.

I was thoroughly exhausted from studying like mad, and I planned on just sleeping through the noise coming through my window from the plaza—the crisscrossed walkway where Allie and I walked on our first date—which was a painful reminder of what I had tried so hard to forget.

I groaned.

Allie.

It had been almost two weeks since our last date, and our last moments together plagued my mind, even in my dreams. I had spotted her a few times on campus, and any time I tried to walk in her direction, she turned away quickly. I didn't know if she was embarrassed about what was on the tape, hurt that I didn't go after her, or a mix of the two. But I hoped to talk with her before finals ended. I couldn't go all summer without talking to her. It hurt even more because things seemed to be going so well up until that point.

"Oh, God!" I exclaimed. Those melancholic thoughts were cured temporarily by a giant weight that fell on me, pulling me into a bear hug.

"Get up, Ben!" Spencer yelled in my ear. He was sweaty and smelled like rust and rotten eggs. I gagged as he pushed his armpit near my mouth. "Can you taste it?" he teased.

Swimming in a pitiful (no pun intended) odor, my body seized, searching for an escape from my best friend's lack of deodorant. I gasped for air and strained for the cool, uncontaminated side of my pillow. I plunged my face into its soft exterior and coughed to survive his stench.

"Get off of me, you swine!"

"Come on, they're showing *The Princess Bride* at the plaza!" Spencer whined, tugging at my shirt sleeve.

"Are you a child?" I asked. "Get off me!"

"Go with me. We've gone every year! It'll be fun!" he exclaimed. "Now, get up!"

"I'm tired from exams," I whined. "Not everyone's exam is saving a fellow lifeguard from a pool!" Spencer's major was Recreational Sports, and he worked as a lifeguard as part of his classes. "Seriously, off!"

"You told me to get off you," Spencer said as he pulled my limp body up and shoved me toward the door. He smirked and pulled on his gray windbreaker to match his black and dark green MHU baseball shirt.

"I don't want to go," I tried to protest but I followed him; I didn't want to deal with sweaty, smelly Spencer again. Spencer's social battery was fully charged after finishing finals and wanted to celebrate the end of the year. Mine was completely drained, consumed with thoughts of Allie and what I could do to fix the situation. I wasn't in my normal end-of-the-year jovial mood. "The party isn't even fun. And I hate *The Princess Bride*."

Spencer touched a hand to his heart.

"You've hurt me, and you've hurt Buttercup."

I sighed and ran my hands through my hair, trying to look presentable, but without a mirror, my waves would have a mind of their own.

"Fine," I agreed. "Let's just get this over with."

At six in the evening, the party was in full swing. Girls in short plaid skirts with stick straight hair paraded around the grass. Some people stretched out on blankets to the side, but the center was completely filled with people talking and dancing to Cyndi Lauper.

President McCarrell was with them, before he was nicknamed McGrumpy, dancing around in the little mob of students.

Just at the spritely age of thirty-two, our President tended to go a little crazy when the end of the year came around.

"Beauty," Spencer stated as McCarrell slapped his ass. We both burst into laughter. "Told you this would be fun."

"It's only fun because President McCarrell is crazy!"

McCarrell never aged past twenty. He played the goofy guy persona well and used that to his advantage to get the students to like him. Most of the time, it worked.

Spencer clapped me on the back.

"Hey, I'm gonna get a slice. Do you want anything?"

"Nah, I'm good."

"You sure? You only ate one quesadilla at dinner last night, so don't think I haven't noticed something is up." Spencer tried.

"Just not hungry I guess" I shrugged.

As Spencer walked away, I spotted a familiar face through the throngs of people. She sat on the grass, with a camera in hand and a bag of popcorn between her knees.

My stomach flipped, but I knew this could be my one final chance to talk to Allie before summer break. And I had to do it. But finally facing her made me realize just how much I liked her, and how nervous I was about saying the wrong thing.

But I walked over to her, deciding it was now or never.

"Hey," I whispered, hoping for the best.

"Hey stranger. Or should I say, 'person in my debt,'" she teased.

Whether Allie had just needed time, or she didn't want to bring up what had happened at the ice cream truck when everyone around us was having fun, I was glad to get a warmer reception than I had anticipated.

"I am, aren't I? That's a shame. I don't have twenty-five cents."

"Tsk, tsk, tsk, Ben Asan, what will I have to do with you? I'm so thirsty for lemonade, but I don't have a quarter."

At that, I broke our little charade and squatted down next to her. She moved over to the side to give me space, welcoming me to sit next to her.

"About what happened..." I tried to explain.

"Where did you get that tape?" Allie interjected.

I scratched my neck. I wasn't sure if Brennan was okay with me sharing, but I had to be honest to Allie.

"Brennan... kind of helped me get it. He took it from your car the other day. He knew you liked that worship music, and I thought it would be the perfect end to our date."

Allie's eyebrows scrunched. "Brennan? My cousin?"

"Yeah, he's one of my roommates. When he found out we had been seeing each other a few times, he kind of... cornered me wanting to find out what my intentions were with you."

Allie let out a snort. "He cornered you? Gosh, I'm so sorry. He saw us walking away from the library one time and asked me about it. We grew up together, so he loves to act like an older brother." She paused, then quietly added, "what did he say?"

"Oh, you know..." I stammered. "Just that I should leave you alone, especially if I'm just trying to add you to my 'lay list,' is what he called it."

"And are you?"

Allie looked at me with wide eyes. The barrier between us had broken down, especially on that last date. This was her asking, wanting to know if my intentions with her would be the same as any other girl, and what she probably expected them to be.

I sighed. "Maybe it was that initially, but now?" I met her eyes. "Allie, when you walked away—again, I'm sorry about the tape, I had no idea what was on it—it felt terrible. These past few weeks, I've had so much fun with you, in a way I realized I never looked for with other girls. You make me laugh. I get nervous trying to talk to you, but when I start talking, I don't want to stop. I want to say things to make you laugh. To hear your laugh. And you can ask my friends, or my reputation, I'm never like this. When I told Brennan I was serious about you, he offered advice, so I could do my best by you. Because you deserve it."

Allie had covered her hand with her mouth, but her eyes were upturned, and I knew she was smiling. She sighed again, still keeping her eyes on mine.

"Ben, you're sure? About me? Even after I screamed and cried and now refuse to tell you what it's all about?"

I shrugged. "If it's something I need to know, I trust you'll tell me in time."

Allie took her hand and placed it on mine. I froze. She rarely was this forward. Her eyes dropped down to our hands as she spoke.

"I'm sorry for avoiding you these last few days. I-I was just so embarrassed. So ashamed of how I acted and that I stormed off without an explanation. I promise I'll give one just not now, okay?" She squeezed my hand, and I reciprocated. "Then I got so stressed with my finals coming up. I had a migraine all day on Sunday, I couldn't even go to church. But… I'm glad you came over here. I'm glad you still want to take a chance on me. Because," she glanced back up at me, "I want to take a chance on you, too."

I wanted to kiss her right then and there. But I knew Allie well enough now, that with nearly the entire student body all around celebrating the end of the year, it would make her uncomfortable, so I didn't dare.

"You have no idea how happy that makes me," I said and squeezed her hand once more before she pulled it away.

I glanced around—there was popcorn, corn dogs, lemonade, and soda pop stands set up, each with a price point.

"Do you still want lemonade?"

Allie shrugged. "I mean, kind of, but I used my only spare change on the popcorn," she held up her bag, nearly full. "It's kind of stale."

"I have some change back in my room, the house just past the library. I can go get it," I said as I got to my feet.

But Allie stood up as well. "Is it okay if I come with you?"

My eyebrows raised. "You're sure?"

Allie nodded and took my hand. "Positive. If you're telling the truth about how you feel…?"

I crossed my heart with my free hand. "I'm honestly just as surprised by it as you are," I promised, and we made our way over there.

"So, this is your place?" Allie asked as we ventured behind Mt. Hope's grand library. The plaza stood directly in front of the library, so it took no time at all before I was venturing to the room I'd so sorely left.

Allie spotted my plain white home and stepped up to the front mat. The 'Welcome' slowly faded to 'Wecoe' with the shoe marks, and it usually left scratches on bare feet.

"Nice. Small," she pointed out.

I supposed it was small. Smaller than the other campus houses, definitely, since ours housed three guys instead of the usual fifteen. But it was roomy enough for Brennan, Spencer, and me.

"This way," I said as I motioned her to follow me to my room.

Litter lined around the trash basket where my far-fetched three-pointers had missed, clothing lay on my bed and floor, and even without much furniture, it still seemed like the ceiling was hardly tall enough for a six-foot person.

"Your dorm must be smaller, though. My dorm was."

She shrugged as her eyes traced the side in wonder.

"My ceiling is taller, but that's about it."

I let go of her hand and shook mine out. Summer heat made my palms sweat more than any part of my body.

I pulled at the sock drawer and combed through until my fingertips recognized the silver canister that I kept loose change in.

My eyes glanced at Allie as I dug my stubborn fingers beneath the lid to pry it open.

As I struggled, Allie's eyes kept scanning my room, staring at each poster of famous Olympic runners of the ages, like Carl Lewis, Abebe Bikila, and Jesse Owens, all with glorious medals around their necks.

"Are these all Olympians?" she asked after a moment. There was a small pop, and the top clattered to the floor. I celebrated in silence.

"What?" I asked as I sifted through the rupees and Canadian loonies, looking for my fifty-cent coin with JFK's profile. I tried to ignore the several quarters my fingers brushed. I didn't want us to be out of debt to one another just yet.

"These are Olympians? Are they all runners like you?" she repeated, pointing to a large poster of Owens.

"Yeah, yeah," I said, still rooting around in the can. I pointed to the poster next to the head of my bed. "That's Carl Lewis. He won gold in Seoul in the one-hundred meter with a time of nine-point-nine-two seconds. These posters keep me motivated—or they try to. My PR was eleven-point-three-two at the last meet. I still need to lower it by nearly a second."

I grasped the silver edges and pulled the coin from the bottom of the can.

"Got it," I said and turned to hand it to Allie.

She stared at me, a smile wide throughout her face, and her eyes lifted, with her right eyebrow raised ever so slightly.

"What?" I asked.

"Oh," Allie grabbed the silver coin. She rolled it over her fingers and pouted. "Are you sure you want to give this up to someone like me? It seems pretty special."

I shrugged and took her hand. "This is nothing. If you asked to borrow my gold medal, that I'm going to win at the 1992 Barcelona Olympics, then that's a definite no."

"Maybe I can come watch you," she offered, with the coin in one hand and her other in mine. "In Barcelona. Traveling is fun."

I smirked at the idea of Allie being in my life two years from now as we made our way back to the party.

"Sure. If you want to cheer me on."

"Oh, I was thinking about booing you instead. You know, a healthy distraction."

"Ha, I appreciate it," I said as I leapt over a giant limb of a tree which had fallen during a March storm. No one seemed to want to pick it up, so it became a sort of jungle-gym for the brave.

Allie attempted to jump the branch, but tripped midway, and I caught her hand.

Allie's laughter reverberated with mine. The sound of her laugh was the most transfixing thing in the world.

With the rare fifty-cent piece, Allie bought a can of lemonade for her and then water for me.

"Are you staying to watch the movie?" I asked Allie in a loudish shout; the DJ decided it was a perfect time to blast some AC/DC.

"Definitely. I love *The Princess Bride*. It is tied for my favorite movie."

Her comment jolted me.

"Shoot, I just remembered, I came here with my best friend, Spencer, and I totally ditched him. Is it okay with you if I track him down?"

Allie shrugged. "Sure, that's really nice of you to go find him. I'll just be over by my blanket, okay?"

I squeezed her hand as we departed. I looked around the food area, but Spencer wasn't there. He wasn't near the group of students playing four square. I was about to give up until I spotted him settling down on a blanket next to Brennan.

I jogged over to him. "Hey, Spence," I said. "So sorry I went AWOL."

"Hey, long time no see, it's Ben Asan," he laughed. "I see you're in a better mood now. Not just finals getting you down, then?" Spencer tilted his head over to the direction of Allie.

Brennan shared a knowing smile with Spencer. Of course, they would talk. But getting Allie back made me on cloud nine.

I laughed. "Yeah, a little… But things are better. I was going to watch the movie with Allie, but you can join us if you want?"

Spencer shook his head. "Nah, it's okay. Enjoy your evening. I'm just glad you got out of bed."

"I owe you for that, thanks." We shared a smile, and I left him, Brennan, and some other baseball guys to watch the movie together, then I headed over and plopped down next to Allie.

"Tied with what?" I asked.

"Huh?" she spoke with a mouthful of popcorn. Guess it wasn't too stale after all.

"You said *The Princess Bride* is tied for your favorite movie. What's the other movie?"

Allie's cheeks tinted.

"*Dirty Dancing*." She took a long sip before laughing, and I felt instantly jealous of the can. "I know, I'm a typical romantic."

"There's nothing bad about a little romance."

She continued to sip on the lemonade that never seemed to end. The blue sky began to turn gray and cloudy, so I led us toward the library where I spotted a spare tent, normally used for food and drinks. I pulled it over toward us to protect from the rain I knew was coming. Michigan never got this warm without some rain.

"What's your favorite movie, Ben?"

My insides tingled at the sound of my name. Whenever she spoke it, I felt so pure and gentle, as if everyone else had been careless with it.

"Me? I don't know… I like *Top Gun*… And *The Outsiders*… And lots of Bollywood films I used to watch when I was younger. Sort of like how you feel about Disney, or something."

Allie pressed herself into my chest as we talked.

"Like what movies?"

I kissed her cheek. "Maybe I'll show you one day."

Her smile returned and she wrapped her arms around my neck.

"It'd really like that," she whispered.

I had no plans to kiss Allie. Taking things slow, like Brennan's suggestion, would be my next course of action. It's one thing to want a girl, and another for her to want you.

But then Allie pressed her lips to mine, just for a moment, and breathed out a sigh when we parted. She rested her head on my chest, and I wrapped my arms around and pulled her closer.

The Princess Bride wouldn't be too bad after all.

"I'll walk you home," I suggested to Allie as the end credits rolled from *The Princess Bride*. "As a little, end-of-our-fifth-date thing."

"Whatever," Allie laughed.

"We watched a movie, ate some popcorn, kissed, I even let you in my room! Date."

Allie's signature blush showed.

"*Fine,* it was a date."

I held my arm out at a nice ninety-degree angle for her, and she slipped her arm through.

"A kiss, fine lady?" I asked, giving my best impression of a Renaissance knight.

Allie rolled her eyes playfully and let me kiss her hand.

"When shall we see each other once more, my Juliet?" I asked as we trekked through the rain.

"Actually, I'll be home next week. You know, for summer vacation."

My face fell. In the joy of being back with Allie, my mind had pushed away the thought of her not in Mt. Hope for the summer. I knew she lived further up north, but so many students stayed back in Mt. Hope for break, I was hoping she would be one of them.

"Oh. Well, when are you leaving?"

"The nineteenth at eleven a.m." That was just two days away.

"Well, that's specific," I laughed. "Well, what about tomorrow?"

"Probably not. I'll be packing, returning my schoolbooks, and I promised Audrey we would have a movie and spa night our last night. Then the day after I have to leave," Allie explained. "I really wish I could, though."

"And is eleven a.m. the definite time you'll be leaving?"

"It's not set, but I have to leave early, at least before noon," she answered. "I live like, three hours away," she explained, "I'm really, *really* sorry, Ben," she said. "I do want to see you again."

"Well, could we meet up, possibly? You could tell me where you live, and we could hang out—"

"I...can't," she whispered. "I have a full-time job during the summertime. I sort of...babysit," she said.

"Babysitting..."

"That's right."

"Full-time?"

"Yep," she said. "So, I've really got no time for anything else. Maybe a day or two when I get back, but after that, I'll be busy beyond belief."

I frowned.

"Don't you ever get a break? Summer is the time to relax."

"I'm really sorry. I mean it. This is just something I can't get out of."

I sighed. If ten days without Allie was difficult, I couldn't imagine a whole summer. My stomach tightened at the thought.

"But what if I give you my home phone number? We could at least talk?"

I smiled slightly. Talking, of course, like Allie loved to do. But it was worth it, to get to talk to her.

"Of course."

13

"It had been four weeks since our first date, but I knew how I felt about Allie. Even if it was new, I couldn't help but find myself wanting to be with her," Dr. Asan explained as he washed out his coffee cup.

Devon handed over his own to be cleaned. "Then what is the point of your love story? You seemed to be getting better already," Devon said.

Dr. Asan raised his eyebrows in surprise.

"Oh come on," Devon laughed. "I know why you're telling me your story. I'm you before getting your life together. I know it, too."

"That may be true, but there's always more to learn," Dr. Asan added. "I wasn't done learning, yet."

"You met your wife. You became a better person," Devon listed. "What more could happen?"

Dr. Asan smirked and turned to face Devon. He crossed his arms in front of himself and cleared his throat.

"Perhaps you know how it ends. But what's a better story? The other side of the river, or the wade?"

"I guess, I would say—"

"It was rhetorical," Dr. Asan cut in, drying the mugs with a towel. It was past midnight now, the bags under his eyes were darker, enunciated by the glow of the kitchen lights. He had yet to sit down, impassioned by sharing the story of Allie, one which Devon was sure Dr. Asan and his wife had plenty of practice sharing.

As if he could read Devon's mind, Dr. Asan changed the subject.

"Do you ever wonder, Camburn," Asan began, still staring at his feet; his baritone voice shook with each syllable, "why do we sit through life, collecting memories? Why do we attach ourselves to people and feel love and safety with them, only to be ripped apart by some overpowering force?" He swallowed and never dared to glance up.

Devon wondered if Dr. Asan had already figured out what Devon had done. The way in which he had betrayed Lindsey. He tried to hold himself together.

"Someone once told me that the human race is time-conscious," Dr. Asan continued. "We always seem to be running around, trying to juggle five things at once to save *time,* because time is the only thing that is constantly *running out.*" Asan ran his hands over what was left of his hair and grasped it. "It can't be rewound like an odometer. Time has passed with each breath, and you cannot stop its ways. We are simultaneously the oldest we've ever been and the youngest we'll ever be again. Some people live to be old, and that's good. But I can't tell you how strange it is to watch someone die when it didn't seem like they were sick at all..."

It was at that moment Devon realized Asan was a cracked man about to break.

"Don't you think that's wrong?" Asan whispered as he slowly lifted his head.

Maybe Devon wasn't the only person who needed this story. He swallowed.

"Completely."

There was another pause, and then Asan spoke again with a loud sigh.

"In the space of being totally transparent—and again, this is not an excuse for me to learn what's going on between you and Miss Huff—I want to apologize for being a bit more impatient toward you recently. I guess what I'm trying to say is..." Asan took a deep breath and paused again. "Remembering all of this has made me realize just how different of a person I've been lately. How I've lost touch with who I am."

Devon held his breath. He had never seen Asan's face so dejected before, and he never wanted to again.

"My mother died last week. She had a really long battle with Alzheimer's that stripped away at her mind for years… I felt like I was strong enough to face going to work this week. I've gone through harder times, but…" he sighed. "Today I took out my last straw on you, and I am very sorry for that."

Devon didn't know what to say. He wasn't good with sad emotions—his own or others—hence the bucket still in his lap. So, he held out the bucket.

Asan chuckled.

"Thank you, but I already used one a week ago, by her bedside."

Devon put the bucket back down.

"I—"

"You're not obligated to share, at all, Mr. Camburn, about you and Miss Huff. I just wanted to apologize and explain myself, both my misty eyes now and my inexcusable treatment of you. I was too harsh in class earlier and should have been more understanding."

Devon looked up at Dr. Asan—normally this looming figure in his life that often reminded him of his irresponsibility—and saw him differently. He saw him as a grieving son, a family man who had an old wooden bird clock and a little elephant from visiting India, the land of his father. Devon saw him as not only an expert in history, but an expert in life. A wise father, a patient and selfless man, and passionate. He could see the cracks of kindness that Allie saw, and he knew Dr. Asan was someone he could trust. He needed someone to listen to what had happened—to help him sort through the storm of emotions inside of him. He opened his mouth but was drowned out by the sound of the front door opening.

Asan immediately perked up. Devon saw him wipe his eyes.

Whoever pulled in took the living room route toward the kitchen, looking down at her phone. Unaware of the drunk college student in her kitchen, she crashed directly into Devon.

"Oh, sorry!" she said with a slight lisp as she finally looked up. Her dark tresses fell just to her shoulders, and she had a complexion to match.

It took Devon only a few seconds to recognize her round eyes and curly hair to realize the girl before him must be Asan's daughter. She looked to be in her late teens or early twenties. Her eyes spotted her father.

"Uh, Dad? Why is there some random guy in our kitchen?"

"Thank you, Vidya," Asan exclaimed sarcastically, "for your tact. This is my student, Devon. We're just talking about history."

Technically not wrong.

Now seeing his daughter, and the picture of Asan younger, he could almost picture them together, that young Ben Asan with a baby tucked in his arms.

Vidya rolled her eyes.

"Okay, boring. Is Mom home yet?"

"No, I'm still waiting. She said midnight, but you know how things go."

Devon and Dr. Asan both eyed the clock. It was nearing the Song Sparrow—getting ever closer to 1 a.m.

Vidya shrugged, waved to Devon out of politeness more than anything else, and brushed past her father toward her room.

Once Asan was assured his daughter could not hear any more, he continued.

"Sorry for the inconvenience with Vidya. She is notoriously late everywhere, *especially* coming home. She works at the movie theater in Flower City. Her third job this year—Vidya keeps getting fired. Do you know why?"

Devon was not sure if he should answer.

"Theft?" He took a wild guess.

Asan howled with laughter at the idea. His watery eyes were gone after seeing his daughter.

"No, no. Tardiness," he said with a smirk. "She's like you in that way. She's had this job for about three months now, her longest yet. I'm hoping she's turned a corner." He winked toward Devon, who shifted uncomfortably in his seat at the mention of tardiness. "There's always time, remember, Mr. Camburn."

14

May 19th, 1990

The day of Allie's departure arrived much too quickly. I woke up at 8 am, and with determination, got out of bed. I had only three hours before Allie left for the summer, and I needed to see her again.

The sun was peeking through the clouds, and I stood outside of Allie's dorm room, the number of which I got from Audrey. I gave three knocks and waited.

"Just a minute!" came her voice. The lock jiggled, and then Allie stood in the doorway. "Hi, Ben." She did not seem surprised to see me, almost as if she had been expecting me just as much as I was her. "Is something wrong?"

Allie was most definitely a morning person. By the way she spoke and how she looked, you would think she spent her favorite times watching the sun rise while singing to chirping bluebirds. Still, seeing Allie this early in the day, I realized how human she looked.

She had slight bags under her eyes that she hadn't bothered to cover; although still pretty, she wasn't wearing any makeup, and she had a few groupings of tiny pimples on her porcelain skin. Human, but still beautiful.

"No, everything's fine," I said, regaining myself. "I just wanted to take you somewhere before you left to go home."

Allie bit her lip and her eyes darted away from my face as she battled internally. "I don't think I can… I still have a bunch of things to pack—I haven't even cleaned my bathroom!"

I took her hand and stroked my thumb against it. "I promise you'll be back far before eleven."

"Promise?"

We headed toward the church, first. We walked, just like we always did. If I wanted to sit, Allie would want to move. On the rare occasion she sat down, like at the movie, her feet tapped impatiently like there was a bug inside her, desperate to fly out. Even as we walked, her fingers jittered.

"Hi!" she exclaimed as we walked past a guy holding a guitar case. He had curly brown hair, a matching beard, and square glasses. "That was Kendall, did you know?" she mentioned. "He sings with me at the church."

"Yeah? What's your favorite song to sing?"

"Oh, 'Rock of Ages,' for sure. I just love the melody and the powerful words about God, you know?"

I swallowed hard and nodded.

"Oh yeah, for sure. It's one of my favorites, too. Will you sing it for me?"

Allie laughed.

"Maybe another time, Ben."

I reached for her hand blindly as I glanced up at the oncoming road for a break in traffic. As my eyes scanned back to the right, Allie jumped into the road and sprinted across, laughing like a mad woman as she did.

"Allie!" I called after her once she reached the other end. "You're crazy!"

Again, she laughed like she was having the time of her life.

"Run, Ben! You're a great sprinter. C'mon, it's just a little way!"

I glanced back and forth. I could cross after the gray Ford… No, there was a red VW Beetle coming down at the other end. It took a good minute until a Buick passed, and I could run through before a clanky, beaten-down, discolored van drove by.

"About time," Allie teased. She looked both ways down the sidewalk. "Where are we going?" she asked.

I pointed left, and we headed off.

"The elementary school?" she asked as we walked into the parking lot of Casey Elementary—my old school. Students had a late start every Friday, meaning there wouldn't be any students for an hour at least, so we were in the clear.

"Close," I said and headed behind it. "The playground…"

Allie rolled her eyes as we made our way behind a fence and to the playground.

"How come every time you take me somewhere, we end up breaking into property that isn't ours?"

"Psh… We aren't breaking in," I assured her. "We're just… not using the direct way of entry. Completely different," I insisted.

Even after her comment, Allie still followed me onto the playground.

When I offered Allie her choice of playground entertainment, she plopped onto the nearest swing and began pumping her legs in and out.

"Swings, huh?" I asked as I wrangled one with my hand and sat beside her. "Never really was a fan of them growing up."

Allie reached higher bounds as she lofted through the spring air. Her hands nearly touched a nearby tree's leaves, and if she had been reaching, she could've held on forever.

"I like them." Her simple answer was not unlike what I would hear Fatima, my younger sister, say. "It's one of the only human gateways to Heaven." I thought she was serious until she laughed, so I did too.

"So, you don't like swings?" Allie asked from so high above her hair mingled with the clouds.

I kept myself at a height that left my toes brushing the worn-down ground if I didn't lift my feet in time.

"Nope."

"And you brought me to a playground, even though swings are arguably the best part?" Allie asked with a raised eyebrow.

"I thought you would like it. A good way to get your energy out before your road trip," I said with a wink.

"What am I, a dog?"

"You have the energy of one..." I mumbled.

"Well," she hmphed, "why don't you like swings?" she asked, almost as if she had never met someone who disliked flailing back and forth like a pendulum.

"Well, when I was six," I began and pushed off the ground as I passed through, "I saw a kid jump off a swing and hit the ground like a belly flop." I slapped my palms together for effect. "And his two front teeth soared out of his mouth and landed directly in front of me. His mouth was all covered in blood and dripped all over the playground." I shuddered in memory. "That's why. Seeing that would make any kid hate swings."

Allie grinned.

"That sounds like the best story ever. Tell me, are you the life of the party?" Allie said sarcastically.

And just like that, after a satisfactory number of pushes, Allie flew. Her arms spread out to reach the sunlight. Her legs poised beneath her, in a sort of jumping-jack position, and her hair stood on end like a halo. When she stuck the landing with a soft thud on the rubbery ground, her silver smile erupted through a waterfall of blonde hair.

"Close your mouth, Ben," she said. "Don't want to catch flies."

I clicked my jaw shut.

"Don't do that again."

Allie laughed as she settled herself back onto the swing.

"Why? Were you afraid I'd lose my teeth?" She gave a mighty grin and then stuck out her tongue. "You have to let go of the past and forget about what you're afraid of and just do things, Ben," she said. "If you're going to be a runner, you can't be afraid of things that might stop you or hurt you. You can't let your mental game affect you." She pumped her legs again. "You're too good."

I gave her my greatest Ben Asan-worthy smirk.

"Allison Johncox, did you just compliment me?"

She raised one eyebrow and smirked.

"Don't expect any more from me. You talk like a caveman."

I rolled my eyes.

"And you talk like we're on an English moor."

"Wow, I had no idea you knew what a moor was," Allie said in awe.

I shoved her playfully, and she howled as her swing twisted around and around. With each twist, the struggle to hold the swing increased until she couldn't twist anymore and faced me.

"Hi," I whispered and cupped her face with my hands. My rough palms brushed her soft cheeks.

"Hi," she said back. Allie's face contorted though when I leaned in to kiss her. Her nose scrunched up, her eyes narrowed, and her forehead wrinkled into mountains and valleys. "Don't. Don't kiss me."

I pulled away.

"Sorry," Allie whispered, her face half-longing and half-satisfied. "I-I don't know why I..." The sentence seemed to disappear as she twisted around. Her body spun in a blurred whirl before gently falling to a stop.

"It's okay," I promised. "I was just thinking... We aren't going to see each other the rest of the summer. We're just running out of time—"

"Time!" Allie groaned and threw her hands up to the sky. "What *is* it with people and *time*?" Her enthusiasm flipped her backward until her halo of hair kissed the ground. She wrapped her legs in the chains like an aerial silk performer and let her hands hang. "'We're going to be late!' 'What *time* is it?' 'How much *time* is left?' Humans are the most time-conscious species, and I swear, this country is up there on time-consciousness. 'Every second counts.' 'You can't waste your day!'" Allie groaned. "I call bullcrap. Time has messed everyone up, including me."

I paused to take in everything.

"Time?"

"Yes!" she exclaimed, whipping her body back upward. The chains rattled from the sudden motion. "When I was sixteen, I went to Costa Rica with my youth group at church," she began. "And days lasted years there. Time didn't seem like an issue. You woke up with the sun and fell asleep when you were tired."

I raised an eyebrow at her.

"Okay, listen," she said. "There—you know, Costa Rica —they run on 'Tico-time,' Otherwise known as 'you get there when you get there.' It's this culturally accepted way to go through life—without time and strict schedules holding you back from a meaningful conversation or helping your neighbor. And do you know what I noticed more often when I got home?"

I shook my head.

"Clocks. They tick so incessantly loudly, almost mocking you for sitting around not attempting to solve world hunger. It's so..." For a moment, I thought Allie would curse, which I hadn't heard her do, yet. "Distracting. Everyone has twenty-four hours in one day, but we spend hours worrying about being 'on time' for the next event! No one takes time to just savor life anymore."

Alie gave a loud sigh and dropped back down again, her hair fleetingly gracing the ground.

"We are a time-conscious species, Ben. So, I won't kiss you because we don't need to worry about time running out—I refuse to. I trust in God's timing."

Never had I thought that leaning in to kiss a girl would make me question the concept of time. But I respected Allie and felt buoyed by her comments that we were going to have plenty of time together.

After a few more minutes of swinging and jumping—Allie only, of course—we slowly made our way back toward campus. It was almost completely deserted now, and the last of the packed cars were heading out. Mt. Hope was always quietest at these hours, minus the passing local walking with a shaggy brown dog.

"I need to leave in the next hour, so would you mind helping me pack?" Allie asked.

I couldn't say no.

The first thing I noticed when we entered Allie's dorm was the drastic difference between Allie and her room. Allie, whose clothes never had wrinkles, had a messier room than me.

Allie's bed, decorations, and desk all had various shades of yellow and purple. However, amidst all the matching colors, clothes were askew everywhere—on the bed, by her closet—there was even a black undershirt caught in a mini yellow safe. Books, probably from late-night cram sessions, still sat on her desk chair and cluttered her shelves.

The other half of the room was completely clear.

"So sorry for the mess," Allie groaned and grabbed a purple hamper from the inside of her closet. I only got a brief look of the catastrophe inside; shoes sideways and every which way, shirts half-hanging off hangers. "I get sort of untidy during finals when I'm studying and haven't had time to pick up."

Allie artistically flipped the clothes into the hamper. I saw her cheeks reddened when she hastily threw in a bra and a tiny pink lacy item I realized was a pair of underwear.

"Um, could you grab my suitcase from under the bed?"

"Sure."

It was yellow. Of course. Easily Allie's favorite color, I had realized, as her fingers and toenails were always painted yellow. And it suited her, so cheery, a true ray of sunshine.

We spent a good fifteen to twenty minutes dematerializing her room; we unpinned pictures and notes from a corkboard, packed up multiple teaching textbooks—"I need to sell the rest of these..." Allie muttered—and took out many, many articles of clothing out and stuffed them in her Jeep.

"Don't you wish you had a bigger car?" I asked Allie as she stuffed undershirts and socks in some boots to save room and tucked them in the back of the driver's seat.

She shrugged and balled up a yellow camisole in a pair of combat boots.

"I like my car. I've had it since I was 17."

After stuffing an Army hat on her head she had spotted at the bottom of her car, Allie smiled.

"Well, this is where I go..." she said in an unconvincing tone. It seemed I wasn't the only one hesitant for her to leave.

A part of me wanted to tell Allie to stay because I couldn't face a summer without someone sane, but I just watched her climb into her Jeep.

"Can I come with you?" The words came out before I had a chance to stop them. I knew the answer, but the question hung in the air.

Allie laughed.

"What in the world? Ben, no, you'll be fine—"

"No," I interjected. "You don't have to spend a summer with my dad. I would honestly rather be stuck in a box all summer than spend it with him." I sighed. This was not the time to get into the issues with my father, but I just couldn't bear the thought of not seeing Allie for the rest of summer. "It'll be fun. You can show me around…"

Allie leant back against her Jeep door. Her eyes stared up at the blue sky, contemplating.

"And how will you get home after tomorrow? I'm not driving six hours in one day—"

"I'll walk."

She snorted.

"Ben…"

"I don't know. I'll see if Spencer can swing by—he's from up in Traverse City—and I'll just hang out there." I exclaimed as the plan began to form. "Allie, if there's a boy standing here wanting to spend time with you and willing to walk all the way home, it's a sin not to be with him," I joked. "But seriously, Allie, I can't stand the thought of not seeing you for months."

Allie's eyes rolled up to the back of her head at my joke, but she bit her lip as she thought about it. Then her eyes popped open and met mine. Each line and inch of her face glowed, and when she finally said, "Just this once and just for today."

I pecked her golden cheek.

"What about your things?" she asked.

"I'll buy some clothes when I'm up there, or just wear these again tomorrow. It isn't a big deal."

Allie's face flashed into a scowl, but it must have been a trick of the light.

"Oh, alright," she grinned. "You're getting very hard to say no to. Let's get in."

I gave a celebratory fist pump into the air and hopped into the passenger seat.

Twenty minutes into our journey, Allie let out a rather loud, "Oh!" and reached into her glove box.

"My address book. I gave you my number the other night, but I didn't get yours."

I flipped through Allie's address book and it was filled with numbers and names, but all were random famous people of history. FDR, Amelia Earhart, Marilyn Monroe.

"Uh, you do realize you have the numbers of dead people, right?"

"Oh," Allie laughed. "I just like to give my family and friends special names, for fun."

"Okay, can I just write my own name?" I teased the pen in a blank space.

"No, you'll be Gandhi."

"Why, because I'm Indian?" I teased.

She laughed.

"Oh gosh, Ben, no. Because you can make a change."

15

May 19th, 1990

"You know what I hate?" I called to Allie from the passenger seat.

Allie was outside of the car, pumping gas.

"These gas station-restaurant combos. Like, every gas station has a little restaurant in it. I don't want something going in my mouth to be near gasoline."

"Mhm…" she mused, her eyes on the gas pump.

"What?"

"Nothing…"

I gasped and pressed my hand to my chest.

"You *like* them?" I asked in play-disgust.

Allie shrugged.

"I don't know, they're just convenient, you know? Get gas and a sandwich. It saves time." Her bottom lip pouted, and she grabbed a pamphlet about oil changes from next to the pump.

I groaned.

"There you go with time again. I thought you were against it?"

"I'm from this century too, genius. I am too involved in time for my own good."

As Allie stepped back into the car, she turned up the radio and let out a velociraptor shriek.

"MR. BLUE SKY!" she screamed the title of the song and jumped back out of the car. I turned up the volume and watched her skip around her yellow Jeep, belting along with the song. I was reminded of her funny faces when she raced me, when she was just lost in the moment of being free.

Allie sang out as she pressed her hands on either side of my face and squished my cheeks side to side.

Allie finished her dance number when the electronic instrumental kicked in and hopped back into her Jeep, and drove away, still humming along.

I hoped this meant one day she would really sing for me.

Just like with her funny faces before, I could not control the bellows that erupted out of me as we turned out of the gas station.

"What's so funny?" Allie laughed along. "It's obligatory to dance like a crazy person when any British pop rock song comes on. I'm being me," she teased.

"Well," I said through my laughter, "one day I hope to feel so good about myself I can obey that made-up rule."

Something about Allie always filled me with some crazy euphoria, and if I didn't scream it to the world the magic she used on me, I would surely explode.

Once again, I was reminded of Allie's need for movement. She patted her fingers against the dashboard, pantomiming a piano, unable to sit still.

"Hey," I joked, "technically you sang for me."

"It was car radio singing," Allie teased back. "I never sing well on purpose."

And Allie held true to her word, even during "Strawberry Fields Forever," in which she changed keys incorrectly three times.

Finally, we got to Petoskey, a small town on the shore of Lake Michigan, right at the top of the Lower Peninsula. It was just as Allie had described it to me—a rustic lake town full of trees, boats, and a cute downtown with flowers that lined the sidewalks in the spring. We drove through downtown Petoskey, and low and behold were bushes of begonias, lilacs, and lilies. Gorgeous green trees on the cusp of the beach passed us by.

Allie relaxed into her seat from the familiarity of being home. She honked her horn as she drove downtown and a woman holding groceries waved at her.

I wondered how people just knew it was Allie honking at them, but then I remembered how rare it must have been to see a yellow Jeep drive around town.

"We're almost to my place—it's just a little further outside town," she said.

"How are your parents going to respond to a boy you've brought home unexpectedly?" I checked.

"Oh, I told them," Allie said. "Payphone at the last gas station," she explained when I looked at her puzzled.

Allie was right. We left the east part of town, caught sight of Lake Michigan, and almost immediately she slowed down to a driveway.

At first, I thought we had turned into the wrong house. There was no way Allie Johncox lived here. Beautiful, artistic, and somewhat rebellious Allison Johncox did not live in a shack.

Okay, so it wasn't totally a shack, but it looked rustic in comparison to the three mansions I'd spotted nearby. Obviously, Allie had wealthy neighbors.

It just took me by surprise that the girl with a thousand cameras who was so colorful, lived in a gray one-floor trailer home with no garage, a flag as a decoration, and a splinter-covered ramp. As I walked in, I noticed the small kitchen and modest living room, which felt a bit too small to be comfortable. There was no possible way Allie could live here if she went to one of the most expensive schools in the state. She couldn't—

Oh.

The Army hat. The American flag hanging in front of the house. The ramp. FDR.

I turned and spotted two adults coming in from the hallway, and my stomach tightened.

"Ben," Allie began, gesturing toward her parents. "This is my mother, Hannah, and my father, Samuel."

I was never one of those people that passed veterans in the street or at school and muttered, "Thank you" or gave a half-salute of appreciation. It's not that I didn't respect what they did or what they went through, I just thought if I was a veteran, I would get annoyed with the constant reminders of war and being treated differently. Plus, I didn't know what these men would be forced to remember if I recognized their heroic actions. Maybe they sent out friendly fire. Or carried someone miles just for their ally to die. Or maybe they were bashful and couldn't be brave like everyone else, and it ate away at them for years. So, I always thought maybe I was doing the veterans a favor for not being that way.

But when I saw Allie's father seated uncomfortably in his wheelchair, my spine lowered, and soon I was bowing to this man I didn't know. All I knew was that he had made a sacrifice for my life and should be respected.

"Thank you, sir," I croaked out.

When I stood straight again and met his eyes—green with a tint of brown like Allie's—his face broke into a wide grin.

"Al, you've trained him well. But I think the bowing was a little much—I'm no King of England," he chuckled.

I let out a laugh in relief. I noticed that Samuel's jaw was sharper than a bone whittled down to a point. When he wasn't smiling, his five o'clock shadow gave him the impression of a pissed-off lumberjack. If it wasn't for his kind green eyes, I'd assume he spent his free time sharpening axes to practice on every boy Allie brought home.

Hannah was the exact opposite of her husband—so much so that I was intrigued on how they ended up together. Her hair matched Allie's as did her warm smile, but her face was longer and her eyes brown. Allie really looked like a mix of both.

"Hello," I directed to Hannah with a nod, and she laughed.

"What? I don't get a bow?"

I chuckled and gave her a curtsy instead, which sent both Hannah and Allie into fits of laughter. Only when Samuel brought up the inevitable, the silence reared.

"So, Al, you were sort of vague on the phone earlier. You said Ben was a friend?"

Allie's cheeks turned rosy.

"Sort of. Mom, we talked about this." In the corner of my eye, I saw Hannah give a slight nod and—was that a wink? "Ben and I are kind of together. And he wanted to meet you two."

"I hope it's okay I came, I've just heard so much about where Allie is from, I wanted to see it for myself," I added, hoping to ease the tension setting back in Samuel's face.

"He'll be gone by tomorrow," Allie added. "His friend, Spencer…" she hesitated. I completely forgot she barely knew him. When I confirmed his name with a nod, she continued, "lives in Traverse City, and said he can pick Ben up tomorrow to hang out. Ben lives…" She trailed off and up to me.

"In Mt. Hope," I finished. "But Spence and I usually go up to his place on Lake Michigan sometime during the summer, so this works out perfectly."

Samuel glanced at his wife, as if asking permission to refuse my stay, but Hannah's smile brightened, and she pulled me in for a hug. Great. A hugger.

"Of course, you can stay here. It would be great to get to know the infamous Ben who Allie's been raving about."

I raised my eyebrows at Allie.

"You've been raving about me, hmm?"

She just stared at the floor, not wanting to meet my eye.

"Okay, well, I'm going to go and unpack," Allie said, swiftly changing the subject. I was about to go and follow Allie when Samuel spoke up.

"Ben, why don't you and I have a chat?"

Oh no. This was it. The dreaded talk. The "If-You-Hurt-My-Daughter-The-Cops-Won't-Find-Your-Body" talk. I'd gone through a few of them, especially in high school. One father was a urologist and had scissors sharp enough to cut off human balls.

I considered changing my name and moving to Canada after I broke up with that girl.

"Now, Sam—don't terrify him," Hannah chuckled and rubbed her husband's shoulder gently. Apparently, my face had paled more than I expected.

He rolled his eyes and gestured for me to follow him into the living room.

Hannah gently patted my back.

"He won't bite. Just tell the truth."

The truth. God, at this point, I wish what he expected was the truth. Allie probably came from one of those families that married the first person they dated and—oh no. What if he expected that Allie didn't even *kiss* that person until the wedding day?

I was screwed.

As I was debating the perfect way to escape before they noticed—out the window or perhaps hiding under the couch until further notice—Samuel spoke up.

"Are you paralyzed or something?"

I laughed at his joke for a second before stopping myself. A semi-paralyzed man just made a joke about paralysis to ease the tension. I sighed in relief. Someone with a sense of humor in the family would bode me well. Samuel Johncox seemed decent enough.

Then I realized why he asked me. While contemplating my future escape, I stood in the exact same spot, my eyes almost glazed over.

"Oh, um." How do you answer that? No? "Sorry," I said and followed Samuel to the living room.

Yellow. Everything was some shade of yellow. The couches were a dark shade of mustard, the walls were a faint baby yellow, the floor (and the rug on the floor) were complementary hues of amber.

I blinked and more yellow appeared like a genie wish. There was even a yellow desk and matching chair in the corner. I peered in every cranny but couldn't find a single different color—not even a hint of white, gray, or black—every inch of the room was cloaked in yellow so much I swore this was what the center of the sun looked like.

"Sorry, it's a bit bright in here," Samuel said as he fixed the brake on his chair. "When I came home from the war, Allie had painted and redecorated this entire room and my office desk." He gestured to the eye-melting yellow desk behind him,

"Why so yellow?" I asked him as my gaze continued along the walls. Every picture frame was yellow with a dark yellow Bible verse printed in it. The one closest to Samuel read 'Psalm 18:2' with the verse before it. A few others lined the others, like '2 Corinthians 7:9-10' or 'Romans 8:18.'

Samuel's fingers brushed a golden letter opener beside some neatly opened envelopes.

"It's been Al's favorite color since she learned the word, 'yellow.' Every dress she wore for dances was yellow. Her car is yellow—one year she tried to convince Hannah and I if she could dye her hair yellow." He chuckled at the memory. "We told her we didn't want to be sued for another student's eye damage."

"Wow," I said, "how did she take that joke?"

"Quite well, actually. Al loves to tease. But she's been through a lot. She's been hurt, and she doesn't make friends easily." He held up his hands quickly. "Don't get me wrong, she's a lovely girl, but she has a tough exterior. Once you break that down, she's a sweetie pie. Like, oh, what's a food that's hard on the outside but sweet inside?" He thought for a moment.

After another moment without coming up with anything, Samuel turned his head and called into the kitchen where Allie and Hannah were setting down boxes.

"Hey! What's a food that is tough on the outside but sweet on the inside?"

"A coconut?" Hannah called back.

"No, sweeter!"

"A Tootsie pop!" Allie exclaimed.

Samuel smiled and turned back to me. "A Tootsie Pop, that's what she is. Once you break through the hard exterior with your teeth, you can enjoy the sweetness."

"So, you want me to bite your daughter?" I joked.

Samuel chuckled. Oh, God, good, that wasn't cheesy, it just came out weird.

"I think you've already made it. This? Meeting us? This never happens—you should feel special."

For a brief second, I thought the interrogation was over.

I held out my hand to Samuel.

"Well, it was great talking to you…"

Samuel took my hand but squeezed it so hard that my entire body winced. Why I thought a veteran in a wheelchair wouldn't be strong, I'll never know.

"I got lucky with my older daughter's husband being her first boyfriend. I don't expect too much from you, Ben," he said through gritted teeth and a forced smile, "but if you aren't pursuing my daughter seriously, get the hell out, because I am not going to see her heart be broken."

I would have sworn my heart had stopped beating. My fingers began to numb. I had to say something, anything to get my hand and feeling back.

"Of course, sir," I hastily assured him, with a nod and a firm shake before our hands returned to our sides. We headed back over to the kitchen. I was aware that Allie and Hannah would hear our conversation as we were just inches away, but I tried to flex my hand out subtly.

"Ben, would you like a sandwich?" Hannah asked. She was slicing homemade bread on the countertop.

"Oh, sure, Mrs. Johncox."

Hannah pointed her finger at me and raised an eyebrow.

"Ah, ah, ah, I am too young to be called 'Mrs. Johncox' like that. Please, call me Hannah."

I chuckled. "Sorry, Hannah…"

"Salami work?" she asked as her hands rummaged around in the fridge drawers.

"Sure," I said and made my way to the kitchen table. It was round and wooden, a nice break from the army of *amarillo* in the adjacent room.

"Anything else on it?" Hannah asked as she pulled out a package of deli salami. "We have pepperoni, lettuce, mozzarella, and mayo or Catalina."

My lips curled. "Man, they're all my favorites. How did you know? Pepperoni, lettuce, and Catalina, please."

Hannah whirred around the kitchen, pulling at different drawers and cupboards until almost everything was left open except the ones beneath the sink.

Beside the refrigerator was the cereal and bread, where Hannah snatched a plastic bag of whole wheat sub buns. I couldn't help noticing as I watched Hannah whirring around the kitchen, that it was probably a fourth of the size of my parents' back in Mt. Hope. But I'd never seen such efficiency from them making food for a guest.

Almost as soon as she began, Hannah spun around the kitchen slapping all of the open drawers and cupboards closed. I glanced down at the plate in front of me—the sub was sliced in half—then back up at Hannah who whirled over to the stove top and punched a large white button on a red popped-up timer I hadn't noticed before.

Allie emerged and spotted her mother almost doubled over, panting to catch her breath.

"Time?" Allie asked casually and set down her purple laundry basket.

"One minute, forty-five seconds, and fifty-three milliseconds," Hannah responded through thick gulps of air.

I stared between the two women. My eyes searched for an obvious explanation that just wasn't there.

Allie smirked and swaggered into the kitchen.

"Still not beating the master, you amateur."

"You know I pushed your giant melon head out of me, right?"

"Okay, too many images," I said and closed my eyes in horror at the thought. "What's with the timer?"

I opened my eyes to see Allie sitting down beside me. I yearned to reach my hand out and grab hers.

"We always time each other to see how quickly we can make deli sandwiches—it's a silly competition my sister started." Her chest puffed out with pride, and I swore she was a queen. "I'm in the lead with a minute and twenty-two seconds exactly. I'm like Carl Lewis," she said with a grin over to me.

"So, Ben," Hannah settled down, her breath now back to normal. "You're from Mt. Hope?"

I nodded.

"And do you live at home or on campus? I know commuting can save a lot of money."

I shook my head. "I live on campus. I grew up there with my parents, grandparents, and my three younger siblings, and I needed a bit of a break."

"That's a big family," Hannah guffawed. "And I thought having two kids was busy."

"Well," I shrugged, "that's how we do it in India."

"That's where Ben's family is from," Allie explained.

"Actually, just my dad's side," I said. "My mom is American—she's half Irish actually, with bright red hair—and I was born in Flower City, just next door to Mt. Hope."

"How fascinating!" Hannah exclaimed as she leant forward with her hand on her chin. "Have you ever been to India?"

My face felt warm. I knew I shouldn't have been so embarrassed, but when I was in elementary school, kids weren't too interested in where the brown kid was from.

"No," I said after hesitating.

The wait seemed longer in my head.

"Samuel and I went to India several years ago before Essie was born," she began. "What state is your dad from?"

Little five-year-old Ben who was made fun of for having aloo gobi in his lunch pail was beaming from inside me. Not even my closest friends at Mt. Hope cared to ask.

"They're from South India. Kerala—Thiruvananthapuram, the capital," I sped out. "My father came from a wealthier family, and they came to America when he and his siblings got scholarships to the University of Michigan. There he met my mom, and shortly afterward, they were married."

"Do they speak Hindi there?" Hannah questioned. "We were mostly in North India, and I know it's popular there."

"No, it's called Malayalam. My dad mostly speaks it in the house."

"Can you speak Malayalam?" Allie spoke up. "I mean, if your dad uses it…"

"Yeah, I do. All us kids do."

Hannah set her fist on her chin and smiled as if remembering a better time.

"Samuel and I were in New Delhi for Diwali during our semester abroad."

"It must have been amazing to witness Diwali in India. Was it crowded?" My smile was growing. Outside of my family, I never talked about Diwali, and it was my favorite holiday growing up.

Hannah chuckled and ran a finger over her wedding band in thought.

"Every day was crowded there, but, yes, quite crowded. I didn't really understand many of the cultural things they were doing, but everything was so fascinating."

"I bet it was…"

"Maybe you should go to India," Allie suggested. "You only have one year of school left. Go for a semester."

"I couldn't do that," I said slowly. I finally remembered the sandwich in front of me and took a bite—it was delicious.

"Oh, why not?" Hannah asked. "Don't you want to see Kerala or New Delhi or just, you know, experience it?"

To be honest, I would have loved to go to India. But India was the Daisy to my Gatsby. I was too afraid of how my perception would change if I got too close, I was equally satisfied and dissatisfied about never crossing the Indian border and watching the Diwali lights from afar.

Also, I couldn't help feeling sick at the thought of not seeing a certain someone every day. My gaze fell on the upturn of Allie's nose, and I smiled. This girl had gotten a hold of me, and I didn't want to let go.

"Hey, where's Linus?" Allie asked after a moment of silence. "Linus!" She looked around the corner and frowned.

"Honey…" Hannah began. "He's…"

"No!" Allie exclaimed, her mouth agape, eyes wide in horror.

"In the backyard. I didn't want him to jump on your car."

"Linus!" Allie ran outside of the home and tripped over the steps that led to the backyard. A rickety old Golden Retriever clambered out and shimmied through Allie's legs.

I had never felt jealous of a dog before.

"Hi, Linus! Hi, buddy! Did you miss me?" Allie cooed as she rubbed and scratched his ears, stomach, and back.

And that little bastard just smiled at me, reveling in being Allie's favorite and showing me who was top dog around here.

However, I definitely did not expect this next thing to come out of Allie's mouth, at least not yet.

"Come on, Ben, let's go to my room."

16

Devon stared at Asan as he stayed silent, perhaps pondering about the weight of the world as the snow gathered against the window or debating the political and social norms in the modern day versus the past; a past in which Devon could only get a glimpse of from far, far away, like a passerby of a finished story.

Asan flared his nostrils slightly, which Devon thought perhaps it was by accident.

"I loved celebrating Diwali as a kid," he said finally, his voice quiet. "My dad would find some sparklers at a discount fireworks store, and I'd run around our front yard chanting and singing Indian songs into the middle of the night while wearing a traditional *kurta*. Our neighbors yelled at me, and Mom would plead for me to put on a coat because, 'For goodness' sake it was October,'" Asan chuckled sadly at the mention of his mother.

Devon had an overwhelming urge to reach out and put a comforting hand on his professor's shoulder but refrained. He didn't know how to comfort his grieving professor.

"My father encouraged me, and my mother took photographs. She hung up one of her favorites above our mantle. I think I was about eight."

Dr. Asan sighed and rubbed the back of his neck, a sign Devon had noticed meant he was about to share something uncomfortable.

"I think, at some point, Mom missed me running around screaming prayers and songs, because on my sixteenth Diwali, I came home with my hair all messed up, my shirt on backwards, and with my sparkler burnt out. I didn't answer my mother when she asked where I'd been," Dr. Asan sighed. "That was the start for me, that night. A party, a girl, the inability to say no. The desire to seem cool, not the weird kid who can speak another language that sounded like 'gibberish.'"

Devon cleared his throat.

"I, uh, know what you mean, a little bit," he shared. "My dad is this big lawyer over in Flower City. Camburn & Associates?"

Dr. Asan's mouth gaped in recognition.

"He's a defense attorney for corporate companies near Detroit, including one that—and I probably don't need to name names—had a bit of a scandal a few years ago, when I was a freshman," he sighed. He looked up at Dr. Asan, who nodded in recognition and encouragement to go on.

"The CEO had been accused of laundering money and inaccurately paying his employees for years." Devon rubbed his eyes. "When my dad won the case, nearly a hundred employees who were the whistleblowers lost their jobs, and my dad acted like it was nothing. He was *proud* of how well he did for his client." He shook his head, wishing he could shake away the memory. "I told myself I would become a lawyer, a *better* lawyer than him. But I-I started drinking to forget the way my dad destroyed those families, and I've taken it too far. I..." Devon sighed again. "I've let it consume me. Now I don't know if I could ever achieve my goals, now."

Dr. Asan crouched in front of Devon now, meeting him eye to eye, level, as equals.

"I'm so sorry, Mr. Camburn. Truly, I am. My father was many things to me, but I cannot imagine the burden of the legacy that you carry." Dr. Asan placed an encouraging hand on his shoulder. "If you are determined, I know you can change. You can still be proud of yourself."

Devon felt his eyes water. He hadn't cried in years, and he tried to blink them away.

Dr. Asan stepped back, turned toward the kitchen counter, and grabbed a small plastic storage container.

"Would you like a cookie? They're sugar. My wife made them. They're her signature," Dr. Asan said as he held out the container. They were holiday shapes—a Christmas tree, a Santa Claus, and a reindeer, all decorated with precision.

Devon grabbed a Christmas tree and bit the star off the top. It melted on his tongue and was the burst of sugar he needed.

"I understand why," he chuckled.

"Families can be complicated, Camburn." Asan said gently. "Sometimes you might not feel like you fit, sometimes you might want to prove them wrong, or perhaps you even create your own. The most important thing is to be true to yourself, and I can see that you still have that in you. You just need to believe it for yourself."

17

May 19th, 1990

Allie collapsed onto her bed, shortly followed by Linus—who had limped behind us—who quickly scraped his back legs against the bed to gain momentum and plop next to her. By the several scratch marks from his paws tattooed into the wood of the bed frame, I assumed it was a common ritual.

Everything in Allie's room was in its place and organized. All of the cameras Allie apparently hadn't taken with her to school were all carefully placed in a little row on a wooden desk in the corner. Her shoes, about five pairs, were all under her bed—also neatly made—with each pair evenly spaced along the frame.

My mouth agape, I turned my attention to Allie, who threw one of the pillows to the floor. Her toes flipped her sandals to the ground, both landing several feet apart and at funny angles.

"Your room's very...neat," I noted in confusion. Allie, with her path of destruction, couldn't have made her room so organized.

"Yeah," she sat up and rubbed Linus' belly. "I spend two hours each day here cleaning and picking up when I'm home." Her face remained stoic as she stared at me.

"Really?"

Allie snorted and giggled before falling back down and hugging her dog closer.

"Of course not. You're lucky it's not a pig sty in here. No, my dad loves to straighten out my room, and my mom's side of theirs. He's a big guy on symmetry. In the Army, he'd clean and fold all of his roommate's linens and pick up after them. Every night he'd iron and lay out the uniforms for his troops. They'd sit at each person's foot of the bed with their socks in their combat boots, unlaced and with the tongue out already."

I raised my eyebrows. Samuel, who'd seemed so tough and protective, spent his time daintily organizing shoes and socks? What was next? That he stole candy to give it to babies?

"It kept his mind off of his impending death," Allie furthered explained, and the joke in my throat died. Her tone was so matter of fact, it shocked me. "He was sent to Vietnam when I was just three and didn't come home until I was close to six. I had to get acquainted with the idea of death at an early age."

"I'm... I'm really sorry."

She shrugged. "It was normal to me." Allie finally pressed a kiss to the side of Linus' face. She had been trying the past few minutes, but he'd kept slowly moving away.

"So, what did you want to show me in your room?" I asked.

"Well, you showed me yours and what inspires you, so I thought I could show you mine," Allie gestured past my head toward the wall behind me, and I turned.

My eyes widened as I took in the art before me. And it *was* art. Allie had multiple canvases on her wall, clearly all shots she had taken herself. One was a sunset that rivaled The Sunset That Got Away, spread out across the lakeshore. Another was a close-up black and white portrait of a woman with a single tear running down her cheek. And my favorite one was one of Mt. Hope, with its recognizable clock tower in the backdrop, and the sun shining through at dawn.

"These are beautiful," I gasped. Allie smiled at me knowingly. "Your photographic eye is so insightful and emotional. I don't even know what the crying woman is going through, and I feel for her."

"That's Essie," Allie added in explanation. "We were watching *Fox and the Hound*, it's a very sad movie."

"Well, you captured it beautifully," I said, and in a moment, caught her lips as well.

Around five in the afternoon, Hannah realized she had forgotten to purchase ravioli for dinner, so Allie and I hopped into her yellow Jeep and headed into downtown Petoskey.

Allie parallel parked on a random street in front of a large brick building. It didn't look like the stores around Flower City. Everything in Petoskey seemed like it was from another decade.

"Am I close enough to the curb, do you think?" Allie asked as she scrutinized her parking job.

I rolled my eyes and grabbed her hand.

"Don't worry. C'mon, we want cheese ravioli, don't forget."

Allie let her worries about her parking go and led me into the building. Immediately, I was hit with a scent of freshly baked chips and salsa. There was a lady standing near the entrance, handing out samples of the homemade salsa with the chips she was baking in a toaster oven.

"This place is full of locally produced food," Allie explained when she saw me looking in awe at the woman practically governing her own salsa stand. "We try to support the farmers and businesses around here as best as we can."

Despite its modest appearance from the outside, it was full of aisles with fully stocked shelves, and even a refrigerated section. I somehow got lost, my eyes constantly caught on another person running their own little stand selling peanut butter, bacon, or jam.

Finally, I heard her lilting voice.

"Ben!" Allie called, holding up a bag of cheese ravioli. "Do you want anything?" she asked from the end of the aisle.

I glanced around at the shelf in front of me. Allie was offering, and I didn't want to disappoint.

"Sure. This…," my eyes fell on the first thing in front of me, "bag of almonds." I grabbed the small pack of roasted nuts and tossed it over to her.

Allie stuck them under her arm and walked over.

"Anything else?" she asked, grabbing a toffee chocolate bar for herself.

I shook my head.

"Alright," Allie shrugged and placed the three items on the belt. "Don't say I didn't offer." She pulled at her flowery purse and gave a sigh of relief when her yellow wallet came free from whatever junk she'd stuffed in that small bag. She removed the five-dollar bill Hannah had given her. "Hold on," she mumbled to the cashier, "I think I have a couple quarters somewhere..." Allie rummaged through her wallet, checking every crevice.

"I've got it," I said, pulling out my own leather wallet.

"No, I'm fine," Allie shot back.

I stepped away.

After one more failed attempt at making perfect change, Allie silently and begrudgingly grabbed a dollar from her wallet and handed it over, receiving ten cents from the cashier.

Back in the Jeep, Allie fiddled with her keys. Her hands shook as she started up the car.

"Allie..." I began.

"Don't."

"It's not a big deal. I just didn't want you to get stressed in front of the cashier so I thought it was easier to offer and then you could have paid me back if you wanted to."

"I'm already in debt to you twenty-five cents from the Funyuns, Ben. I can't be in debt to you anymore."

"It's just twenty-five cents, Allie, it's not a big deal," I reiterated and reached for her hand, but she didn't reply.

Allie's eyes were watering now, and she pulled over to the side of the road. Her driveway was just out of view.

"Allie, what are you..." She was foraging through her wallet again.

She unzipped her change compartment with a shaky hand and tipped it upside down. She raked through the change but couldn't come up with the equivalent of a quarter. "Just take it!" she exclaimed and thrusted her ten cents at me.

"Allie, it's just twenty-five cents! I don't need it!" I said firmly, trying to push it back into her clenched fists.

"No! Take the money!"

Suddenly, I was brought back to the incident at the ice cream truck, but this time she had nowhere to run to. Her breathing was labored, and she was shaking as if it were negative fifteen degrees. I tried to take her hand, to give her some sort of comfort, but it was ice cold and speckled like the cracks of a frozen window.

"Allie… Allie, it's okay, it's all okay. Please." I pulled her into a hug, and she whimpered against me. "I'll drive you home," I whispered, jumping out of my seat. I opened the driver door and helped Allie into the passenger side.

It took almost twenty minutes for me to finally navigate back toward the Johncox residence—I passed it twice. By that time, Allie had calmed down, but the moment we entered the house, she retreated to her room, muttering something to Hannah I couldn't hear.

"Hannah," I said as I handed her the ravioli.

"Thanks, Ben," she said and immediately ripped the bag open. She didn't seem concerned over Allie's strange behavior.

"Um…" How was I supposed to explain that Allie had a breakdown in the car? *Hey, Hannah, your daughter just freaked out about less-than-a-dollar debt and now is refusing to talk to me for the second time in a few weeks?*

"What happened?" Samuel asked as he came into the room. His eyebrows were raised in a way that made my palms start to feel clammy.

"Um, well… She needed change to pay for the food, and I offered to pay for it, but she refused, so she used another dollar." I explained quickly, as if getting the story out faster would lead to a resolution. "She already owed me some change from a bag of Funyuns from before we got together. I tried to tell her it wasn't a big deal, and then she freaked out because she already owed me twenty-five cents and threw her change at me." I shuddered remembering what happened next. "Then she started breathing heavily, and she became so cold…"

"It was a panic attack," Samuel explained. "Don't worry yourself. It's not your fault, it happens."

"A-are you sure?"

Hannah set down her wooden spoon from the pasta sauce and chimed in.

"We know that's what happened because she's always talking to us. She's social. She never goes to her room without saying hello. That's how we would know if she had one if she just storms off and shuts herself away."

Samuel sat forward and rubbed his eyes.

"Allie is beautiful and wonderful and our happy little girl. But she is stubborn. She doesn't want to *need* help," Samuel sighed. "It reminds her of some rougher times. She can get panic attacks when she feels out of control. And money is a big trigger for her."

Hannah and Samuel glanced at each other knowingly. Meanwhile, I was still completely confused.

"I think we need to explain a bit more," Hannah said softly. "Allie is very prideful. Back when Samuel was overseas, and then after his accident, people treated our family with kindness, but Allie felt like it was charity."

"If Allie forgot her lunch, the school gave her a free one. Or her friends, during church, would take her car and get her gas, even years after the accident," Samuel elaborated. "Well, Allie didn't want those gifts. She hated feeling obligated to pay them back."

"She didn't have to pay them back—or me," I added.

Hannah sighed and pinched the bridge of her nose.

"But that's not Allie," Hannah sighed. "She wanted to be treated the same, not pitied or treated differently because Samuel is disabled. So, she got a job, and every cent she made went to paying back anyone who helped us over the years."

"There's a pattern to her behavior," Samuel explained. "She should be fine in—"

"I'm fine now," Allie interjected as she walked into the kitchen. "You guys made me sound like a basket case," she teased. She was back to her old self, and it just made me want to hold her close to let her know that it was okay.

But I didn't want to make a big deal about it. If she was fine, I was fine. And if Allie wanted to talk about it later, I would be there for her.

Dinner was nice. The ravioli was tasty, but the best part of dinner was Allie initiating a long game of footsie. As much as I wanted to comfort her from how she felt, I could tell she wasn't there yet, but it reassured me that everything would be alright between us.

After dinner, I excused myself to the bathroom. When I returned, Allie was holding what looked like a parachute, but I soon realized it was a tent.

"That's your home for the night," Samuel said.

"Just so you know, Ben, I advocated for you to sleep in Essie's old room."

"It's right next to Allie's, Hannah—"

"It's fine," I said and smiled at Allie. "A tent sounds good."

The sun was just beginning to set as we carried out the tent.

"Why doesn't your mom help us?" I asked Allie as I held down one side with my foot and another with my hand. The musty tent was becoming even less appealing as we put it together, but I tried to be grateful. They could have left me to sleep in Allie's Jeep as I was the first guy Allie ever brought home.

"She takes care of my dad when I'm not around."

She relieved me of my strained leg with a peg. She put a few hammers into the ground, and she clipped the black hooks onto the silver pole.

"What about school? You study three hours away."

"My mom takes care of him during the week, and then I babysit my dad every other weekend when my mom works," she said. At the term, 'babysit,' she blushed and refocused on the tent.

"Babysit." I repeated it as I remembered how Allie said she spent her summers.

"Well, there's a lot my dad can't do any more," she explained as she grabbed another pole. "The cabinets are too high, so he can't reach his medicine or some food. I have to aid him in buying things at the store or other simple things, like mowing the lawn and cleaning the house and gutters. Dad jokes that I babysit him, but I guess I kind of do."

When Allie placed the pole back in, I clicked the hooks and stood up straight.

"So, that Friday when you were in a hurry, the one where I asked for a date...?"

"My mom had an emergency at the hospital, and I found out late. I was rushing to get home in case my dad needed me," she clarified, as if her dad being dependent on her was no big deal.

My eyebrows furrowed.

"Can't he do stuff like go to the bathroom on his own or take a bath? Couldn't he handle being alone?"

Allie bit her lip and looked up at me.

"Um, no, he could," she said, her voice beginning to shake. "It's just a precaution, because of history. W-when I was twelve, my dad insisted that Mom and I go to the farmer's market together to get fruits and vegetables for the week and enjoy some mother-daughter time," she sighed and toyed with her hair.

Maybe I didn't want to hear this story anymore.

"And when we came back, he had tried to make us dinner as a surprise, but he fell out of his chair trying to reach the stove top." She tucked that piece of hair behind her ear. "He broke his hip."

The words I should've said got caught in my throat. I'd heard worse stories, of course. But something about Allie sharing all of these memories with her voice breaking made it worse than anything I could imagine.

"Allie, I'm—"

"Sorry?" she supplied. "I've heard it all." Allie leant over the tent to fix at a few rips with some bright yellow duct tape. "I know that my dad is in a wheelchair. I know he's disabled and that makes things a little harder. When it first happened, everyone was telling my mom how awful it must be and how they were praying for us," she sighed. "And I got so sick of it. They had no idea what life was like for us. Dad had to have hours of counseling just to be civil around others. When he first came back, Dad was a different person. He drank all the time, swore nearly every sentence, and blew up at the smallest things. If it wasn't enough to see my dad struggling with his new life every day, it was the cherry on top to constantly be reminded of it whenever he wasn't around."

My experience when girls got emotional was minimal, but with Allie, the desire to comfort her was almost instinctual. I reached for her hand, and she let me take it.

"How did it happen?"

Too many people must have asked Allie this question over the years. She had her answer rehearsed.

"He was in Vietnam, and it was early in the morning. My dad was asleep on his bed, and some of the other U.S. troops were goofing off outside—they were young kids. One accidentally set off a grenade..." She rubbed the back of her neck. "We don't know how it went off, but three people died."

Allie's eyes watered more, teetering on the edge of crying, but she held it in. I wanted desperately to tell her she could cry, but Allie didn't need my permission.

"The shrapnel went through his tent and severed his spinal cord. The doctors on site tried their best, but now Dad's paralyzed from the waist down."

Allie weakly continued setting up the tent, taping piece after piece. It was about two minutes before I could say anything else, being so scared of saying the wrong thing made me say nothing at all.

"What was he like before?" I finally asked.

And Allie's face lit up. The tears had dried. I had said the right thing.

"He was the best dad ever. I mean, he still is, but in different ways. He joined ROTC at Mt. Hope where he met my mom. They fell in love and got married at nineteen, just after knowing each other for a year." She chuckled. "They often tease that I'm just like them, that I'll marry my husband after a short amount of time. But Essie and Jack dated for, gosh, eight years before they finally married. So, who knows..."

"Nineteen?" I exclaimed. "Isn't that a bit young?"

"Not to them." Allie beamed. "Before, when we were little, Dad would take Essie and I out on this trampoline we used to have, and we'd ride on his back, holding on while he tried to buck us off. Essie was always better, but I had fun, just as a little kid."

As the sun's bright light started growing only visible through the cracks in the forest, Allie and I finished setting up the tent to the music of our childhood memories.

I shared about all the teasing I got for wearing glasses in elementary school so that eventually I just kept them in my backpack.

Allie told me about how Essie and her used to ride their bikes, pretending they were horses, all along the yard.

We ended up talking on the porch until midnight when Samuel called Allie inside.

"You are an adult, now, you know," I told Allie as she began to stand. "He can't control when you go inside."

"I know," Allie said and stood up to gently brush her lips with mine. "But I don't know if I can control myself with you," she whispered and headed in for the night.

18

"Do you believe at this point you know Allie enough?" Asan asked as he stood and brushed down his sleeves clean.

"I mean, I've never met her, but—"

"Based on what I've told you, do you know Allie well enough, Mr. Camburn?" Asan narrowed his eyes, almost as if he was scrutinizing him for the right reaction.

"Um," Devon coughed. "No, I guess."

"Mr. Camburn, you said you want to be a better lawyer than your father, correct?"

"Yes," Devon said without a beat. "I have to be."

"And what do you think is the key aspect to being a lawyer?" Dr. Asan queried.

Devon shrugged and looked up to the ceiling as he tried to remember anything from his classes that would help. He sighed.

"Being able to lie well?" he suggested, thinking of his father. Asan's face stayed still, so he tried again. "Looking good in a suit? Wait!" He smirked. "Being good at history?"

Asan let out a chuckle at Devon's brown nosing. "This answer isn't one of flattery, Mr. Camburn, no. It's understanding that everyone comes from a slightly different background than yourself, and until and unless you get to know that side of them, you will never truly know them."

Devon stared at him. "Why does it matter if I feel like I know Allie? Is there going to be a quiz when she gets home?"

Asan shook his head.

"I tell you this because my idea of Allie changed over and over again with anything she'd tell me," he explained. "In retrospect, it all seems silly, but when Allie had panic attacks, I questioned if I was even qualified to be with her. I came from lots of money that my parents worked hard for. But I was never desperate for it like she was."

Asan rubbed his beard in thought.

"Back at the vending machine, she was desperate to get home to Samuel and bring him his favorite snack—the Funyuns. Where I saw quirky, odd behaviors related to money, Allie was experiencing distress in a way I could never understand," Dr. Asan explained. "But I could control how I approached things with her. So I learned, fairly quickly, how to respond to her, to truly know her, despite our differences, and to overcome how either of us may have behaved in our worst moments. We continued to choose each other—to choose to understand and to care."

Devon shifted uncomfortably in his seat. He wondered if Dr. Asan had somehow read his mind and knew Devon was wondering if Lindsey would continue to choose him, in spite of what happened.

His phone began to vibrate in his pocket.

Lindsey. Shit, he hadn't responded to her texts. It was nearly one-thirty now.

"I have to take this," he told Dr. Asan and excused himself once more to the bathroom.

"Hello?" he answered, his voice cracking.

"Devon, thank goodness, where are you?" Lindsey didn't sound angry. Her voice cut through, sharply, likely her concern for Devon had sobered her up. "I've called you like ten times already!"

She had?

Devon checked his phone—yes, there were about ten missed calls from Lindsey. He must have been so focused on Asan's story that he didn't feel his phone go off.

"I-I'm so sorry, Lindsey, I didn't realize…"

"I'm just glad you're not dead, Devon!" she exclaimed. "Where are you? Are you still at the party?"

"No, no…" Devon trailed off, unsure of what to say. How could he explain to Lindsey he was at his history professor's house without her asking him to just leave? And he couldn't leave, not yet.

Dr. Asan's words of wisdom were the kind he had needed from his father. His insights into life, as well as similarities to Devon at his age, made him hopeful with every moment of the story. "I'm just at a friend's house. I got sick, and I'm worried it might be contagious. I'm just gonna stay here for a little bit until I feel better, but I promise I'll be home soon, okay?" A little white lie, but he hoped when all the truth came out to Lindsey, she wouldn't care too much about this one.

"Okay. Feel better, alright?"

"I will. Please, don't stay up waiting for me," he insisted. "I love you."

"I love you too," Lindsey said through a yawn. Devon hoped she would be asleep soon. But he had to go back to Dr. Asan.

As his sobriety was approaching the horizon, he was worried he was going to lose the nerve to finally share and receive guidance from someone he was now learning was wiser than he had ever known.

19

May 20th, 1990

As a child, my least favorite day of the week was Monday. I don't think I ever met a kid who liked coming into school after the weekend.

But the moment my parents tried to force their religions on me, my least favorite days of the week easily became Sunday. My stomach pitted every time the morning shone on a bright Sunday morning.

That's exactly how I felt when I walked into Allie's home church. A part of me drowned in a sea of active churchgoers who checked up on the young kids by name and would be mortified if they heard the things I'd done.

"Here," Allie said and offered me the sweet solace of her hand. She led me to the front pew.

Beside it, there was a large space that Samuel wheeled into. Before us were a few Bibles and hymnals placed in the front of the space for people like Allie's father. Allie hurried away to go talk to a few older couples near Hannah.

The band began to play softly, so Allie said goodbye to the couples before bustling over to sit beside me. As a greeting, I leaned in to kiss her, but she pulled back.

"No, no kissing in church."

Of course, I just hadn't been thinking.

Allie's hometown church was physically smaller than I'd expected, but by the time the band had begun to play "Old Rugged Cross "everyone was scooting together to accompany the large congregation.

Allie stood among the flowers, all singing their praises, eyes closed, palms up. Even her friends behind us were blooming.

I felt like a weed.

"What's wrong?" Allie asked once the pastor came up and the band disappeared. She took my hand as she sat down, squeezed between myself and Hannah.

"What do you mean?" I asked and, as a cover, picked up the nearest Bible in front of me. I had to at least act like I cared in front of Allie. I had slipped up with her on our second date that my mom was a Christian, and I had started to recognize that Allie thought the same applied to me. Too afraid to let her go, I summoned my memories of Sunday School as a kid to get through the service.

"You aren't standing during the songs. Do you not feel well or something?"

"No, no… I just… I slept wrong. My back hurts." Which wasn't entirely a lie. It just wasn't the reason I didn't stand.

"Okay…" Allie pulled out a yellow Bible and yellow notebook and yellow pen.

The pastor spoke quicker than anyone I'd ever heard, but somehow, Allie, with her head down and her yellow pen skirting across the page in her yellow notebook, caught every word.

I couldn't understand what the pastor was talking about, so I just looked to my left at Allie.

Her profile was the most beautiful part about her. Her nose slightly turned up; her eyebrows full and perfectly shaped; her lips sat in a small pout when her head was down. It was almost like a rhythm. She'd glance up, her smile lengthening at the words of the sermon, and a few seconds later it dropped down as her hand sped across the page, leaving ink smudges on her wrist. I hadn't even noticed she was left-handed.

The words of the sermon went on, stretching horizontally in the waves of ink. In large letters at the bottom of the page, Allie wrote: LET IT BE BY THE LORD'S WILL.

I didn't know what she meant by that, but I wanted that tattooed everywhere in Allie's handwriting.

I wrapped my arm around her and held her close. Before I could stop myself, I pecked her cheek.

Allie's eyes widened.

"I told you not to—"

"I know, sorry. It's just," I sighed and pressed my lips to her ear. "You're so beautiful, Allie. In this moment, the love you are expelling is intoxicating."

Allie blushed and looked at her feet. "That's so sweet, but I'm just being me."

"You are beautiful no matter what the reason is," I whispered.

After church and a brief lunch at Allie's, Spencer called and said he was about thirty minutes from her house.

"I can help you take down the tent," I offered to Allie as I headed outside.

"Don't bother with it," she said, following me out. "I'd rather spend this time just together."

"I just feel like we couldn't do any of this stuff with my parents around," she said and situated herself crossed-legged on the grass.

"Stuff like what?" I asked and sat beside her. Our skin brushed, and Allie blushed.

Then Allie initiated a real, lengthy kiss for the first time all weekend. Her hand found mine and squeezed it as she pulled away.

"How's that?"

"That was," I breathed out, "unexpected."

Allie smirked and laid back, letting her fingers and toes brush the emerald grass.

"I thought I'd get you back from this morning."

"You had to admit I was smooth."

"I was caught off-guard," she corrected and pointed a finger at me. When I gave a playful bite, she laughed and pulled away. "Bad puppy!"

There were some things about Allie I never tired of. And one of those things was her voice. It was sweet and low, almost like a hum. But it was more than the lilt of her voice. It was what she said and the conversations we had. I could never think of enough things to ask her, and time flew by whenever we were together.

My entire time with women was based on one thing, and when that one thing was taken out of the picture, I found I could not stop using my mouth for talking.

Never in my life had I ever been so disappointed to see Spencer. I ached to stay in that moment with Allie as long as I could.

"Ben, come on!" Spencer honked and yelled through a smirk. His sorry head poked out of the window of his truck.

I rolled my eyes and sat up, taking Allie with me.

"Well, I suppose this is goodbye," I said as I enfolded her into a hug. When she didn't relax, I leaned in and said, "This is where you kiss me."

She pressed a soft kiss to my lips.

"Until August."

"August?" I guffawed. "But it's summer. When do I get to see you—"

"Ben. Come on, we need to go!" Spencer called.

Okay, this wasn't the sweet send-off I expected any more.

"You honestly won't be back in Mt. Hope until August?" I asked.

Allie chewed her lip and shook her head.

"My dad..."

"What are you doing on the Fourth of July? I can come here, so you don't have to leave your family." It came to me out of the blue. But for some reason, I wanted to see Allie's smile surrounded by sparklers and fireworks.

"I-I, um, I suppose that would be fine..." she said with a sneaky grin. I knew she wanted it, too.

"Great." I pecked her cheek. "I'll be here."

And somehow, I landed myself in the passenger seat of Spencer's truck, barreling down the highway, counting down the days until I was reunited with Allie again.

20

Devon took another cookie from the container. Now that he knew Lindsey was asleep, he felt a little more at ease, and perhaps Dr. Asan could sense that.

"Would you feel more comfortable moving over to the living room? I can keep an eye on the driveway then, too," Asan offered.

"Oh, sure," Devon said as Asan gestured to him into the living room. The pictures he had noticed on the mantle were now turned facedown.

"Pick any seat," Asan said as he settled himself into a leather armchair facing the door.

Devon ended up on a large yellow couch, next to the Victrola. It smelled like lemons.

Dr. Asan was doing a great job at pretending like he couldn't hear Devon's conversation to Lindsey in the bathroom, but Devon had been able to hear Vidya on the phone with a friend earlier in the night, and her bedroom was much further away. He wasn't oblivious to the thin walls in the house, but he appreciated Asan's discretion.

"Aren't you tired, sir? I'm used to being up late, but I can't imagine you staying up until the early hours of the morning very often," Devon reasoned.

Dr. Asan shrugged and sat further back in the armchair. "I've gotten used to it, over the years. There's always a late night every month or two, so I'm not worried. If the sun's out and she's not here, that would be new," he said with a chuckle. "But I like staying up and waiting. It's worth it to see my wife walk through the door. I fell in love with her much earlier than she did with me, and so therefore, I always want to be the first one to greet her when she walks through the door. Everyday I'm grateful to be in her presence."

Devon bit his lip at the thought of love so pure that Dr. Asan would stay up for hours just to wait for Allie to get home.

"Do you feel that way about Miss Huff?" Dr. Asan spoke to what Devon was thinking.

"I—" he stuttered. "I'm not sure. I love Lindsey, I really do. But the love you have for Allie… It's from a fairytale. It's so pure. And… I don't know if I deserve that kind of love. I've made some mistakes."

Dr. Asan sat forward now and met Devon's eye. The words he spoke were full of such purpose, such passion, as if bellowing up from the depths of his soul.

"Everyone deserves that kind of love."

21

July 4th, 1990

"Would you like a hotdog, Ben?" Hannah offered.

I had a hard time convincing my mom to let me spend the holiday with the Johncoxes.

"You'll miss the fireworks in Flower City—and you and Fatima always chase Jared around with sparklers," my mother had said. But when I'd explained about Allie, how she made me feel, and promised I would just make it a day trip, she obliged.

"I'm actually more of a chicken guy," I answered as I helped Samuel hang up the American flag. The sun was shining as we hoisted the flag into its holder. I knew today must have been difficult for Samuel. Allie had let slip to me once, during one of our long phone calls, that anything that could vaguely remind Samuel of the war bothered him.

"Thanks, Allie," I said as a besides, "that you didn't force us to go to the parade earlier. Jared and Fatima always insist on going to the one at home and trying to get as much candy as possible. Last year, Jared almost got trampled by a horse to get a Whatchamacallit."

Hannah snorted.

"Jared sounds like an ambitious young kid."

"Mom, where's the aspirin?" Allie called as she headed inside.

We were in the backyard, setting up for our lunch. Allie had found a picnic table and had set it up in the corner of the lawn. Linus had stationed himself directly beneath the table, enjoying the shade.

"In the medicine cabinet near the back!"

"Is the Jell-O ready, yet?" Samuel asked Hannah who had taken the initiative to set the table. She had laid a red, white, and blue plaid tablecloth over it.

I swatted away a few flies that were circling the table and grabbed another ice cube to run along my neck. The temperature was only in the eighties, but I could not stop sweating. Allie teased earlier saying I must have been part-ice cream.

Allie was decked out in white shorts, a red shirt, and blue and white starred flip-flops. She had painted an American flag on one cheek and red, white, and blue fireworks on the other.

"Babe," she laughed as she flopped out to the yard. "Did you run through a sprinkler?"

I looked down at my shirt, just streaked with sweat from my underarms and chest.

"What, you don't sweat this much?" I teased.

Allie gagged.

"I try to control mine," she said with a chuckle, and I earned a kiss. "You're properly melted. Let's see if you can borrow one of my dad's shirts—Dad?"

When we received the thumbs-up from Samuel, Allie raced inside with her hand in mine. Three months with Allie and her gentle touch was still a welcome feeling.

"You can put on one of his shirts that are Fourth of July appropriate. Take off that soaked gray shirt—it's so boring."

Allie rustled through her dad's closet. Meanwhile, I slipped the damp shirt off and let it fall to the ground. I shrugged my tank off, too, which was soaked, and balled them both.

"This one should work," Allie said as she turned around with a white tee that said, 'Veterans Fourth of July Parade.' She paused for half a second with a micro-expression of pleased shock before turning back to casual Allie. "Um, anyway, here." She snapped it off the hook and started to push it over my head, but I stopped her.

"Allie, I'm a big boy." I laughed and slid the shirt on by myself. "But thanks for the shirt." I kissed her gently. She pressed her palms to my cheeks, and my hands drifted downward. I paused.

"Hey, do I smell something burning?"

"The food!" Allie sprinted out of the room, her legs flailing like a sick duck, and I was left to smirk at the satisfaction of how my body made her smile.

Hannah had bought some fireworks at the local big box store.

"I never go there to shop, but the fireworks tent was set up in the parking lot," she had explained when both Allie and I were shocked at her choice of shop.

At nine, we set them off into the dusk. Some colors, like the dark blues and greens, barely showed up in the background. But the reds and oranges proved most beautiful as their short lives met their purpose before dying.

One firework lasted for about a minute as it kept snapping new patterns. Others were fast and short but left their smokey skeletons behind.

As the fireworks were exhausted, Samuel reached his hand up to his wife. Without a word, driven by some unspoken code, Hannah helped her husband back into the house, with Samuel's head in his hands.

When she emerged with s'mores supplies, Allie stood up.

"Is Dad—?"

Hannah nodded.

"I started up a bath for him to calm down. I tell him every year he doesn't have to watch but he insists—he still loves the colors, and how happy they make you," she added with a smile. "Do you want to toast marshmallows?" Hannah held up the half-empty marshmallow bag sealed with a twist-tie.

"Not tonight," Allie said. I agreed with her. Hannah's Independence Day buffet of food had stuffed me up.

"Well, I'm going to go watch some TV, and you two can watch a movie or something in the basement. But if it's *Steel Magnolias*, you're gonna have to let me join," Hannah teased and went back into the house.

I let my hand drift to Allie's as we walked down into her basement. Just beneath the stairs was a church organ Allie earlier explained Essie used to play when she was younger.

"Promise me we won't be watching *Steel Magnolias*," I said as I flopped onto the faux-leather couch.

"Definitely not," Allie chuckled as she plopped beside me and tucked her legs to the side. She stretched over the edge and came back up with a handful of movies on VHS. "We've got... *When Harry Met Sally, The Little Mermaid, Casablanca, Howard the Duck,* and *Yoga for Beginners.*"

I wrapped my arms around Allie's waist and tugged her closer to my chest.

"I don't know. That yoga one sounds nice. Soft colors..."

"Mmm... New-age music."

"Women in yoga pants."

Allie playfully slapped me.

She jumped to her feet and, after pressing start, found her place now in my arms. At first, we both watched the screen. Allie giggled whenever the instructor took a long breath and then proceeded to cover my eyes whenever the woman stretched downward.

And then I kissed her for no reason other than purse desire. I took her cheek in my hand and slowly our bodies pushed together and down further into the length of the couch.

The video ended without our notice. In short periods, our lips relaxed, but didn't break apart. When we had regained our energy, I let myself escape into Allie's kisses.

My hands reached beneath her shirt and ran my fingertips along the small of her back. Without fail, my fingers unclasped her bra, and a small moan emitted from Allie as I palmed her skin.

"Allie! Ben! Going to bed now; just so you know!"

Allie flinched beneath me, and I pushed myself off of her. She became a blur as she raced around the corner with her hands snaking up her back to redo the clasp.

"We're coming!" she called.

I had to stifle a laugh at that one.

The rest was a haze. We spent about twenty minutes upstairs chatting with Hannah. I remained quiet except for a few laughs or agreeing statements. Then Allie and I were alone in the kitchen, and somehow, I felt we didn't deserve our shared solitude.

Allie stared down at the wooden table and traced circles with her finger. When I excused myself to leave, she followed me out the front door and to my car.

"So," Allie sang once we made it to my car. "I am actually glad we found a time to see each other before the school year started," she admitted.

"You are?" I smirked and raised an eyebrow. "Are you telling me Miss Allie Johncox actually enjoys spending time with Mr. Ben Asan?"

Allie laughed and playfully slapped my arm. "I think you knew that already." She bit her lip, contemplating, then looked up into my eyes. "And... I think it's time the rest of the world knows, too."

My eyes widened in surprise. Allie and I had talked openly about our relationship—what it was, and what it wasn't—while on the phone this summer. But there was one stipulation to making things official.

Allie took a deep breath. "Ben... I want to be your girlfriend if you'll have me."

Despite my reputation, I hadn't ever had a committed girlfriend. I could count on one hand how many girls I had spent more than a week with. But I had not waited so eagerly for anything in so long as I did this moment.

"Yes, of course I will," I accepted. I picked her up and spun her around until both of us were in fits of laughter. Allie Johncox was officially my girlfriend, and I never wanted that to change.

I was still on cloud nine as I got in my car and received a goodbye blown kiss from Allie.

Yet, as I spent the night driving home, I couldn't stop thinking about what might have happened with Allie if Hannah had not interrupted us.

22

August 25th, 1990

Allie and I spoke nearly every day at three and at eight if she wasn't home alone with Samuel. A routine we had fallen into over the summer after Allie called me the day I returned from her house in May at three. Her father and mother went to town from three to five every day to run errands and let Samuel see some friends. Then at eight, Hannah and Samuel watched *Cheers*.

I had longed to see her even more with every conversation.

"Tell me your biggest secret," Allie whispered one June night.

I bit my tongue as I thought. I didn't need to guess my biggest secret—I knew it. It plagued me. I contemplated telling Allie that I didn't actually believe in God. But I didn't want to ruin her perception of me, especially as our relationship was going so well.

"Never mind. That was super personal. So, how was your day?"

Allie moved fast—not physically in my sense, but emotionally. We took things at a slower pace than I was used to physically, but now that our feelings for each other were so open, her emotions were, too.

Every day we would tell each other personal things that sometimes I wished we were together to say.

"I failed math in eighth grade and had to retake it over the summer."

"I had a lisp when I was young."

"I peed myself during a marathon."

We both laughed then.

But despite our often discussions of quite uncomfortable memories, we grew much closer.

In late July, when I registered for a mini-marathon, Allie called me at five in the morning to give support. "I'll pray your bladder controls itself," she said, both a joke and a confirmation of real prayer.

So, when I saw Allie's Jeep rounding the corner of Mt. Hope's campus in August for move-in weekend, my stomach flipped. She was more beautiful than ever to me and seeing her yellow Jeep signaled the arrival of her sunny self back into my life. Her summer at home helping outside at home in the garden and mowing the lawn had tanned her skin nicely, and her dirty blonde hair had lightened to a light strawy blonde.

As usual, she had her camera bag with her, and a camera swinging from her neck strap. When she saw me, my heart sang.

"Welcome back, m'love," I said, holding out a hand to her as she stepped out of her car.

"Don't mind as if I do. My parents are right behind—oh! Wait! Essie's pregnant!"

Allie had mentioned that Essie and her husband Jack had been trying for a baby for a few years, so this was very happy news.

"She's due like, end of January, early February, okay?" Allie said.

"I will make absolutely sure I will be available in January in case you need anything from me."

Two cars pulled up next to Allie's.

A tall woman came out first. Her hair was dark, down in a single thick braid, and she had large, bright blue eyes. She immediately ran up to Allie and hugged her. Allie screamed with delight. The two women held each other tight and jumped around, both talking at lightning speed to one another.

Next an even taller man emerged from the same car, glancing briefly at the two excited women, and giving me a nod. He held out his hand.

"I'm Jack, Essie's husband," he introduced himself.

"Oh." I cleared my throat. I hadn't understood that the news about Essie also meant she would be present today. I looked over at Allie hugging her sister, then back at Jack. "So that's Essie."

Jack nodded. "We're here to move her in for the last time—Hannah made it a surprise. Essie told Allie we'd be gone for a business event."

I glanced at Allie who had been crying happy tears and chatting away excitedly with Essie.

"She seems pretty surprised. When was the last time they were together?"

"Christmas," Jack chuckled. "It's my fault. I'm involved with international affairs. I'm a pilot, and Essie likes to join, so we're always traveling."

"Wow, that's so cool. Must be fun." I lied. That did not seem fun to me whatsoever. I would constantly have motion sickness.

He shrugged.

"It's work. But Essie's busy working at the dentist's office when she isn't traveling, and now we're expecting a baby." Jack grinned at the thought of becoming a father. "It's been difficult. But those two are closer than my wife and me. You'll have to learn to share your time."

After a moment of watching Allie with her sister, I realized I'd been rude.

"I'm Ben, sorry. Allie's—"

"I know."

My eyes widened.

"She and Essie talk often. You've been the newest subject," Jack said with a wink. "She really likes you if you can't tell. First real boyfriend."

Heat spread through my body when the two girls looked at Jack and I as if they knew what we were talking about.

"Ben," Allie called me over.

Jack clapped me on the back for support, and I walked over to the giggle-sisters.

"Ben, this is Esther, my fantastic older sister."

"Essie," she corrected when she shook my hand. "I'm going to stay Essie even when I need dentures." For thirty, Essie barely looked a few years older than Allie. She had high cheekbones that framed her face nicely when she laughed with Allie. Although she had more angular features like Samuel, her smile matched Allie's.

"Nice to meet you," I said, "oh, and congrats on your baby." Essie was so tall and thin; her belly barely had a bump.

"Thank you. I can't believe I'm pregnant at an age not considered unfit. I'm a real 'mom' age." She rubbed her stomach, then pulled Allie into a hug. "It's crazy how old my little sis is getting, too!"

The two continued to chatter away animatedly. I turned to Jack to see if he also felt like an outsider, but he was laughing along with them. I tried not to let it bother me—I would fit in in time.

Essie handed Allie a box with a bow on it, which Allie eagerly opened. In her hands she held a new camera.

"Essie buys me a new one every school year," Allie explained. Of course, I was the only one who wouldn't know of this tradition. "Hence why I have so many cameras. And I try to make the first photo with it be significant."

"So," Essie said with a grin. "What'll your first photo be this time?" She stood to the side and cupped her bump with a wink. "I'm ready for my close up, dahling."

Allie giggled at her sister and put the camera to her face and then paused.

"I've changed my mind," she trailed off before turning to face me. "I want my first picture of this year to be of you."

I must have looked taken aback, because Allie said quickly, "If you don't mind, I mean," she blushed.

"Of course not," I said. "I might not look my best being this sweaty, though."

My smile always brightened when I made Allie laugh.

"Don't worry—you look perfect."

I plastered on my best cheesy smile—all teeth, squinty eyes. But then Allie stuck her tongue out at me, and my mouth turned into a natural grin. With a flash, the moment and my joy were captured forever.

"Well, these boxes won't unpack themselves," Essie announced, bringing us all back to reality. Allie, Jack, and I grabbed some boxes and hit the stairs, while Hannah and Samuel, who had been getting the vehicles unpacked, took the elevator.

We got most of Allie's clothes unpacked and half of her books before Essie sat down to take a break. She smirked over at me and Allie.

"When's the wedding?" Essie teased.

"In your dreams," Allie laughed, but she blushed and turned away.

I wrapped Allie in a hug.

"No, we'll get married eighty years from now when we're old and Allie's face isn't red anymore."

Everyone laughed, even Allie, although she playfully shook her fist at me.

As we continued to unpack, we happily chatted away. I told Essie most of the things Hannah and Sam already knew about me, like how my family was from Kerala.

"Are you gonna go there, do you think?" Essie interrupted.

I stuttered.

"That's what I keep telling him," Allie said. "But he doesn't want his façade to be ruined, you know?"

"Completely," Essie said with a nod. "Okay, this pregnant lady has to pee, and if I'm going to leave, it's also going to be so I can go get some tea from the café down the street."

"Oh! Can you grab me an iced coffee?" Allie asked with a pout.

"Make that two?" Jack added.

"You know what," Essie said as she rubbed her belly. "I think someone else needs to come with the pregnant lady," she winked over at Allie and I, "and maybe give these lovebirds some space."

Hannah's eyebrows raised. "Ah, I understand... You know what, I want to see if they have any muffins. Honey?"

"Right behind you," Samuel said as he followed the group out. With the door closed, it was just the two of us. I was ready to pull Allie close to me, but she spoke first.

"Do you really never want to go to India?" she asked, sounding surprised as she plopped down on the couch next to me and began playing with my hair. "I know what you've said before but... really never?"

"I mean," I began, "I actually talked to my dad about it recently." Allie's eyebrows rose. "I could've studied in Mumbai for the fall semester."

Allie jumped up immediately, but the momentum and gravity collided, and she fell back.

"Oh my gosh, do it! Do it, Ben!"

"It's too late now," I said. "The deadline to apply was a month ago, and classes start Monday. Besides, this gives me more of a chance to spend my last year in Mt. Hope before I move."

Allie, who had resumed playing with my curls, stopped.

"Move? Where are you moving?"

I cleared my throat. No one knew my plans to move away after school, not even my own mother.

"Well, I actually wanted to move to Colorado."

"What? What's in Colorado that's not here?" Allie rebutted.

I could list several things. Mountains, Denver, good roads. But I only answered, "The United States Olympic Training Center in Colorado Springs."

Allie remained silent, so I continued.

"I've been tracked by scouts since middle school and have been making my way up in the ranks for the Olympics. If I beat my personal time next season at the trials, I'm eligible to train at an Olympic Center."

Allie blinked and spoke up.

"But are there any centers in Michigan? Maybe close by?" Her hands clamped in nervous fists, and her knuckles were turning white.

"Yes, two, actually." Her face lifted. "But Colorado Springs is one of the main ones, and it's at an elevation of 6,250 feet above sea level, so running there can improve my SpO2, or the capacity of my lungs to breathe while running."

"But what about us?" Allie hesitated.

"We've only been together a few months, Allie. I haven't had a chance to think about what our relationship would do to change this dream I've had for years. You can't really expect—" I stopped mid-sentence at the sight of Allie's face changing before me. It had squashed together so much I thought she was going to cry. But then it smoothed out, and she took a deep breath.

"Excuse me," Allie muttered and got up from her bed. She stepped out into the hall and the door thunked behind her.

In the hallway, I could hear the voice of Essie call out to Allie—they must not have gone far. But I was frozen in my seat. I was an idiot. How could I not think of how Allie would feel? I was a bit flabbergasted still—but then I heard voices grow, and Essie and Allie re-entered her room. If I hadn't felt on the outside of their relationship before, I sure did now.

"Allie?"

"Ben, can I talk to you?"

I swore at that moment I reverted back to eight-year-old Ben who was sentenced to the principal's office for running with scissors.

"Sure."

Allie and I went outside, not touching. She didn't seem at all like she had before. There was a lightness back to her again, but her calmness unnerved me.

"Do you want to just sit here with me, on this bench?" Allie asked.

"That-that's it?"

"Let's just sit first, okay?"

I took a deep breath and sat beside her. I waited for her to speak. I had already said enough to mess with the day.

It felt like an eternity before Allie took a deep breath, and when I caught her eyes, I saw that they were watering.

I couldn't stop myself. I pulled her close to me, and she melted into my chest.

She wrapped her arms around me, still not speaking. My blood was rushing as I caught my breath. Even my ear had a heartbeat.

"You're going to Colorado," she finally whispered, muffled against me.

"And you're upset about it." I rested my chin on top of her head and rubbed her back gently. "Talk to me, Allie, please."

Allie let out another loud sigh as she struggled to hold back her tears.

"You can cry," I whispered to her.

"N-no, I'm f-fine," she stuttered.

"Okay, I won't make you," I said and gently kissed her hair. Across the quad, I spotted groups of students carrying boxes up staircases just like we were, moments ago. "But please," I implored. "If we are going to work as a couple, I need you to trust me and talk to me about what upsets you. I might not be able to fix it, but I at least want to know."

Allie's body, initially tense, slowly began to relax into my touch. For moments, I just held her, until she cleared her throat, and spoke.

"I don't want you to go to Colorado because I would miss you," she whispered as if it were a sin. "I would miss you even more than I did this summer."

I could barely register what came out of my mouth next.

"You could come with me," I whispered.

Allie didn't bat an eye.

"I can't. My dad..."

"Has your mom."

"But when she works..."

"He's a grown man, Allie! You guys can't keep babying him, I'm sure he hates it." She pulled away from me, but I had to tell her. "If that happened to you, you wouldn't like being helped—you can't even take a few cents from me. And Samuel is the same way—I can see it. You would die being dependent like that, and Samuel hates it, too."

Allie looked down. She knew I was right, but there was no way she would admit it while so vulnerable.

"That is not the only reason." Her voice grew smaller. I had brought down her only defense, and it gave me a pang in my chest. "I-I'm trying to get a job in Petoskey at my old elementary school. They have an opening that's being filled by a temp this year, and they've already offered me the job."

I cupped her cheek.

"Allie, that's great." I reached for her hand, but she pulled away.

"Ben, I—" she gasped out. "Ben, I don't let people into my life easily," she whispered, and it sliced the air. "It's miraculous for me to even care about you this much without pulling myself out of the situation. I'm not throwing that away if you can train here."

"I'm not even 100% sure I'll be eligible—"

"Ben, I know you. You're on the track to the Olympics. And you're not going to give up until you qualify. You've put so much time and energy into your dream." Her eyes magnified and glimmered like stars even through her tears. "All you have to do is break your record, and whenever I see you," Allie caught my gaze for a moment, "you run faster to me than you have in any meet." She looked away, and I lost the stars. "I make my judgments too quickly. I thought you were a different person, and now I couldn't be happier being with you, and I have taken time to get to know you and invest in our relationship. I don't want it to just go away. Everyone else has left me, please, not you, too."

I pulled my arms around her. No matter how mad she was, I knew Allie could not resist a hug.

"Who else has left you?" I asked quietly.

Allie sighed. "Only because Essie encouraged me to share, I'll tell you..."

She sat up and put her head in her hands, almost in pain at what she was about to share.

"It's not even—it's so dumb that I still let it bother me..." she trailed off. "I was your typical weird kid. I liked climbing trees during recess. I enjoyed art class, obviously. And I was a pushover. I didn't really know how to speak up for myself, and Essie was so much older, I was alone at school. No one really interacted with me.

"By middle school, I had really gotten into photography, and looking back," Allie gave a small chuckle, "those first pictures were so bad. But I was proud of the photos I took. So, I used my allowance to print off copies at the local print shop and passed them out to kids at school," Allie's voice grew quiet again. "They ripped them up in front of me."

I had seen Allie's work as an artist, and her eye for photography was beautiful. I'm sure even at a young age her work showed promise. The thought of random middle schoolers destroying what she had worked hard for and paid for made me nauseated.

"What did you do? Could you move schools?" I asked. Allie let me take her hand now, and I stroked the back of it in support.

"I did in high school," she explained. "We thought it would be best for a fresh start when everyone else was moving into a new building too, but… The other school was smaller, further away from Petoskey, and most people already knew each other, so I was excluded…"

I squeezed her hand reassuringly.

"In art class, I remember one day, we had to do a group project. But everyone was slacking off, so I coordinated everyone to come to my house to finish it," Allie explained. I had a sickening feeling I knew where this was headed. "No one showed up. I completed the project all by myself. I stayed up for hours using five different mediums to create a mountain landscape sculpture. I just remember," she bit her lip, "just being so tired and feeling absolutely so alone."

"Allie," I sighed, "did you tell anyone?"

She bit her lip and shook her head.

"Why not?"

"I-I couldn't," she whispered. "I didn't need more pity. I-I had to prove to everyone that I wasn't just the girl whose dad was disabled. The VA checks every month didn't always cut it. I couldn't let what people thought of me win." Her lips trembled. "But the reason the idea of you moving to Colorado bothers me so much is because I actually had a friend, someone who I thought understood me, sophomore year."

My heart lifted for a moment at Allie having someone to support her.

"Her name was René, she was new. I befriended her right away. I even brought her to church once and introduced René to all my friends there."

I raised my eyebrows.

Allie rubbed her temples.

"One day during sophomore year, René started talking to some girls on the basketball team. They told awful lies about me—just said awful things, I-I can't even think about..." Allie took a deep breath. "René stopped hanging out with me after that, and then... She's the reason that boy from school assaulted me."

My eyebrows furrowed. "What? Who assaulted you?" I exclaimed. A vivid image flashed in my mind of what I would do if I ever laid my hands on whoever hurt Allie.

Then, as if my body already knew, a memory popped in my head about our first date talking about our first kisses and the boy who kissed her in the corner with no one looking.

"It was a dare," Allie croaked out. "My first kiss. René thought it would be funny if...if the most popular guy on the football team pretended to be into me." She sighed and ran her hands through her hair. "He cornered me one day after school when I was finishing up a project in the art studio. He cornered me, pressed his lips and body against mine, and thrusted against me for...I don't know how long. Until I started to cry."

My stomach dropped. "Allie, did he...?"

"He kept our clothes on, but only just..." she winced. "He only got off me after René got nervous about getting caught and called out to him to stop." Allie took a shuddering breath. "I knew I couldn't trust anyone there again. I kept to myself the rest of high school and the moment I graduated, I never went back to that town again, and I decided to go away to the furthest public university I could that was still in Michigan."

Allie's earlier defenses fell into place in my mind. Why wouldn't she think the star track player wanted to hurt her just like the footballer in high school?

"Did you ever tell your parents?" I asked Allie. She was so close with Samuel and Hannah; I couldn't imagine her keeping this from them.

Thankfully, she nodded.

"That afternoon, when I came home, I cried the moment I walked in the door," Allie explained. The relief she must have felt in that moment mirrored her face now as the weight of carrying her story from me lifted. "It was the hardest thing I could have ever done—to tell them—but also, I felt so calm, somehow? My dad obviously threatened to hurt the guy—and I even told him his name—but to my knowledge he never did anything." She caught my eye. "And my mom, well, she's so practical, that after lots of tears and hugs and prayers, decided to give me a way to process everything, even when she and dad couldn't be there for me, or if I didn't feel ready to share with them, but still needed to talk about it."

I furrowed my eyebrows. "What is it?"

"Well..." she began. "My mom gave me a tape and microphone, so I could record myself, as I was feeling, fresh in the moment, and that I could share with them when I was ready. I ended up," she swallowed, "adding worship music to the tape, as a way of talking to God and using the lyrics to remind me of my prayers in hard times."

Allie glanced away from me, but I gently tipped her chin toward me.

"So, the ice cream truck music…?"

"Was one of those tapes, yes," Allie sighed. "That's why I…freaked out. That was private. It was me at my most vulnerable."

My chest grew tight as I imagined what Allie was thinking in the moment, as the shame wound its way into her heart at having her emotions so obviously on display.

"I'm so, so, sorry, Allie. If I had known—"

"You couldn't have known," Allie insisted. "Only my parents and Essie did—so of course you, and even Brennan, didn't know what was on that tape. Honestly," Allie continued, "it was jarring hearing it back. I haven't used my recorder in so long—except, I did after the panic attack at the grocery store this summer," she admitted. So that's what Allie had been doing in her room. "I'm so much stronger now. I'm confident in myself. It was hard to hear it again and go back to that place, to who I was then." Allie swallowed. "Just like it was hard to think of someone truly caring for me, romantically, being just a temporary stop in my life," she said with a chuckle, trying to ease the tension.

My stomach tightened.

"So, I've just basically ruined your life even more," I scolded myself.

Allie bit her lip, but then spoke, "N-no, Ben, that's not true," she whispered. "Y-you've brought so much joy to my life, that I can't imagine being without it—without *you*."

My throat tightened. I felt the same way. Despite it just being a few months with Allie, I didn't want to even think of my life without her. If Ben from six months ago knew I felt this way about a girl I hadn't even slept with yet, he would have thought I'd gone crazy.

Allie continued. "T-the fact that you are just *here*, that you care about me, that I've told you about my past and you're still *sitting* here, lets me know at least, that no matter what happens—if we break up or get married or however this all shakes out—at one point, s-someone *loved* me. And… I feel the same way," Allie stated. She met my eyes, now empty of tears but full of expectation, of confirmation.

I wanted nothing more in that moment than to remind Allie, to affirm to her, that I cared about her and wanted the best not just for her, but for us. I reached, pulling her towards me, and kissed her.

When I pulled away, hand cupping her cheek, I whispered, "I've thought about my future for so long, it's been second nature to me. But now?" I kissed her again. "Now, I need to remember to mold it to fit not just me, but us. Because I don't want you going anywhere out of my life, Allie Johncox. Not for a long, long time."

This time, Allie initiated the kiss, and I felt myself melt into her touch. When we pulled apart, her green eyes stared deeply into mine.

"I don't know what the future has for us," Allie began, her mouth widening into her perfect, beautiful smile, "but… I trust God has placed you in my life for a reason, Ben Asan. And I want to obey Him. We will figure it out in time, between jobs, between the Olympics, whatever will happen. I will follow you wherever you go if you'll have me."

I squeezed her hand and shrugged. "And who knows, maybe Colorado will feel too far for me. But I'm committed to being with you, all of you, this year. We will figure it out together when the time comes."

23

August-November 1990

When school started, I wasted no time with Allie. We spent as much time together as we could. Between mealtimes and study sessions, I even began attending church with her, albeit out of a desire to please Allie more than anything. I still didn't have the heart to tell her I didn't share her faith, and I was too scared of how she would take the truth to tell her. I had thankfully convinced her to go to the later service, as I knew my mom always attended the early one, to avoid awkward run-ins.

We continued to go on walking dates, which Allie loved as we could talk freely, and one of mine because I could loosen up after long runs, but we also began to become integrated into each other's lives in new ways.

"...and the kids are so sweet! One little girl, Valerie, comes up to me every day and gives me a big hug! And Jared, he's a stinker—"

"Wait, Jared as in my younger brother, Jared?"

Allie snickered. "I wanted to see how long it lasted before you found out. Yes, Jared Asan, your brother is in my student-teaching class."

"Guess I got a spy on the inside," I chuckled and kissed her cheek, but Allie was far too focused on her story to notice.

"I love working with kids. When Essie has her baby, I'm going to be such a happy aunt. I'll photograph her every waking moment." As per typical Allie, she had a camera around her neck, bouncing with every step we took along the pavement.

"Speaking of photography, what are you doing for your art major final project? I know this semester is all about your elementary education major."

"I'm not spilling," Allie said. "But I will need your help on a project for this semester about nature. Will you?"

I pecked her lips.

"Of course."

"Okay, I know this is artsy, but you really expect me to be okay with my naked body floating around the gallery?" Allie had asked me to meet her in the art studio a few days later, but now I felt exposed.

Allie rolled her eyes.

"For the last time, you will not be naked. That's why I asked you to wear flesh-colored underwear. I'll edit appropriately."

I shrugged off the robe.

"Okay, so I just...pose?"

Allie shook her head.

"You're not camera ready. You need to be made up first."

I raised my eyebrows as Allie pulled out a paint brush and blue paint.

"I forgot to tell you: I'm painting you like ocean waves."

Obviously, I was opposed to being painted on.

"So, I'm your human canvas?"

"That's the project!" she exclaimed, like I'd guessed correctly at twenty questions. "Use another thing as a canvas. One other student is using a person, but a lot are using rocks and walls and such. Someone else I think is using their car, but I wanted to use you."

"So," I smirked, "I could say you've been *using* me?"

Allie slapped my chest playfully.

"Stop," she laughed. "Now, stay still."

The brush's soft strokes glided smoothly along my chest. The blue paint—navy, sky blue, cerulean, I learned as Allie named with each stroke—spread across my skin, making waves with white foam along the sides.

"You know I have bigger boobs than you," I teased as Allie drew around my chest.

"Oh, totally a double D, at least, hmm?"

"I think you mean double E," I insisted.

She snorted.

"Shush." Allie dipped her brush back into the white pail and slashed it across my mouth. "Stop!" she squealed when, without missing a beat, I leaned in to kiss her with my painted lips.

Allie ducked out of the way, but I chased after her, running laps around the empty art studio trying to catch her.

"Stop! You're not dry! Ben, no! Oh my… Ah!"

I planted a kiss on Allie's forehead and smudged

my lips across her skin to rub off the excess paint before I pressed them to her lips.

The paint on my chest had gotten onto Allie's shirt, so she made me stand extra still while she repainted.

"Allie?"

"Don't move, you're breathing."

"Maybe you should have grabbed a cadaver from the bio labs."

"Alright, fine," Allie said, putting her hands on her hips. "If you keep moving around and being a bad model for me, no more kisses today."

My eyebrows rose. "If I stand super still, you're going to let me kiss you?"

Allie's rosy lips upturned.

"Maybe..."

I became a statue.

Allie went headfirst into almost everything. She had her guard up in the beginning, but ever since that talk on the bench the day she got back to campus when Allie had bared her feelings to me, she was one-hundred-percent in.

And I could see that determination in her eyes, that ambition to finish what she started. The ocean reflected in her squinted gaze at my cheek as she lightly caressed an itty-bitty brush to define my cheekbones.

"Why are you squinting? I think you need glasses."

Allie ran the brush through my eyebrows.

"Shut up," she said with a laugh. She nicked along the scar in my eyebrow and paused.

"What happened here?" she asked.

"Bicycle accident when I was six," I spoke through gritted teeth—I didn't want to disrupt her from moving my face muscles. "For some reason, I didn't see the tree and flew right into it."

Allie's use of my body as foamy ocean waves was a hit. During the art show near midterms, everyone was impressed —the other student that used a body tried to paint trees with the use of armpit hair as the leaves, but it didn't have the same artistic touch as Allie's did.

When the weather started turning colder, and the leaves that had graced the trees in bountiful colors began to fall, I had to use the weight room or indoor track for exercise. Not one for extreme heat nor extreme cold, I was a man who loved temperate weather.

Since Allie was gone all day student-teaching, we used the few seconds I had when I ran by her seat in the bleachers by the indoor track to talk, shouting back and forth to each other whenever I crossed her path.

"...so, Essie's having a girl! "Allie shouted to me.

"Wow! That's…" I ran the length of the indoor track again, waiting until I was closer to Allie again to yell back. "Great! Have they thought of a name?"

Another lap.

"They like Mila or maybe Katherine!" Allie called down to me.

It wasn't quality time, but it was time, and every moment I heard Allie's voice hollering down at me, I smiled.

"Hey," Spencer said one night near Thanksgiving break as he was washing some dirty dishes. "Can I ask you something?"

"Hmm?" I asked. I was flipping through the channels, stretching out, and searching for anything good to watch that wasn't some strange documentary.

"Do you love Allie?"

Mostly Spencer tried to talk to me about sports, so I was completely surprised to hear Allie's name come out of his mouth. We rarely navigated girl territory, despite how blatant my love life had been for the last few months. I didn't usually bring Allie over—a house full of college boys didn't always smell the best—but we spent most of our time together, either in the library, the art studio, or just walking around campus.

"What?"

"Okay, don't act like you didn't hear me," Spencer said. "I know you heard me. You're sitting five feet away."

I slowly turned around and stared Spencer down. I could tell he wasn't joking.

"Why does it matter to you?" I said with a chuckle, trying to diffuse the tension.

Spencer raised his eyebrow at me. "Just curious."

Brennan walked past us, headed to the cupboard, and grabbed a bag of Hot Fries.

"I-I don't know," I said, although I did know, but wouldn't dare admit it to them. While I didn't care how my relationship with Allie had soiled my reputation as a womanizer, talking about Allie with my friends required a whole different type of vulnerability. "You can't expect me to fall in love with someone this quickly. It took years for me to even love myself."

"Ooh, did you finally ask him if he loves Allie?" Brennan questioned Spencer with a mouthful of the salty snack I was pretty sure had my name on.

"Wait, have you guys talked about this?"

Spencer turned back to the dishes.

"We might have talked about it once or twice…"

Brennan shoved in more Hot Fries.

"Do you, or don't you?" he mumbled as he chewed.

"Why do you guys care so much?" I laughed.

"Cousin!" Brennan exclaimed with a hand raised.

"And I'm your friend," Spencer said. "I care for your well-being, and I fear Brennan might kill you if you hurt her."

Brennan snorted, then coughed.

"F-fry down the wrong pipe," he barked.

"No, but Brennan? What did Allie say to you?" I asked. "Is this something she put you up to?"

After he'd finished *my* bag of chips, Brennan lopped it into the trash and cheered over his successful basket before answering.

"Nothing," Brennan explained. "I just know my cousin. And I feel like I deserve a heads up if I need to get my machete sharpened."

Spencer rubbed his eyes and sighed. "Brennan, I told you we can't kill Ben if he breaks Allie's heart."

"I was just gonna castrate him!"

"Hey!" I exclaimed with one hand over my front.

"Obviously a joke," Brennan insisted. "We just want to know if what's happening with Allie is serious or not."

"I know you, Ben. You're my best friend," Spencer elaborated, "but I also know your history. And if this is just some long-game scheme to get in her pants and then never see her again, we're going to have to have a serious talk."

Spencer never spoke his mind. I expected this from Brennan, but not Spencer. He never gave a mean comment when I'd come home drunk, with a girl, or high, or even all three. He would even clean up my vomit. He bought me new sheets after an episode left mine covered in menstrual blood. He always made me food when I got the munchies. And all the same, he never said a word.

"No," I said after a pause. "Maybe when this first started sex is what I had on my mind, but I've gotten to know Allie. I don't want to pursue her like that. I know that's not what she wants." It had been months since I got laid, and somehow, I didn't care.

"She's kind and genuine and fun to be with," I continued. A chuckle bubbled up as I thought of all the times we'd joked around together. "But I could never, ever think of hurting her like that now. She's the only girl I've ever met who is so comfortable in her own skin that the words of others have no effect on her—anymore," I added as I thought about how much she had grown into herself after high school. "She's humble and beautiful…"

"Ben," Spencer began with a smile on his face, "are you sure you're not in love with her?" He and Brennan shared a knowing look, satisfied in my answer.

I paused, smirked in their direction, and turned back to the TV.

Allie had a bad day at school during the following week, and we were medicating with a pint of Ben & Jerry's Cherry Garcia on a walk. The blustery autumn wind had abated, and the last rays of sun were shining through the barren trees. Unlike our earlier walking dates, we were bundled up against the cold, though Allie still insisted ice cream was the best remedy, even in forty degrees.

"What are you doing for Thanksgiving?" Allie asked as she cleaned her spoon.

"I don't really celebrate Thanksgiving," I said. "My dad and grandparents don't care for it."

"What holidays do you celebrate, then?"

"Just traditional Indian holidays. Like Diwali or Holi or Navaratri…"

"Lots of holidays that end in 'ee.'"

"Hey, I also celebrate Pongal!" I said with a chuckle and wrapped Allie closer to me to help her avoid a puddle.

"Doesn't your mom miss celebrating holidays?" she asked as she dug in for a piece of black cherry. "What do you do for Christmas? Is it just you kids and her?"

I shrugged, not ready to admit to Allie again that I didn't celebrate Christian holidays. "Not really. She goes to her sister's house for Thanksgiving but has never forced us kids to go. She still celebrates Christmas at home and gives us Christmas gifts, but it's never been a big affair." I reached over for Allie's spoon and slurped up the ice cream before she could.

"Hey!" Allie exclaimed, "I already gave you your ice cream tax," she joked. "But honestly, Ben, I'd still like to meet your family. Can't I at least come and meet them during Winter Break, even if it's not for festivities?" Allie popped out her bottom lip. At that moment, her eyes shone in the moonlight. The light breeze swept her long hair to the side, and I was struck by how beautiful she looked.

A strand of her golden hair wound around my finger before I tucked it behind her ear. "Break it is."

24

December 13th, 1990

"Now, Mom," I muttered as I scurried around the living room, picking up Dad's stack of books on human anatomy and tossing them into a collection of his other trinkets I'd collected into a bin, "please try and talk to Dad about acting at least a little bit normal—Allie's not used to people who are emotionless and robotic." I tossed a statue of Shiva that typically graced our piano into the bin as well. I winced as it clattered against the textbooks. Dad was not going to be happy.

My mother was a beautiful but tired woman. Where baby blue eyes used to shine, now left a dull ghost of its color. The bags beneath her eyes were poorly covered to regain a youthful appearance, but her makeup was unsuccessful at hiding her fatigue. And although the gray hair of age had not speckled itself in her mane of ginger, the shade had lost its luster, making my mother look like she belonged in a sepia photograph.

"I can try," she said, grabbing a new bag of pull-ups from the storage room. Already I could smell the stench of whatever Kit made in his pants.

"He's still not potty-trained?" I asked as I grabbed the package for her before Kit could fall out of her arms.

Mom sighed and brushed Kit's dark hair out of his eyes.

"I've been trying, but it's getting even harder for me to get him to leave my arms for a second, let alone use the toilet on his own."

I knew my mother loved Kit, my youngest sibling, who was almost three, but she had been all in career mode when she became pregnant for him, having thought her days of being a new mom were over after Jared, who was five when Kit was born, that she felt so unprepared to be a mother again to a baby.

"What do you do at work?" I grabbed Kit from her arms and carried him over to the changer to clean him up.

"Hold him as I take pictures. Sometimes I use him as a point for the little kids to smile at." Mom watched over my shoulder as if she was criticizing my art of changing pull-ups.

I gave a forced laugh and paused to glare at her.

"I can change a pull-up on my own, you know."

"Okay, okay!" she said with a chuckle.

My mother and I had gotten along well when I was growing up, much closer than I was with my father. Mom was a natural parent, which was easy to feel as a child and tell as an adult watching my mother parent my younger siblings. My dad did not have a parental bone in his body, and I knew it bothered my mom. Part of the reason I wasn't so keen to have Allie meet my family was because of that tension. I barely came home anymore; I didn't want to witness my parents' marriage falling apart.

"When will Allie get here?" Mom asked, and as she moved toward the kitchen, I was reminded of how different my home was to Allie's. Our kitchen was crowded, not just with food, but mini statues of Annapurna, the Hindu goddess of nourishment. Considering nearly half of the house was practicing Hindus, I was used to the gods being displayed since I was young. I doubted the Johncox house had ever heard of Annapurna. That aside, our kitchens couldn't be more different. We had two ovens, a large refrigerator always fully stocked, and a breakfast nook. It was nearly the size of the entire Johncox house.

"I told her seven."

"Seven?" Mom exclaimed as she bent down to clean up the plastic baby toys scattered around the kitchen. "It's December, Ben! It'll be pitch black by the time she arrives. Make it five."

My eyes flashed to the clock light on the oven: it was 3:26.

"That's in an hour and a half. And dinner isn't even ready yet."

Mom waved her hand at me.

"Let me worry about dinner," she snapped and sighed, full of immediate regret. A toy squeaked and slipped out of her fingers. Trying to manage a house with three young children was hard enough, but my mom was not just trying to impress Allie, but my grandparents, as well, who had never been big fans of hers, despite the fact they had lived in our house since I was a baby.

"Ugh, I'm sorry, Benny," my mom groaned. "I just want things to be perfect for you and Allie." With reluctance on Kit's part, Mom passed him to me to clean efficiently. "Wake up your grandparents and tell them the change. Oh, and make sure to tell Allie, too."

When I called Allie to tell her about the change in plans, she was happy to come over earlier. "Perfect! More time to get to know your family!" The dorms had closed, so instead of traveling back to Petoskey, Allie was staying with Audrey until tomorrow, so the switch was feasible.

As I rounded the hallway down to my grandparents' den, my stomach flipped thinking about how soon Allie would be padding around the carpet I learned to walk on, integrating herself into a life I had kept from her for months, for good reason.

"C'mon, *Muttassi*," I urged my grandmother from her slumber. Her afternoon nap could continue into the following afternoon if no one woke her.

"Let me sleep," she snarled back with a quick whisper before muttering, "*nayinte mone*."

Ah, yes. This wasn't the first time my *muttassi* had insulted my mother.

"Get up!" I exclaimed.

But she grunted and kept her eyes shut, so I gave up and woke my *muttachan* instead.

"Why are we up so early?" my *muttachan* asked as he pulled himself into his wheelchair. He grabbed a blanket from his bed to keep him warm.

"He's got a girl coming, some *velutta bicc...*"

"Kunti, language!" *Muttachan* exclaimed. "Be kind to your *anantaravan*, he really likes this one." I thanked my grandfather for correcting my grandmother's words. I wished for a moment I didn't know Malayalam. I didn't need to hear my grandmother call Allie a 'white bitch,' an insult I had heard far too many times thrown at my own mother.

I'd have to thank *Muttachan* later for stepping in.

At five exactly, Allie knocked on the door. I almost jumped to meet her. Instead, I took a deep breath, ran my hands through my curls, and walked to the door with my heart spinning in my chest.

"Hey," I greeted Allie, opening the door. How much I missed her still surprised me. I knew Allie wasn't big into public displays of affection, but to my surprise, she pecked my lips.

"Hi!"

Hidden under Allie's arm was something tufty and green and sparkling. She must have followed my gaze, so she pulled out the object.

A tree. She brought a freaking tree.

Okay, so it was a two-foot-high fake Christmas tree, but the lights were multicolored and flashing—I had a right to be taken aback. Perched on the topmost plastic branch was an angel, too, staring down at me like my worst idea of a conversation starter.

"Isn't it adorable?" Allie asked with a smile too wide to be real.

To be honest, it was more shocking than anything, but I held a grin and felt the coarse faux fir.

"Fantastic."

"I know you said your family doesn't celebrate Christmas, but your mom does, so I wanted to get her something small."

I wasn't too sure how my father and grandparents would feel about something in their house that was so blatantly Christian. My mother compromised a lot when she married my father. Since he was big on idols instead of religious texts, he got the statues, and my mother got to keep her Bible. But I had never seen Christmas trees save for television shows or the occasional window tree down the roads.

Allie glanced over my shoulder and into the house.

"Can I meet your family now, or…?"

"Calm down, eager beaver." Allie raised one eyebrow. "I'm kidding. Set down your tree in the hall, and you can meet them."

That was about the quickest I'd seen Allie do anything.

I had to force back a laugh.

"Ben? The food's not *entirely* ready, so we're in the living room waiting!" Crap, I couldn't use food as a distraction.

"That's my mom," I supplied before Allie could even ask.

As we tiptoed into the room, Allie whispered, "Your mom sounds pretty."

We shuffled in through the back door to the living area where everyone's backs were to us. I cleared my throat to gain their attention. Unfortunately, seven pairs of eyes turned to look at us at once.

"Well… Hi, family. This is Allie." I'd never brought a girl home to meet my family before. They knew I'd been with girls before, but I'd never been serious enough to bring one home. And mainly I was always embarrassed about how tense our family was. Let alone being the only Indian kid in school, I also preferred my mom and siblings and didn't want to subject many other people to my father.

My mom smiled and waved, her hands full holding Kit. "Welcome, Allie! We're so excited to meet you!"

"That's my mom," I introduced her.

"Just Julie," my mother said to Allie. Of course, she'd want to seem hip.

My father barely looked at Allie. When he heard she was a Christian, he looked sick. My father disliked a display of religion other than Hinduism—of course, that didn't apply to his own marriage—just as long as Mom kept her Bible hidden.

The silence hung heavy in the room until a small giggle broke it.

"Are you Ben's girlfriend?" Fatima squealed.

Oh, gosh.

"Um," I began and ignored my sister's question, "that's my little sister, Fatima. She's ten and very excited. And next to her is my brother, Jared, but you know him."

The love I had for my younger siblings was unfathomable, but Fatima's question was so direct, it had thrown me off.

"And Kit is the baby. Well, he's two, but he's still a baby to me."

Now were the difficult members.

"Well, there's my dad, Mustafa. You can call him Dr. Asan, he's a surgeon, if you couldn't tell," I quickly turned us away from my father in his scrubs, just home from work. "And those are my grandparents, *Muttachan* and *Muttassi*—that's grandpa and grandma in Malayalam."

Allie didn't hesitate to give her brightest greeting to them all, even my father and grandparents whose faces were stone. I could tell how happy that made Mom. And me, of course. Allie wasn't faking her enthusiasm. Having someone accept my family, even when it was hard for me to do the same, filled me with joy I hadn't expected.

After some niceties, Allie made a beeline for my mom.

"So, I hear you have your own photography business." Her eyes widened like a puppy staring up at its master. "Tell me all about it!"

Mom's eyes lit up at Allie's interest. "Goodness me, Ben wasn't lying, you are a photography girl!"

I pulled Allie closer to me and chuckled. "Actually, this is the first time in a long time I've seen her without a camera." Allie's cheeks blushed as I rested my palm on her hips.

"Not entirely true," Allie admitted and pulled a small disposable from her pocket. "I can't go anywhere without one." Mom's eyebrows rose at the disposable camera, but Allie quickly dashed away any thoughts of naivety. "No, I'm a serious photographer, I have a Canon EOS 10 back at home."

"Oh, I believe you," my mother laughed. "I'm just surprised. Sometimes I can't wait to be away from my cameras after a long day."

"Really?" Allie asked. She glanced, agape, between my mother and me. "Gosh, I love being with my cameras, more than people, sometimes."

I nudged her.

"Except Ben, of course," she said with an eye roll. "I love being with Ben."

Mom shrugged and moved Kit to her other hip.

"Well, when it's your job and you spend hours and hours taking pictures of happy couples or crying babies that ruin the clicking sound of a camera, it's hard to love picking them up sometimes." She motioned to Allie's little camera. "I hope you don't plan on making your career out of it—I'd hate for you to be like me, your passion deflated by monotony."

Oh, no, Mom was scaring her. I knew it.

But Allie laughed and replaced the camera.

"No, of course not. It's just a hobby. Actually, I'm planning on being an elementary teacher. I'm Jared's student-teacher."

"A teacher?" Except Mom didn't say this, the shout came from the other side of the living room.

Allie and I turned around to see my father sitting further forward in his seat on the couch. His fingers rested on his hands, and he studied Allie like a painting.

"Don't you think you could do so much better in the STEM field?" He scoffed dismissively. When he made that sound, something usually condescending followed. "Statistics show that your age should be trying to create futures in the sciences, as they will have the most available jobs."

Allie raised her eyebrows.

"You don't say? Who came up with those statistics, then?"

"Well, statisticians, of course, and—"

"Don't you think they could have changed the stats to favor their own field? By being a part of their field now and ensuring future employees, it's cause for more upper management positions to cover new kids right out of college. I mean, it's a smart move, but do you know if everyone goes into science, there will be no one of this generation out there teaching kids from a young age. And you know who those big management guys used to be? Kids."

I had never seen my father so lost for words.

I got the STEM lecture every other month from my dad—typically paired with his lecture of me disappointing him—but I had never found a surefire way to shut him up before.

I should have brought Allie home sooner, I smirked to myself.

Dad scratched at his collar before sitting back against the dark leather couch. It was brand new—he had insisted on having the best of the best. The couch still smelled like the furniture store which is probably why our house felt like a showroom rather than a home like Allie's.

His eyes were shot red from the long working hours, and unlike my mother, he didn't care to cover up his dark purple bags. Mom, for years, had insisted Dad stop working lengthy shifts, but as their love had started to flicker, Mom had given up and resigned herself to not spending time together and being left to deal with us kids single-handedly.

"Seems like Ben has caught himself a live one. What do you think, Jules? Should we kick her to the curb?"

"Father…" I pleaded.

But Allie laughed. I knew Dad was impressed with her, maybe even a little scared of her intelligence, but he would never like her in the genuine way Mom would. Mom would photograph us for free, she would give her unconditional support, and she would dance with me on our wedding day.

"Mustafa, that was not kind," Mom chided him, despite Allie still laughing, albeit uncomfortably. I pulled her away before she could hear my father's true feelings.

"He shouldn't be with her…" was all I heard before I spun Allie and myself away from that storm that was brewing. Despite himself marrying my mom, my dad had insisted I marry an Indian woman since I was young.

I was used to constantly disappointing my father for failing to be a carbon copy of himself as his firstborn son in following his religious and vocational footsteps, but after experiencing kindness from Samuel and Hannah, I couldn't let Allie hear what untruths my father would say.

Unfortunately, going back into the living room wasn't the reprieve I was looking for. We barely stepped twice before Jared exclaimed, "Hi, Miss Johncox! Why are you holding my brother's hand?" Jared had inherited the Asan hair that wouldn't ever stay a normal length. I brushed his bangs off his face and smiled.

"It's because we like each other, Jare," I explained. "Fly high?" I let my hand go from Allie's when he nodded and flipped my brother up over my shoulder. "Let's go, Superman!"

As a young kid, I had always wanted my dad to play games with me, to lift me up, spin me around, and help me act like an airplane. The kind of father I got was the one who, if I needed money or a favor, I had to bring his favorite food and ask at a specific time when he wasn't tired or grumpy. Only then did I have a fifty-percent chance of an acknowledgement. With Jared, Fatima, and now with Kit, I strived to give them the father-figure I never had and bring joy and playfulness into our house.

Jared zoomed through the sky and into the sitting room, connected to the kitchen, and he landed safely on the sofa runway.

"Whoosh! Yay, Superman!" My fingers flew around his belly until he screamed in giggles.

"Stop!" Jared squealed.

"Stop means go!"

"Let me help!" Fatima ran in behind us and tickled under Jared's chin.

"No, get his feet, they are his weakness!"

"Nooooo!"

Jared failed to hide his soles, and he kicked his legs as we tickled both feet together. After a soft blow to my jaw, I lifted him back up. "Okay, okay, enough tickling."

"Before Fatima joined the party, she was telling me about her rock collection. She was about to show me a Petoskey stone before you two interfered." Allie stood in the door, resting her back against the jamb.

Before, nothing could distract me from my younger siblings. But now, everything froze when I saw Allie.

"Yeah, she's got quite the collection…" I pulled Fatima into my arms and lifted her. She was getting older and heavier, but I wanted to hold onto her youth. "Up we go!" I rested her on my left hip with Jared on my right as I followed Allie back into the living room. "Allie, this way."

I set down my siblings at the feet of my grandparents.

"*Muttachan, Muttassi,* this is Allie, as I said before. They live with us," I explained to her.

"Well, we *used* to live in Thiruvananthapuram before my *idiyarr* of a son and his siblings got scholarships and insisted we move here. America," *Muttassi* spat.

My *muttachan* scolded his wife in quick hushed Malayalam so Allie didn't hear.

Muttachan turned toward Allie and spoke Malayalam in the soft, gentle way that always inspired me to practice more. *Muttachan* wasn't as skilled at English—*Muttassi* had picked it up through watching television programs—so I had to translate for Allie.

Heat rushed to my brown cheeks. I cut out the part about us being happy together for a million lifetimes and translated the former half. "He says you are a beautiful and kind girl." When my *muttassi* cursed at Allie in Malayalam, I simply swapped her unpleasant words for the complete opposite, although I knew Allie could tell—tone translates.

Mom announced dinner was ready, but before everyone made their way over to the table, she stopped us.

"Wait! Before dinner, let's take a group picture!"

At the sound of a picture, Allie perked right up.

"Oh, I can take it!"

"No, no!" Mom laughed. "Allie, I want you in it. I'll take it. Just sit by Ben and look cute!"

I plopped on the couch and looked for Allie to join me, but instead saw her shuffling quickly back into the room with her idiotic Christmas tree. Now the lights were twinkling.

"Is that a Christmas tree?" Fatima interrogated immediately. "Are you a Christian?"

She *had* to learn context clues.

Allie wasn't fazed by the questions as I was.

"Yes, it is. I thought it would be festive for the season. And yes, I am, just like your brother and mother."

I swallowed hard at the lie. I just hoped my mother hadn't heard Allie.

But Fatima simply nodded. I had an inkling she would choose Christianity instead of finding herself stuck in the middle like me. She went to Sunday School and church with Mom, and seemed fascinated by all the stories, the same as I was as a kid. For my mother's sake, I hope she followed her lead.

"Okay, are we all ready?" Mom asked, changing the subject from religion, the most heated subject in our house. "Mustafa, can you look at the camera? How does your two-year-old son understand commands better than—hmph. Never mind, then."

My father dropped his finger.

Mother blinked long and hard. Kit squirmed in her arms, making the camera unsteady. "Okay, Ben, can you and Allie, although it is extremely cute, stop giggling together and look this way?"

My face didn't stop feeling warm.

"Cheese!" *Click.*

Dinner was better than expected. Mom had prepared some traditional Indian dishes and Irish desserts. My mother took her fifty percent Irish heritage seriously considering she was the only redhead in her family.

Allie ate everything on her plate, even the *mascot dal,* a spicy red lentil curry. Even *Muttassi* seemed impressed with that. At one point, Allie did squeeze my hand under the table, and I squeezed back in moral support.

When the final dish was cleared—Allie insisted on helping my mother—she hugged everyone goodbye.

"Thank you so much for such a delicious meal. I'm so glad to have met you all! You're all so great—tell me when your tooth falls out, Jared! —and I pray you all have a safe holiday season."

I followed Allie out of my house, and we sat on the wrap-around porch. I had strayed away from giving Allie a tour of my house—it was three stories with more amenities than needed; I didn't want her to be uncomfortable at the differences in our homes.

After about five minutes of keeping each other warm and chatting, Allie pulled away.

"I have a gift for you," she said and pulled something small from her pocket.

"Oh, no. I haven't bought you a present...I just kind of forget because we don't really…"

Allie chuckled, clearly on some sort of cloud nine from meeting my family, which I would never understand.

"It's fine. Just take it."

Hesitantly, I reached for the folded paper. I rolled the piece through my fingers, trying to guess what it was, before prying apart the thick sheet.

The top words said: Mt. Hope University India January Term 1991 Trip Final Packing List and Information.

"What's this?" My mouth dried so quickly it was curious that a spell hadn't been cast to remove its moisture.

"I thought you deserved to visit the place half of your family calls home." Allie's smile widened. "Everything's paid for—I helped fundraise it by selling some of my photographs. All you have to do is go to the two pre-trip meetings—both the first week of January—and then be at the airport on January 8th to fly out. And you'll fly home on the 27th."

"This can't be… What about my ticket and passport information?" I questioned. I was determined to prove this was an awful practical joke.

Allie's ears turned red as she glanced away.

"I may have used the university files for that…"

I stared at the slip before me, my brain refusing to acknowledge what had happened. I still couldn't believe her—not yet. I flipped the paper over to read the list of students going—and my name was printed clearly on the top, thanks to the alphabet. My eyes darted up and down the list for the last name 'Johncox' but there weren't any J's going on the trip.

Allie had the unfortunate habit of reading my mind.

"I couldn't go— I've got my senior project, remember?" I knew it was more than that, most likely the cost. Frankly, I could pay for my education wholly and then some. The fact that Allie used her own money for me to go was a true gift.

"What am I gonna do without you?" I pouted.

"Be awfully miserable," she teased and squeezed my hand in reassurance. "No. You'll have a great time. I know it. And one of the places they're going is Kerala where—"

"My family's from, yeah." I stared at the itinerary. Kerala was listed under the destinations.

"Mostly you'll be doing work for people in the villages, studying Hinduism, and there's also some sightseeing—I think there's a mosque visit planned…" Allie said as she turned over the paper back into her hand.

For the first time, I drowned Allie out. Then, in a strangled voice, I whispered, "Thank you."

Allie watched me. Her lips relaxed, and her eyebrows grew closer.

"Are you okay?" she checked.

I nodded and rested my hand on her check. I leant until our foreheads and tips of our noses touched.

"I'm great. Sorry, this is just… Are you sure you can't come? I'll feel bad going without you," I pleaded.

"I'm sure. Go have your adventure! I'll be here when you get back," Allie encouraged.

25

Asan's eyes watered, and Devon couldn't help thinking he had seen the same face on him just hours ago when talking about his mom.

"Um, Dr. Asan? Is everything alright?" he mumbled.

Devon fully expected Dr. Asan to brush everything off, to deny the tears wavering on the cusp of falling. But it seemed that something in the story had made him uncontrollably sad.

"I..." He stuttered. "It's just hard, talking about my mom I guess, now that she's gone."

Devon cleared his throat. His stomach was starting to gurgle, not dissimilar to the feeling right before he had vomited earlier, but he knew it was not because of something that was going to come from his stomach, but deep within himself. He needed an excuse to leave, before the truth tumbled out. He was afraid now of what Dr. Asan would think of Devon.

"Dr. Asan, it's getting late. I would love to hear the ending but if you need space—"

"No, no," Asan insisted and motioned Devon to stay. "It helps. Truly. If I relive my life, maybe I won't forget it, too."

Devon bit his lip. He couldn't keep it in any longer. He just hoped Dr. Asan's kindness and wisdom didn't falter when the façade of Devon's life shattered. But Dr. Asan had shared enough personal information tonight. It was Devon's turn.

"I cheated on my girlfriend tonight," he whispered, almost afraid to say it out loud and solidify it in history.

Asan raised an eyebrow of curiosity.

"It was an accident," Devon insisted. "I was drunk, and a girl came up to me. I thought it was Lindsey. I didn't know until we were already…involved. Then, I kissed her and suddenly knew it was a mistake." His eyes began to water. "Hearing what you have with Allie just—I want that, too. With Lindsey. Do you think I have any chance of getting her back?"

Asan gave a soft smile and nodded.

"Yes, Mr. Camburn. There's always a chance." Dr. Asan sat back, his hands resting on his stomach and sighed. "I'm guessing that inebriation is not the only reason then, that you were ill when I found you?"

Devon bobbed his head in agreement.

Asan gave another contemplative sigh, one like a father who was hearing an admission from their child, confessing to having broken a lamp or disobeying their curfew. It was the look of disappointment, but one that showed a glimmer of pride from being honest.

"I'm also guessing Miss Huff is unaware of your mistake, right?"

"So far," Devon croaked out. "I-I don't know how I can tell her. But I won't be able to hold it in. To lie to her. I'm t-terrified that she will leave me when she finds out I slept with someone else, even if it was for two seconds and when I was drunk."

"You're right, or half-right," Dr. Asan began and leaned forward toward Devon. The light of the moon shone through the window, and its reflection off the snow carpeting the ground wrapped Dr. Asan in a calming blue hue. "You won't be able to hold it in, but also you *shouldn't* hold it in. You shouldn't keep this from her. Lindsey deserves to know the truth."

"I-I understand," Devon said.

"It's not just about whether you can comfortably continue this relationship without sharing the truth," Dr. Asan specified, "but it's that Lindsey has the right to know everything that may impact her decision to stay in or to leave your relationship, and that I'm afraid includes any infidelity on your part—accidental as it may be. She deserves all the information she needs to make a fair decision of how she feels about you." Dr Asan sighed and spoke almost to himself then. "Even if you feel like keeping the secret will hurt her less or make her happier..."

Devon waited, holding onto every word. He wondered how Allie felt, seeing Dr. Asan grow from the Ben she knew in college to the wise man before him. She must be proud. Devon wanted someone to be proud of him like that.

"I just wish I had never gone to that party," Devon grumbled. "I-I wish that I actually cared as much about my education and success as I used to. Now it's just drinking, partying, sex... High school Devon would be so embarrassed," he admitted.

Dr. Asan shrugged. "And pre-Allie college Ben would be shocked that I'm a stuffy old professor still living in his hometown. But," he continued, "we grow as we're meant to, with the soil we give ourselves and the sunlight we spend time in. I don't know why you were meant to have this terrible night," he encouraged, "but I know that there will be good to come from it."

Devon felt grateful for Asan's kind advice although a little embarrassed, but mainly an overwhelming sense of relief for getting this off his chest. Now that was out of the way, he wanted to bring up something else. He glanced around Asan's living room until he spotted the elephant, back on the windowsill in the kitchen—its home.

"What else did you get when you visited India besides the elephant?"

"Oh, you know. Some candy. A shirt. Mostly things for other people." Asan sniffled, clearing his throat.

"A-are you sure you want to go on?"

But Asan had already plunged into his past.

26

January 7th, 1991

The day before I was meant to leave for India, Allie finally found out a big secret:

"Wait, you've lived in Mt. Hope all your life and you've never gone sledding down *Mt. Hope*?"

I sighed. People always found that so shocking.

"It's not like it's an actual mountain. This town is named after a slightly biggish hill. You've also never gone sledding down it," I pointed out. We were currently dismounting two sleds from the straps on top of my car. Allie had insisted that we went sledding before I left for India. As I parked, I admitted my secret.

"No, but I wasn't born here."

"Hey," I pointed a finger to her, "I was born in Flower City."

"Technicalities," Allie tutted, taking the rope from one sled, and tying it around her fist.

I chuckled and took Allie's free gloved hand.

"C'mon—we'll lose our Mt. Hope sledding virginity together."

"Ah, yes," Allie giggled. "I must have been waiting to lose it with you."

I gave her hand a squeeze as we began to walk up the hill.

If I were a child, I would be in awe at the steepness of the hill, marveling at the sparkling white snow, and sprinting up the side with childish adrenaline. But I was older now, with a girl to impress, so I trudged up the hill as manly as I could muster.

Allie, on the other hand, maintained her childlike wonder. "Oh my gosh, this is so fun! Ben, look! There are *snow ramps*. Oh! Fresh snow!" Allie scooped up a handful of untainted snow and stuffed it in her mouth.

I laughed.

"Is that good, hm?"

She nodded.

"You enjoy your snow—*I'm* going up to the top." I sprinted up the hill several yards before I heard Allie crunching behind me, yelling, "Wait!" through a mouthful of snow.

I bit my lip to suppress a laugh.

"C'mon, wait! Ugh—Benjamin!"

I turned around with my bottom lip firmly held down by my top teeth in an attempt to hold back a smile.

"That is not even my name," I enunciated slowly.

Allie grunted and swallowed the snow.

"What? Then is it just Ben?"

I shook my head, but a smile still creeped up on my face.

"Then what?"

"Benji. My full name is Benji Mustafa Asan. Not Benjamin."

"Oh." Allie hurried quickly up to meet me. Our knit hands found each other once more.

We crunched our way up to the top just as the sun began to set over the treetops surrounding the hill. In the distance, I spotted the clock tower, looming over the brick buildings of campus. The stark white of the church steeple stood out, too, against the shadowy downtown, barely lit with streetlamps.

Once we reached the peak, I paused and leant up against an off-centered wooden pole.

"Allison Charlotte Johncox, by the way. If we're saying middle names."

"Allison Charlotte. That's beautiful."

Allie shrugged.

"I just prefer Allie."

She plopped her sled—the larger one—on the ground.

"I say we go down together first. That way we're losing our Mt. Hope sledding virginity at the same time."

I sat down in the front to protect her from flying snow and crossed my legs.

"Sounds good to me."

Allie clambered behind me. I wrapped her arms beneath mine to tug on the chest of my gray parka.

"Ready?" Allie's feet planted themselves on either side for take-off.

"Ready."

We soared off the tip of the hill, speeding down and twisting along the path. Allie's hands pushed against my chest, and she squealed when a large amount of snow flew up the front of the sled. Her chin jutted next to my shoulder, and I could almost feel her gaze ahead of mine, eagerly enjoying the ride and taking in the view.

And in the seconds our journey began, it ended with a sideways tip, and we toppled into the clean snow.

Allie burst into laughter when her head popped up. Her pale cheeks were already turning pink from the cold and pieces of snow clung to her yellow knit wool hat.

"That was awesome!" she cheered.

I had to admit, it was fun.

"It *was* pretty awesome." I pulled her close to me to situate her on my snow-covered lap. "Mostly because of you."

Allie's cheeks turned even pinker, and I bent my head down to peck them.

"Are you cold?"

She shrugged.

"I mean, we *are* sitting on a snowbank."

I looked around us. The white was blinding but beautiful as the snow sparkled in the setting sun. Behind us, skeletal trees lined the practice hockey rink. The words I had been pondering on rose into my throat. The background was perfect, but the timing was off. I coughed, and they left.

"What a comic you are." I kissed her nose and rubbed my gloved hands along her arms. I pressed my lips against her hair and took a long breath. She still smelled the lemons from our walk so long ago. "How am I going to go to India without you?"

Allie snuggled closer.

"You keep saying that."

"It's true. Maybe I shouldn't go…"

"Now, that's stupid." Allie pushed away to face me. "You have to go—you *need* to go, Ben."

I sighed.

"Allie…"

"Embrace India. I'll be here when you come back. Promise."

I finally kissed her lips. They were shivering cold, like she had just unstuck her tongue from a frozen pole. I tried my best to warm her up.

With a sigh, I pulled away.

"Okay." I pecked her lips once more before helping Allie to her feet. "Let's go again. A race?"

Allie smirked.

"Sure. You know I'll win, right?" She stood and headed toward the hill. After watching Allie struggle to grip the snow and climb back up, I gave in.

"You sure you're strong enough to pull me? You're just a runner."

Allie was seated in the sled, her legs splayed in front of her, and she leaned forward to watch my body attempt to pull her up.

"Yeah, like you're three hundred pounds," I teased, but felt the pain in my lungs. "I'm fine… Don't need to work out tomorrow," I mumbled to myself. Her muffled laugh pulled at the corners of my mouth.

"Are you sure that you're okay? I didn't know how little traction my boots had." Allie was wearing galoshes—what a surprise.

"I mean," I huffed, "if only my legs were my arms, I'd have no problem."

It took determination and more butt clenching than I'd wish to admit, but we made it to the top.

"It'll get easier every time," I assured Allie.

We tried everything in the book. Sledding over a ramp, faux-snowboarding, faux-snowboarding over a ramp, backwards, backwards over a ramp, and a horrible attempt at a two-person train; halfway down, Allie climbed into my sled while hers spun out of control and did a little flip off the ramp.

After all four sets of cheeks were red, and we had lost all energy, Allie and I retired, side by side, lying beneath the wooden pole at the top of the hill, which the setting sun had revealed to be a light post.

In the middle of a wonderfully odd conversation about Allie's fear of needles, which was the reason she didn't have her ears pierced, she squealed and pointed up to the massive sky.

"Look!"

At first, I was puzzled. Look? At what? My eyes trained on the bug encased in the light graveyard above us, but Allie specified.

"The stars! Oh, I think I can see a constellation..." Her hands seized the stars and threw them into organization. "Yes—oh, it's Orion's Belt, don't you see?"

Nope. To be honest, I saw none of it. It just looked like someone had flung grains of sand at the sky.

But Allie didn't wait for my response. She turned to me, her beaming smile blocking out any other feature.

"Essie and I used to make our own stories about the constellations."

"Like what?"

"Like..." She lay back on her back and stared up to the sky. "Like Orion's Belt. How did Orion get his belt?"

When I shrugged, Allie continued.

"Orion, in Greek mythology, was a hunter, right?"

I nodded—I actually knew that.

"Okay, so one day Orion was hunting in… Do they have woods in Greece? I'll just say woods. He was hunting in the woods." And as Allie spoke, her eyes lit up the story—she was no longer present. "There he came upon, say, a goat. But the goat was different than any other he'd stumbled upon. It was covered in ivy and jumping around. So, instead of killing it like he planned, he followed the goat to a clearing. There was a hidden mansion. And sitting on a throne was… Which god had goats?"

"Dionysus."

"Dionysus! god of…"

"Wine."

"Wine! Wine?" She gasped. I urged her to continue. "Fine. There was Dionysus—the god of wine—drunk. He saw Orion and laughed. 'You're so funny, hunter! Relax, enjoy some wine!' He acted jolly, for he was so drunk," Allie continued. "Afraid Dionysus would hurt himself; Orion raised his sword and killed the goat."

"What?" I exclaimed. "Why?"

"Oh. Because the goat was giving Dionysus wine. Did I forget that?"

"The god of wine needed a goat to give him wine?" I chuckled. "Couldn't he just—"

"Shush. My story."

Gosh, I wanted to kiss her.

"Anyway, Dionysus was so angry, but hid it. He congratulated Orion on his kill and gave him a belt as a reward. However, the belt was cursed. When Orion put it on, it thrust him into the stars." She smiled sweetly, so strangely after such a tragic story. "The end."

I chuckled and pulled her closer.

"Such a positive story. You know, the myth is Zeus placed him in the sky to guard it."

"Eh. Mine's better."

Her head rested on my chest, and my hand trailed along her hair.

"Yeah, I think it is."

We studied the stars. When I came upon another reason to talk, I was worried about what Allie would say.

"I think I want to die at night, so I can look at the stars." I confessed. When she said nothing, I cringed. "Is that weird?" Still nothing. "Oh, gosh, it *is* weird."

Allie squeezed my hand.

"No, it's not weird. It's interesting. I've thought about what I'd like, too."

I squeezed back.

"And what would that be, Miss Allie?" I teased.

"Well, probably on a sunny day. I love the sun. And it's beautiful outside, and it's just me and God, nobody else." Her eyes scanned the sky before falling on me.

"No family at all? Not your kids or husband?" The words made me squirm with anticipation.

Allie shrugged.

"Like I said, just God and me. Dying is a private thing. And I think by that point, I will have said all the goodbyes I need."

After a few moments enjoying each other's presence, Allie sighed.

"I lied to you."

My brain raced. Was she really coming to India with me? Her name wasn't on the documents though, and she hadn't attended the two pre-trip meetings. My heart fell as quickly as it had fluttered.

"Oh, really? What about?"

Allie bit her lip.

"I actually have sled on Mt. Hope."

I gasped, "I can't believe you!"

"I'm sorry!" she squealed, burying her head in my chest. Her body convulsed in laughter. "I remember sledding last year but I didn't know the hill. I recognize it now."

I crossed my arms and turned away.

"And to think, I waited just for you! Hmph!"

We exploded in giggles.

"You're truly interesting, Allison Charlotte Johncox. And I'm grateful for you." My throat tightened, and that's all I could say at the moment. I knew Spencer was right, but the words that described how I felt about Allie were slipping out of my grasp.

Allie smiled and clambered to her feet again.

"I'm getting so tired. But I still want to try snowboarding-sledding before we're done."

Before, Allie had been too nervous to try faux snowboarding out; instead, she resolved to stand on top and laugh as I failed time and time again.

"Go ahead. I'll put the other sled away."

I didn't have time. Allie fell almost immediately, failing to dodge the ramp.

I let out a slew of swears as I raced down the hill to Allie. Even from far away I saw her foot at an odd angle it shouldn't have been.

Allie should have been crying. She should have been freaking out. But when I carried her over to my car, she was more in shock than anything else.

"How badly does it hurt?" I pulled her snow pants up a few inches and gently removed her boot. She hissed—her ankle was already swelling.

"Extremely bad," Allie winced.

"Okay. I'll get you to the Flower City Hospital right away."

Allie slapped at my arms, which were already positioned to turn left.

"No. Not there." When my eyebrows knit together, puzzled, she elaborated. "It's always busy there—we'll be stuck for hours, and your flight is at five am tomorrow..."

She had a point. I sighed.

"Okay... I guess the hospital in Colby isn't too far... Twenty-five minutes I think, only five more... Hang tight."

Firmly grasping Allie's hand, I drove one-handed to Colby's hospital. Allie was right—it wasn't busy there.

I assisted a limping, pained, but all-together calm Allie into the emergency room.

"Excuse me," I told the woman behind the counter. "She's fallen from a sled—I think her ankle might be broken."

The receptionist nodded.

"She needs these forms to be filled out before she meets with our physician." She typed some information into a computer. "But first, name?"

"Allison Charlotte Johncox."

"Age?"

"Twenty-one."

"And what is your relationship to her?"

"Me?" My face flushed wildly. "I'm her, um, she's my, well... She's my girlfriend."

My stomach twirled inside of me. It had been the first time I'd used such formal terms about Allie to a stranger.

The woman just nodded and handed me a clipboard with a pen attached to it by a metal chain.

"Here are the forms."

The emergency room—at least the section I wheeled Allie into—was a lot less hectic than I imagined. Perhaps because Colby was so small. Nobody seemed hurried like on *General Hospital*. In fact, I noticed only one other person waiting—a middle-aged man with what looked like a surgical mask across his mouth.

I was forced to fill out as much information about her that I knew.

Name: Allison Charlotte Johncox. Date of birth: 08/23/69. Gender: Female. I finished her home address and parents' names before I had to ask for the things I didn't.

"Allie," I whispered, "what's your Social Security number? Insurance? Number…? Okay, I'll call your mom."

I decided I should call Allie's parents to let them know what had happened and used the pay phone, dialing Hannah's number which was written on a napkin.

Naturally, Hannah was worried. Samuel's kind voice didn't match his gruff exterior, but he was mainly using sarcasm to cover up his concern.

"Everything's okay… The physician believes it's just a hairline fracture… No, no surgery needed… Okay, I'll tell her you said that. Bye."

I also called Audrey, then Brennan, wanting to make sure that with me about to head off on my trip, that

Allie would have a couple of people looking after her for the next three weeks.

When I got back, Allie looked up at me from her seat. A nurse was currently wrapping her left ankle up.

"...is temporary, of course. You'll need to come in for a sturdier cast in a few days once the swelling has gone down, but your ankle should heal nicely."

Allie stammered.

"A-Actually, I'll be home in a few days, up in Petoskey. Is it possible to get the cast done there?"

The nurse cinched the wrap snugly before standing up from her crouched position.

"Of course. We'll just fax your information to your home hospital. I'm afraid we can't prescribe anything stronger than over-the-counter medication with your insurance..."

Allie shrugged.

"It's about a 'three' anyway."

That was stretching the truth. If there was a scale to five, maybe...

The nurse nodded and rubbed her hands together.

"Well, then you're free to leave. Here are your papers on how to keep further damage to a minimum," she said as she handed Allie some brochures on cast care as well. "You'll need that soon. Have a nice night."

Night, I thought, and it hit me. By the time I went to bed, I'd have four short hours to rest before I had to wake up to head to the airport and leave for India.

I supported Allie's left side as she climbed in my car before heading to the driver's seat.

I sighed.

"What an awful way to end our last night together before I leave," I said as I turned down the road to Audrey's house. Audrey had volunteered to look after Allie for the night, much to my relief. The car ride back had been silent besides the humming of the heater.

Allie looked over to me, eyebrows raised.

"I'm coming with you to the airport tomorrow."

I turned off my car when I reached Audrey's house. My eyes caught Allie's, whose face read the opposite of mine—calm, alert, and completely serious.

"Um, what? You know I have to leave at three in the morning, right? You're not getting up that early. That's in just over three hours from now."

"I am. I'm heading to Petoskey for a dentist's appointment at eight, so I'll be up early anyway. And" she ducked her head, blushing, "I want to be with you, Ben, to see you off before your big trip."

Her hand squeezed mine, and I gave her a weak smile.

"That's kind of you, Allie. But I'd prefer you to get some sleep." That's how our relationship had evolved. I cared more about her well-being than being with her.

"And I'd prefer to spend all night up with you laughing and spending time together before you're gone for three weeks. But we can't do that." Allie said as she grabbed her gloves from the backseat.

My thumb stroked the back of Allie's hand before I got out to open the door for her and assist her up the stairs to Audrey. I wasn't going to argue with her. I wanted her there.

Back in town, Allie's sled lay in the snow at the bottom of Mt. Hope, forgotten.

"Say cheese!"

I grimaced in Allie's direction; a camera flashed what I could bet was the worst photo its owner would ever take.

Overwhelmed with thoughts of Allie, I hadn't fallen asleep until midnight. Now, clutching a coffee at DTW, I was running on barely three hours of sleep. Dark bags were already forming beneath my eyes—I needed beauty sleep.

Allie seemed as perky as if she had slept twelve hours and was wearing five caffeine patches. Maybe excessive hyperness was the way Allie's body dealt with sleep deprivation.

Her bobbing, bouncy self was waiting with us at the gate, balancing just on one leg. I wished now more than ever that she could be on this trip.

"This picture is so ridiculous," she said as she clutched the Polaroid, "I think I'll look at it every day just to remember that handsome Ben Asan can look," she gasped, "normal!"

I scoffed.

"Liar. You read that in a tabloid."

Allie chuckled and smoothed down my jacket. I had almost forgotten to wear it, but the blustery wind of January reminded me quickly.

"Did you pack enough warm clothes?"

"Yes, Mom," I said with a fake groan.

My father had said goodbye to me before we went sledding, since he was on shift in the morning. He had sat me down before my date with Allie that night, and we had a short conversation in Malayalam about upholding my heritage and culture. It was the most I had ever seen my father show genuine love for his country that wasn't rooted in his disappointment in me as his son.

At the airport that morning, Mom asked for pictures—lots of them—and stuffed one of her best cameras into my carry-on, much to my disapproval.

"Ben, I have several cameras, and if God forbid I run out, I'll ring up Allie for one of her one-hundred," Mom had said as I tried to hand it back. I rolled my eyes affectionately and zipped the bag closed.

Mom embraced me and sighed.

"I'll miss you, Benny. I love you so much, do you know that?"

I felt myself melting into her hug. I'd always been a mama's boy, even when mama was tuckered out and dealing with problems of her own.

"Of course, I love you, too."

"I'll miss you."

"I... won't," I admitted.

Mom had feigned her grief before brushing hair out of my eyes.

"I know. And I'm proud."

Allie and I had waved to her as she left us at departures, unable to join as at that gate with Kit screaming loudly from the back seat.

Allie stopped smoothing out creases on my shirt now and played with my hair.

"Maybe you'll see some famous Bollywood actors in India," she said hopefully.

She sensed my hesitancy. Who hadn't? I was purposely lagging behind in our group to avoid the reality of having to say goodbye. A laugh escaped my lips half-heartedly.

"Maybe one of the billion Khans."

We both fell into silence. Before I could tell her what I really wanted Allie to know, she cleared her throat.

"I suppose I should let you back to your herd. It's nearly boarding time."

Allie's smile had fallen now. Neither of us were trying to hide how hard this separation would be after being around each other every single day of the semester. I wrapped my arms around her tightly, as if she would slip through my grip like soap and inhaled her scent—still of the lemon from our first kiss.

Now I knew those around us must've found our affection annoying, gag-inducing, and repulsive. But all I knew was I would be in drought from Allie for three weeks, and I wanted to drink in as much of her positivity before I left.

"I'll call you as soon as we land back in the States."

Allie shook her head. "You won't have to. I'll be here for you."

As the distance between us grew, I watched Allie's face break down more and more through my own watering eyes. When I turned my back, she turned hers and began to sob. I only knew that because she told me weeks later.

As our plane took off, I glanced back down to Detroit, saying goodbye to Allie and my life there as I braced myself for this new adventure.

27

The clock continued to tick into the deep of night. Obviously, Dr. Asan had seemed to already plan to be up until Allie got home, but Devon worried they wouldn't get to the end of the story before then.

"You know, sir," he began, as he sat back down in his chair. He had begun to pace around the time of the sledding accident, and his sobriety was in full force. "You're spending a Friday night talking about your wife and your time at college to a junior whose life is falling apart without any guarantee that this will be worth it at all."

Asan shrugged and placed his feet upon the ottoman. His tears had dried up, and his usual expression of feigned curiosity had returned.

"You're right. I have no idea if tonight will be worth my time. You might walk out of here and make all the same mistakes that I made. This story might mean nothing to you at all."

Devon paused. He had not wanted his professor to actually think that.

"But," Asan continued, "I don't think it means nothing to you. If it meant nothing to you, the first romantic phrase I said about Allie would have been more than enough for you to leave, sober or not." Asan's fingers fiddled together as he spoke. "But you haven't, which shows that you're interested, even if just to see where I end the story. And that means all the difference. Because even if you're just willing to listen, it means you're willing to grow. The lessons you learn and the themes you take can change your life, Mr. Camburn. I really believe that my life story can affect yours for the better."

Devon blushed, embarrassed at being outed. His least favorite professor had suddenly turned into the one he could not stop listening to.

"And even if you learn nothing from the story of Allie and me, I hope that my advice on how to deal with Miss Huff will be a sufficient way to spend your evening," Dr. Asan added as an afterthought.

"But," Devon began, now thinking of the opposite, "what do you get to gain from talking to me tonight?"

Dr. Asan chuckled and shrugged. "Company? A listening ear? A chance to reminisce with someone who never used a TV guide?"

Devon grinned at the joke. "Do you think we'll be able to finish it before Allie comes home? I-I do want to get to the end."

Dr. Asan sat back, checked his watch for a brief moment, and said, "We just might. Now, shall I continue? I promise we're almost to the point."

"Yes, please, sir."

Asan smirked. "Good, good… Well, I truly thought I would die before the plane landed…"

"Because of how long it was?" Devon guessed.

"Well, partly," Dr. Asan answered. "We spent a solid twenty-four hours flying. But most of it—or at least the moments I was awake—was solid turbulence..."

28

January 8th, 1991

"Psst..." came a voice right next to my ear. I jerked away and then groaned at the sight in front of me. The digital map showed our plane was just hovering over the Russia-Mongolia border. We still had eight hours until we landed in Hong Kong for our connection. Why the flight path went up over the Arctic Circle still boggled me.

"Psst!" came the voice again, and I finally turned to see the guy who was sitting in the aisle seat next to me.

"What?" My voice cracked, so I cleared it and tried again. "Um, what?"

But my question disappeared when Mark's face appeared, as if it popped out of nowhere in the aisle. I had forgotten he sat one seat behind us.

Mark and Heather were a pair of married refugee studies professors at MHU, and our cheery trip leaders to India.

"Sorry to wake you, dude," he began. This man was in his early forties. "Just wanted to ask you. You look a bit pale. Anything I can do, just let me know. You guys are doing great."

As soon as Mark's head was there, it was gone as he plopped back into his seat without another word. The guy beside me and I made eye contact. We sniggered. He pulled off his headphones and held out his hand.

"That was so random," he said. "Uh, I'm Franco, by the way, the guy you've been sleeping next to for hours." He looked vaguely familiar from the pre-trip meetings, but I hadn't given my full attention as I always wanted to just get back to Allie. "But I go by Fran mostly. You're Ben," he cut me off as I began to open my mouth. "Track extraordinaire, headed to the Olympics."

"Possibly. It's not a given though," I added.

Fran just shrugged.

"Stay positive," he explained.

"Preach it, brother," said an accented voice in the window seat. The mop of dirty blond hair that had fallen asleep with his head down on the tray table the moment we'd taken off had finally woken up. He'd earlier introduced himself as Willem from Holland before saying something in Dutch and ducking out.

I could tell I'd like these guys already.

After a moment of silence, Will burst out, "Of course you are," across my lap at Fran. I had no idea what this was about, but then I followed Will's pointed finger—it led directly to Fran's plane screen where the subtitled movie was still paused.

"You know I had to!" Fran exclaimed in return.

Before I even had a chance to ask what was going on, Willem read my mind and explained, "Darling Franco here is a very jealous person."

"Am not!"

"Shush," Willem said as he held up a finger to his friend. "Franco is a very jealous person," he reiterated. "He was born in Italy and came to America as a baby. His family never spoke Italian at home to assimilate better, and he was fine with that. Until we became friends."

"I was trying to learn before—"

"No, you were not," Will insisted, and I saw Fran's face turn red. He smiled slyly after being caught in his lie and spoke no more.

"Anyway, Fran and I became friends freshman year. We were both involved in the group for international students or students of other cultures. He loved that I'm from Holland and speak Dutch, and after we became friends, he became determined to learn Italian. He asked his parents to teach him, they said—"

"No," Fran supplemented.

"He asked his grandparents for money for lessons, they said—"

"No."

"He tried to use an *Italian-English Dictionary* and all he could learn was—"

"*No,*" Fran spoke with a heavy Italian accent.

"So," Willem rhymed, "he turned to the only thing he could think of: movies. And the only Italian movie he chooses to watch is the tragic World War II film, *Life is Beautiful.*"

"Is that what's playing now?" I asked. The film sounded familiar, though I didn't remember the scene frozen before Fran, with a white horse covered in spray paint.

Both guys nodded on either side of me.

Thus, began my friendship with Fran and Will. When I mentioned I spoke Malayalam, Fran's face scrunched together, and he gripped at his heart with a wail, but soon we were laughing and keeping each other company until our descents into Hong Kong, and finally, Delhi.

When we arrived in India, it was nearly midnight, and as we exited out of the airport, I tried to withhold my smiles of surprise. I'd heard enough stories from my dad and grandparents to know what to expect, but they didn't tell me that leaving the airport felt like you were a Bollywood star.

Hordes of families surrounded the exit, barred only by another family a little bit closer to the travelers. Several of them had cameras or phones and began snapping pictures of us. The flashes of light left my head spinning and fuzzy. One man attempted to grab my arm and started speaking in rapid Hindi. By the time I had tried to tell him I didn't speak Hindi, he realized he'd mistaken me for someone else and released me back to my group.

At nearly two in the morning, we made it to the small hostel we'd be staying at for our time in Delhi. Our itinerary had us traveling to two other states besides the capital, with our time in Delhi bookending it all together.

Despite what I'd heard about India from my father and grandparents, it still was breathtaking and even more bursting with life than I imagined.

In the morning, as we stepped out onto the streets for our first day in Delhi, you could smell the nearby stands making *chai,* with its signature scent of cardamom and cinnamon that immediately reminded me of my childhood when dad would insist it had been far too long since he'd had proper food. *Muttassi* would spend all afternoon creating a feast—starting with cutlets and ending with *chai* and Good Day cashew cookies from the international market. As we passed a stand, I made my team hold up a moment so I could pay for a cup.

As we walked along the sidewalk, full of cracks with each section more uneven than the last, covered by a canopy of *kanju* trees, my ears received something different on each side. On the left, I heard voices shout out to us, holding out various fried foods, scarves, and copies of famous books with no covers. To the right, innumerable rickshaws, motorcycles, and cars honked and whizzed past us with the occasional marimba music coming from a floral-painted truck in reverse. The traffic was organized chaos; from the outside, there seemed to be no rights or wrongs to driving. As I tried to remedy that thought, I realized the unspoken rule was focused solely on getting to each person's destination without dying.

The longer we walked, the more I became mesmerized by each vehicle, like dancers weaving in and out of a complicated routine. They all had a space, a purpose, and a path that fit perfectly, yet remained a mystery to me.

The other thing that surprised me in India was that I benefited greatly from my dark skin for the first time. After living in a predominately white town in Michigan, I finally knew what it was like to blend in with others.

Satya, the only other South Asian on our trip, was from Sri Lanka and spoke Tamil, and as both of us didn't know Hindi, the first few days in North India while everyone else was looking at Hindi phrases, we were discussing the differences in our languages.

We visited a few mosques as part of the historical context of our trip. Haley, our spunky, eccentric, and arguably most talkative member of our group, constantly reminded us on our last day in Delhi, "I still can't believe Fran forgot to get out of the mosque during evening prayers at Jamma Masjid!"

Most of us had gotten over being ushered out of the mosque and losing Fran in the process, who had to hide to avoid being seen not praying toward Mecca. However, he theorized differently.

"I think Haley keeps bringing it up to distract from when she fell and ripped her elephant pants," Fran mumbled to Will and me with a laugh.

Will, who had gone over to Haley's aid and proffered his zip-up for coverage, defended her.

The way he looked back at Haley reminded me of how I viewed Allie after Sam and Hannah explained about her panic attacks.

A few times, I'd have to correct some team members when they made assumptions about me. When Kelly asked me if the *chole bhature* was good while seated together in a restaurant for lunch, I explained the differences in North and South Indian cuisine. Joel wanted to know what the Hindi word for water was, and I answered *pannee* correctly, but told him that was the extent of what I knew.

Before any of us could feel settled, we were back on a plane headed for Mumbai. Mid-flight, Shannon, who had been feeling ill that morning, vomited on a flight attendant while asking for water. Heather was immediately by her side. With two kids of her own, she knew how to handle the situation, and since Shannon was better at joking about her own misfortune, Haley's pants situation was forgotten.

In our January meetings, we had run through things to expect while in India. We were given a packing list, as well as a list of cultural expectations. The most emphasized one was illness related to food and water.

Under no circumstances should we drink water not from a plastic bottle—which was self-explanatory. Heather and Mark had explained that the spiciness and the change in the type of food we'd be eating would be no excuse to have a negative attitude—Shannon had turned red, for she had just complained—but that usually a few people got sick because their digestive systems weren't used to the bacteria in other countries.

However, Shannon's illness was only the first of many. On the drive to our homestay in Mumbai, Todd and Keith had to open the rear door in the back of the second van and vomit on the side of the road. Haley, unfortunately, couldn't escape from new pants-related drama after an uncontrollable bout of diarrhea, and even Heather spent a day back at the hotel by the toilet.

"I really hope people stop getting sick," Willem said once we were back on the road. "Not that it makes me sick, I just want everyone to have a good experience."

"Getting sick is all a part of the authentic Indian experience," Mark sang out from the front seat.

And we were getting an authentic Indian experience. Besides the main sight-seeing in Delhi and Mumbai, to get school credit we were also spending some time with local non-profit organizations to learn about the work they were doing in India to help combat abandoned children and poverty, which was at our next location, outside of Mumbai.

When we arrived at our destination, we were directed to a series of different, smaller buildings from the organization we were visiting. Heather had told us this place rescued people from difficult situations to provide school, shelter, and food.

"Is it kind of like a university?" Shannon had asked.

"More like a safehouse—just on a much grander scale," Heather explained as she gestured to the buildings on the left, where clothing was hanging out to dry on the railing of the balcony. "Usually, the residents have trouble going back into normal life without counseling and rehabilitation from whatever they have gone through, so they take classes to either continue their education if they're young enough or take courses to help them get jobs at many of the shops established exclusively for them."

We would be sleeping a few to a room hosted by a few Indian residents around our ages. I was with Joel, a curly-haired basketball player giant Shannon had nicknamed 'The Gentle Giant' because he was an early development education student, and Mark. Fran, unluckily for him, got placed with both Todd and Keith, who were still struggling with their stomachs, and Willem with just Patrick, an Irish international student.

I bumped my head as I stepped into our room. Despite being part-Indian, I had inherited my height from my mom's side of the family.

It was half the size of my bedroom, yet somehow, they had fit six mats on the floor. Three for the Indian men—but now that I looked at them, they were more like boys—rescued through the organization, and three for us.

I clasped my hands together and bowed my head.

"*Namaste*," I addressed them. Thankfully, they knew a bit of English, and soon we learned their names—Harish, Lalit, and Chandan. Harish was only sixteen, and from the scars on his arms and hands, had suffered severe burns. Lalit and Chandan were brothers, seventeen and twenty-seven, but both had such youthful faces hidden behind their eyes that had suffered too much.

All three of them were laughing and smiling immediately at ease with Mark, which surprised me. I didn't know much about what the people here had endured to need an institution like this, but from their familiarity with Mark, I knew he had met them before.

I had barely unzipped my bag to attempt to find my journal—which we were required to keep for the class credits of the trip—when an Indian man, just as tall as me, but older, walked into our room. Immediately, I could tell he was mixed, like me, with even lighter skin.

"Hey guys," and—it seemed, by his accent—had grown up in North America. "Mark, Heather," he greeted our leaders with a friendly smile. "I wanted to introduce myself really quickly." He fixed the boxy black glasses that had slipped down his nose. Wearing glasses in this heat seemed impossible.

"I'm Daniel Forrester, one of the directors of WeRefugee—an organization with a history of helping refugees in Mumbai who are caught in bondage slavery, human trafficking, and orphan abandonment." He smiled far too brightly for someone who had just said 'orphan abandonment,' but he lit up the room like someone else I knew. "Now we've broadened our help to anyone in those situations, not just refugees." The glasses slipped again. "The name's just kinda stuck."

"I like to call this place WeGee," Mark added. "If you look on the side of the kitchen, I wrote 'I love WeGee' on it back in '87."

"Yes," Daniel said. "Nella is *still* in timeout from telling you the cement was wet."

"Is she here this year?" Mark asked, then added, "Nella is Dan's oldest, and she was away at university last year."

"Her engagement party is going to be on Saturday, then she'll come in—you'll be there, right?"

"We wouldn't miss it—paid a little extra for the train to Kerala on a Sunday…"

And with that, the two men were lost in conversation. I overheard a few vague descriptions of Nella's fiancé, with Mark, in undulation, gripping his strawberry blond hair in surprise.

"He's studying architecture, really?"

"Well, of course their first date would be at the Fruit Shop on Greams Road—there's no better fruit shop in Chennai!"

"From Kolkata! Well, what does your mother think?"

"She's basically living her dream for me, but through my daughter instead," Daniel responded.

Joel cleared his throat.

"D'ya think we could—"

But I never knew what Joel would say, because, without missing a beat from the conversation, Daniel turned to us, with the same excited tone and said, "Well, c'mon guys!"

"What?" Joel asked. Clearly Daniel had not realized his tangent with Mark had left us all a bit in the dark, and we weren't sure what was going on.

"We're having dinner, then the children of WeRefugee would love to play Kabaddi with you guys. In fact," Daniel looked past us to our forgotten roommates. I felt a twinge in my gut as I remembered the boys' joy talking to us. "It was actually Harish's idea! He told me about it a few nights ago, when I asked if these guys wouldn't mind sharing with you three."

Harish's sharp profile dropped to his lap in embarrassment.

"I thought it was a great idea!" Daniel exclaimed. "So great in fact, the younger kids spent this afternoon clearing up the big field we usually reserve for larger events so everyone can have a chance to play!"

Daniel spoke with such gusto and enthusiasm; I could picture him perfectly as the dad who would dress up as Santa Claus to keep up the charade for his kids and prance around the house swearing Santa could be brown.

"That sounds great, right guys?" Mark said.

I hadn't played Kabaddi since I was a kid. But after grabbing food, I was whisked away to memories of my Indian cousins visiting from Minnesota as we tackled each other to the ground. Once, when I was eight, my older cousin Harmeet grabbed me from a large squat and lifted me up into the air before slamming me into the grass that was only soft in theory.

Harish explained the rules to us visitors—the game was simple: the raider crosses the line and tries to tag as many people from the opposite team as possible before they, in turn, tackle the raider.

"And to make things fun, you have to say 'Kabaddi' over and over until you run out of breath. If you don't tag anyone, you have to get back over," Daniel added.

As the teams assembled based on random choice, I noticed I had both Harish and Lalit on my team.

Needless to say, we won.

The three of us became a powerhouse. Harish was skinny and quick, and surprised several of the American girls by charging at them from the back. Chandan tagged his brother at one point, so I brought Lalit back in by getting both Joel and Willem out in one turn. I barely made it over the line—Mark had been at my tail.

As I laid my head down to bed that night, amidst the sounds of distant rickshaws and the whispers of insects, I thought of the young kids we played with, and how much Allie would have enjoyed being here, too. My heart ached with the weight of her absence.

29

January 18th, 1991

I hadn't been entirely sure what the trip would entail. I knew from the meetings it would be full of sightseeing, as well as education about the refugee crisis in India. I was holding onto hope for the moments of joy in connecting with my heritage, and although we weren't in Kerala yet, my soul was relaxing into the beat of Indian life. I didn't feel like I had to put on a mask or a persona to fit each person I met—I could be just me, and that was enough.

But there were some physical aspects to the trip that I wasn't expecting—like sorting out leaves of palm to be made into rope or helping organize and clean the classrooms. Mark and Heather always wanted to give back to the communities we'd been welcomed into.

We also helped financially. We donated our leftover rupees at the end of the stay at WeGee. They had a small candy shop set up to teach the residents about business, and I bought a bag of chocolate covered toffees called Chococlairs every day to replenish each bag I devoured before sunset.

But mostly we were just there—to play, to observe, to be.

The day before Nella's engagement party, we spoke in several of the classrooms at a partner school. The students' English was good, and they asked several questions about what the United States is like and what we liked most about India. On the way out after taking a picture with the fourth class of the day, I caught up with Heather and Mark.

"What purpose do we have here?" I whispered to Heather as we strolled across the schoolyard. Groups of playing students waved to us. "I thought these trips were all educational."

Heather was dressed in traditional Indian clothing—she had been since we first landed in Delhi. Today, she was wearing a purple *kurti* with silver vines along the side slits, with matching purple pants and a silver scarf.

"You're the third person to ask on this trip! Funny, we usually get more by this point," Heather said as she flicked the scarf up over his shoulder. It trapped some of her long, graying blonde hair.

"Like a lot of cross-cultural classes at Mt. Hope, the India trip is a class. There's the class portion—like keeping a journal and understanding Hinduism," —which I knew enough of already— "but unlike other trips, we take things a step further."

Heather politely nodded to the security guard as we passed out of the gates of the school before continuing.

"Mark and I have come to India every year for ten years. And there's something that always sticks with us. Do you remember what that girl in the eighth standard class at the local school asked earlier?"

I nodded. Of course—it had been the most in-depth question we had.

"What's one thing you would change about India?" the girl asked as she played with her braid.

"Yeah, we all joked about the traffic," I answered Heather with a laugh.

"Yes, but what else did we say?"

I thought back and remembered Haley speaking up about what the refugees and others had struggled through. Not naming names, but she mentioned brief stories of those we had met at WeRefugee like young kids caught in sex trafficking and the inequalities of the caste system.

"The thing is," Heather explained as we turned left to walk back to WeGee, "these students ask these questions because they want to see you care about their country. That you see the things they see."

I thought back to the boys from my room—I saw the brokenness Harish, Lalit, and Chandan had gone through to get saved.

"These kids need hope that if an American could recognize and figure out ways to improve India, then why couldn't they, some young Mumbai kids, be the ones to do it? They all look up to you and will remember this day for the rest of their lives." She dodged a branch as we continued to walk on.

In the distance, I saw the gates of WeRefugee and the lights being hung up for the reception. The corners of my mouth twitched upward.

"Our interest in their lives as an outsider," Heather continued, "pushes these kids to do their best and focus on excelling. But the changes come from within." Heather smiled, full of hope. "All we do is encourage future leaders and world changers."

I took what Heather said to heart and tucked it in the recesses of my mind. I wasn't sure I believed I could be a world changer but maybe I could start smaller by talking to others in all ways of life, but I just wasn't sure how.

When I woke up the next day, I stuck my head out the door, and Daniel was running around frantically, exclaiming, "Nella is coming!" He slung his arm around Mark, crying out, "I didn't even think I was old enough to have a daughter that could get married."

I must have missed her arrival, but I didn't mind. I'd been to my fair share of Indian parties—not in India of course, but between all of my Minnesota cousins' weddings—but they were still beautiful. From the variation of food, the astonishingly bright *saris*, and the presents, each engagement party was a fun sneak peek of the wedding to come.

Despite the excitement and music now radiating through the campus, my brain immediately reminded me of Heather's words yesterday.

I never thought of myself as someone who would change the world. Mostly, I thought only about myself. Allie had begun to change that in me. I still felt like an imposter though and doubted myself and if I was a good enough person.

Altogether unsettled, like a foreigner in my own body, I bunched up my hair in my hands as I tried to reconcile the mistakes I'd made and the potential that others like Allie and Heather saw in me. What had I done?

Really, a lot of nothing. I talked, spent time with Harish —who taught me a fun game that felt like a form of Duck Duck Goose mixed with repetitive rhyming—and when one day I woke up a little earlier than planned, I asked Daniel if he needed help serving up breakfast.

"Sure, that'd be great, Ben!" he had answered, grateful for another pair of hands.

Daniel had led me to the kitchen, where his younger daughter, Priya, was already finishing up the rice for a dish I'd never heard of, called *poha*.

"You can chop up the onions," she had said as she handed me a bag as big as my garbage bag after forgetting to leave it on the curb for a month.

"All of these?"

"That's just one of five bags," she responded without missing a beat.

I held Priya's gaze for roughly thirty seconds, waiting for her to admit to the joke, but when she didn't, Daniel and I sat out on the steps and began to cut and sort them into large wooden baskets.

During that two hours of cutting onions, Daniel and I talked—but I wouldn't call it world-changing. It was simple stuff—like how he grew up in Queens with his mom and dad. His mom's family was from Mumbai, and his dad from Manhattan. He was the youngest of four boys, and when I said, "Oh, that sucks," Daniel's eyebrows fell together and he looked past me, as if unwilling to accept my sympathy.

"No, actually, I loved it," Daniel had said when he met my eyes again. "My brothers taught me so much about what it means to be a good man. To be someone who looks at what's broken and chooses not to deepen the destruction, but to mend it. Our dad taught them that, but he didn't get a chance to teach me."

I didn't push further.

"We all doted on my mom, too, like she was a princess we were all trying to woo," he laughed at his own simile. "While her dad was still running WeRefugee, we'd visit every few years, but when it was time to pass it on, there was no doubt that I'd get it," Daniel said as he plopped another cut onion into his basket.

"You seem like you're doing really great work here," I had encouraged after a moment of silence. "I'm sure your dad would be proud. This is life-changing stuff."

"Oh, yeah, he would be," Daniel had agreed immediately. "But I'd say calling this stuff 'life-changing' in a positive way is a stretch. Sometimes I wonder if I chose my life right." He looked down at the onion in his hand, and I spotted him playing with the ghost of a wedding ring.

I thought back to something Allie said, when I had begged her for the fiftieth time if she could somehow come to India with me. *God is directing me rightly. He just asks me to take His hand and walk.*

Allie's inner peace and certainty was haunting me. Around Daniel, I felt that same peace.

"Well, um, you've done so much for others. Do you think maybe that was meant to be, even if not entirely what you wanted?" I had asked Daniel.

The man that had sat before me, with his black glasses slipping against his snow-touched hair, who shrugged and had said, "Probably," was now gesturing to me, calling out, "Ben! Come and join the party! We have *gulab jamun*." That serious conversation was not even a ghost on his joyous face.

I smirked from the doorway of my room. I had slipped to Daniel on the porch that I liked the sweet, sticky dessert.

I headed out to join the celebration, dreaming of *gulab jamun* and wondering if my talk with Daniel made me a world changer like him.

In the giant white tent, I met up with Fran and Willem, who had both been gorging themselves on *samosas*, a favorite of Nella's. Being a big fan of them myself, I snatched one up. The party was in its latter half, which meant it probably would last only four more hours.

"Isn't this so cool?" Fran exclaimed. "I've learned so much about what Nella's wedding will look like. Did you know Indian brides wore red instead of white?" Fran, already a loud fellow, was a touch softer than shouting like a sergeant over the layers of conversations and music around us.

"Surprisingly, yes, I did know that."

Fran laughed at his misstep.

"Duh. Guess this isn't new for you!"

"Nope," I said with a smile, though I still felt unsettled from within seeing the love and joy on display, though I wasn't sure why. I just missed Allie.

The field where we had played Kabaddi now had a tent and shimmering gold decorations—from the tables down to the little spoons for *chutney*. In the distance, I spotted Mark and Heather talking to who I assumed was Nella, draped in a *sari* of gold to match, with her fiancé next to her. As I watched them laugh, overjoyed at their union, I felt a hollowness fill my stomach that could not be remedied with *samosas*.

I looked away.

"Do you think you and Allie will have an Indian wedding?" Will asked, as if he could read my mind.

I only talked about my relationship with Allie casually with the two, usually to relate with Fran about missing Maria, his longtime girlfriend of four years who was always busy talking about their future wedding—not that they were even engaged.

Not only that, but I hadn't even spoken to anyone, especially Allie, about the little moments I imagined us as a married couple. I thought about Allie and I, at home in a small house that was our own, maybe with a dog, and a baby or two, sleeping in late on Saturday mornings and cooking pancakes together with our little rascals running around…

Having been around people like Heather and Mark lately, whose marriage was agonizingly sweet and honest, I had begun to worry that my beliefs didn't fit with Allie's. I was still undecided about religion whereas she thought I was a committed Christian.

"Oh, um, I—"

"Probably not—girls usually get the say, huh?" Fran interjected. "Maria already decided we're dancing to "Eternal Flame" and our colors are seafoam green and pink." He jokingly gagged himself.

But I had already left the tent. So much for being there for a few more hours. Every time I looked over to Nella, I couldn't see anyone but Allie, dressed in a wedding sari.

I started stalking toward my room, thinking over everything. I couldn't do this. I couldn't think of Allie that way. I wasn't a world changer. With each passing moment in India, I felt sicker with myself at those around me living good, decent lives. Everyone felt genuine, while I was tormented with the lies I'd told.

I had come to India with a selfish mindset, unlike people like Mark and Heather and Daniel. I was thinking only of what I could gain from getting to experience the country of my father, without recognizing the great privilege I had to impact the lives around me. In fact, I never thought much about how my presence and words affected others, prior to Allie, at least. She had given me a chance and had found a way to soften the rigid parts of me, while opening her heart to me.

The Ben from a year ago would not have been as patient, loving, and caring to Daniel and Priya, to Lalit, Chandran, and Harish, to the school children we met. Maybe I could be a world changer, but only because Allie had initially changed mine. And week by week, church service by church service, studying with Allie and her worship music, I continued to hide the part of myself that I knew would break Allie. I was too afraid to tell her that I had let the idea of God fall far away as I focused on physical pleasures. Being pulled between my parents' beliefs, feeling forced to choose a side, had made me turn away from either in order to find who I thought I was. But I never gave it much thought about what I believed if I gave myself the chance to really think about it.

Even though I'd changed so much, I still worried that Allie deserved someone better than me. My stomach rolled even thinking about letting Allie go, but I could never entrap her in a relationship like my parents—with false hope that I could come around to Christianity for her, like my mother and father both hoped for one another. I didn't want to have children with Allie who felt conflicted in pleasing their parents as I did.

But I didn't have time to dwell on it, because a hand touched my shoulder, and I turned. It was Daniel.

I didn't know why I did this—maybe Daniel seemed like the kind of father I could have had—or even the friend I needed—but I began to cry.

"Ben," he spoke softly.

I tried to shove him away, but to no avail, Daniel stepped closer.

"I saw you leave," he sighed. "Please talk to me."

"You won't u-understand—" I stuttered as I tried to stem the flow of tears.

"That's okay. God will, and He'll tell me what to say."

I paused. The first mention of the Christian God since I was with Allie, and it felt so comforting and familiar, like her, like my mother.

I laughed inside. I had suspected Daniel might have been a Christian, due to his American upbringing, but this confirmed it.

"I-I act like my life is fine, but it's not," I sniffed as my eyes began to water again. I fought back the tears, but they caught in my throat. "M-my girlfriend is amazing. She's the greatest thing ever to happen to me, and I've l-lied to her. S-she's a Christian, and I'm not. I've pretended to be, I go to church with her, I listen to her talk about her faith, but I-I can't keep pretending. Not for her, not for me." I shuddered out another cry, silent but like breathing in ice. "I can't do this to her."

"Hm," he said, as he sat down. "That is a stumper," he said, as if in fascination. "Do you love this girl?"

I nodded.

"Gotcha. Hm." More silence, then he spoke again. "Why is this bothering you now?"

I shrugged and slowly lowered myself beside him. In the silence, the tears ended.

"I guess, just, you know, being with everyone and seeing the hardship here, but all the—I don't know—the j-joy? I didn't realize it, but Allie's specialness isn't hers alone—I feel it talking to you, to the kids here. It's like she's here with me. And I feel s-so useless. I've had this p-privileged l-life, so much so that I didn't n-need faith or h-hope.

"I didn't realize how many differences there were between A-Allie and I until I felt it here, too, with people who aren't her. P-people who are l-living in wonder at e-each day of life. Suddenly, I just feel so unworthy." I sighed and pulled my knees to my chest and let the tears run freely.

Daniel placed a hand on my back, and I looked up to see him gazing at the stars above.

"I think you've unlocked something really special, Ben, being with Allie *and* being apart right now. Being able to recognize that is huge," he explained. "Do you think you feel this way because you want to stop pretending to be the way she thinks of you, or to go back to who you've been?"

"I don't know," I croaked out. "I don't wanna be who I was again. But I've never—at least I don't think so—felt God's presence or joy or optimism like s-she does..."

When Daniel walked away, his response hung in the air, so corporeal and thick with potential, if I tried, I thought I could grab it.

"Maybe you never knew what to feel for."

Caught between Hinduism and Christianity, between Indian culture and American, between pleasing my father to never stop pursuing my goals and pleasing my mother to simply spend time doing what I enjoy, made it incredibly difficult to sort out what to feel and how to think.

But, as I stared at the stars above, Orion's Belt blinking down at me, I imagined I could finally become who I was destined to be: myself, in all my glorious flaws and strengths.

30

January 21st, 1991

"...then Tuesday, Willem and Ben will lead the book..." Mark rattled off from the front seat of our rental bus. Despite having traveled mostly in two vans, Heather insisted we use one vehicle in Kerala to make less traffic going to the village.

"Yes!" Will and I exclaimed simultaneously and high-fived. I had extensive knowledge on Hinduism, and one night in Delhi, Willem asked me if Hindus believe in unicorns as a joke. We had been waiting to use that as a question in a book discussion, but never got the chance—but here it was.

"Ooo, you guys, look! There's got to be at least seven people on that motorcycle," Haley exclaimed, but touched only Willem's arm.

"How close are we?" Shannon called out. "I forgot to pee before we left the hostel!"

It took three rooms on the trip for Willem, Fran, and I to finally be roommates. Mostly due to the fact that when Mark tried to announce Willem would be with Todd, Fran jumped on Mark's words and called our names instead. Everyone was too exhausted to argue.

"We're almost there," Heather confirmed.

We'd taken an early morning train from Mumbai and were now headed to the village where Heather and Mark had become connected with three years prior. Unlike the bustling streets of the bigger cities, or the extensive compound of WeGee, the Kerala we had seen so far had been mostly country, covered in banyan trees, tall grass, and rice fields filled with workers knee high in the flooding waters.

Kerala smelled clean and fresh, like laundry in the spring air. I was falling in love with it by the second as we bussed past winding rivers and banana trees.

Heather had bought the group a huge clump of bananas when we had gotten off the overnight train that morning, and Willem passed me two small ones to munch on as we stared out the window in awe.

I could've spent the rest of the trip just watching the greenery before us, but before we knew it, we pulled into our last stop, the school of the village.

Heather led the charge with a stack of coloring pages, books, and snacks as a gift. While I had approached most of our trip to India with wonder and curiosity, finally finding myself in Kerala filled me with a type of anticipation I had not expected. I had loved watching the landscape change through the safety of the window seat, but my nervousness rose as we passed through the large wooden door gate. What if it wasn't what I was expecting?

But I reminded myself, as Heather said before, we were here to encourage. If that meant I just had to sit next to kids and color, I could do it—swallow the existential dread until bedtime, I hoped.

As we walked in, hundreds of voices rose up, growing in volume as the school came into sight.

On the main level stood roughly two hundred kids, boys and girls, all clapping, smiling, and chanting out the same song—one I understood.

Of course, I knew we were in Kerala, but in my excitement, I had forgotten that they would be speaking the language of my father, and it felt like home. After being surrounded by Hindi for two weeks, I'd forgotten how beautiful it was to hear Malayalam.

"Can you understand them, Ben?" Heather asked me, her grin wide and eyes eager. I expected she had been anticipating this moment.

I nodded and stepped closer to the singing—as familiar and comforting as a warm blanket fresh from the dryer.

The voices united into the repeated line, and its words dissipated the ball of anxiety that had worn its way into my stomach. I felt the release of my dead flee. I was home.

Welcome to Kerala, Welcome to Kerala, Welcome to Kerala – God's Own Country.

Within moments, I found myself on my knees, next to two girls that could have been twins in their matching green dresses, singing along. The lump in my throat had erupted, not into tears, but into song.

If any of them were surprised to see one of their visitors speaking Malayalam with them, none showed it.

Before long, I had a young boy sitting in my lap, speaking too quickly for me to catch everything he said, and when I asked him to slow down, I learned that he was Ishan, he was seven, and he thought my hair was really cool.

Eleven-year-old Ashwini shouted into my ear that she was so excited to meet me and immediately began to make small braids in my curls.

Navin, who was three, simply stared at me and kept repeating those two facts about himself.

I tried to keep up a conversation with a young girl named Sandhya who was asking me if I was a tour guide with the Americans, but soon I was drowning in giggling children, all shouting louder than the others in an attempt to get my attention.

When I glanced over at the rest of the team, they were all surrounded by excited children, too. Heather's hair was braided into an intricate rope of straw with streaks of gray, like a delicate painting. She was talking animatedly to the older girl doing it, who must have known some English. Haley had two kids on her hips, one on her back, and two on either leg. They all shrieked with joy. Shannon was bouncing with a little girl, even smaller than Navin, whose short hair was dusted with dandruff. Mark was enthusiastically talking to some older children, who had snuggled up beside him like a father entertaining his kids during a thunderstorm. They spoke alongside him at open points, and he kept pulling them closer with the crowd somehow constantly growing.

Fran and Willem came to my rescue, pulled a few of the kids off me, and asked, "How do you say hello?" There was a swarm of kids around them already.

"*Hlea,*" I responded, just as a chorus of children surrounded Haley roared in laughter, chanting, "*Hlea* Haley *Hlea* Haley!"

I caught her confused gaze.

"What are they laughing about?" she called. I stifled a laugh. The girl on her back had pulled out several strands of Haley's dark brown hair and had begun to clip pieces to stick out.

"Your name sounds like 'hello!'"

We didn't get to the coloring books the first day, nor the second day. The kids had been too excited to show us the monkey bars and slides they had at the back of the building.

These kids knew Kabaddi, too, and insisted we play. In fact, after losing four games of our team versus about fifty of the children, Ashwini pleaded with me that we played again, and our team proceeded to lose six more times.

We all left tired, but from the moment we left the van in the morning to when we packed back up near dusk, everyone was laughing, smiling, and altogether happy.

As I walked about every day, no matter where I was outside of Kabaddi, Navin was next to me with his small hand enclosed in mine.

When the kids had calmed down a bit more between tea times, Heather pulled out the games and coloring books, and I sat down with Sandhya and Navin to color a picture of a young girl riding a bicycle.

"Blue," I spoke in English to them as I held up a sky-blue crayon and scribbled a bit of sky.

Sandhya's head bobbed from side to side in understanding and grabbed the crayon from my grip. Her blue was much lighter than mine as the tip of the crayon barely brushed the paper.

"Blue," she repeated back. She fished in the box for another color and held up one the color of her dress. "*Nī pchchyayi pṟyu nnthennne?*"

"Green," I answered.

"Green." She rolled the 'r.'

"GREEN!" Navin exclaimed before collapsing in my arms like a puppet. The sheer force of his excitement seemed to drain all his energy.

As I explained the difference between 'yellow' and 'hello' to Ashwini, who had then joined us, I thought about Allie working in a classroom so different from the room I was in now: dark, cement walls, and with an aroma of *masala* as if baked into the walls.

But whether in a large classroom with desks and motivational kids' posters or sitting on a cement step coloring from a used coloring book, I could see why people chose to teach. There was such a rush of pride when something you've said sticks with someone, especially these kids.

On Friday, our last day in the village, Navin would not let go of me. Even the wives and husbands doing various jobs in the market watched us walk around like conjoined twins.

"I wish they could understand me," Willem groaned after struggling to translate again. "You're lucky," he told me.

"It's definitely been easy since there's no language barrier," I said, "but still a cultural one. I guess all those years of my father rapping my knuckles when I used the wrong past participle worked," I chuckled.

"Hey, don't forget we have to meet tonight to prepare for the book discussion," Willem reminded me.

"Are we still good on the unicorn question?"

Willem scoffed and stared at me like I had asked him if he'd ever seen *Star Wars*. Everyone had seen *Star Wars*.

"Duh, of course."

I swaggered away to find one of the kids who had become part of my posse, but I could feel my intestines tying themselves together like a cherry stem with every minute that went by.

It hadn't hit most of the group that today was the last day until our normal activities ceased. Instead of playing games, coloring, or letting the girls go hog wild on doing hair, Mark and Heather called for everyone to gather—our group, as well as all the villagers.

"We've had the best time being back here with you all," Mark called out, and his interpreter did his best to match his booming bravado. Mark's voice had great projection, yet still gave off the gentle spirit of a calming father. "My wife and I love to see you all every year. How you grow, how you learn, and how much you love." The last word he choked on as runaway tears fell.

I had bet Fran a hundred rupees that Mark would cry before the afternoon. I checked my watch and saw it was 12:45.

Dang.

"Sometimes I cannot believe how lucky we are, that we get to come across the world to be with you all. And now, for the fourth year in a row…"

The kids, even the younger ones like Navin, knew instinctively what to do. Mark opened his arms out wide, as did Heather, as did every one of us in return as we enveloped every person in that room.

All I remember was hearing my heartbeat, barely a threading sound amongst the rapidity and frequency of the little ones around me. Navin was right under my arm, and in the stillness, we caught each other's gaze. I had to look away almost immediately. Other people crying was a certain gateway for me, too.

We held them all for what felt like hours but lasted only minutes. I wished it could have been longer. I wished for it in the last moments at the school when Ashwini tugged on my shirt and asked if I would be back tomorrow. I wished it when Ishan showed me he had parted his hair to look like mine. I wished it in Sandhya's small note, written in a mixture of Malayalam and English, hoping we had a safe journey.

Most of all I wished for it in the last moments with Navin when I had to watch him cry as we all waved goodbye for the seventh time. Neither group was willing to let go.

Haley broke down when one of the younger girls refused to take back her own hair clip and gave it to her. Strangely, though not so surprisingly, Will disappeared from Fran's and my side after that.

The ride back was somber.

Will sat next to Haley, comforting her. As I watched him let her lay her head on his shoulder, I thought of Allie. Which of the kids would she have spent time with? Or would she have done like Shannon, and chatted and sewn clothing with some of the village women?

In the light of day, I could see how foolish I'd been to question my relationship with Allie. I couldn't throw her aside like that, like girls from the past. Daniel had been right—it was time to see where my heart lay. I'd changed so much since I'd met Allie and felt like we could get through anything. I could only hope when I told her the truth, it would all work out okay.

It was late by the time we returned to the hostel. Everyone was either physically exhausted or emotionally exhausted from the day. We moved through our book discussion rather quickly, with everyone ready to spend some time resting before it was time once again to travel. Before we headed up to our rooms to pack and rest, Willem pulled me aside.

"Hey, Ben, do you want to go up to the roof?" Willem asked.

I didn't know what Willem wanted, but I didn't want to say no, so I followed him up to the roof of the hostel.

Kerala truly was beautiful. A few stars were visible tonight, ahead of us, just along the tree top line. Although we were staying outside the village in a city smaller than Delhi or Mumbai, the whizzing sound of passing vehicles and the distant sounds of conversations on the street still harmonized beautifully. India was always alive, and it filled me with new life I couldn't have imagined for myself.

"Okay," Willem cut through the music, and my attention turned. He had a journal with him.

Then Willem spoke.

"Studying Hinduism was hard for me," he said. "I know you understand it much better, but I've really only studied the Christian God. I can't understand polytheism. I just wanted more of a personal take on it, really."

"Well, Hindu theory isn't polytheistic," I offered. "Not really. The idea is more that the gods are all one ocean, made of many drops. And those drops are represented in the different gods." That had always been my father's explanation. "I thought Christianity is polytheistic, isn't there God the Son and God the Father?" I reiterated the little I remembered from Sunday School

"No, it's different," Willem added, "kind of similar. to Hinduism, I guess. One God, three ways He connects to us. As the Spirit in us, the Father in Heaven, and the Son that died."

As Willem explained what I would later learn as an overly simplified version of the Trinity, I could see what drew my parents to find each other. How their similarities didn't feel as big as their differences.

But they were. And they had brought me to this space. To choose. To forge my own path or follow theirs, in more ways than one, now complicating the one relationship I cared about. And of course, it was all spiraling during my first trip to India.

Willem and I continued to discuss the two religions, although my knowledge on Hinduism was shallow compared to his on Christianity. I should have felt peace.

Instead, I felt confused. The confusion I felt about my relationship with Allie resurfaced. I barely slept that night. What would I be subjecting Allie and I to, our future family to, by repeating the mistake my parents made in choosing to try and overcome their differences? I wanted to be honest with her, but I wasn't sure if I was brave enough to potentially lose her by doing so.

Saturday afternoon was going to be spent just shopping, which was a great way to end the trip.

Despite stopping at a few bazaars earlier in the trip, I hadn't done much buying of souvenirs. I'd wanted to find Allie something authentic and art-related, but not many potters enjoyed enameling clay cameras.

We arrived at a large, indoor mall with several wings branching off each other. I hadn't expected the shopping to be a maze, but I followed along with Fran and Willem to explore.

Like typical guys, we bought the first few things we saw. I spotted a cricket jersey for Spencer, and since I spoke Malayalam, I was able to barter with the seller for only one hundred rupees for the shirt and, with a little added twist to keep things interesting, I had him throw in the wooden cup Willem had been looking at.

"You didn't have to do that, Ben," Will whined, but I ignored him.

Since we weren't too keen on getting lost, the three of us only ventured to one of the branches. There were every kind of store there: tattoo parlors, piercing bars, a cinema, furniture stores, boutiques, tourist trap knick knack stores, an extensive food court, and even a spa.

"This is the life," Fran muttered as we passed a masseuse kiddy corner to a gelato shop.

I still had trouble finding anything photography related for Allie, so I quickly bought a postcard just in case we ran out of time. We still had an hour left to shop, but I was nervous.

Just as our trio was about to leave another tiny storefront, something caught my eye. It was a beautiful ornate ring. The golden setting held an opal, with its array of pinks and blues floating in a background of white. The exact kind of ring I knew Allie would want one day.

I shook my head and looked away. I couldn't entertain thoughts of marrying Allie while also simultaneously not knowing where our relationship would stand when I told her the truth. I was hopeful, but not stupid.

Eventually, I figured Allie needed something better than the lazy postcard. I haggled a wooden elephant down to seventy rupees, then grabbed a blue scarf for my mom for just over one hundred.

We were heading back toward our meeting spot when Fran got separated somehow. He reappeared with just two minutes to spare before we left; most of the team had arrived early or on time. Heather and Mark came by last, both clutching fruit smoothies.

By the time we had eaten dinner and began packing and weighing our bags, it finally hit me that we were really leaving India tomorrow.

In a moment of solitude, I slipped away from our room, onto the balcony, and breathed in the amazing scent and sights of India. Now I knew the true beauty my dad talked about when he mentioned how the trees ran up for miles, competing for the tallest. The sea, splashing in the distance, so blue it seemed animated. The smell of cloves and a *tandoor* oven filled my nostrils.

And the sky. Now a dark, continuous, star-splattered black canvas seemed so close, so real and tangible, like if I truly tried hard enough, I could stand on my tippy toes and brush Heaven.

I imagined it felt something like velvet lips.

31

January 27th, 1991

Willem's alarm went off at one in the morning. He had gone to bed at ten that night, claiming even three hours of sleep would be enough, but Fran and I couldn't sleep. So, when the alarm went off, and Willem groaned awake, Fran and I were in the middle of a game of poker.

"Morning, sunshine," I said cheerily to Will.

"Ugh."

"Do you regret sleeping, *principessa*?" Fran asked, gathering up the cards.

"Whoa whoa whoa! I had a full house!" I exclaimed.

"And I need to shower before we leave, *principessa*."

"Glad you clarified," I joked as I fished my toothbrush out of my suitcase to get ready to continue our long night.

As I scrubbed my tongue, Mark knocked on our door. I thought back to my first impression of Mark on the airplane and remembered it differently—not an annoyingly positive man waking me up from sleep, but a kind professor who wanted to make sure I was doing as best as I could.

"How're you guys? All awake?" he asked as he stuck his head through the crack in our door. Mark, like Willem, seemed to have slept a bit, considering they were both rubbing their eyes.

I sent him a thumbs-up from the sink, and from behind me, Willem muttered, "Good... Tired."

Mark sent his wide smile our way. "That's what I like to hear. Meet downstairs in ten minutes." Then he was gone. Regimented-schedule Mark replaced fun-loving Mark, but still left the ghost of positivity in his wake.

The air in our little room felt even more stale as I knew we were closing upon our leave of it. It became harder to breathe, difficult to imagine not being in India. Zipping my suitcase shut, I tried to focus on anything but saying goodbye to this wonderful country. It had become like a home, and bonding with Willem and Fran and the rest of the group made them my family.

The three of us never said it aloud, but we all thought it. We all ran with different crowds back at school—Fran with his buds in the Village, Willem with his tennis friends and other history majors, and me with Allie. Will and Fran barely saw each other outside the Multicultural Club. But I had grown so close to them—I wasn't prepared for our friendships to end after feeling so close to them on this trip.

"Pass me the souvenir bag, wouldya, Fran?"

I rummaged through it, like sifting through weights, until I found the elephant and the India Cricket Team jersey. I folded the elephant with the jersey and scarf and set them down gently within the open crevices of my carry-on. I decided to give my dad the postcard.

"And now that our last group has arrived," Mark began as Fran, Willem, and I descended the stairs, "we can head out."

As we boarded the bus to the airport, I took one look back at the streets of India. Despite being the middle of the night, the bright red taillights of individuals living out the evening on their motorcycles shone back at me. Before the rain could bury itself in my eyes, I looked away.

Willem sneaked over to Haley, and I caught him saying, "Your *mehndi* still looks great!" as he pointed to the intricate henna design on her hand. As we began to drive, I glanced back and saw them seated together, talking passionately about the village.

"Ready to see Allie again?" Fran asked me. He must have noticed Willem and Haley, too.

"Of course. What about Maria?"

Fran shifted in his seat and glanced briefly at his hands, which were rubbing together as if trying to start a fire.

"Excited. Nervous." At my wrinkled forehead, he paused and looked back over his shoulder. Willem was still talking. "I bought a ring while we were at the marketplace last night," he whispered. "I'm finally going to ask Maria to marry me."

"That's great, Fran," I said, genuinely happy for him.

With boyish anticipation, he asked, "Wanna see the ring?"

Without an answer, Fran plucked a wooden box from his carry-on pocket. He popped it open and there it was—the ornate-set opal engagement ring I had seen before. My stomach dropped.

"It's…"

"Breathtaking, right?"

I nodded, unsure of what else to say.

"It's incredible. She's a lucky girl."

Fran stuffed the ring back to his bag clumsily, accidentally zipping half of the pocket fabric, and I was filled with a moment of envy, of his solid relationship and the certainty of its future.

We made it to our gate with time to spare, and after the plane took off, I chatted to Joel and Haley, who were next to me.

"How'd you enjoy the trip, Ben?" Joel asked as he righted the instruction manual before him. The poor guy's knees nearly knocked the TV.

"I really loved it," I answered. "It wasn't what I'd expected, but in a good way. My dad told me all these stories about India when he was a kid, so I thought life in India was mainly like his. But this gave me a completely new perspective. You?"

"Same. I think everyone loved it. Mark called it one of his best," he replied.

"Really? I'm flattered."

We laughed. And that's what I loved about this trip—learning how to talk to anyone. I felt a pang of regret for spending my time at Mt. Hope focusing solely on myself and running. On this trip I'd been surrounded by so many of my great people, who I could have met earlier if I'd made more of an effort with college life.

After a moment, I added, thinking about Allie, "I'm ready to be home, though."

The plane lurched into the air, and I felt my stomach flip.

"Why's that? Missing your family?"

I chuckled, and my smile grew wider.

"More like my girlfriend."

Joel nodded and rested his head back.

"I suppose that's a great reason. So, you graduate this year, right?" he asked as he turned to face me. "What do you plan on doing?" I forgot Joel was only a sophomore.

I thought back to my conversation with Willem on the roof in Kerala, to my one with Daniel on the steps and at the party, to the words about being a world changer from Heather. What did I really want?

The Olympics were a crazy possibility, but what about Allie? What about if the Olympics didn't work out? I wasn't sure where my Bachelor's in Business Management would get me, considering I wasn't too interested in it. The only things I was passionate about were Allie and running.

"I'm not sure. If my athletic goals don't work out, I might need to go back to school. I didn't choose the best major."

"What would you go back for?"

It came to me much too quickly, but it felt right. Just knowing how Mark and Heather made such an impact on me, even in their small positions as professors of history and refugee studies, had caused me to rethink. I hadn't shared my thoughts with anyone else, yet, but the idea was still there, tumbling around in my mind, half-formed, but promising.

"Higher Education. Yeah…" I ruminated over it. "Higher Ed. Possibly to do what these two," I motioned to our trip leaders, "did for us."

Joel shrugged. His young age showed.

"Sounds cool. I hope things work out for you."

It took me the first time I threw up to remember I hadn't taken Dramamine. Thankfully, I made it to the bathroom with the partially full vomit bag before I emptied my stomach anymore.

On my walk of shame back, Fran nodded sympathetically. Oh well. At least I had gone three weeks without getting sick.

I spent a good twelve hours of the flight knocked out, and the other eight I spent watching movies or eating the packaged food they provided for us.

When we finally landed in Detroit, we carried our bags and rolled our suitcases over toward customs, passports in hands.

When Fran, the last person, came running out with a Rocky impression, we hollered and clapped him on the back. At one point, Joel lifted him in the air with excitement.

"Well then," Mark bellowed, and we silenced, but Fran was still smiling. "Now that we've had a little reunion, I just want to say thank you for being such a great group. You guys are truly world changers. I hope this trip broadened your horizons and helped you see things with a fresh perspective."

I spotted a few teary faces, and although we all went to school together, it would never be like this again. While everyone else was leaving the trip filled with knowledge and perspective, I was leaving even more unsure of who I wanted to be.

With plans to reconnect as a group, make homemade *palak paneer,* and look at everyone's developed pictures, we broke off, one by one. I thought about my mom's camera, still tucked away in my carry-on. I had been so focused on the trip; I had barely taken any photos.

"Do you need a ride back?" Willem asked. "Maria is picking up me and Fran."

"Thank you, but Allie should be here."

I turned to Fran, who, though grinning, still exhibited high nerves.

"Good luck with Maria," I told him. "You, me, and Willem should meet up sometime."

"Of course, man. This can't end here."

I swallowed, nodded, and waved goodbye. My eyes scanned the crowd as my friends left, and instead of spotting a flop of dark blonde hair with a camera, I saw my mother's watered-down red.

"Hi sweetie! How was India?" my mom called as she waved me over.

Dad had his arms wrapped around Kit, whose hair was curling around his ears.

No Allie.

I tried not to let my smile slip, but my heart began to race in my chest. Was something wrong? Why wasn't Allie here? If I missed her this much when she wasn't at the airport, I could imagine how bad losing her would feel when I told her the truth. My conversation with Willem had opened my eyes to Christianity more than Sunday School ever had, and I only hoped it was the saving grace I needed. I didn't want to lose Allie.

"Hi, Mom…" I wheeled my suitcase over.

Mom wrapped her arms around me in a squeezing hug. Kit squirmed in my father's grasp. Neither were happy with the situation, for Dad stared at me with disdain.

"I missed you so much! Seriously, how was your trip?" she asked once she finally let me breathe again.

"It was so good. I'll tell you more about it later."

Like thunder, my dad's voice ripped through the conversation.

"Did your trip to India change your opinion?" Dad asked as he shifted Kit to Mom. I knew what he expected me to say. That he was right. That India was the place to live and that I should be grateful yet sad we immigrated.

But I didn't.

"Yes." Dad tensed his jaw. "For the better sometimes, other times for the worse. But it opened my eyes. And Kerala was beautiful."

Apparently, that was enough to satisfy him.

"Maybe you could sense your roots there. We can go together one day, show you where I grew up."

A genuine offer to return to India, from my dad—the man who acted like I barely existed—no less. I couldn't refuse.

"Yeah… I'd like that."

Mom broke the moment between Dad and I, her face scrunched up, deepening the wrinkles of her forehead. She brushed a piece of her faded red hair behind her ear.

"Allie sends her apologies. She had some last-minute family things. Hannah called and told me." Our mothers had gotten chummy, it seemed.

My stomach tightened. "Samuel?"

"She didn't say—I'm sure it's okay though." Mom hesitated before leaning forward and patting her hand on my shoulder.

I sat with Kit in the backseat on the way home, mostly keeping an eye on him. He blew spit bubbles and giggled, showing them off to me. Too many times, he tried to unbuckle his car seat and crawl over to my lap, but I always stopped him mid-crawl as he giggled. My throat closed at the thought of Navin back in Kerala.

Later that night, Allie called my parents' line to apologize and told me she was at Audrey's. I drove there a bit too eagerly.

At the sound of my name called out from the front door, the corners of my lips upturned. I glanced up to see Allie's face light up as I exited my car. Her cute little ankle was in a walking boot, yet that wasn't what surprised me.

"You cut your hair!" I exclaimed as I hurried to her. Allie's honey hair was cut just above her chin in a sophisticated fashion that reminded me of a French model I'd seen on my mother's camera roll.

Somehow, she was even more beautiful than before. My mind jumbled with some adage about distance and hearts.

Allie stepped back self-consciously and tucked a strand behind her ear as I reached for it.

"What do you think? Cute? Or too middle school?"

I looked at her for a moment before leaning forward to give her a kiss on the forehead, and I was in heaven.

"You're spectacular. Even more gorgeous than before."

Her mouth went agape, perhaps to refute the claim, but I beat her to the punch.

I couldn't imagine how I could miss a pair of lips for so long but considering how desperately I had missed the person attached to them attested for my feelings about Allie.

It felt like only seconds had passed before a high-pitched whistle broke our embrace. Audrey leaned out of a window, staring at us, her glasses creating a bug-eyed look of surprise. I thought momentarily of Daniel, and my grin grew.

"You guys were going fifty-three seconds without breathing. I saved your lives."

We laughed before deciding to take a walk so we could catch up properly, without Audrey's watchful eye.

"I forgot to ask," I began, "what was the family emergency thing?"

Allie covered her hand with her mouth. "Oh, I totally forgot. Essie slipped on some ice—she's totally fine!—" she exclaimed when my mouth went agape. "But I rushed to be with her just in case. They monitored the baby at her hospital in Grand Rapids, but she's home now."

I breathed a sigh of relief. "Well, I'm glad to hear. And glad you're here," I said with a kiss. "I missed you so much while I was in India. Gosh, I can't believe I was in India. It feels like a lifetime ago, but also just yesterday. I haven't really talked about it yet. It still feels surreal."

Allie swung our arms between us. As we walked, she twisted her hips playfully, clearly happy I was home.

"Really? Not even your parents?"

I bit my lip.

"No, not… Not the stuff that really matters." My feet stopped, barely a mile from my house. Was a mile safe enough to say everything I ever thought? It had to be.

I took a breath.

"Allie, I need you to understand something. The relationship you have with your parents is great. But I don't have that with my family. The people I'm closest to are my little siblings, and only because I want to protect them from becoming, well, me." My hand dropped from her grasp, my fingers ran through my hair, nervously. "My parents fell in love, both believing they could convert the other to their religion. I think my mom has given up now… But their differences have always been a source of tension all my life."

"In what way?" Allie asked. Her voice was starting to lift, curious where this was headed.

"Just in little things, you know? Holidays, as I told you, keeping Sundays the Sabbath, my dad's worship, the idols around my house… Every time my dad sees my mom with a Bible he cuts her down with stinging words." I flinched at the reminder of what I dealt with for years. "And every night my dad would ignore my mother and stay up late praying to Krishna while my mom would cry alone in her room."

But she just pressed on, asking, "What about you kids?"

I mistook her question.

"They must still love each other, I guess. Kit's two. I don't, like, *know* what goes on between them, but I think at some points they just get so stressed and mad at each other that their, I guess—passions—come back out."

Allie's face went vibrant red.

"I meant the differences in religions affecting you kids."

Now I was the one blushing.

"Oh. Um... They have a sort of pact that they can't influence the kids one way or another. They choose for themselves. Fatima and Jared and Kit are all too young to decide yet."

I sighed and rubbed my hands together. This was it, this could be the time. But I slowly felt my resolve fading.

"Anyway, my entire house is always tense. Nothing is carefree like yours. Only the younger kids laugh. So, telling my family about my trip to my dad's home country is just a grenade ready for disaster."

I wished I could cut my tongue the moment I said it for how insensitive it was.

Allie looked away.

"I didn't mean it like that..." I reached for her hand, now thinking of Samuel.

Her voice came out softer than I'd ever heard it, a whisper in a thunderstorm.

"I know. It's fine."

Tears stained her cheeks, leaving red rings around her eyes.

"The grenade thing didn't bother me, it's just..." She took a deep breath and closed her eyes. Her eyes batted back and forth beneath her lids, probably overthinking any possible response. A single tear escaped when she looked back up at me.

"My only support in my life has been from my family. I can't even fathom who I would be or where I would be or *if* I'd even be without them." She took a shaky breath and continued. "Then I wouldn't have met you and had the best—what?—not even a year of my life. I can't *imagine* how you feel and the pain you've gone through."

I had to tell her the truth soon. But I selfishly just wanted a few more moments. A few more days of Allie and me before I could risk losing her again.

I pulled Allie close to my chest and pressed a kiss to her forehead. Her breathing was ragged, so I rubbed circles on her back, trying to get her to calm down.

"But Allie, listen, okay?" I whispered, barely loud enough next to her ear. "I'm not in pain. I'm not—I'm used to it. It's my life, and until recently I didn't know how it could be so different. But I'm not sad. I'm grateful that I know there's someone else I can be when I have my own family." I tensed for a moment at the thought. I still pictured Allie in my future, cheering me on at the Olympics, holding our future child in a hospital bed, smiling up at me. If I couldn't have her in those dreams, I wasn't sure I wanted them with someone else.

Allie nodded into my chest, still trying to control her tears.

"And I am completely, undeniably, and unforgivably happy with you, the woman I love."

Allie's eyebrows raised. "B-Ben, you…?"

"I do. I love you, Allison Johncox."

Allie's tears turned into ones of joy, and we kept sneaking kisses in as we walked. I didn't even care that she hadn't reciprocated the words. I knew she felt the same.

We continued on as I talked about India, holding hands—and swinging them once again—but the air was different.

We ended up seated on the bench outside her dorm again.

I tugged her into my arms and reached for the pocket of my parka and pulled out the small wooden elephant.

"I wanted to get you something photography related, but I thought a postcard wasn't special enough."

Allie pressed a kiss to my cheek.

"You know me so well." She snatched the elephant from my hand and studied every inch of the artwork. Her eyes surveyed its golden details painted over the carved wrinkles, the red decorative dressing, and its head staring up at the sky before turning back to me.

"I really love it." Allie pressed her cheek against my chest. "I missed you so much." Her whisper was a tickle that resonated throughout my body. "It feels like nothing has changed. That even after three weeks apart and no talking, we have come back together so seamlessly. We could be apart for thirty years and nothing would change."

But something had. My desires had shifted—to honesty, to wanting to understand God better, the way that Allie did, the way that Willem explained to me. Taking the feud of my parents' expectations out of the equation, I wondered if I could actually find some solace in the faith Allie called home.

"You should meet Willem and Fran sometime," I mentioned. "They're great guys."

Allie's gaze seemed to be looking off in another direction, stuck in a different dimension. When her brain brought her back, she nodded.

"Sounds great."

I dropped Allie back off at Audrey's before heading home.

Spencer was cooking in the kitchen—the smell of garlic bread hit me immediately, and my smile grew. Any other college student would cook ramen for dinner, but not fancy shmancy Spencer. My throat tightened at the thought of graduation looming just months ago, and the end of the era of living with Spencer as well.

My parents had dropped off my luggage and carry-on, but the haphazard treatment meant it was a last-minute thought, and they were laying on the foyer covering the mess of shoes.

I slung the carry-on around my back and walked through the living room to the kitchen.

"Spence," I called out.

My best friend's back did not respond at first. Then, he slowly turned around with a half-smile on his face. Last time we had an in-depth conversation, he and Brennan accused me of not having genuine feelings for Allie.

"Hey, Ben." Spencer set down the wooden spoon he'd been stirring spaghetti sauce with and looked back at me. He crossed one ankle over the other and his arms followed suit. "How was India?"

"It was great—amazing, really," I sped through. "But we can talk about that later. What I really want to tell you is I'm sorry." The words barely registered in my head before they were out, waiting in the space between us.

A pause. Spencer's eyebrows rose.

"What for?"

I sighed, and the words tipped out.

"For everything. I'm a terrible friend, I don't do anything for you. You've always cleaned up after me, helped me when I was hungover, and I never said a single thank you. And I am so, so sorry. This trip has made me realize how awful of a person I've been."

Spencer sighed, as if he knew all of this would come out one day.

"You're not an awful person, Ben. Don't say that—don't even think about it. We're just different. I never expected thanks for what I did. I did it because you're my best friend." Spencer stepped away from the stove. "I don't do things for recognition. These past few years at Mt. Hope, you've been a fantastic friend. You always listen, you give me advice, and you definitely make my days a little more interesting," he chuckled.

I was taken aback. My mind tried to search for a response, but Spencer was too quick.

"You're a good friend, Ben. But if this is part of some self-realization and personal growth thing," he placed a hand on my shoulder, "I'm in."

"I'm trying, I really am, you'll see. I promise—oh, wait," I slang my bag off my shoulder and dug around until I found the jersey. "I got you something in India." Not exactly baseball, but cricket was close enough.

"Thanks," Spencer smiled, staring at the jersey, "but… this?" He motioned between us. "This is better."

As I grabbed my luggage and headed to my room, I turned back to spot Spencer adding more sauce into the pan—enough for two.

Despite not taking the chance to get to know more people in college, I was glad I had at least been able to hold onto the one friendship that mattered so much to me.

32

"Allie works late hours, huh?" Devon asked as the clock was rounding into three in the morning. "What does she do now? This is a little late at night to teach."

Asan chuckled.

"Yes, yes, it is. I'm used to it at this point, but I am getting more concerned with this weather. I love winter, but snow makes me nervous. My love isn't the best winter driver."

"Yeah, me too," Devon agreed. "I-I don't have many other friends except Lindsey, nobody like Willem or Fran or Spencer, even. We got together so early in freshman year, I kind of blocked off all chances of making good friends."

"You play soccer here, though, right?" Dr. Asan queried. "It's been many years since I was on a team sport, but I figured you must have some friends from there."

"I mean, I wouldn't call them close friends," Devon expanded. "They're also part of the party scene—and probably a big reason why I got into it, too. Nobody in my life is there to really ground me, you know?" He sighed. "Ironically, you're the only person in my life that seems to care if I even get out of bed to class on time."

Dr. Asan scoffed. "I'm sure that's not true, Mr. Camburn," he said. "But if so, I really do recommend getting good friends as well, who are your age, not your stuffy professor," he teased.

"I mean, you're not that old, Dr. Asan, what, forty-five?"

"I'm fifty-four," Dr. Asan said with a laugh. "I'll be fifty-five in April. But I appreciate the compliment."

"Are you still connected with those friends?" Devon asked. "Even so many years later?"

Dr. Asan's eyes twinkled once again. If he was tired, his demeanor and body didn't show it. "Willem lives back in Holland, but we visit him every two years or so. Spencer lives in Arizona, but we talk every few months. But Fran?" he chuckled. "Fran and Maria come over every Wednesday for Lasagna Night."

"Sounds like some good friendships," Devon muttered. "I wish I hadn't put all my attention on one person."

Dr. Asan shrugged. "I didn't even meet Willem nor Fran until senior year, and we later found out we even had some of the same classes over the years!" He exclaimed. "You can always find friends, even in the hardest, toughest moments of your life. In fact," he smiled to himself, "those moments may even be the best time."

"Like how you felt in India?" Devon asked.

"Exactly."

33

February-March 1991

I had been hoping for a calm few weeks before classes began, but like life with Allie, it never calmed down. Shortly after coming back to the United States, Essie had her baby.

Allie fell in love with her baby niece immediately. I knew they'd be inseparable.

She showed me pictures on a walk, a few days after coming back from Grand Rapids to visit. Several pictures were just of Mila, in a cute pink onesie, held by her parents. For a moment, I wished it were Allie and me with a baby instead of Essie and Jack.

Allie, holding Mila, grinned. She was a natural. She would make a great mother one day.

We made it back to her dorm as it started to grow chilly.

I hugged Allie to my chest and rubbed her shoulders.

"You cold?"

"Mm..."

"I'll warm you."

With a kiss, Allie smiled, and we parted. She had been talking about Mila the whole walk, I barely said a word.

As the warmer weather came around in March, Allie became so busy with her senior project, we spent less time together except for late-night calls and the occasional kiss before I raced as track season got into full swing.

But on a nice, cool afternoon, my life changed.

Allie stood by the fence to wish me good luck before the race. We drove to one of the Olympic training centers in Michigan. Several other hopefuls stood beside me—we were all hoping to qualify for the trials.

"You're gonna do great, Ben," Allie whispered. "I'll be cheering you on the whole time." She pressed a firm kiss to my lips, and I started to believe her.

"I'm gonna do great."

"Perfect. Just keep saying that, okay?"

With Allie as my rabbit's foot, I hustled over to the third lane. One hundred meters, that's all. I had this. I *had* to have this. I needed to be fast enough—to be good enough.

Then a memory popped into my head from Allie, all those weeks ago when I had mentioned moving to Colorado Springs. The idea made me laugh—how could I ever leave her now? But that's not what stuck with me.

Whenever I see you, you run faster to me than you have in any meet.

I lifted my head up to meet her eyes. Allie waved.

Using her advice, I envisioned Allie standing at the finish line, and my legs sprang out at the sound of the gun. I raced toward the imaginative Allie—I didn't even notice the other guys beside me, nor did I realize once I crossed the finish why everyone was cheering so loudly. The mere force of the screams stopped me in my tracks.

"Ben! Oh, Ben!" Allie screamed. In one moment, she was calling from the stands, and in the next, her beautiful self was tripping over to me.

I nearly toppled over when she jumped into my arms. but I still had no idea what was going on.

Then my eyes caught the scoreboard, shining with my time next to Asan, Ben.

10.03.

I qualified for the Olympic trials. I was one step closer to the 1992 Barcelona Olympics.

I spun Allie and kissed her with such ferocity, it was by grace she didn't fall over.

"I'm going to the trials!" I exclaimed once we parted. Allie slid from my grasp and nodded, tears pooling in her eyes.

"You're going," she whispered.

Tears fell down her face. I reached up to her cheek, to brush her hair aside, but she caught my hand instead.

My stomach dropped, and every red flag went up. My other thumb came up and caught her falling tears.

"What's going on? What's wrong?" Allie must've been upset about what would happen next.

I glanced around the crowd—two other guys had qualified, and their supporters were cheering along with Fran, Willem, Spencer, and Brennan, who had come to support. My parents eagerly talked to a man with a notepad, planning out my future.

But at the moment, I only had eyes for Allie.

"I'm just happy for you," Allie said, but it came out as a whimper. I pulled her to my chest. I decided not to say more. Instead, I let her silently cry as I waved to the roaring crowd, happy and celebratory that Ben Asan had a chance for the Olympics.

Allie took me out to a celebratory dinner. When I offered to pay, she insisted, claiming it was her treat. I didn't fight back. I knew January Ben still had to keep me accountable. I promised myself I would tell Allie the truth soon.

Two days later, after the high of qualifying for trials left, I decided I couldn't put it off any longer. I had to be honest with Allie. But before I could even go back into my room and prep what to say, I paused at the driveway and stared straight at my house.

Was this even allowed? The university owned it. This certainly wasn't, then. But there was Allie, standing on a ladder, painting my house yellow.

Half of the house was already painted yellow, and the door was drying in the sun, with a trim the color of fresh mustard. Allie, humming to herself, was painting my house her favorite color.

"Um, babe?" I called out. "What are you doing?"

Allie smiled and turned around with the brush in hand.

"Your house was such a drab color. It needed a makeover."

Still confused, I stepped up to the rickety ladder and held it for her.

"Did you get permission to do this?" I asked, my voice sounding unsure.

Silence.

"Did you get permission to paint my house, or will I have to pay a fine at the end of the year?" I repeated.

Allie breathed out to bring her back to reality and said, "I made a little deal with President McCarrell. I planted some begonias at *his* house in exchange to paint *your* house." Her left hand held the brush, and she moved it in slow strokes along the exterior. Her wrist bent with every motion, and her eyes scrutinized each speckle until the whole section turned yellow. The sun shone against the bright colors of the house.

"That's an interesting trade," I chuckled. "But, Allie, can we go for a walk? I need to talk to you about something, and it's important."

She plopped the brush into the yellow paint can, and the sound of the wood against tin rang into my ear.

"Sure. Should I be concerned?"

I helped her down the ladder.

"Let's just walk."

My heart was beating so fast I thought it would burst out of my chest. I didn't even know how I would go about this. Despite the many conversations I had in India about changing into a person I was proud to be, nothing had prepared me for admitting my lies to Allie.

Though a million things ran through my head, I couldn't form a single word.

We headed down a familiar path, one we traveled along often, to a familiar spot, where just months earlier, Allie hurt her now healed ankle from sledding. The top of Mt. Hope would be the perfect place.

"Is this seat beside you open?" I teased as we laid down on the edge of the hill.

Allie chuckled and settled beside me. "I think that's your weakest joke yet."

I shrugged and wrapped my arms around her to pull her close. "Guess I've got a lot on my mind is all." I sighed and ran my hands through my hair.

"So, I just need to be honest with you," I began. "We aren't the same." Allie's body immediately tensed beside me, and I let out a long breath.

"You know that Holy Day, Diwali? I-I sort of lost my virginity on that day, when I was sixteen," I said in a scratchy voice. "It's actually the last time I celebrated it. And it was my last time celebrating it as a Hindu."

If I thought Allie had been tense before, she was frozen now.

I wanted to curse and scream and reel those words back into my mouth, but the line got caught. This was not good.

Allie sat up, out of my arms now, and looked out at Mt. Hope, now bathed in afternoon light, but just as beautiful as coated in the black of night.

"Allie, please just—just listen. I know I said the younger kids didn't really choose a religion, b-but I chose early in life. I think I was twelve, or so. My whole family on my dad's side are practicing Hindus—so I felt an immense amount of pressure to do the same," I sighed. "I don't even practice Hinduism any more… After that night, I told myself those gods weren't real, and I didn't believe in them any more…"

Ugh. Bringing that back in. I shut my mouth to prevent myself from digging myself into a deeper hole.

Allie turned, and I gave her a moment to think things through. After a few breaths, she spoke out, facing away from me to the trees lining the base of the hill.

"So, after you weren't a Hindu anymore, when did you come to Christ? Later, right, in college after you were done sleeping around?"

That's when I heard it. The doubt. The worry that had been plaguing Allie. This was something she had thought over, lost sleep over—if I had slept with all these women she had heard rumors about, how did I get to be who I am today, someone who wanted to date her? Someone who went to church with her most Sundays and listened to her read passages of her Bible while being mesmerized at the sound of her voice?

She had figured it out, but I was about to put the nail in the coffin.

"Um, actually, I sort of became an atheist."

Silence before the storm lasted all of the time it took for me to say that word.

"Atheist?" Allie whispered, as if the word belonged to a foreign tongue. She stared forward, utterly unable to speak.

"Allie…" I reached for her hand.

She closed her eyes tight and still did not look at me.

"You're an atheist? After all this time, after I've told you how happy I was to be with another believer, it was all a lie?" The betrayal clearly cut deep.

I looked down at my hands shamefully.

"I didn't ever say that I was or wasn't… I just didn't correct you when you assumed. Which is equally bad. But I didn't do it on purpose," I insisted. "And then when I realized I was in love with you, I was scared to ever tell you. I didn't want to lose you, Allie."

"Lose a chance at sleeping with me, you mean?" she snapped and finally looked over at me. "I *was* right. This really was all this was about." Allie finally stood up with tears running down her face. "It's pathetic." Her voice started to become sharper and hoarse as she fought back her sobs. "I really thought that you…you *liked* me. That you were *like* me. But instead, you *lied* to me." She almost slipped on the edge of the hill as she began to pace as she got more worked up.

I caught her arm.

"I-I never lied…" I repeated.

"But you withheld the truth. You came to church with me. You listened to me sing and talk about things about my faith and nodded like you agreed," Allie spat. "It doesn't matter that you never said it with words. You know I'm someone who cares about actions, and your actions spoke differently."

Allie pushed me away. Her breathing became more labored, but I didn't speak again. I couldn't. I knew I didn't deserve to try and convince Allie. Her eyes were welling with the tears that had been plaguing her more and more lately. I wanted to reach out to her, but I held back.

"You've been an atheist *all* this time?"

Again, I said nothing. I was too afraid—too scared that if I tried to say anything, Allie would pull further away.

"I let you kiss me a-and touch me! And I thought I'd found such a good guy for me, no matter what your past was… None of it mattered because I thought you were feeling ready to change your ways, be more… I don't know what to..." Her mumblings wandered off, making about as much sense as the lies I had told myself about this going well.

I tried my hardest to never make Allie cry. I could almost feel the parts of my heart ripping off with every sob that broke through.

"Does it even matter?" I asked. "You've gotten to know me, the *real* me," I exclaimed. "Shouldn't how I treat you be more important?" I was grasping at straws and we both knew it.

Her tears halted for a moment, and she glared at me.

"It's not just that you're an atheist, I know and love so many," she barked. "It's that you didn't *tell* me," she emphasized. "You led me to believe you were the kind of person I'd want to be with—the kind of person who hit the most important requirement for me. You let me..."

I knew she was right. I knew it in the same way that I knew the clock tower would strike three o'clock soon. In the same way that I knew the moon would rise and the sun would set. But with everything in my soul, I wanted to deny the inevitable.

"What?" I proclaimed. "I let you fall in love with me by being who I am?"

I wanted Allie to scream. I wanted her to feel anger. But all she showed was sadness.

"We're done, Ben. I can't be with a liar." She didn't even give me a chance to speak. When Allie made up her mind, it was serious. She really was stubborn.

In an instant, she turned and left, leaving the words I wanted to say dissolve into the wind.

I sat back on the edge of the hill, and my hands scraped at my hair and neck until I saw blood under my fingernails. I felt increasingly hot even though the early spring weather was chilly. I shuddered when I heard the piercing wail of Allie's cries reverberate in my ears.

She had distracted me. My heart tore at the seams barely keeping me alive. I hadn't even had a chance to tell her about my conversations with Willem and Daniel, that I was toying with the idea of God, if only she would teach me, separated from any pressure from my family.

It was dusk by the time I made my jelly legs move. When I rounded the corner to the house, my heart ached even more; the whole thing was now yellow, with the paintbrush thrusted to the ground, brushing the green grass lighter.

34

April 6th, 1991

Senior year was ending far too quickly, yet every day felt like it dragged on without Allie in my life. Before I knew what had happened, I was twenty-two, and Allie and I had been broken up for over a month.

The night before Allie's senior project presentation, I brought her a coffee from the café in the library. I had kept my distance, but I knew she would be stressing about her deadline.

I had spent multiple nights late at the library with Willem. We had studied the works of C. S. Lewis and N. T. Wright, and he had walked me through the basics of the Gospels. He had gotten me to see through the words on the page to the life that they led. I spotted Allie in the behaviors of Jesus, and I understood now why my deception had hurt her so badly—it had gotten to the core of her being. While I wasn't converted, I was interested, and I hoped to make amends with Allie.

I stepped into the doorway and smiled upon seeing her. She sat, sprawled along the floor of the circular gallery, clipping upside-down photographs into even frames. Her hair was in a little bun at the base of her head, and her finger sat at her lip as she studied the photographs with such intensity it made my heart swell.

"Coffee break?" I offered nervously.

Allie looked up. Her eyes met mine for a moment before she snatched the coffee with a shaky hand. They were already filled with tears.

"Thank you, but please leave," she said, her voice cracking. She winced as she sipped her coffee—burned the roof of her mouth, most likely—and set it aside before craning her neck down and setting a picture into a frame. "We're not together anymore, Ben." She didn't say she didn't want me around, I noted.

"I know," I sighed and scratched the back of my neck. "I just figured you'd need a coffee…"

But Allie just shook her head and continued to ignore me. I waited for a moment—I knew she wasn't good at being rude.

Allie looked up at me briefly.

"I appreciate your kindness, Ben. But I still need my space, please."

I listened to her and left. But I planned on being back tomorrow. I wanted to support her no matter what.

Allie's senior project presentation was in the afternoon at the main art gallery. I was waiting at the door fifteen minutes before it began, watching her walk across the floor and stare up at her photographs, continuing to analyze them on the gallery walls. Above the gallery read "The Celebration of Life." Allie had told me the gist of her senior project idea, but we'd broken up before I'd seen any of the photographs.

My heart swelled seeing Allie again. She wore bright yellow heels and a slimming little black dress. Her short hair was still at her chin, not having grown out much, and clipped half-up.

I wavered, watching her nervously pace, before pushing open the door to the gallery. I was wearing a yellow tie in support.

"Allie..."

She turned and her face fell when she noticed me.

I tried to use the previous night to break the tension, but I wasn't sure how well it worked.

"Ben, please stop..." Allie whispered.

"I'm just here to support you," I explained quickly. "I-I couldn't let this day go by without seeing your project."

Allie's eyes widened in surprise. "Oh... Um, I appreciate it..."

"And... I was hoping we could talk after, just... I have some things I really need to say," I blurted out. "But I didn't want to take away from your big day."

Allie bit her lip and looked up at me before quickly glancing to the ground.

"That was... very considerate of you, Ben." Allie looked back up at the clock. "I'll have to see... I've just got such a busy—"

"Allie, hey!" shouted a voice, interrupting her before she could answer. It came from Chantel, another senior sharing the time slot with Allie for her project. Their reception would be the same, but they had their separate galleries. Piles of frames sat in her arms as she shimmied by, wearing an ankle-length white dress fit for the red carpet.

Allie forced a smile to Chantel.

"Hi, Chan. Have you been working all night?"

"Nah, I've had them under my bed for a week—just kept forgetting to set them up!" she called as she shimmied past us.

I waved to Allie and stepped out to give her a chance to finish getting prepared, hoping she would take me up on my offer after the presentation.

When the doors opened, I hesitated to go inside. I let a few people pass me into the gallery. Their eyes widened, they gasped or laughed, and I even saw someone wiping away tears near the end. Not only did students and family come, but so did citizens of Mt. Hope. I spotted Hannah, Samuel, Essie, Jack, and Mila. Only Jack gave me a half-hearted smile of acknowledgement. I figured Allie had told them about us.

I had my fingers full of chocolate-covered pretzels from the dessert table when my mother walked through the glass doors to the art exhibits with Kit. I forgot that I had invited her months ago.

"Hi," she said as I kissed her cheek.

"How are you?" I began, but Mom saw through my pleasantries.

"Why aren't you inside to support Allie?" she shot as she grabbed some cheese and crackers. She glanced up at me as she waited for an answer and nibbled a whole wheat cracker. I'd avoided the gallery so long that the buttery crackers were all gone.

"Uh, we kinda broke up."

Kit poked at my cheek, creating a dent, and in turn, a smile.

"It's not a big deal," I said hastily.

"Benji! This is a big deal."

"No, but I—"

"Why didn't you tell me?" Mom asked. "I wouldn't have come—I don't want to upset her."

"It's fine," I whispered, hands out to try and calm her, "Allie would want your support. She loves that you understand her on an artistic level. She knows I'm here, and we're going to talk later. I just... I'll go in when I'm ready."

But she took me by the collar instead.

I let Mom believe she was strong as she dragged me into the gallery. I smiled at her effort, and at the doorway, I spotted Allie.

But my eyes quickly focused on something else as I stepped into the gallery to experience life.

To my left, the story began with a baby, whom I recognized as Mila almost immediately. She lay on a bed with a teddy bear beside her.

After a second baby I didn't know, I saw a class of elementary students, and the sight of my brother grinning with his holey smile confirmed who they were.

Lockers from my old middle school flashed at me, as did a few school buses.

Later on were high school students, dressed in their best, laughing and in love.

Then came a picture of Allie's dorm—cleaned up, thankfully—and odd to see in black and white. And in the corner was a shaded hand, which I recognized as my own, waving blurrily at the camera.

Allie stood around the center of the gallery, smiling, and greeting people who hugged her and insisted that her work was good enough for the Chicago Art Institute, The Museum of Modern Art, or The Maison Européenne de la Photographie.

Essie, with a sleepy Mila wrapped around her torso, hugged Allie, her face bright and gushing over her younger sister's work.

As I moved on, I noticed pictures of the familiar Mt. Hope campus. I recognized myself posed and ready to run on the track and a warm feeling bloomed in my chest. Other aspects of the campus followed it, such as the classrooms and dining commons. There was even a photo of last year's graduates tossing their caps in the air.

"Hello again," I said as I walked over to Allie, trying to be casual, although my heart felt like it was about to spill out of my chest.

My eyes just dashed to the end, with a coffin and the cross from church, a symbol of resurrection.

"I love this. How'd you think of it?"

Allie feigned politeness.

"Just kind of came to me."

My eyes fell upon the wedding photos—Essie and Jack, I could tell—and then Essie, pregnant.

"Essie and Mila are in these quite a bit."

Allie glanced over to the newborn photo of Mila.

"Yeah, well, Essie's had more life events, so…"

I shrugged.

"You have all the time in the world."

The pictures grew somber. They aged. Then I stared at my *muttachan*, smiling.

I hadn't expected my family to inspire Allie.

There, at the end, as I saw before, the cross, shining from a spotlight on the stage.

Before, a cross would make me roll my eyes. Now, I was intrigued. Out of politeness, I headed to the other end of the foyer to look at Chantel's project. She painted, and it was beautiful. But as I stared at a realistic painting of a man reading, I found myself yearning for The Celebration of Life.

Mom had found Allie, and they chatted away about the exhibition with Hannah. I kept Kit busy to give my mother a moment of peace.

When the final visitors and family left, wishing Allie good fortune with her work, and waving their compliments, I wandered back over to her.

"You really liked it?" Allie whispered, her eyes focusing over my shoulder. They studied some photographs behind me, but I never asked which ones.

I met her eyes.

"It's tremendous—just like you."

But before I could say anything else, Allie jumped in.

"What do you have to say, Ben?" she said pointedly. Her earlier friendliness had disappeared along with the attendees. It was just the two of us now, and our history reverberated between us.

"I just want to explain. And if you're still mad at me, I will leave. I gave you a month of distance, but I can't do it anymore, Allie. I can't." My voice cracked.

Allie crossed her arms, but her eyebrows lifted in curiosity. Gosh, she was so beautiful. I had nearly forgotten how her presence could make me feel after a month without it.

I looked down at my shoes for a moment to gather my thoughts before saying everything I had been ruminating on for weeks.

"Allie, before you hear anything else, I need to tell you how sorry I am," I started on advice from Willem and

Haley. "I am sorry that I lied to you. I am sorry that I kept information about my life and my past from you. It's inexcusable. But I want to have the opportunity to explain it to you." I looked up. I still had her attention, thankfully. "I will admit, in the beginning, you were just another woman I wanted to sleep with. I knew you were different—you would be hard to catch."

"I've heard enough—"

"Please," I begged, and my voice cracked, "please just let me finish." She bit her lip in silence.

"I'm not proud of myself. I'm not proud of how I've treated women in the past. I was selfish and immature. But when I met you? You… you have enchanted me, Allie, right from the start. You are kind, caring, and confident. You are so sure of who you are because you know that God has created you to be exactly as you are. And it's admirable. It's attractive." I admitted. "Allie, you are the most attractive woman I've ever known just from your personality. But your looks help, too."

Allie's cheeks blushed involuntarily, but her expression still looked stern.

"I know you've been hurt. I know your past, and I don't ever want to hurt you again. I am so sorry for lying to you. But once we were together, I was so afraid to lose you, like… like now." I ran my hands through my hair and made eye contact again. I took a few steps forward, and tentatively reached for her hand. She hesitated for a second, then took it. I prayed she still cared for me.

"I'm never going to be able to live down the fact I lied. And I know I'm not the type of guy you imagined being with. But, Allie, after my trip to India… I've never been more unsure about the existence of God—in a good way. And if you'll have me, I want to try and learn. Teach me what you love about him. Help me to understand. And have me back. Please."

My hand traveled up to stroke her cheek. She stared at me with watering eyes.

"I-I don't know what to say, Ben…" She stepped back from me, and her eyes met mine. "C-can I think about it?"

I didn't expect that. Honestly, I was hoping for a fairy-tale ending. I stepped back as well.

"S-sure. Yes, of course. Please, think about it." It was better than an outright no, at least.

I'd hoped this would have gone better, but I wanted to respect Allie. I knew it was a lot to think about. I just hoped she would decide quickly—I hated being in this purgatory.

I was halfway toward my house when the sound of feet hitting the pavement caught my attention.

I looked over my shoulder, and there was Allie. One hand carried her yellow heels. The other clutched her pinned up hair. She was doubling over, catching her breath. I smirked, remembering how little of a runner Allie was.

"Was that enough time to think?" I asked cautiously. Maybe I had forgotten something at the gallery. I felt in my pockets, but nope, I had my wallet and keys.

Allie slowly stood up as her breathing slowed back to normal. She took a deep breath, her eyes tightly shut, then her body relaxed in a sigh. She caught my gaze.

"No more lies?" Allie whispered.

I nodded. "No more lies. I'm willing to learn. I want to grow. And I want to grow with you, nobody else."

I reached for her hand, and she let me take it. She even squeezed it.

"Okay," she whispered, so quietly I thought I had misheard her.

"Okay?!" I exclaimed. I wasn't ready to believe it.

Allie nodded but it took mere seconds for me to embrace her. She melted into my arms, and I held her as she released the tension through her tears. I hadn't thought how hard this month had been on her. She had held such a strong front, but it seemed she had missed me just as much as I did her.

"I love you, Allie," I said for the second time and kissed her forehead, cheek, and lips. "I love you, I love you, I love you. And I am forever sorry."

I would proclaim my love forever. I wasn't going to mess this up again. I was all in.

35

May 10th, 1991

Allie sat hunched over her education textbook, studying for her final exam, while simultaneously tapping her foot to "December 1963" playing from her stereo. I was laying across her bed, watching her jive to the faint music, and I reminded myself of how lucky I was. After a month away from Allie, I couldn't get enough, and we slowly settled back into our old routines over the last few weeks.

Allie rested back for a five-minute break, and I stepped over and kissed her cheek.

"You look so beautiful tonight," I cooed, but Allie groaned. "What?" I asked.

"It's this—this stupid practice test. I keep going over and over it, erasing my answers and restarting but…" she sighed and took a fistful of her hair. "I can't remember the answers."

Allie had been more stressed since we got back together. I had never seen her so frustrated every day. She had nearly failed a test last week, chalking it up to nerves as her college education came to a close. But I tried my best to support her however I could.

Allie had taken her practical exam for her Elementary Education degree earlier that day, where she thought she did well.

"Just think about how you would answer the test as if you were in a classroom," I suggested. I snuggled my head up to hers, but she pushed me away.

"It's not that easy, okay? I know you're trying to be sweet, but it's distracting. Leave me alone." Allie stopped her break early and pushed back into her work.

So, I sat listening to Frankie Valli and the Four Seasons, not saying a word. After twenty minutes of watching Allie sweat over her final and mouth the lyrics, I stood up and swayed over to her.

My hand found her waist and pulled her up.

"Ben, what are you doing?" Allie exclaimed.

"Dancing with you, of course," I teased and pulled her into my arms as we swayed together for a moment.

But only for a moment.

"Ben, stop. I really need to focus," Allie pleaded and sat back in her desk chair. Before, she would have laughed and joined me, even if just for a moment. Now, she just sighed.

"Why don't you just—"

"Why don't *you* just go run!" she barked.

"Allie, I—"

"Just go!"

I didn't know what was wrong with her, but I did what she asked me to. I swore, and I didn't care to hear her call after me as I slammed the door. Allie's muffled cries of discomfort put my hair on end, and I nearly turned back then just to hold her and let her cry. But I turned and stalked off. If she wanted to stress herself into infinity she could, but I wasn't going to subject myself if she wanted space.

Then Allie wanted me as a handkerchief the next day. So, I stood there, as she cried over how awfully she'd done and how she'd never be a teacher after that, while I held her to comfort her.

Once she was watered out, I suggested talking to her professor and felt her absence when she nodded, wiped the snot from her nose, and pulled herself out of my arms to go do so.

Later that night, Allie called me, sounding brighter. She passed with no reason to worry.

"I'm so sorry I'm so back and forth lately. I didn't think I'd be so stressed about it all," Allie admitted.

"It's okay. Finals are a stressful time," I reassured her. "I'm here for you, always, Allie."

I let myself feel happy, relieved to be back with Allie after everything. I let my frustration about how Allie had been pushing me away subside. She was stressed and struggling, so I just needed to be there, like I knew she would be there for me.

Graduation from college felt so different than graduating from high school.

First off, I knew I would want to see these people again. Most of my friends from high school I didn't speak to after we crossed that stage. But I knew I would seek out Fran, Willem, Spencer, and even Brennan.

And there was Allie.

In high school, graduation is a sign of independence. You have an open house, partying over the fact that you're going to Whatsoever School, majoring in

Something You'll Probably Change But Woo! Let's Go College!

After you graduate college, there's no big party, and you're filled with fear of either more college or attempting to merge into the real world with piles of student loan debt.

Graduation in both ways unraveled regrets. Regrets of never going to the after-prom party or regrets in not studying abroad.

But my regret was far different.

I regretted not knowing Allie earlier. Not changing my behavior to women from day one. I wished I'd gone to India sooner.

I expressed my regrets to Spencer as we got dressed on that sunny Saturday morning the day of graduation. I secured my tie before putting on my graduation gown and cap that mussed up my perfect hair.

"You don't have to leave. You could become a resident director. That would be fun. Or you can get your Master's here."

I shrugged and tried to fix my hair back to acceptable.

"I know, but it won't be the same."

Spencer shrugged in agreement and turned back to the refrigerator. He checked off a box on the To-Do list whiteboard he kept. Next to the tick mark said 'graduation.'

Maybe he felt the same uneasiness as me. Four years was enough time to get situated in one spot. Even being on campus was different than growing up in town. I was comfortable here, now I even yearned to stay and soak up everything Mt. Hope University could give me in the last few hours.

So, we walked slowly through the crowded streets to the field house, the only building big enough for graduation. It was void of its normal stench of sweat and feet, and the gym had been cleaned up more than I had ever seen it.

During graduation practice, we lined up alphabetically by degree type. I headed over with the Bachelor of Arts degrees. Spencer departed to catch up with the Bachelor of Science ones.

Graduation began at noon. As we processed, my eyes wandered, trying to find my family in the crowd. Once we sat, I spotted Mom, smiling and waving to me with Dad by her side. Kit was squirming, but for once, Mom didn't look stressed. Fatima and Jared were the first to catch my gaze, and they waved so enthusiastically I was worried Jared's flapping wrist would break.

By the time President McCarrell reached the podium, I had forgotten to look for Allie.

"Welcome to the graduation of Mt. Hope University's Class of 1991. Today we are here to celebrate these great minds and people and congratulate them on these past few years of achievements." A pause as his hand slipped up to tighten his tie. "Each class is special in their own way. But this year, I must say, has astounded me." McCarrell then continued to rattle off a list of names, and I was disappointed not to hear Allie's name in there.

"And let us not forget our future Olympian, Ben Asan, hopeful to compete at the Barcelona Olympics next summer!" The crowd applauded at my achievement, and my chest puffed out.

When McCarrell ended with a reference to the women's soccer team, the board members stood, and the mountain of diplomas all numbered and ready, filled me with anxiety.

My last moment at Mt. Hope University was here, and I wished my surname started with Z.

"Andrea Michelle Affen," the girl two people before me stood and walked up to the stage to receive her degree.

"Cory Anthony Anderson."

My palms began to sweat, and I felt my chest tense up.

"Benji Mustafa Asan."

Like flipping a switch, my nerves shut off, and I shakily moved forward. The girl behind me gave me a little push of encouragement.

A diploma. Check. A handshake and a smile toward the parents and camera. Check. The steps we had practiced now whirred around me, and I moved through them like a robot.

President McCarrell leaned into me, and his voice rang in my ears.

"You're going to do great things."

With a clap on my back, I jerked my body forward and to the spot to get a professionally taken shot with my diploma, then back to my seat. I sat, pondering over what McCarrell told me. It reminded me vaguely of Mark and Heather's staunch beliefs I could be a world changer.

The audience clapped politely, but every so often, a few people whooped and hollered for their best friends and family members. So, when Spencer went up, I shouted his name. When Fran received his degree, I heard Willem's cheers from behind and followed suit.

Allie went up the stairs with a wide smile upon her face. It was nice to see her back to her usual cheery self, the weight of finals being over meaning she was no longer irritated or stressed.

I took a deep breath, thinking through my plans with Allie for the day.

After graduation, her family was treating us to lunch at Red Lobster, but before then, I was going to surprise Allie with a visit to my house, and there I'd tell her my news.

Allie walked back, one hand on the railing and her other hand juggling her the black leather case holding her degrees. I wanted to pick her up and kiss her then, but "Emma Leigh Johnson" was crossing the stage.

I clapped for her and urged Allie to catch my gaze, but she waved to her parents instead, sitting in the front row of the bleachers where Samuel could wheel up.

Graduation lasted another hour, and I sat, wriggling impatiently in my seat, clutching my diploma.

When McCarrell finally said his last words and dismissed us, Allie ran over to me. I thought how funny we all were, that all the money we spent, time that passed, worries that plagued us, all boiled down to a sheet or two of thick, bound paper.

"I did it!" Allie exclaimed. She flung her arms around me for a kiss, and I had to hold her up from falling against my body. Her boisterous energy almost toppled me over. "I did it—I'm gonna be a teacher! Well, I have to pass my licensing exam first but then I will be!"

I closed my eyes and breathed a sigh of relief.

"Yeah, you will. Congrats, love." I pressed a kiss to her cheek before letting Allie slide back to the ground.

Straining my neck, I spotted the Johncox family rushing over with smiles on their faces.

Hannah embraced her daughter and I heard, through her muffled voice, "Oh, Allie baby, I'm so proud of you!"

Samuel waited his turn, a smiling, proud father.

"Congratulations, Ben," he said as he caught my eye. Making sure Allie wasn't noticing, he leaned forward and whispered, "Have you told her yet?"

I shook my head.

Samuel knew about the surprise—he had basically arranged it. I had rented an apartment in Petoskey to be near Allie while she worked, and I trained for the upcoming Olympic trials.

"She'll love it," Samuel mouthed before wheeling over to Allie for a hug.

"Ben, oh, I'm so happy!" cried my mom as she walked over, her eyes shining with tears. Kit sat uncomfortably in my dad's arms with Fatima and Jared playing tag circling behind him. My mother's smile brightened her face, giving way to a glimpse of the old light of youth in her eyes.

My father gave me a nod of approval.

Our mothers insisted on taking close to ten thousand pictures of Allie and me decked in cap and gown. We spent most of the time darting our gazes between the cameras, trying to figure out if the clicks came from Hannah's or Mom's.

"Now, with no gowns on!" Mom exclaimed, and I was glad to hear Allie's own groan of relief matching mine as we removed the heavy black gowns.

We smiled for the cameras, and my impatience drew me to kiss Allie, leaving our mothers' gasping in awe.

When our families had dispersed, I turned to Allie.

"Hey…"

"We're meeting at Red Lobster, right?" she asked as her eyebrows rose.

Every part of her drove me mad with adoration.

"Actually," I began and pulled her closer, "could you come by my house before your family meets us there?"

"Can my parents come?"

"Of course."

My hands were sweating as I drove home, following my parents. Allie and her family were behind me, and I had to force myself to watch the road and not Allie's reflection.

When we pulled into the driveway, I parked and took a deep breath. I saw in my rearview mirror Hannah helping Allie get out of the car, and they were whispering together. My nerves were growing with each moment that passed, so I got out and made my way over.

Allie smiled at me, and my heart rushed with affection like lightning.

"So, why are we here?" Allie asked as we walked toward the front door.

"You'll see—"

We only took a few steps up to the porch, then Allie's grip slipped from mine.

My body knew that something was wrong before my mind. Allie's absence triggered a reflex, and I spun around. My eyes gazed down at hers, staring blankly at nothing.

Her body twitched, shook, shivered. As she fell and hit the bottom step, a line of dark red led from the back of her beautiful blonde head to the ground. I stared frozen, mouth agape, at my convulsing girlfriend.

In the distance, across some canyon, Hannah screamed.

"Not again!"

The Johncoxes rushed forward with Olympic speed, but I was still in slow motion. I melted into the staircase as my voice broke out, crying her name. Hannah held Allie's face in the hands of both a nurse and mother, and my eyes widened in horror from her to Samuel. His shoulders slumped forward, and the color drained from his face.

The time between the call and the ambulance's arrival spanned my lifetime. I crouched by Allie, clutching her pale hand, watching her body seize with such force. Hannah did her best to keep Allie safe by turning her to her side.

I stroked Allie's palm slowly trying to stay calm even if inside I was freaking out about what was happening.

When the ambulance pulled into the driveway, I could spot the nosy neighbors trying to not seem like they were looking out at the commotion.

The EMTs raced over, and soon Allie had on an oxygen mask. They strapped it to Allie's face so forcefully it must have bruised. I wanted to yell and scream, to let them know that her face was sensitive, that didn't they know about the time the bees stung her face so much it swelled? But they were doing their job so efficiently I stepped back to let them work. My eyes focused on Allie; now shivering like it was freezing, was like a rag doll to them as they hoisted her moving body into the back of the ambulance.

The sirens wailed, and I followed in my car as we passed through every red light like a funeral parade.

I sat in the ER with Hannah and Samuel beside me, holding hands, whispering to each other. Before I could stop myself, I interrupted them. I needed to know something, anything, and they clearly knew what was happening.

Hannah told me this was Allie's third seizure. The doctors had hoped it would stop.

I called Willem, Fran, Spencer, and Brennan from the payphone.

Willem prayed Bible verses for me and for Allie. I wasn't sure how I felt about it but accepted it all the same.

Fran tried to tell me jokes to make me feel better.

Spencer tried to help me think through the situation logically and assured me Allie would be okay. He insisted on bringing some food for me, but I declined. My stomach wouldn't be able to handle it.

Brennan wanted updates to send to the family and promised he would be up there as soon as he had finished dinner with his parents. I had forgotten they were all celebrating graduation, just like we were supposed to.

Brennan came to the hospital later that evening with his parents to check in with his aunt and uncle. Hannah's sister provided her comfort and a coffee.

Jack sat in the car with a sleeping Mila while Essie paced in the waiting room. She and I made eye contact every few moments. She had been the one to tell me everything. The diagnosis. The treatment. The probabilities. Everything the doctors had explained to them over the last few months.

By one in the morning, I was caught up on Allie's medical history, and she was moved to the seventh floor of a special care unit. And I finally got to see her.

The hospital gown made her washed-out face gleam whiter. An oxygen mask still covered her nose, and her lips were breaking and bleeding. Her beautiful eyes stayed shut, but they fluttered ever so often. I sat forward in my chair, hoping she'd wake up.

Her hair was shaved short and wrapped in tons of gauze with wires poking out beneath the bandage. My stomach twisted when she had another scar that was still healing.

Everything had a purpose, but the tubes ticking out of her arms and the monitors around her made me feel sick. How was this the Allie from merely twelve hours earlier, proudly exclaiming her excitement to begin a teaching job? How was the same girl I had kissed, hugged, and rejoiced with then now lying on a hospital bed, looking as if she had been admitted for months, not mere minutes?

I wanted, every time a nurse came in to administer a new IV medication, just to jump up and scream, tell them to leave Allie alone, and rip the tube from her bruising hand. Hadn't they seen she'd gone through enough? What would her students say when they saw those dark, staining bruises?

But I just sat, gave a half-hearted smile to the nurse, and they'd shoot back a sympathetic nod and turn their back to check her vitals. And with every concerned nurse's face leaving her room, I felt worse.

They suggested I could perhaps rub Allie's feet or move her legs around until she awoke.

My hands ran over her bristled legs and bent and straightened her knees. My palms pushed along the arch of her foot, running along the slopes of her metatarsals, and down the bottoms to her heels. The steady inhale and exhalation of her breathing kept me going.

It was around seven in the morning when she finally woke up. Hannah had curled up in a corner—her eyes enlarged through a pair of glasses that aged her greatly—and was filling out a sudoku she'd bought from the hospital gift shop. None of us had slept.

Hannah's voice, quiet from lack of use, gasped when Allie began to cough.

My thumb pressed the nurse call button as if it was a well-known reflex. In moments, two nurses were around Allie, supporting her from the back and sides as she threw up into a basin at her feet.

A third nurse entered with an oral prescription, and Allie threw up half of it before being given IV medication.

I stepped back by the windows, watching with eyes wide and a hand cupped against my mouth. Hannah and Samuel stared at the scene, wordlessly. That left me more unsettled than anything. They watched Allie as if she'd been in a hospital bed for the past year, like it was just another normal day watching their daughter throw up in a plastic bin. It was all so new for me, though I knew it would not be soon, just like it was not to them.

When all Allie could vomit was stomach acid, she sank back in her bed and let out a scream. She howled in pain, and I was reminded of a lone wolf, straying from the pack, and crying out in refuge.

The vultures swarmed her, so when I got to holding Allie's hand again, she was skin and bones, so weak she could not speak.

"Allie…" I whispered and kissed her forehead. The nurses had replaced the oxygen mask, which had before been covered in vomit, and it misted with condensation with each breath Allie took.

Her face relaxed, and her lips formed a weak smile; her eyes spoke the most. They watered and darted around my face. Mine moved with them, following her gorgeous hue.

I laughed at this ridiculous situation, ignoring the tears in my own eyes. Allie tried, but it came out as a wheeze. I didn't have a care in the world. Our foreheads gently pressed together, and after a moment, I kissed her mask. Just us. The room we were in—the building our bodies occupied—didn't matter.

Samuel cleared his throat and shifted in his chair. Our moment broke, and I glanced back to Allie's father, who watched his daughter with tear tracks marking his face.

"Ben, I think you should get some breakfast, maybe check-in with your parents? You've been up all night."

I didn't even think to fight him.

My knees cracked as I stood, and I gave Allie's palm one last kiss before heading to the elevator. I tried not to focus on what they were talking about behind closed doors.

The mess hall was only on the second floor, but the journey lasted much longer because the elevator picked up passengers on every floor. We all emptied out at the cafeteria. A few were hospital staff grabbing breakfast after a long shift. One other was a frazzled man, perhaps an expectant dad grabbing food after hearing his wife scream for hours. And then there was a middle-aged woman who looked as if she was only eating because she had to.

I related the most to her. A single fruit cup sat in the refrigerator, so I grabbed that and a piece of burnt toast.

Nurses and doctors moved around in groups, chatting, eating, not even thinking about the several lives balanced on their shoulders. One moment, and a life was gone. And it was just another day to them.

I longed to scream at them, to all of them to go to my Allie, to devote all their time to healing her. Food could come later but all that mattered was Allie and her health.

I stared down at my meager breakfast, but I couldn't find the energy to take a single bite. I threw it all away, and although nauseated at the thought of all the machines and tubes five floors above me, I needed to be with Allie.

36

June 2nd, 1991

"Good morning, Ben," Karen, the receptionist on the seventh floor, greeted me. "Begonias today?"

I nodded down to the small bouquet in my hand. "She grew them herself. Thought they'd like to meet their planter now that they've bloomed."

Karen smiled politely. "That's very kind, Ben, but I'm afraid flowers aren't allowed in patient rooms, remember?"

I had totally forgotten. I looked around, unsure what to do with the bouquet in my hands.

"I can keep them here by the desk, and she can see them on her walks?" Karen suggested.

"Thank you, that would be great," I said and handed her the flowers, though my gaze lingered. There were so many little rules it was so hard to keep track of them all.

I stepped into Allie's private room, number 730. They'd moved her around a few times in the three weeks she had been at Flower City Hospital. First, to a semi-private room, but the other patient complained about a lack of privacy—that definitely had *nothing* to do with her roommate's ever-present boyfriend—and Allie was then moved to a smaller single room.

My knuckles drummed the door lightly.

"She's bathing, Ben. Give us a few minutes?" called her nurse.

I bit my lip.

"Of course."

It happened every day. After I went to bed, I'd forget how dependent she'd become. My initial excitement to see her would be deflated when I remembered how she couldn't even use the bathroom on her own now. The once vibrant, energetic body Allie lived in was now a shell of what it once was.

I stood awkwardly, glancing around at the gray-speckled walls of the hospital hall as I heard through the door the faint sound of a soaked towel against skin and a squeeze out of soapy water.

I tried not to picture it.

"We're all set. Come on in!"

My hand gripped and turned the brass knob with ease. As I shut the door, I clicked the knob to the right to keep it in place, something I'd learned the second day that unless so, the door popped back open.

Allie sat up with oxygen tubes coming out of her nose attached to a tank. She insisted she didn't need them, but the doctors assured her the last thing they needed was for her to hyperventilate. Sometimes, when we were alone, I slipped the tubes off and let them breathe oxygen into the atmosphere.

"Hey," I began, and the word stretched itself into my smile. My lips pressed softly to the top of her bald head, and I sniffed. "Peach body wash today?" I missed the lemons.

"They keep shaving my head for my EEGs," she began, "but I insist on still smelling good."

"You smell great and still look beautiful."

Allie's face flushed, and I pecked her lips before she could protest my compliment.

Her nurse, Paula, stepped over to the patient board and uncapped a pink erasable marker.

"Now, Allie, how are you today?"

Allie flitted her eyes over to Paula, standing, waiting with her marker tip in preparation to circle one of the several emoticons depicting various feelings of pain.

"Um…maybe the face with a straight smile, not up nor down. Just kind of uncomfortable, right?"

I smirked at Allie's rhetorical question; she spoke as if Paula knew how she felt. Despite her physical body losing strength each day, Allie's mind had not suffered from the latest seizure as badly as the doctors anticipated.

Paula nodded and circled the number five emoticon. Next, the marker hovered over the notes section of the board, where the doctor could check for any changing symptoms.

"And the migraine?" Paula asked.

"What migraine?" I snapped, glancing between Allie and her nurse. "When did this happen?"

Allie sighed and shifted her gaze to the windows.

Paula turned on her nurse-mode, spitting out information.

"Allie woke up in the middle of the night with a migraine near her frontal lobe. She was administered a strong pain reliever, and then fell back asleep."

I swiveled and stared at Allie, though she avoided my eyes.

"Your *frontal* lobe?"

Her head jerked around, her eyes glaring red with tears pooling.

"Don't stare at me like it's my fault!" she barked, clearly trying to cover up the fear we both felt. "And it's been feeling better!"

My eyes narrowed, but Paula rushed over to Allie. She reached for a damp cloth and ran it along Allie's forehead. It was already sweating.

"Take deep breaths. Deep breaths..." When Allie's face stopped flushing, Paula turned to me.

"Dr. Culver ordered another MRI," Paula added. Allie groaned—she hated getting MRIs. She always complained about how claustrophobic she was.

"It might be nothing, right?" I asked, more worry in my voice than I had wished to show.

Paula smiled kindly.

"Might be."

"Could.... If it.... Could that be why she lashed out?" I whispered to Paula as she checked Allie's monitors for anything abnormal for her condition.

"I didn't lash out!" Allie shouted defensively. I guess I hadn't whispered quietly enough.

But Paula pressed the washcloth back to Allie's forehead until she had calmed down, then turned to me and nodded.

My eyes ran along the bed, staring at Allie's body. It was so different from just months ago. She'd gained about thirty pounds due to the effects of her metabolism.

Her face seemed fuller, and her stomach acted like a cyst; each day it expanded more, bloating without reason.

Although Allie had physically changed, whenever I saw her, I saw *her*. The Allie from a year ago—driving up to her house with an Army hat on, dancing in the gas station, my personal ray of sunshine, the girl in yellow who lights up every room…

I had promised myself to be with her always.

"Okay, heart rate is going down… Breathe, Allie, breathe…. There you go—much better." Paula watched the monitor as she spoke and stroked Allie's hand.

Paula was a sweet nurse, but she had been a nurse for several years in this field. She knew the right amount of relationship to give to her patients and their families.

Visiting hours started at 7 a.m. They ended, at least in Allie's case, at 10 p.m. When she was first admitted, they were lenient on it, but after Allie stabilized, the rules were set in place. Initially, I asked to get an extension.

"She's at therapy from one until four, and I'm not allowed back there. Could I stay until eleven, at least?" I had asked the manager of the wing. But policies were policies.

So, I woke up at five every morning, ran for twenty minutes, then drove to the hospital. I'd wait outside her wing, ten, maybe fifteen minutes before Karen let me in at exactly seven on the dot, and I'd sprint down to Allie's room and give her a kiss.

Some mornings Allie wouldn't be awake. I'd sit in the chair at the front of her bed, waiting for the sun to greet her.

I had only grown more curious about life and the life hereafter while vigil at Allie's bedside.

Often, I wouldn't notice Allie waking until she stirred, and my head would snap up to see her first movements of the day.

Allie had stared back at me one morning, while her parents were getting some breakfast, and I was alone with her. I didn't mind sharing my time with her, but when Hannah and Samuel were around, time with Allie wasn't the same.

"Ben," she had called out. "Can you read to me?"

I would do anything for her, and when she asked me to read, I knew what she meant: her Bible.

"*'Now if we are children, then we are heirs – heirs of God and co-heirs with Christ, if indeed we share in his sufferings in order that we may also share in his glory. I consider that our present sufferings are not worth comparing with the glory that will be revealed in us. For the creation waits in eager expectation for the children of God to be revealed. For the creation was subjected to frustration, not by its own choice, but by the will of the one who subjected it, in hope that the creation itself will be liberated from its bondage to decay and brought into the freedom and glory of the children of God.'*"

Allie's eyes had begun to water, and I put my Bible aside. I rested my knee upon her bed and pushed myself closer to her until my lips pressed against hers. Her tears fell in multiple tracks, racing down to her quivering chin. I pushed one along the edge of my finger, and it traveled down my knuckle.

She didn't say what was on her mind.

Allie often encouraged me to leave her and go run. I wanted to stay and hold her.

"You need to go to Colorado Springs," she had argued another day when I dismissed it.

"I'm staying here until you leave."

"Ben! This is your shot!"

"But I'd rather be here." My thumb ran the length of her palm, and I pressed a single kiss to the soft pad of her skin. "And I'm still training. I will go to Barcelona."

Allie had glanced away but hadn't moved her hand away.

"You shouldn't keep coming here."

I couldn't think about the worst-case scenario. I wouldn't let myself. I wanted to be one of the first people to welcome Allie home from the hospital, and I couldn't do that from Colorado Springs.

As I watched Paula lull Allie to sleep with the washcloth, I thought back to my response.

"But I want to."

37

June 29th-July 2nd, 1991

Allie went for a walk around the ward after complaining that her legs felt heavy.

My arm acted as Allie's crutch, yet she initially declined, as stubborn as ever. However, when we stepped onto a ramp and she stumbled, I caught her immediately and she clung to me like a handrail. Actually, she called me her *muscular* handrail.

We walked along the halls chatting, like we had done when we first met. Allie had two drips on wheels that followed her. I pushed along the rolling IV pole and held Allie's hand that wasn't infested with tubes. After three more failed attempts of getting food to stay down, Allie had elected for a tube down her nose, now feeding straight into her stomach.

"Wait, we can't go this way," Allie paused in her tracks, and the IV pole and I jerked forward. Her face was drained with color.

"Okay, why not?"

She pointed to a sign: Caution, MRI Zone.

I nodded and turned to latch my arm with her other one in a regal manner.

"Of course. Let's circle around a few more times, then maybe it'll be bath time." Sometimes I'd catch myself saying things like this and would realize it sounded like I was speaking to a child whose parents had asked me to babysit. We would play for a bit, then bath time, and I'd sneak her a few tastes of ice cream before tucking her into bed and collecting my pay.

How quickly our relationship had changed. At points, my heart sank when I thought of what Allie and I had been doing just a year ago. Talking twice a day, giggling about our childhood and embarrassing memories. Almost a year ago I had visited for the Fourth of July. I caught myself thinking when the last time Allie had even seen her dog, Linus, was. I wondered if he missed her, or if he could sense something was wrong.

I sat in a chair in the hall when Allie took baths. The nurses bustled around, sharing laughs with one another. The nurses had got used to me always being at the hospital during visiting hours and sometimes we'd chat a little as they headed for their breaks.

Kevin, a nurse with spiky blonde hair, had twin daughters in second grade. Tracy, her pregnant belly ever-growing, was working for a few more months before moving to California with her husband. Susanne had retired last year, but after finding that she wasn't patient enough to keep a garden, she came back to the hospital with open arms and enthusiastic hugs.

Today, Kevin sat in the nurse's station, swallowing a sandwich wholly—he never took long breaks. He waved to me, and I waved back.

"Bath time already?"

I wondered how much practice it took for them to be so casual about the daily ways of hospital life.

"We went for a walk because Al was feeling a bit stiff. She's taking a bath now and the physical therapist is rubbing out her muscles." I tried to give a weak smile, but the corners of my mouth didn't seem to want to lift.

"It's about time she'd start feeling stiff," Kevin said as he nodded understandingly.

I bit my lip.

"What do you think, Kevin?"

"Honestly, I'm not paid the big bucks. I don't have the official word," he replied and bit back into his sandwich.

I rubbed my eyes and nodded. Gosh, I was exhausted. Seeing Kevin devore his sandwich, my stomach grumbled. When did I last eat?

"I get it, but…unofficially? From what I've asked you about when you took care of her last week…?"

Kevin gave a simple shrug as he swallowed down what looked like the ham and cheese sandwich from the cafeteria fridge.

"I've seen what you might classify as miracles happen before. So, I wouldn't stop sending good vibes to the stars." Kevin rolled the cling wrap up into a ball and dunked it to the waste basket behind the nurse's station desk.

"Or prayers to God," I whispered. The faith and hope that Allie impressed in me was starting to take root.

Two days later, Allie stared at the walls in her room, her nose pinched, her eyes scrutinizing the room.

"Everything here is so… so… so," she struggled to speak. Allie closed her eyes, swallowed, and my chest hurt. Her eyes looked glazed over when she opened them.

Her mouth gaped, and finally, through her struggle to form one word in her mouth, she breathed out, "plain," as if it had taken her the energy to light a house to emit a spark.

I pointed to the drawing my brother Jared had made for her.

"It's very colorful there."

But she just rolled her eyes.

"When therapy is done, I promise it won't be plain." I'd had an idea, prepared to do anything to help cheer Allie up and make the room brighter.

Once Allie headed off to therapy, I drove into Flower City.

Even as I walked through the store, excitedly grabbing the supplies for the surprise, my stomach twisted, wishing Allie was beside me, laughing over the ridiculous names for yellow paint.

With the supplies in hand, I draped my sweatshirt over them and headed back to the hospital. When I got to Allie's empty room, I dumped the paint cans and brushes on the floor and got to work.

After my legs became too sore to get up and down off the chair to grab the paint can, I let it hang from the crevices in my fingers.

I was not an artist. The trees—with leaves that were far too big for the branches—and the fence that was much too short proved that. The sunset, I must admit, was the highlight, a beautiful mixture of purples, oranges, and yellows, like a sea of bursting light.

Then the door opened.

"Ben—!"

"Oh, Ben, what are you doing?"

Allie was sitting in a wheelchair—therapy now left her too weak to walk back—smiling, her eyes watering and roving around, trying to soak up my sad attempt at a mural before it was gone.

"Oh Ben, you can't paint hospital walls," Paula gasped, stepping forward to inspect my handiwork. I surrendered the brush with a smile on my face. If Allie loved it, half-finished as it was, that was enough for me, even if it couldn't stay permanently.

But Paula caught Allie's gaze of pure joy and her shocked expression softened. "Well… I guess it'll have to dry before we can do anything…" She chewed her lips. "I didn't see anything if someone asks," she said and winked at Allie before leaving us.

When the door was shut, I turned around to face the painting and wheeled Allie closer to it. I stood in silence for a while, then Allie grabbed my hand. Her grip was growing weaker, and I had to be careful with her bruised hand.

"This looks familiar…." she whispered, and my heart sank. "But… is it a memory?"

I dropped her hand and nodded.

"Well, sort of. It's a place." I stepped up to the mural and turned to face her. "We were on our first date, and the sunset was beautiful. You ran down to the fence in front of the track, and I helped you up to get a picture, but—"

"The Sunset That Got Away," she whispered in realization. "My camera was out of film."

I closed my eyes in thanksgiving, beating back tears that were forming in my eyes. She remembered.

"Yes, yes. You remember?" But when I opened my eyes, Allie was just staring at the floor in horror.

My arms wrapped around her immediately.

As she sat, and I held her, she whispered, pleading, murmuring, "I forgot.... I forgot.... I forgot..."

I just stroked her cheek until she calmed down, until the tear stains on my shirt dried, until her shaking ceased. My forehead pressed against hers, and the uneven surface swirled my insides.

"Maybe you did for a moment," I whispered, and when I opened my eyes, hers were already staring back at me. "But you remembered."

They watered, and I was there to catch the tears that never fell.

"But...but..."

"But you remembered. Remember what the doctor said? Elasticity." I kissed her gently. "It doesn't matter if you forgot because then you remembered." Before Allie could protest again, I pressed my lips to hers between my words, and she calmed down.

"You painted this for me..." she said softly as she tried to push herself around me. The wheel ran over my toes, and we winced simultaneously. "Oh, Ben. I'm sorry—your running toes..."

I laughed out loud, and even Allie's extremely concerned face couldn't make me stop.

"Running toes?" I snorted.

"What?" She frowned. "You need your toes to run."

I smiled and helped her up from her wheelchair. She stumbled into my arms, but I held her as we stared at the mural together. Allie stepped over to it and pressed her hand to the damp wall. A bit of sun stained her finger. I held Allie's back to steady her, and I pressed my lips on her cheek. She blushed for a moment.

I glanced at the painting, wishing, if only for her, this was real.

The custodians of the hospital painted over my mural a few days later. Allie must have seen my disappointed look that morning because she ushered me over and showed me her Polaroid picture: the mural. It didn't get away this time.

Before we could have a moment of peace, Allie's IV pump started beeping, a common occurrence I'd gotten used to. Half of the time Allie had to get a new IV, it was because her monitors were beeping, and she would get scared and try to rip it out. The nurses came in and quickly put yet another IV in her arm to replace the one in her grip. Because of this, Allie's arms were littered with bruises from trying to stick her with needles.

It had always made me feel sick seeing her like that, as if her body was merely an obstacle to get to the essence of her life.

Allie was sleeping one day in July when I thought about this. She had just had an episode where I came in the early morning and several nurses were surrounding her, holding her flailing body down enough to poke her again. I knew they were doing their job, and my mind probably exaggerated it, but I had to look away. I couldn't bear it. After we had just gotten back together, it felt like now I'd lost Allie in a whole new way, one I had not predicted could happen.

After they left, I stared down at Allie, my mind rewinding that scene, and I still felt sick. A purple bruise was already forming in the folds of her elbow, and I withheld the urge to cover it up with a towel.

Allie had been in the hospital for almost two months now, endlessly poked and prodded and despite my hopes, her condition continued to deteriorate.

I brushed my hands along her hair, barely a quarter of an inch long, then down her cheek. And then my pinky brushed her ear, and my thumb slowly found itself on her earlobe.

Then I remembered why Allie had not ever gotten her ears pierced, something I had learned months before, but it felt like a lifetime.

She was terrified of needles.

Being reminded of this as she spent every day attached to wires and needing new IVs or blood tests tore my heart even more. I wished I could take all the pain away.

I leaned forward and pressed a gentle kiss to her bruise and whispered a prayer of healing for her.

38

July 25th, 1991

While Allie was at therapy, I often went and trained with Coach Nickels. He even seemed to pity me. I tried to brush it off, but it was tiring having everyone in Mt. Hope ask me how Allie was doing. It was worse when they asked about me. I felt like I was holding it together by a thread but at any moment it could snap, and I could finally break.

"You okay today, Asan?"

I groaned and shrugged, though I told myself it would be okay, somehow. I had to practice my patience, just like Allie would.

"Okay, then," Coach said, now focusing back on our session. "Now, finish stretching and do twelve by one hundred meters."

I did as I was told and just barely finished before Coach came out with his stopwatch in hand.

"Okay, Asan, pace yourself. Try and get under fourteen seconds for this one."

Fourteen was easy. I finished at 13.53, slow enough for a warmup, but fast enough to reach my goal. I wiped the already forming sweat beads falling from my face and jogged back to the starting line. With barely enough time to rest, Coach was at my throat. Again, I ran.

"Twelve-point-four-one!"

Again.

"Twelve-point-one-six!"

Again.

"Eleven-point-six-eight!"

My shirt was coated in sweat by then. Barely twenty minutes had passed between running and resting but I was already a waterfall.

"Now," Coach began, "I really want you to book it. Pretend you're in Barcelona competing for the world to see your talents. It'll happen."

At the start, my eyes closed, I imagined all the people cheering around me and the other runners beside me.

I wished them luck.

Then I was off. The rhythm of my running faster than my heartbeat created drumming in my mind. The shining lights blinded me, but I kept on going. My mind was clear of my worries as my legs pumped beneath me. There was no fear, no illness, no uncertainty when I was running. Just my feet hitting the ground. I imagined my name, barely audible through the chants, but still there, pierced through—like fuel, it kept me going. It pushed me to run faster, further, and further up, past a runner from Ethiopia and one from the UK. I just kept going for myself and the girl I envisioned hopefully cheering me on from the stands.

And I hit the fence, the façade gone.

Coach smiled.

"Ten-point-four-nine! Amazing."

"No, I can do better," I insisted as I jogged back. At the start, I re-stretched, rested for not nearly long enough, and imagined the stands again.

"Ten-point-four-five!"

"Ten-point-four-three!"

"Ten-point-four!"

I collapsed on the ground, my throat felt dry and I was breathing heavily from my big efforts. It wasn't, of course, from the running, but the images that stayed in my head. For, as I ran faster, the people around me blurred, and the only person I saw clearly was Allie, smiling and healthy, yet it pained me. It seemed unachievable, so distant I could barely remember a time when she lived just five minutes away from me, happy and fully herself. The hospital visits had caught up with me.

Coach stepped over to me and glanced down with the only true look of concern he had ever shown.

"Hey, Asan, talk to me. What's wrong?"

I couldn't hold it in. I told him the amount of pressure I felt, needing to keep running, to do something with my life, and be there for Allie.

"You ran well out there. Your future looks bright—"

"No," I bellowed, then paused. "No... I don't care about that. I could run a hundred miles in a second and still not be proud unless it helped her." I couldn't and wouldn't boast of my skills while she was still sick. "I just feel useless. I don't know how I can do better, not with running, but with Allie. Nothing matters to me, nothing at all, while she's sick. I just sit and watch her, not only because I love her, but out of selfishness. I want her to get better—*need* her to get better so I don't have to go back there and see the woman I love keep deteriorating before my eyes."

Coach Nickels was silent for a while. At first, I expected him to tell me to put it aside, to start back and try to beat my time. Coach didn't care much about our personal lives as long as it didn't interfere with running. But I wasn't proud of my running. Only when I walked in each day and Allie could remember me did I feel worthy enough to boast.

But then Coach crouched beside me and ran his hands through his thinning hair. His coal black eyes startled me, less intimidating than normal, but as if he could stare right into my soul.

"Can I pray with you, Ben?"

The weight that had settled on my chest escaped. I had known nothing of Coach's personal life. Never would I have imagined this. I said yes without hesitating. Never had Ben from a year ago imagined that response, either.

Coach's low rumble of a voice began, and the peace I longed for slowly flowed its way like a downpour on my head. Like droplets of rain on the window of a car, calmness spread to the base of my neck and branched out to each curve of my body. It slid down my arms and stopped my fingers from shaking. It gushed through my chest like a sharp wave and swooshed along my legs, and to the tips of my toes.

After running for another hour, I headed back to the hospital, eager to spend time with Allie.

Allie was sitting up in her bed when I kissed her hello.

"Hi, baby," she said, her speech slow and her breathing heavy, "h-how was your run?" she slurred.

Determined not to seem prideful or boasting, I shrugged.

"Pretty good. Could have been better."

In my excitement to see Allie, I didn't even notice her family sitting around, just as eager as I was. My stomach dropped for only a moment. I had so much time with Allie, that I knew what was coming.

"Hey, Ben? Essie and Jack are only here for the afternoon," Samuel began, "so could we spend some time with Allie alone?"

I knew why Samuel always insisted they spent their time with Allie without me—I wasn't a part of their family, and when it came to Allie's health, he didn't want me to influence what they discussed regarding Allie's treatment. Allie and I still debated about it all, of course, like we talked about everything, but Samuel and Hannah were her parents, and I didn't want to overstep. Or, when it was a visit like this, they didn't want me constantly distracting Allie. For whenever we were all together, Allie tried her best to listen to her parents, but her eyes would constantly flit over to me—too often for Samuel.

"Oh, um, sure. I actually needed to call my mom about her birthday dinner," I said, trying to hide my disappointment. I stepped over and kissed Allie once more before heading out to the telephone.

I did need to call my mom, but our conversation on birthday dinners was rather short.

"Doesn't it bother you," Mom began when I told her the Johncoxes had asked me to leave with a crack in my voice, "that they just rudely told you to get out? Don't you think they should include you?"

I stood in the lobby, watching people move around me. The many stories of their day at the hospital plastered on their weary faces. No one seemed happy here. And as I spent more and more days at Allie's bedside, watching her body bloat and her breathing become more labored, I understood their dejection.

My first thought was if she was healthy, Allie's smile would have brightened any room.

Shifting my attention away from a young boy tugging on his mother's skirt, I said, "It sucks, of course it does. But she's their daughter. I'm just her boyfriend. It's their choice, their family. If they'd like to speak to Allie without me, I have to respect them if I'm ever going to get her and her dad's permission."

There it was: the sigh at the other end of the phone.

"Ben…"

"I know, Mom. I know." I breathed in deeply and held it, with my eyes closed, until the exhale. "But I have to believe, even if everyone else doesn't." I sighed and scratched my head, pushing down my hair, which was long in need of a haircut, but I never seemed to have the time. "I will bear this entire struggle for her. I want to be there for her. I've promised Allie and myself. She's going to make it, I know it."

Mom was silent for a moment. Then she gave another long sigh.

"As long as you're aware of the odds, I'm okay."

My feet scuffed the ground, kicking a pebble on the ground like a soccer ball.

"Trust me. I'm very aware. I just don't want to dwell on it. I have hope."

When Allie's family left to get dinner, it was around seven in the evening. I only had three more hours with her. When I walked in, Paula was standing over Allie, pressing a damp washcloth over her swollen forehead.

"She's got an infection," Paula explained. "She started getting a fever about an hour ago."

Without missing a beat, I stepped forward.

"What can I do to help?"

After Allie had been given antibiotics and a pill to make her sleep, I sat by her side and became her nurse. I fluffed her pillow, kindly adjusted the blankets when her body pushed them off and tucked the sheet around her body snuggly. A couple hours later, she finally relaxed. Allie wouldn't wake in time for me to talk with her at all, so I opened up her yellow Bible next to her and read it for myself.

At ten, Paula ceremoniously opened the door, and I left, looking back at Allie sleeping.

That night, as I headed to the bathroom to brush my teeth, the phone rang.

It was Samuel.

I stepped past Fatima and Jared, who were busy chasing each other through the hallway, and picked the phone up.

"Hello, Ben," he began. Before I could say a word, he continued. "I just want to apologize for earlier. I should never have told you to leave. We see each other often in that room, and I don't know why I became so protective of my time with Allie today. I'm so sorry. I don't want to close you off from her care like that again."

I leaned against the wall and twirled my fingers in my hair, an old habit of mine when I'm tired.

"Samuel, don't worry about it, honestly. I forgive you, and I respect your decision. We're all there for Allie," I said, hoping he would understand my point. I thought of the verses I read to Allie, about forgiveness and withholding grudges and tried to take them to heart. "I appreciate your apology. Thank you."

I seemed to have thrown Samuel off-guard, because he cleared his throat and took a moment to respond.

"Well, then. Goodnight, Ben. We had to go back home tonight, but we'll be back the day after tomorrow. Tell Allie hello for me."

Satisfied, I hung up and grabbed my new yellow toothbrush.

A couple of days later, I came to the hospital as usual and found Allie had escaped to therapy early because she had tried to ask for water, and when her mouth failed to form the word, she had a panic attack.

When she returned to her room, it was around noon, and she was working her mouth and forming it into different shapes to speak or ask for things. Allie addressed me, though I looked up at her before she had finished my name. Her 'e's were much longer than needed, but she just had to work at it.

"Yes?" My chipper and short response was a hummingbird to her tortoise. I reminded myself, not for the first time, to slow down. Allie would still be there at the end of a word.

"Do…you…hear?"

"What?"

Allie just grew silent. For a moment, I thought she was just having a hard time forming words again. But then I heard it, the faint noise that needed no explanation.

I stepped up on my chair, though the analog clock was just barely an arm's length away. Closer, the ticking was even more evident. I let the batteries fall into my palm after opening its casing, and Allie let out a sigh of relief.

In her case, the sound of ticking must have been like the sands of time plastered before her eyes.

I sank back to her side and let the batteries roll out of my hand, one at a faster pace than the other, and along her tray table before they clinked together on the other side.

"Better?"

Allie barely nodded, and I pressed a single kiss to her forehead.

Before, we used to talk a lot, to fill the empty time. Allie said it helped to talk, so we would sit together, laugh at each other's attempts at bad jokes, and enjoy the lightness our chatter would bring.

Now, just the mere company of each other sufficed. It was more than most people could even ask for.

Allie had five hours of therapy every day now, per the recommendations from her doctor, as opposed to three, split up in morning and afternoon sessions. This meant I could have extra time to train, but I couldn't muster the strength to. I would run as normal, then head back and wait by Allie's beside for her return.

When Allie returned from afternoon therapy that day, she had a smile on her face—an excited smile.

"Allie found something on the ground she'd like to give you," Paula explained as we helped Allie into bed.

Her hand went to the pocket of her hospital gown and out emerged a few silver coins; the money Allie owed me back from all those months ago.

She pushed them toward me.

"No, keep it," I said with a chuckle. "It's been over a year since I gave you the money for the Funyuns. You've paid me back in much better ways." I pressed a kiss to her cheek as Paula left.

"Take!" Allie exclaimed like a toddler just learning simple words. "Pleeeeease." Her eyes watered as she proffered her hand further. "I... owe."

I shoved her hand back, harder this time, and the coins clattered to the ground.

"You owe me nothing. If you think I base your values on mere cents, then you don't know how much I treasure you." I exhaled, now feeling the frustration of the previous months rearing its head. "I could loan you a million dollars and never expect you to pay back a single penny! If you owe me anything," I continued, "it's an explanation. I have withheld my frustration day in and day out, but you kept your illness from me, Allie, for months! After you made it such a big deal that I lied to you, you kept this huge secret from me. Why did you not tell me?"

I had tried to suppress it for so long, but now my frustration reared its head. I didn't know I had the capacity to yell at Allie the way I did. I had held back my anger for weeks, months, as I sat with the knowledge that Allie knew she was sick and chose to keep it from me, that Hannah and Samuel and Essie and Jack didn't convince her to tell me. I hadn't wanted to bring it up when she was acutely sick and had been waiting until she was better. But my fear got the best of me; I wasn't sure she would get better.

I expected tears. I expected a panic attack—I knew I shouldn't have gotten short with Allie. But then her chin quivered; she was trying to speak. Her teeth bit her lips. I waited, and it was over a minute before she spoke back—the air of frustration I created tightened.

"I... sorry... I... protect...," she struggled through the words, like pulling taffy.

My eyes caught her lips—the bottom one was bleeding.

A roll of paper towel sat on the tray, so I grabbed a piece and pressed it to Allie's lip to soak up the blood. There was barely a cut. No matter how many tears I brushed from Allie's face, she continued to cry, and continued to bleed. Salty tears watered the deserts of her cheeks.

"No, no, I'm sorry," I repeated at least a thousand times. But her eyes forgave me after just once. "I know you were trying to protect me; I know." I kissed her gently. "I just wish I could protect you, Allie. I love you."

I continued to apologize, unable to forgive myself for speaking to Allie that way.

When she'd stopped both bleeding and crying, I helped Allie from her chair to the bed and laid beside her. My hand still clutched a blood and tear-stained paper towel. I couldn't bear to walk to the end of the room to throw it away.

Allie fell asleep. A sentence so simple in my head that I had to think it through before I finally realized what true peace was—trust.

The next morning, the doctor on call stopped me before I could go into Allie's room and told me Allie had another seizure overnight, and from what they saw on MRI and the area of her brain that was affected, she might never speak again.

My throat choked with tears as I processed what the doctor said. I might never hear her lilting voice again, calling out to me, saying my name in the gentlest tone. I tried not to think my yelling had used up all the words from her mind. During her therapy that day, I canceled practice with Coach.

But I still ran.

I ran down the trails of our first dates. Past the reindeer/caribou. Past the Hopso's pool. Past where the ice cream truck had been. I kept on running until my coughs dissolved into the asphalt, where I felt my knees buckle and my breathing heaved to catch up with the pain.

With a lurch, I vomited. My heart and my lungs sat beating on the pavement, stinking up the cool, crisp air. The Mt. Hope campus was now a ghost to me, a distant spirit. Once full of happy memories, it now sickened me to my core.

In the early days of Allie's hospitalization, I met with Willem and Fran, then separately with Spencer. Brennan, I saw enough, since his family visited Allie ever so often.

Spencer had talked with me about the technicalities of Allie's diagnosis and realistic ways this summer would go. I appreciated his third-party outlook, and his ability to see the situation rationally. At the time, I was thankful.

Fran was a tamer version of himself, though he reminded me of all the hospital-related jokes I could use (most involving hand sanitizer or walkers).

Willem asked me questions, worrying about my well-being and how I was holding up.

But more than Spencer's rationality, or Fran's distractions, or Willem's sensitivity, I needed someone to stabilize me, to keep me firm. I had yelled at Allie, the love of my life, and now she couldn't even speak to me. I felt my strength breaking. I tried not to blame myself, but all I could think about was how badly I wished I could take back my words from the day before.

When I returned to Allie, it didn't matter to me anymore if she could or couldn't speak—her eyes said enough. It took just a look to melt my heart. I sat beside her, taking her hand, and opened her Bible to read to her once more. It was a familiar way I'd come to comfort her, but I now looked at it to help me, too.

39

August 8th-12th, 1991

The rain began, and Michigan sighed. The humidity had seemed impossible to bear, and a little rain was just what we needed.

I was sitting in the waiting room with Samuel and Hannah, my mood as gray as the weather outside. It had been a few hours since Allie had gone to therapy, and the doctors planned to meet with us to discuss her current state.

"It shouldn't be much longer now," the doctor said when the door was closed shut. "There's not much to do but wait. We've got some medication to keep her comfortable, and we can continue treatments, but I'm afraid it's just a matter of time."

Hannah burst into tears, and although I felt overwhelmed by the doctor's words, on the outside I was stoic. I couldn't let myself think about life without Allie. Not yet.

The next day, I sat next to Allie, whose eyes were partially open. She was silent, but her hand occasionally squeezed mine. But even when I wasn't there, or when Samuel and Hannah sat beside their daughter, Allie was rarely responsive these days. I never got to hear her sing "Rock of Ages." That realization panged me.

The rain pestered on.

As the sun began to set a few days later, I rested my eyes just for a moment as I lay next to Allie. Just as I felt my body relax against her, her movements woke me. They were jagged, inconsistent, and messy, but determined. I stared at Allie, feeling helpless. Her hand slowly reached for the camera on the metal tray.

I simply watched. Her hands shook, almost as if they were cold and shivering. She clasped the camera firmly in her hands and positioned it toward me. At first, I thought she was trying to take a picture of me. But when the lens focused above my head, I turned my body to see her capture the only thing I'd ever known Allie truly wanted: the sunset.

Her fingers wavered over the button, but no matter how long I watched, how long that scene haunted me, it never clicked down.

Then she broke. Tears gathered along Allie's eyes as the frustration welled within her. She dropped the camera against my chest, and I cradled it into my hands as it fell.

"Shh...Please don't cry. Look, I've got this. *We've* got this." I held the camera up, and with my other hand, guided her to the shutter. With a press, the moment was captured into eternity. With me around, I promised Allie she would never miss another sunset again.

The next morning, Paula stopped me from entering. Or rather, I pushed open the door, a wide smile on my face, only to hear a desperate "No!" and see something I wished I hadn't: two nurses pinning down Allie, who was twitching and crying, while Paula washed Allie's bottom. The sheets below her were already stained.

Allie had lost control over her bowels. A sign of the end, the doctor had told us.

She was no longer the girl I had asked out by the vending machine; the girl who kissed me walking down a road after discussing colors; the girl who would do anything for the ones she cared about whether it be paint their house yellow or drive home nearly every weekend to spend time with her parents. That girl had left me on graduation day. The one lying in bed before me, eyes closed, barely breathing with oxygen while the rain patterned on was not that girl, though my feelings for her had not changed. And that thought ached my heart more than any other. Now, all I wanted was her peace, however that looked. But I still desperately needed her to pull through.

"Hours, now, at the most," the doctor told us that afternoon.

So, Samuel, Hannah, Essie, Jack, Mila, and I waited. We waited for those hours by her side. Then the next day came, and we kept waiting, all while the background thundered behind us, ticking away the hours. There was no more therapy—just waiting.

That night, I drove home, windshield wipers bashing against the rain, the radio as silent as my life. As I got to Mt. Hope's campus, I slowed down glancing at all of the places that reminded me of Allie. As I turned onto the road to my parents' house, I caught a glimpse of that majestic beast, Mt. Hope, and a memory caught hold of me and dragged me down to Earth—how Allie wished she would go one day.

40

August 14th, 1991

The morning of August 14th, the rain dripped from my windowsill, but no longer from the sky, and sunlight shone through my window, partially blinding me as I woke. I was in no hurry.

Searching through my closet, I landed on the suit I had worn to graduation, which seemed so far away now, like a separate life. My hair, a pool of waves, stood fine against my head, and I felt no need to play with it.

On my way to the hospital, I stopped at the local grocery store and bought sunflowers.

When I made it to Allie's floor, twenty minutes later than usual, each nurse I passed gave me a sad smile, and it only confirmed my suspicions.

I saw Paula first. She was tidying up the tubes and machines without a word. Hannah stared at the bed; her eyes so full of tears I couldn't believe they hadn't overflowed yet. Samuel sat in stunned silence, still taking in his surroundings, as if he was not even there. Essie showed the most grief, clinging to Jack while fat tears rolled down her face and neck before disappearing on her shirt. Mila, snuggled up into her father's arms, watched her mother with naïve curiosity.

All I could focus on were Allie's eyes, the ones that always saw the best in everyone, experienced life in a different light than others, and made me feel like the world was full of happiness sprinkled so generously throughout life it was impossible to miss. Those eyes were shut—never again to open.

41

December 1990-August 1991

Allie only did one selfish thing in her short life: she sent me to India.

I had no idea how selfish that act was until months after I returned, after graduation, when Hannah, Samuel, and Essie, in the waiting room of the hospital, told me Allie had brain cancer—she had for quite some time.

To be specific, she had glioblastoma, cancer of the glial cells which aid the nerve cells of the brain. It settled in her limbic system first, attacking the hippocampus, her memory center.

But the symptoms were subtle at first. A headache here or that that turned into a migraine even with medicine. Those began in Spring 1990, around the time we met.

Slowly, but with the cunning ability of a snake, it spread through her, showing itself through seizures.

In early December, Allie was home, and while preparing dinner, she collapsed mid-sentence while telling her father about her day. That was the first seizure.

Unable to drive to the hospital, Samuel dialed 911, and watched in horror as his youngest daughter convulsed on the floor, as if possessed. The crunch of the driveway signaled the arrival of an ambulance, and both Samuel and Allie were carried in.

Though they passed everyone on the road, went far above the speed limit, and ran every red light, it was still the longest ride Samuel ever experienced.

Hannah, an ER nurse, saw her own daughter wheeled in. The doctor tried to tell Hannah to get someone else to do her job, but she simply barked at him, and the doctor left her alone.

Samuel held Hannah when the doctor gave them the news, and once again when Allie woke, when they shared the prognosis.

"She smiled when we told her," Hannah said through tears that graduation night in the hospital. "When I asked why, she said, 'Well, Mom, I either get to see Jesus or thank God for blessing me with knowledge and empathy.'"

I twiddled my thumbs and let a corner of my lips smirk.

"That sounds like something Allie would say when given a diagnosis," I had joked.

Samuel mirrored my weak attempt at a smile.

In that hospital bed, Allie made a defining decision. She could have surgery to remove the cancer or go straight to treatment. The doctor recommended surgery, but it was not required due to the risks of damaging other parts of the brain.

Allie chose surgery, no question. But she had to wait a month, which conveniently landed on the trip to India.

So, Hannah called Heather and explained the situation as subtly as possible.

"Yes... I'm aware we can't get any of our money back... Thank you."

Allie had been on the original list of students going to India. But when January came up as the earliest possible way to get rid of the cancer, she backed out.

The doctors prescribed a high concentration pain medication for her migraines—which limited her insurance from receiving any more strong pain medication—and Allie was fine leading up to the surgery.

Removing the tumor was a success, but the doctor had shaved Allie's head to access her brain.

Allie hadn't gotten a haircut while I was gone but wore a very convincing wig made of her own hair which she never let me get too close to look at.

For the next month, Allie was back to normal. I didn't notice anything had ever been wrong.

But cancer is tricky. It likes to keep its presence known.

Allie felt a seizure coming on in March. She called her own ambulance during Spring Break. When the doctors checked her brain again, not only had the cancer returned in her hippocampus, but it was also now so deep within her brain tissue that further surgery wasn't even a possibility.

"Ethically and scientifically, I cannot perform this procedure," the doctor had told Allie. He'd expected an outburst, a demand that he tries, but Allie had just accepted it. "However," he had said as he looked down at Allie's chart, "chemotherapy is still an option."

Again, it was an easy decision.

Allie began to attend chemotherapy three times a week at Flower City Hospital while I was at track practice. They tried to keep the glioblastoma at bay, while slowly it spread to the innermost workings of her brain. That caused a punch to her personality. Stress, impatience, and unhappiness plagued her during her final months. It wasn't just the pressure of school that was affecting Allie's mood.

Her memory gradually faded as Allie corroded from the inside out.

And, selfishly, she dealt with it all alone. She kept to herself, unwilling to give in to help. I will never forgive her for her stubbornness. But I will always love her.

In the hospital, after graduation, after hours of chemo and speech therapy couldn't prevent her Broca's area from becoming infected, Allie's beautiful voice fled the world.

A woman in Wisconsin got one of Allie's kidneys. A young man in the same hospital took her heart gratefully. And a lucky pair, one in Arizona and the other in New York, received half of the greatest pair of eyes in the world.

As I reflected on the last few months leading up to this, I couldn't listen to the medical team and her family dole out the rest of Allie's organs. I left the hospital for the last time and stepped out into the dreary day—it was raining once more.

42

Devon stared at Asan, whose face was withdrawn. He had gone quiet.

It took Devon a moment to realize Asan was finished talking. For now, or the whole story, Devon didn't know.

"Sir?" he began, but Asan gave a harsh "shush" and pulled himself out of his chair. Slowly, he shuffled over to the mantle, covered in turned down picture frames. He began to lift them up, one by one.

The first frame was a wedding picture. Ben—young Asan—and an Indian woman, draped in a white dress with red accents in the veil. Asan wore a tux, and a smile so huge Devon didn't think it could be possible after experiencing a death like Allie's.

The second was one of a little girl, whose face was familiar. It took Devon a second to realize this was Asan's daughter, Vidya, around elementary school, he guessed.

More frames emerged, and Devon studied each one. Side-by-side were two pictures in a double frame. One showed Asan, younger, crouched into a ball with his head between his knees, surrounded by a blurred crowd. The other had Asan in the same stadium, standing on a track, smiling at the camera. But his eyes were red. He held up a silver medal with the girl from the wedding picture by his side. In her hands was a blue and pink sign that read, "Go, Daddy!" with a rectangle below it—a positive pregnancy test.

Next, he lifted up a fairly recent picture—Asan looked the same if just for a lack of gray hair on the sides, smiling next to a young man who resembled Asan in his youth, but with less wild hair. The man had a graduation cap and robe on as he held up a rectangular diploma bearing the seal of a nearby high school.

A few family Christmas pictures followed—Vidya with braces; the young boy, short one year and a growth spurt the next—leading to a final frame: Asan, hugging an elderly woman with diluted red hair. The background was pale white, like a nursing home, and Devon imagined it must have been taken recently.

"She should've been home a while ago, but this snow..." Asan said, breaking the silence. He stepped out of the living room toward the front door. He stood there for far too long, both men in stillness, waiting.

Finally, lights showed through the black. A jangle of keys pierced through the silence.

Even though Dr. Asan whispered, Devon heard a muffled kiss and "How was your shift?" He tried not to dislike whoever this was but hearing all about Allie and seeing these photographs made Devon feel almost a sense of betrayal for Asan's first love.

The door widened, and an older version of the woman in the pictures stepped out. Her hair was in soft waves but had glints of gray amongst the dark. Her eyes were wide—immediately comforting—and her smile was full and inviting.

Looking at her filled Devon with the comfort and familiarity of a warm drink.

"Devon, this is my wife, Kiah. Honey, this is Devon." Dr Asan explained as he gestured toward the living room. Devon suddenly felt so small sitting on the lemony couch. "He's a student of mine and was having a rough night, so we've been talking."

Devon extended his hand.

"Actually, he's been telling me about Allie," Devon explained.

Kiah smiled, gave Devon's hand two firm shakes, smiled, and said, "I'm glad to see you're doing better, then."

Kiah glanced at her husband to simply look at him, then turned back to Devon.

"Would you like some tea?"

"I'm guessing you're a bit confused," Asan began as they all walked back into the kitchen, where the story had started just hours before.

"Definitely."

Asan chuckled, almost glad at his success surprising his student.

As he spoke to Devon, his eyes wandered over to his wife who busied herself filling the kettle with water.

"I was absolutely devastated when Allie died. That summer was the saddest point of my entire life," he admitted. "She was my first love. And I still love her to this day."

"But you got married!" Devon interjected. "How could you fall in love again after losing the woman you loved at such a young age?" He meant that question to sound curious, it came out more accusatory than he'd planned.

Asan didn't even flinch. He had asked himself the same question through the years. With his body leaning against the island, he glanced at his hands, and his thumbs found themselves twiddling again.

When he finally looked up, he spoke slowly and with precision. "Just because someone dies does not mean you cannot be happy or continue to love them. It means exactly the opposite."

He turned to glance at his wife before continuing. "I was incredibly lost without Allie. I had fallen in love with her, and the idea of her. But I didn't let her death hold me back. But just because she was gone didn't mean I couldn't live. Allie would've been so upset if I had thrown my whole life away because hers had ended.

"But I mourned! Don't get me wrong—I mourned," Dr. Asan cried out. "For two years, most of the time I thought of only Allie. Though she wasn't with me, I still heard her words, and they spurred me on. The peace she felt from her relationship with God was something I wanted. But for the first few months, I was a bird of flight who had lost the ability to fly—still living, but without the thing that made my existence worth it." At that, Asan stood straighter. "But then I realized why I was feeling so awful. I *dwelt* too long. I needed to let Allie go."

"Oolong, echinacea, or chamomile tea, Devon?" Kiah interrupted from the cupboard.

Devon snapped out of the trance he'd been in.

"Um, oolong, thanks."

Kiah handed him a mug with a flamingo neck as the handle.

"Thank you," Devon said as he grabbed the tea bag and bobbed it into the water.

After serving a cup for herself, Kiah sat down, took out her purse, dispensed the items on the counter and began to organize it. Already a small purse with very little in it, Devon suspected organization wasn't her prime reason for distracting herself.

Devon's gaze soon drifted back to Asan, who was staring down at his hands, clasped and clammy.

"You let Allie go? The girl you loved?" Devon ran his free hand through his hair. "How could you even have the strength?" He took a sip of the tea and coughed. He didn't expect it to be so hot.

"Physically?" Asan questioned. Before Devon could clarify, Asan continued. "I often talked to Hannah and Samuel—we were all trying to move on in life without forgetting Allie. I spoke to a grief counselor, and well," a smile broke out on his face, "running always brought me down to earth. Anytime I felt myself begin to panic or grow angry at the memory of Allie's death, I'd stop what I was doing and go run. Even in my Master's program, if I felt the sadness come back, I'd get out of lecture and just take a few laps around the building!" He chuckled at the thought, as though it was a fond memory instead of a coping mechanism.

"Spiritually," Asan continued, "I learned more about God. I began to wish *I* was dead, but I knew if I kept thinking of the 'what-ifs' I'd waste my life. And I didn't want that."

Devon thought back to the camera that he bumped into going to the bathroom.

"But you kept some of her things to remember her by, right? Her camera, the last one, I'm guessing... And the elephant from India?"

Asan glanced away and nodded.

"Yes. I kept a few of her things. Her family insisted I take them." He sighed and rubbed the inner corners of his eyes. "For years, especially when the kids were younger, Allie's things would catch my eye, and I'd feel guilty. She was so good with children. I was living what she had dreamed about her whole life..."

"But Ben couldn't have stopped the cancer."

Kiah had looked up from her purse to interject. Devon imagined this comment came up often, perhaps lying in bed, a consolation when the demons and regrets of the past took hold in the form of insomnia.

"I should know—I'm a nurse practitioner. My specialty is oncology—cancer patient," Kiah clarified.

When Devon glanced back at Asan, he felt a strange uneasiness in his stomach upon hearing Asan's first name. Though he knew it was Ben, hearing it said by someone else when Asan stood here, clearly not in his youth, made everything seem much more personal and rawer.

"No one could do anything. The doctors did their best. It was never your fault." Kiah's voice was so soft and tender, as if each word melted off her lips as if she had said the same words thousands of times before. She was resilient and strong, yet gentle and warm. Even if it was just for her voice, Devon could see now why Asan could have married Kiah. She reminded Devon of the feeling of staying inside on a rainy day.

Asan let out a sigh that traveled down his throat into a groan. Yes, definitely not the first reminder. But

Devon could tell, perhaps the words had not truly sunken in all these years.

Devon shifted his feet, wondering how often over the years Asan pondered what his life would have been like with Allie. Would his daughter have had her green eyes? Would his son share his mother's knack for photography?

Would Asan have lived a happier life?

Kiah shifted uncomfortably, just briefly, but enough so Devon caught it in his peripheral. When he glanced her way, she smiled, albeit sadly.

"I'm sorry," Devon murmured, feeling at fault for Asan bringing up one of his hardest memories. It was quarter to four am now, he noticed the clock. Devon tried not to think of what must have been going down at the hospital to warrant Kiah's late arrival home.

As if now remembering where he was, Asan smiled and tried to make the corners of his eyes rise. His voice shook as he said, "She lived a great life. I will always be honored that I got to be a part of it."

Devon, determined not to meet Asan's gaze, glanced around the kitchen. The little things he noticed now had a deeper meaning. The map of India in the adjoining sitting area, the small cross above the cabinets, and on the fridge, a Christmas card from Spencer Hall and family.

Devon cleared his throat, still wanting answers.

"What happened after Allie died?"

43

August 14th, 1991

The cool rain splashed across the road, picking right up where it had left off, if only for a moment in the early morning. Overcast, a once sunny daybreak constituted a dreary afternoon, and I could not recall the drive home.

When I had left the hospital driveway, I spotted McCarrell exit his car and head inside with the local pastor, no doubt to console Hannah and Samuel.

I pushed myself extra hard as I ran on the indoor track that afternoon. For fleeting moments as I sprinted, I would forget the horrors of the morning. The distraction was a blessing. My legs felt numb as did my mind. I didn't want to face Allie's death. I just kept running to stop myself from dwelling.

When I walked to my car after training, I spotted Spencer, waiting near his own and beneath a large oak tree that shielded him from the rain.

"How'd you know I'm here? Is seeing the future your new superpower?"

Spencer rolled his eyes.

"C'mon, Ben. You know I traded seeing the future for teleportation months ago."

"Ah," I sighed with a nod. "Of course, how could I forget? Is that how you got here from Traverse City so quickly?"

"No, actually," Spencer laughed as he stepped closer. "Brennan called me this morning. I drove down as soon as I heard."

My stomach dropped.

"Allie. I'm so sorry, Ben. This… this completely sucks." Spencer sputtered out. "She was s-so young. Twenty-two?"

"Twenty-one," I croaked, my voice breaking. Her birthday would be next week.

Outside of Allie's family and mine, I hadn't been able to bring myself to say that she had passed. I couldn't say the words. It just didn't feel real. I kept waiting to wake up from this nightmare.

I swallowed back the sob that was forming in my throat.

"Yeah, it does. It really sucks, doesn't it?" I gave a little laugh of frustration. "It *really* sucks." How else do you describe the loss of the love of your life in your twenties? It's inconceivable.

Spencer bit his lip. After I remained silent, he said, "To answer the question you're thinking, I came down to see you."

I shrugged.

"For what? Are you here to console me? Because I can't be comforted. Not now. All I feel is a sort of numbness tearing at me." I placed a hand to my chest, as if feeling the area of pain would help me explain it better. "Can non-feeling hurt?" I cried as my eyes stung with tears.

The pressure on my chest had become so pronounced as we talked about Allie that I felt the pain travel up to my back, my neck, and up to the back of my mouth.

"I know it will wear off, and when it hits me, it'll hit me like a bullet." I swallowed, and I could already feel a hole burrowing itself through my numb shield.

I was stuck between two evils—either feel the pain for the sake of remembering Allie, or choose to ignore the hurt, but perhaps underwhelm the situation and, therefore, Allie.

I knew it would never be the latter.

"Ben..." Spencer began, "I'm here for the next couple of days if you need anything—from a hug to just watching a stupid funny movie. I wanna be here for you—I *am* here for you. Anything you need, just holler."

I bit my lip in thought. "Actually, I could use a hug. There's nothing else I can think of right now."

Spencer softly smiled and pulled me in closely. I held back more tears I felt forming in the corner of my eyes. I squeezed Spencer tighter before we fell apart.

I left without much more to say. The joking manner I'd had when I first saw Spencer quickly left when Allie was in the forefront of my mind.

I ate out to avoid going home to my mother, who was beyond herself—the Johncoxes had stopped by and apparently Allie had requested her cameras be given to my mother. That's how I knew the severity of Allie's life and how few people stuck around.

But I did.

After dinner, I made my way to somewhere I never expected to go without Allie.

The Mt. Hope Methodist church had a quaint prayer chapel, completely covered in plush pillows and blankets surrounding an altar. Above the altar, situated on the wall, was a wooden cross illuminated by two small stage lights set on the ground. While the lighting of the cross was beautiful and symbolic, it didn't fit the mood I needed.

I thought back to all the church services from my youth. How people would come to Christ in crazy moments of joy. I wished for that as I knelt there.

Nothing.

Again, I squeezed my eyes closed tightly, but nothing came to me.

Before I knew it, rage had bubbled inside of me, and the words burst out.

"Why her?"

I hadn't realized I'd said it out loud until I'd repeated it three or four times, each time growing in anger and volume.

"Why her? Why her? WHY *HER*, GOD?" The last yell left my ears ringing, and suddenly the numbness fled. My throat constricted around itself, and I scratched my face and my shirt. My entire body burned from the heat within me. The flames inside started out simple, just sparks, but had now grown into a wildfire, desperate to get out. Suddenly, I wasn't kneeling anymore.

"Why her, God? Why Allison Charlotte Johncox, someone who loved You so much? Why did You do this?" My voice cracked as I screamed toward the cross, as if it would make Him hear better.

"WHY WOULD YOU EVER LET HER SUFFER THROUGH LIFE JUST TO HAVE IT TAKEN FROM HER?

SHE *LOVED* YOU AND *TRUSTED* YOU!" I grew silent, if only to hear the drastic difference. Because when I stopped, nothing responded. My voice formed a growl. "How *dare* you take her… Not just from me, but from this world you made. You made her. AND YOU TOOK HER!"

Without warning my mind what my body planned to do, I grasped the altar, lifted it above my head, and slammed it against the wall. I picked up every pillow and ripped them into fluff, with each satisfied sound of fabric tearing a stimulus to keep going. The chairs along the walls found a similar fate to the altar, and each wooden piece flung across the room led me to another I took my frustration out on, screaming for Allie's life and death. A vase turned into shattered clay. A stand holding the Bible broke when I kicked it to the other end of the room.

Finally, when one of the other stands I forced from my sight hit the bottom of the cross and it tilted to one side, I stopped. Suddenly aware of the insurmountable destruction I was causing, I glanced around the destroyed room and let out a belated wail, a cry of grievance that started deep within my throat, bubbled up and out before exhaling like a banshee shriek.

My knees gave out, and just as soon as I stopped kneeling, I was once more. Through each sob, full of failed efforts to control myself, came out, "*I* trusted You." I pressed my hands to my now swollen eyes, unable to hold back the fear and frustration I had and knew I would always carry for Allie.

Only friends, like Spencer, Brennan, Fran, or Willem dared to speak to me at Allie's funeral. Their lives had continued—in relationships, engagements, job opportunities whereas my life felt like it had been in limbo since graduation day. I felt like my mind was just lifting out of a fog. Heather and Mark briefly came, offering their condolences and their prayers.

Fran, always blunt, approached me directly after the funeral ended. He gave me a hug, and said, "Man I'm not normally a crier, but when her sister spoke about their camping trip to Minnesota in '78? Tears."

I tried to play off Fran's vibrant personality, but my heart wasn't in it. I registered that Will said something, but I didn't comprehend it.

"What?"

"Why didn't you do a eulogy?" Will asked again. This time, Fran added, "Yeah, you talked so much about Allie I was surprised when you didn't go up there."

I shrugged.

"My relationship with Allie was between us," I explained. "It was personal and intimate—I just couldn't bring myself to share it."

Although the answer wasn't what they were looking for, my friends seemed satisfied with the truth, and we made plans to get dinner together in the next few weeks.

The reception was held down the hall in the gymnasium. Despite living in Petoskey, the Johncoxes chose to have the funeral and reception in Mt. Hope, a special place for Allie and closer to their relatives in Ohio. Before the funeral, I'd helped set up several circular tables from a storage closet, and lots of family and friends sat at them, far more than Allie had spoken of.

I sat by myself, but eventually my mom set her food by me on her way to get a drink. Immediately, I grabbed my plate and stalked out of the gym until I was outside—I just needed to be alone.

My head was clouded, focusing only on Allie and the little urn that held her ashes from earlier. There had been a beautiful picture of her framed next to it, but despite seeing her smile again, there was no life—no animated story behind it. It was perhaps even worse than no picture at all.

But unfortunately, the moment I sat down on the curb, Essie followed suit.

I tried to ignore her. Using my fork, I pushed my peas, mashed potatoes, and roast beef around. I refused to look at Allie's sister. I'd just witnessed my girlfriend's funeral—if I wanted to sulk a bit, I could.

"Isn't it funny," Essie said softly, obviously not taking my hint of playing with my food in utter silence, "how funeral food and wedding food are so similar? These 'fancy' dishes, like potatoes and meat, sided with a vegetable no one really likes?"

When I didn't answer, Essie bumped her shoulder against mine.

"Hey, I'm just trying to make conversation. Allie wouldn't want you to isolate yourself." Essie was right, I knew it, but I didn't want to admit it.

I sighed, but she took it as good enough and continued.

"Allie is in a better place right now. I know how cheesy that sounds, and I don't mean it as a placeholder comforting phrase—it's the truth. She's with God, the final goal she always wanted to achieve." Essie stretched out her legs before her, unable to stay still for long—a trait she had shared with her sister.

"Easy for you to—" I began, but she cut through my words so quickly she might have read my mind and prepared a rebuttal in advance.

"If I hadn't spent the last week sobbing and praying, then you know I'd be just like you are now." Although interjectory, Essie's words were soft. "But you have to realize that Allie wouldn't want sadness at her death. I mean," she gestured to our clothing—hers a bright blue dress and mine dress pants with a yellow shirt, "Allie's wishes were no black at her funeral. You knew her, she'd—"

"I thought I knew her," I mumbled. "Or at least, I thought she knew me. That I'd want to know if she was sick. We could've—"

"Enough with your questioning and hypotheticals, Ben," Essie sighed. I was sure she had her own, too. "What happened has happened and there is no use wondering what life would have been like." Essie's words were far from soft now, and my neck tensed from the strength of her voice.

For a moment, I had forgotten Essie knew her sister far better than I did. Despite how strong my feelings were for Allie, it didn't measure up to a relationship built over time like theirs.

"Allie had her reasons for not telling you—one, so you wouldn't worry. While her life was flipping upside down, she needed you to be unchanging and constant. She didn't want to be treated differently, like a fragile flower. She's been that way her whole life." As Essie spoke, my neck relaxed. "I know you must feel like this was all dumped on you, and I'm sorry we've all been grieving for the last nine months while you've had a mere fraction of that."

"Yeah!" I exclaimed, and just as quickly as the release had happened, my shoulders and neck tightened again. "Only three months. I was completely oblivious to everything. I felt like an idiot."

"And secondly," Essie continued her point, "she thought she was protecting you." Peace riddled my body with her touch on my arm, so gentle and familiar like Allie's. "She loved you, you know."

"Exactly," I sighed, "so why did she let me suffer without knowing it? You guys got to be with her during it all, while I was in India or with her at school but oblivious to what was happening until she seized in my arms. I loved her!" I screamed.

Essie pulled away instantly.

"Yeah, and I hated her?" But the harshness didn't last. "Love doesn't give you a right to someone unless they let you. To Allie, not telling you about being sick *was* loving you. She let you continue to thrive, grow, and succeed without the burden of her illness. She still chose to love you through it all. If you push that aside, you're pushing away one of the biggest gestures of love Allie gave."

After a moment of silence, Essie stood up, but left something in her place. I didn't dare look at it for a few minutes, and when I did, I saw Allie's last camera next to me.

44

Asan stared at his hands as he finished, perhaps imagining the initial feel of the camera between his fingers on that August day.

"For all the photos Allie took, I never had any of her. After she passed, I spent so much time running through her features in my mind so I could lock them in my memory." Asan reached for the camera. He opened the small back where the film would go. Instead of film, he pulled out a photo.

"But then I got this one. It's one my mother took when Allie came to the house around Christmas," Asan began. "She had framed it. She didn't show me it until Kiah and I were married—until I'd moved on. But," he gave a sharp intake of breath, "it affected me, more than I knew. I took it out of the frame so as to use it for one of my own pictures, years ago. This photograph is the only one that exists of me and Allie."

Asan held the photograph out to Devon, who took it, nervously about to see Allie for the first time.

In the center, standing out with her lighter skin in Asan's family photo, was Allie. Her eyes were shining even in the faded photograph. Her smile was full and innocent. Her hands gripped the little Christmas tree.

In front of her was little Jared and Fatima. Behind them, Asan's grandparents, and beside them, his father, photographed in the middle of a sentence with his hand coming down, speaking to his wife, the photographer.

And beside Allie, sat young Asan. His eyes were fixed on her, not the camera, with his arms draped around her and pulling her close. There was no doubt: he loved her.

Devon's stomach dropped, thinking about how the beautiful, smiling Allie in the photograph was now gone—she'd died less than a year from that moment.

Devon stirred in his seat. The tea, still full, had gone cold long ago. Life was so unexpected. Asan had no idea what life with Allie was going to look like—and never would have guessed reality. But he spent all the time he could loving her anyway.

"I stuffed it away. When my son, Josh, was packing for college, we removed tons of boxes. Years later, I finally got to put them back when I glanced in and saw the photograph lying there." Asan's eyes had dried up over time, but the emotion behind them stayed. "I looked at it for a while and went on one of our walks, reminiscing. Then I put it there, for safekeeping. I chose to put Allie aside for good. Little did I know, God had other plans." Asan's mouth turned into a smile. "I'm learning now how letting go can be remembering, not forgetting."

No longer did Asan seem like the mysterious professor Devon was used to. No, now he seemed—slumped at his kitchen table—a tired man who'd had to grow up much too quickly.

"But don't mistake him, Devon," Kiah interjected. "I've never felt more loved by anyone my entire life than by Ben. He loves me entirely, and I know that. And I know he loved Allie, but it was different. She was a key part in showing him what living a good, honest life is like, and he exemplifies that every day which has helped our own marriage. Never have I doubted his commitment to me since day one."

"But then, if you loved Allie so much," Devon said as he turned back to Asan, "how did you ever fall in love with someone else?"

Asan went on to share about what happened in the months and years after Allie's death. While he was in his Master's program at Mt. Hope for History Education the following fall, he met Kiah.

"She was in the Nurse Practitioner Program after working as a nurse for a few years. We met one day at the library, when both of us were waiting for someone to come fix the broken printer." Asan chuckled at the memory. They were friends at first, he was still grieving the loss of Allie.

"But I knew there was something special about Kiah. She deeply cared for others. Where Allie was spunky, artsy, and full of energy and joy, Kiah was gentle, willing to listen, and offered the best advice. After almost every interaction, she recommended to me some of the greatest books about faith I've read in life. I'd sit up late at night, reading them, and writing down questions to ask her." Asan's happiness was infectious, and he reached for his wife's hand. "Once when I was sick, Kiah came to my house after working at the hospital, took care of me, and we talked until late at night when my fever broke. Her love for me, even when we were just friends, was relentless. When she learned about Allie, she never wavered in her care and love, despite having to deal with me still grieving."

Asan began to travel and train for the 1996 Atlanta Olympics. In 1992, he wasn't in the mental state to compete. In 1994, he got injured, and Kiah was there to comfort him.

"That's when I realized I cared more for her than a friend," Asan mused. "It's all so funny now, looking back." Discussing his wife and their love story had cheered him up significantly. "The moment I recovered, I asked her out on a date. We were married a year later. Kiah and I wanted a Christian wedding, but it still contained some Indian themes to appease my father and to represent our home, since she was adopted from there."

"When the Atlanta Olympics came around," Kiah began to explain, "I found out I was pregnant shortly before Ben had to leave."

It was that year Asan came in silver in the 100m and bronze in the 200m.

"Where are the medals?" Devon asked curiously.

"In our bathroom," Asan admitted with a chuckle. "There's nothing like brushing your teeth next to some Olympic medals!"

It was also then when Asan glanced up to the crowd after getting the silver and spotted his wife proudly displaying her sign that confirmed they were starting a family.

"It was the happiest moment of my life," Asan admitted. "I cried while singing the National Anthem. To know that one day my child could look back and see their father was an Olympian was one thing, but just knowing I was going to be a father overwhelmed me with joy."

The next day, Devon would watch the very same 100m race on YouTube and see a young Asan cry amongst the cheering crowd. It was like a dream, stepping back in time, to know the story behind the tears, whereas a normal viewer would only see the happiness from getting second place.

Devon glanced between Kiah and Asan and felt his heart expand up into his neck as they met each other's gaze—full of love and understanding. Devon's embarrassment from questioning Asan's choice of letting go of Allie now seemed foolish. He should not have expected Asan to wallow in that sadness forever. Moving on and loving again, as was evident before him, was inevitable.

The choice to embrace or flee love was the true distinction of a fulfilling life.

Devon shifted uncomfortably—he suddenly felt intrusive, despite the fact Asan had willingly opened his life up to Devon. He had, without question, brought in his drunk student, sobered him, and spent hours sharing his personal life in motivation to help him, even in the early hours of the morning.

Asan smiled over to Devon.

"I do wish you good luck with your issues with Miss Huff," he said kindly. Now with his wife home, Dr. Asan yawned, seemingly content and allowing himself to grow tired. "And I trust that in time, you will figure out how to become better. I know you have the drive to become a lawyer—a better one than your father. You just have to surround yourself with the right people—whether that will include Miss Huff or not—but either way, I know you will be okay, Devon."

Devon's chest rose at hearing his first name. He glanced up at his professor, who winked in return.

Devon looked back at the life he'd been living for the past three years of constrained independence not in reminiscence, but in pity for himself. He, and everyone else, deserved better. They all deserved to live fully, unaware of what the future was leading them to, but unafraid to meet it.

Devon finally left Asan's to get some sleep. As he crawled back into the apartment, he was both scared and relieved to see Lindsey under their blankets. She was gently sleeping, clearly knocked out from the nights' events that seemed like ages ago now.

But Devon knew what he had to do if he ever wanted a chance with Lindsey to last. The future was uncertain, but at the same time, so exciting.

He leaned over and gently kissed her head. This couldn't wait.

Lindsey groaned and stirred.

"Dev?" she whispered.

"Mhm," Devon said against her forehead. "It's me. Linds, I need to tell you something, please."

"Ugh, can't it wait until the morning?"

"No, babe, I'm sorry. It's really important I tell you this," Devon said, his voice cracking. His eyes began to well up with tears. He bit his lip. He hadn't cried in years. But with the mix of learning of Allie's death and facing the potential end of his relationship, tears weren't surprising.

"Devon, you're scaring me," Lindsey said as her eyes popped open. Her stomach dropped upon seeing his tears. "Baby, baby talk to me, what's happening?"

So he told her. He told her every detail of what

happened—maybe too many details. He told her about the drinking and the girl and the terrible mistake he had made. He told her about Asan and finding out about Allie and how it made him realize how much he loved Lindsey, would do anything to be with her, and regretted absolutely everything—the excessive drinking, his irresponsibility, and of course, cheating on her that night.

"I swear Lindsey, I swear I thought she was you. I-I would've never…" His sobs escaped, covering anything else he wanted to say.

Lindsey pulled away. The concern for him on her face had disappeared. Devon could not blame her. He would hate himself too.

"Devon, I-I can't… I can't just forgive you like this just because you're upset that your professor's girlfriend died thirty years ago. I can't just pretend you didn't sleep with someone else just because you've realized how much you actually love me."

Devon nodded as tears still ran down his face.

"I understand… I understand, Lindsey, I do. But I didn't know it wasn't you!"

"I know, Devon." Lindsey sighed. "But it's late. I can't do this right now. I'm exhausted… I've already puked like three times tonight, and I'm so weak… I just want to sleep."

"Okay, okay, we'll sleep," Devon said as he began to lay beside her.

"No, I'm going to go on the couch," Lindsey said. "I just need some space. I love you, Devon. I still do. I just need… I just need time."

Devon shook his head and gently kissed her forehead.

"You stay here, I'll go."

"But—"

"I'll go. Stay here, please. I'll leave you be until you're ready to talk about it again, okay?"

Lindsey bit her lip and nodded as she settled back into the bed. Devon slowly crept toward the door, but paused when her voice rang out.

"I'm sorry I can't just forgive you right away," she whispered as she started to cry, too. "But I do love you, too, Devon. I really do. I need some time. Please. I'm not saying things are over, I'm not… I just want space."

Devon chuckled a bit through his tears.

"That's okay. Honestly, I probably would've gotten mad if you did forgive me right away. I don't deserve it." He reached for the doorknob, with as much strength as he could muster, knowing that whatever he faced on the other side he could handle. He could love again. He could love Lindsey forever. "Goodnight, Lindsey. I promise, if you give me a chance, I'm going to prove my worth to be with someone as amazing as you."

45

In the morning, Devon still felt as if something was unfinished. Though his conversation with Lindsey didn't go as well as he had planned, he still had hope for the future. He felt the weight of his secret lift off of his shoulders, and he wondered if Asan felt the same way when he was finally honest with Allie.

At least Devon had a chance to have a future with Lindsey that Asan never got with Allie. Lindsey was still here, present in his world. Asan didn't get that chance. His story was still fresh in his mind and making its home in his memories.

He had woken up early, his back sore from sleeping on the couch. Lindsey was still asleep, but he didn't need her to be awake, not yet. They would sort things out in time, he knew, or go on their own separate journeys. But he needed to prove to himself, and to her, that he was serious.

Devon stepped into the kitchen and fished out the multiple six packs of beer he kept in. He cracked open every single one and watched them foam up and drain into the sink.

Next, he opened up his computer and downloaded every one of his final exam study guides with the goal of spending the rest of the weekend pouring over each one.

Finally, he pulled out his phone and set multiple alarms for every morning so he wouldn't miss any more classes, with loud marimba music that he was sure would wake him up.

Then without really understanding why, Devon began to walk around campus, just like Allie and Ben, thinking about their relationship, his relationship, and time itself. How unfair time was to the best of relationships, and how generous it was to some of the worst.

Devon wandered over to the clock tower, trying to picture what campus must have felt like thirty years ago. But his mind was full of too many things to concentrate on, so he let it buzz on, hoping to figure out its meaning one day.

"Mr. Camburn."

He thought he imagined Asan's voice—there was no way after being up so late he would be out and about at nine in the morning. But after being called to again, he looked up. Asan was walking toward him with his hand outstretched. In it was the photograph.

"Would you like to help me put it in its proper home?" he asked.

Not the camera, then, surely. Nor the frame. No, Devon followed Asan as they trudged across campus, through the clear glass doors of the art gallery, where thirty years ago a young hopeful displayed her senior art project—now memorialized for her in the Allison Charlotte Johncox gallery. Devon halted for a moment at the gallery title but continued walking as he laughed and shook his head—he *had* to explore MHU more often.

There, partially tucked behind a photo of a cross, Asan stuck the photograph. Ben had waited and knew Allie's story could impact people with time, he just hadn't known when. Now, as he and Devon stood side-by-side, peace washed over the pair.

The photograph sat in its rightful place.

ACKNOWLEDGEMENTS

To say that this book wasn't a labor of love would be inaccurate. This was the longest labor that I have endured. I first wrote a simple scene about two college students, obviously romantically involved, making stories about the stars on a winter night, when I was only 14, over 10 years ago. I grew up in a college town and, as a younger sister whose older sister was off at college, my vivid imagination of what life would be like when I was older pushed me into writing what would be the first pages of *Take My Sunshine*.

It looked and read vastly different than it is now. Early manuscripts had odd references to Michael Jackson, characters dying their hair blue in a college fountain, and other little quirks that were fun, but albeit childish and took away from the message of the story.

But through many, many, many rewrites, including scrapping favorite scenes, the novel I am proud to call my debut is complete, and it feels like a weight lifted off my shoulders.

I would be remiss to not mention those who have made this labor and its burdens much easier to carry.

To my first reader, my fellow co-host of Lit Sis, and sister, Haley, who has inspired me and encouraged me through the years, thank you. This book would not be here without you.

To my dad, who first pushed me to look at non-traditional methods of publishing because he just wanted my voice out there, thank you for giving me permission to redirect my dreams so they could become a reality.

To my mom, whose creativity has flowed into me both genealogically and culturally my whole life, who has taken me to countless musicals and plays and libraries to foster that imaginative part of my brain, thank you for never giving up on me.

To my nephews and niece, whose smiles and hearts are an inspiration themselves, and whose competition of getting the dedication forced me to choose no one, thank you for your childlike wonder and joy.

To my Aunt Jenny, thank you for being one of the first people in my life to highlight my writing as a talent.

To Mrs. Rapert, my high school English teacher, I could've spent hours in your class. Thank you for seeing the potential in me that I didn't at the time.

To my editor, Katie Seaman, from our matching striped shirts to our matching ideas on how to make this book a reality, thank you for giving me a chance.

To my designer, Yago Domingues, thank you for being incredibly patient with me as we trudged through multiple rounds of designing the most amazing cover.

To my friends and other family, thank you for listening to me as I talked through plot points for believability and gave me tips on how to really make my book shine.

To Cory, thank you for putting your 100% in supporting me, both in my author endeavors and our marriage. You make me want to be a better person every day.

And of course, to my Abba Father, whose love and devotion is the ultimate inspiration, I thank Him for the grace He bestowed on me all those years.

And to you, reader, thank you for picking up my book and giving the lives of Ben, Allie, and Devon a place in your heart. If you're like me and feel moody after a book, I hope this playlist I listened to while writing and editing will provide the beauty of bittersweet emotions.

About the author

M.E. Glinz has been writing since she could string together a sentence and hasn't stopped since—even when her teachers would get mad at her. Her writing reflects both the nostalgia of youth and the maturity of adulthood and the pangs that come with it. When she's not writing, she's working as a nurse traveling the United States with her husband, although Michigan will always be home. *Take My Sunshine* is her debut novel.

You can connect with her on her Instagram @m.e.glinz_author to learn about what she's writing next or listen to her podcast she co-hosts with her sister, Lit Sis, @litsispodcast.

A note on the type

Book Antiqua was designed Hermann Zapf as a variation of the Palatino typeface. Antiqua means "Roman" and was an original typeface mimicking the style of calligraphers in the 15th and 16th centuries. It is one of two Antiqua typefaces designed by Zapf, who created many other fonts in his lifetime.

www.ingramcontent.com/pod-product-compliance
Lightning Source LLC
Chambersburg PA
CBHW020504310726
48979CB00016B/2778/J

* 9 7 9 8 9 8 8 9 3 8 0 0 2 *